REIGN OF SOULLESS BOOK 1
SHANNON R. LIR

THIS DECEIT OF OURS

THIS DECEIT OF OURS

Reign of Soulless Book 1

Copyright © Shannon R. Lir 2022

All rights reserved. No part of this book may be reproduced in any form or by any electronic or mechanical means, including information storage and retrieval systems, without written permission from the author, except for the use of brief quotations in a book review.

This novel is a work of fiction. Names, characters, and events are the products of the author's imagination. Any resemblance to actual persons, living or dead, or actual events is purely coincidental.

ISBN (hardcover): 979-8-9863802-9-2

ISBN (paperback): 979-8-9863802-0-9

eISBN: 979-8-9863802-8-5

shannonrlir.com
GOLD KNOT PRESS LLC
Copyright © 2022 by Shannon R. Lir

Cover artwork by K.D. Ritchie | Story Wrappers

Print wrap design by Shannon R. Lir

Map by AEKCreates

Character Art by Angelika Nidua Buergo

Copyediting by Jeni Chappelle | Jeni Chappelle Editorial

This Deceit of Ours

GOLD KNOT PRESS

CONTENT WARNINGS

Please note that content warnings may contain mild spoilers.

This book contains strong language and mature content, depictions and themes of mental illness, mentions of pregnancy and menstruation, misogyny, violence, hunting, human trafficking, and death.

For Ma—
No, you're not the ma in this book.

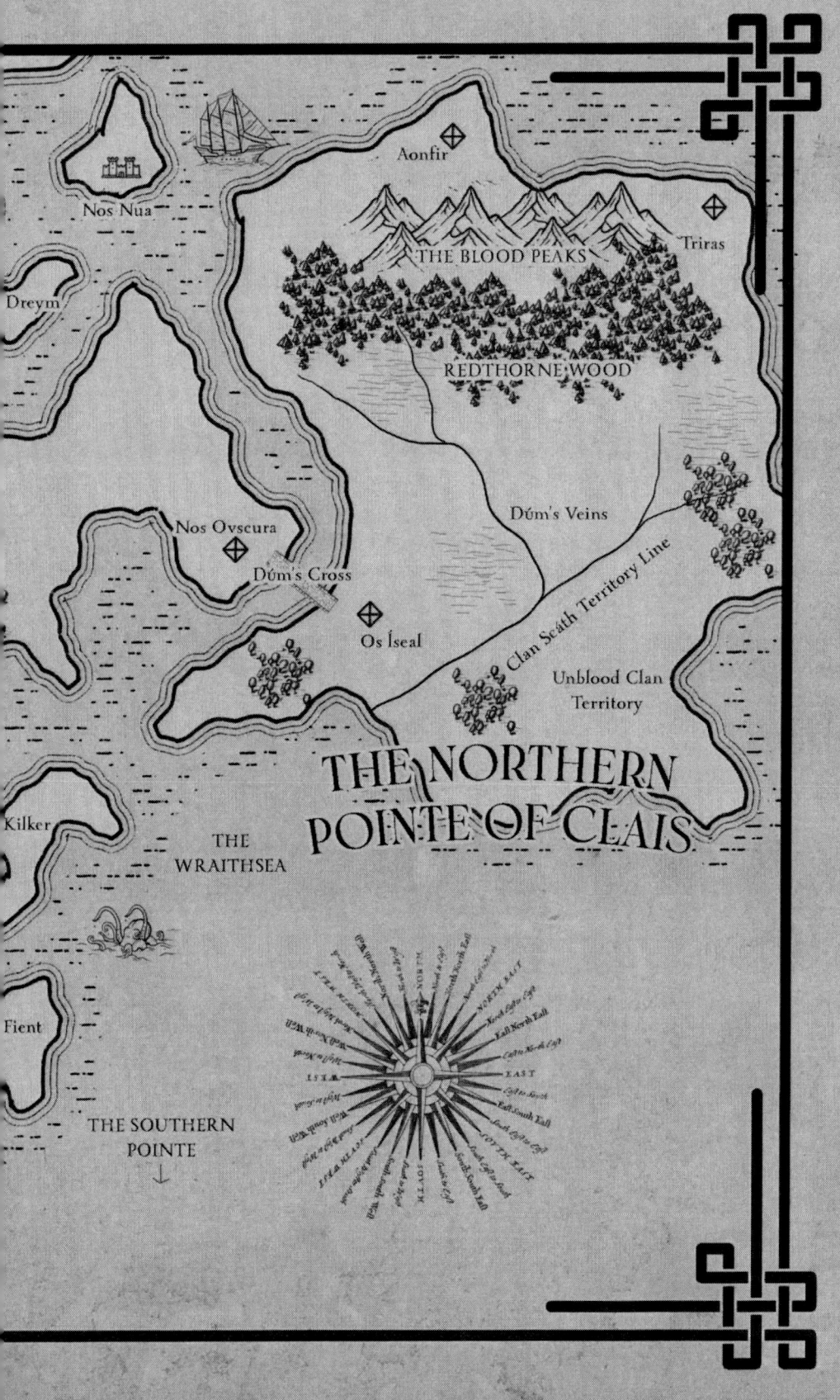

PROLOGUE

My magic shifted to the color of my fleeting moods.
It had for as long as I could remember, ever changing like the dance between the sun and moon. Color was the only way I knew *how* to put words to them, but even then, I often acted before I knew what I was feeling.

Most of my moods and emotions were intense, quick to crescendo, and they blinded me in the moment. They tinted the world I looked upon, and the glasses through which I saw weren't always rose colored.

The deepest, most agonizing sadness imitated a dark blue, profound like the depths of the sea. The first time it drowned me was just after Pa disappeared. Ever since, I always felt some form of it, like being trapped beneath the water while glimpsing the surface. Except no matter how hard I pumped my legs, the waves kept me down.

Rage—a frequent, arduous guest in my mind—came in floods of red. It started as a faint hue but always deepened, spilling over as the emotion surged, flowing free as blood.

And fear. Fear surged black as night, black as ink, like when I stole all my clan's magic without sense, without realizing what I'd done, without a way to give it back.

The wickedest moods and emotions were the hardest to deal with. But among the bad, there was good too.

1

It takes a scoundrel to know one.
 I snorted in the conman's face as he leaned toward me across the bar, trying to pawn what was obviously a fake gemstone necklace. Even a few gold kofs from our home across the bridge could buy him the best meal in the city, lodgings for the night, and maybe even an authentic emerald, unlike the one he was dangling in my face right now. I had half a mind to purchase the counterfeit just to make his night, but I had enough useless things in my life. I didn't need any more.

The necklace swayed before me like a pendulum, and I swatted the conman's hand away.

He straightened, taking a step away from my brother Ciel, whose space he'd invaded to get to me. Unease flashed in the conman's eyes before he stifled it, smoothing out his fancy, tailored coat and breeches—attire that stood in glaring contrast to our scenery for the night.

Or it would have if I hadn't witnessed a dozen acts like his in this pub before.

Everything inside the Devil's Tail was a shade of black or silver, the walls striped in stained upholstered panels, and the chipped marble floors streaked with dark green. It was one of the shoddiest places in the city and notorious for serving watered-down drinks, but I liked it because of that. None of the dueling clans' warlords or the otherwise affluent came to this place. None of the soulless nobles either. The daemons who loitered here were a small price to pay to avoid running into anyone we knew.

I looked up from under my eyelashes at the conman and smirked at Ciel. "Do you remember what Ma always says about scoundrels?"

My brother looked pensive, leaning back in his chair, his eyes on his hands resting on the counter in front of him.

Waiting for Ciel to answer, I returned my eyes to the conman.

Taut skin stretched across his unnaturally high, protruding cheekbones, and magic clung to the rest of him, concealing his true appearance. I would've bet he had horns—most daemons did—but I couldn't see through the glistening magic. Still, I was sure he looked almost mortal beneath it all, with only a split tongue or eyes that lacked pupils. Maybe a barbed tail.

Daemons, unlike wraiths who'd been mortal before death, were born in the Soullands, and many worked for the Daemon King himself, but none could be trusted.

We were beyond the land of the living, after all.

Taking a closer look, I noticed the conman's fine clothes hung off his thin frame like they'd been snatched from a wealthy trader or from a mansion in Gilders Eye. His dirty shoes also gave him away, illuminated by the flickering firelight over the bar. The city's motto was "Look twice. Things are never as they appear."

The citizens' façades were all a show for the living who crossed into the city every night.

I preferred to blend in whenever we visited. Ciel and I had both donned training clothes before leaving home. Not nice enough to garner any assessing stares or find our pockets completely empty later—usually—but also not the sort of garments that would get us kicked out of classier places, should we have any desire to venture out of the slums. My cloak was warm, my white tunic kept me covered, and my leather boots ensured I could run if the need presented itself.

As the persistent conman kept talking, it became obvious we hadn't blended in well enough.

With an impatient sigh, I swirled my pale ginger drink in its frosted glass and took a swig. While the daemons could be a nuisance, the Soullands were a vast improvement from home—a distraction from my problems there. They even had better drinks. Not the boring, bitter ales I was used to. Lemon drifted up under my nose from the glass, but there was something sharper behind the scent. A fiery aftertaste that lingered on my lips.

"Not interested in jewelry then, no?" the conman stammered, his scratchy voice making my skin crawl. "How 'bout this instead? I'll pay *you* the price of this fine necklace if you win a little wager."

He brandished a wad of paper currency from his inner coat pocket. Waving the bills at me, he pointed to the wall behind him without turning.

Three targets hung side by side.

"Hit three bullseyes in a row. One. Two. Three," he said, counting off on his fingers, "and the money is yours, sweetheart. Got it? Looks easy enough, eh?"

I scoffed under my breath.

Not because of the name he'd called me but because of the short distance from the edge of the bar to the wall. It was an insult to my upbringing. Before Pa had disappeared, he'd taught me how to fight with rapiers, short daggers, and how to shoot a bow, while Ma had put a spear in my hand before I could talk. My aim was impeccable because of them, better than most of my clan members who'd been training all their lives, which was double or triple my nineteen years.

Not to mention, what was I to do with currency that wasn't accepted back home?

The targets piqued my interest though.

Bolted to the wall beside them stood a cabinet filled with tarnished knives—most of them broken—with a rickety sign dangling above. *Please, NO THROWING at the bartender*, it read. Risky. Especially for a pub that saw a fight every night.

Surprisingly, we hadn't witnessed one yet. The night had been a wash, mostly. But fun could still be had with this daemon.

"I love a good wager," I interrupted him, still trying to sell me, though I hadn't heard a word he'd said after he'd called me sweetheart. "I could use some fun. What about you, Ciel?"

My brother had kept his black eyes down until now—but now

they studied the conman like he studied his thick tomes, relishing every word and page and the greater sum of them all. I was sure Ciel saw even more details than I did. He'd always been good at reading people.

Unfortunately for me, it meant he could see through my attempts to hide how I was feeling.

The conman's eyes widened with surprise, probably at the fact someone had taken his bait. Confidence restored, he licked his lips, shaking a finger at me. "But," he added slyly, "if you don't hit the targets, you'll buy this lovely one-of-a-kind off me. Deal?"

Ciel snickered under his breath. "How much *does* fake em—"

"Sure," I said over my brother, drowning out his reply. "Authentic Soullander jewels are priceless back home. Shall we, then?"

The daemon conman turned his back to us.

As I stood, my brother slipped me Pa's dagger, which had been hanging from his belt. The white marble hilt resembled mine, both sleek and sturdy, and possessed the proper weight of any good throwing dagger.

I clapped Ciel on the shoulder as I passed behind him. "The night's almost over."

"Be quick, Sersa. It's late." Ciel was right. It was probably close to sunrise. But I'd never excelled at resisting temptation.

Especially when it came to showing a man what I was capable of.

Ciel hated the games I played, said they were dangerous in the city especially, but sensing I was in a mood tonight, he let me have my fun.

My new friend scanned the cabinet of knives with wiggling fingers, suspecting nothing with his back to me. Just as I liked it. His lack of discernment made me grin. He was a mediocre con artist at best for challenging a woman wearing pants.

As I walked past sloshed patrons seated at the bar, I freed the pair of daggers I always carried and twirled them, plus Ciel's, around my fingers. Just as the conman turned, I halted, gripping the hilts like I had no idea what to do with them. He might have missed my dexterity, but his wide eyes didn't miss what I held.

"She brings her own knives. Okay. I like it." Smacking his lips, he returned the ones he'd selected for me to the cabinet.

"Borrowed them off my friend," I said.

It wasn't a complete lie. I'd borrowed the one.

The conman spun on his heel to face me again and clapped. "Ready, sweetheart?"

With a nod, I smiled without showing any teeth. I adeptly threaded the blades between my knuckles and, watching him, tilted my head. Finally registering my mischief for what it was, he backed against the wall, flattening his palms behind him. Worry pooled in his eyes, and his mouth hung slightly open.

"Wait—" he started.

I released the first dagger, quickly followed by the second, and—showing off now—I whirled around and whipped the third over my shoulder at the final target.

Each landed within seconds of the one before it.

Each stood upright, vibrating the target with its force.

Three perfect bullseyes.

"Thrice, you said?" Retrieving our daggers, I called over my shoulder. "What was that saying again, Ciel?"

"It takes a scoundrel to know one," he recited, nudging his empty glass forward with pale knuckles. He shifted in his seat, squaring his wide shoulders with the conman.

I slid a sly hand into his coat pocket and patted him on the chest with the wad of bills I'd swiped. The poor daemon's mouth hung open, but a hard line was forming between his brows as I fanned the money. He watched me walk away.

"Scoundrel? *Me?*" He glanced around at the filled tables in case any other patrons had heard. "I'm no scoundrel. This here is genuine emerald mined from—"

Ciel's dry reply interrupted him. "There are no emerald mines in the entirety of the Soullands."

Back at the bar, I slid into my seat and returned Ciel's weapon. The conman followed me, clearly hoping to recoup his money with another swindle.

"If you're going to try and pawn your junk off someone, you shouldn't pick a Druid," I said smugly, leaning forward in my seat. "They know *everything*."

Ciel shot me a glare. He didn't want me telling everyone he was a

Druid in training—soon to be a member of the learned class dedicated to law, religion, and knowledge—but I couldn't help myself. I was proud of him for relinquishing our mother's path for us, even if I couldn't.

The conman stood taller, reaching for a way out of his lies. "Oh, no. These emeralds aren't from the Soullands. They're from Clais. Don't you want something nice for your...*nice* lady? I'll give you a fair price."

Ciel snorted this time, giving his drink a final push and standing. His chair screeched against the marble as he gathered his cloak off the back and swept it around his shoulders. I hated that he kept growing taller, stronger, and more intimidating while I'd sprouted nothing but hips and heavy breasts the last few years. My growth had stunted on the somewhat shorter side, so I was still swift in a fight and better than anyone I knew with a spear. I supposed my greatest advantage was the element of surprise.

But Ciel was convincing. Daunting when he wanted to be.

He should've been the clan heir.

My brother chuckled as he said, "My *sister* is neither nice nor a lady. Also, it's pronounced *Claash*. Anyone who's been on the other side of the bridge would know that. Better luck with your next customer."

The conman dropped his voice and snarled, "Fine, it's fake. If you knew, why'd you play in the first place?"

"For the thrill," I said, raising my glass. "And because I'm a scoundrel."

The conman's mouth opened in protest as he moved toward me.

"Take another step," said Ciel, "and you'll learn the hard way she's just as good with those daggers up close as she is from afar."

Shaking his head and grumbling, the conman resigned with a wave of a hand. He pushed through the crowd toward the back room, presumably in search of others to scam.

I polished off my drink, ice clinking when I set it back down and stood. "He's lucky I let him keep his jewels at all."

As I replaced my daggers where I'd gotten them, I realized my act had drawn a few too many eyes around the bar. Neither of us had any reason to be afraid of the daemons who roamed the city streets. There were hundreds hoping to make a kof on unsuspecting travelers from across the bridge. Luckily, the daemons couldn't steal souls—unlike the Sluagh spirits.

They, too, belonged to the Daemon King's ranks.

Even so, it was unwise to let your guard down in this city.

"The bridge will be lowered soon, Sersa." Ciel pushed in both our chairs. "We need to go get Ailerby."

I nodded in agreement.

As we made our way toward the door, I dropped a few kofs and the paper bills into the rusty tip jar. Pa always said you could judge a person by how they treated anyone perceived to have less power or lower status, servants especially, and animals. Because of him, I'd tried to bring home one too many sick creatures over the years, and I always tipped well.

Pausing to be sure the money made it into the slot, I jumped when a white-haired *tower* bumped into me. The stranger recovered just fine, barely affected by my existence, but I almost lost my balance.

I teetered on the heels of my leather boots as Ciel steadied me, and I gripped his forearms until I righted myself.

Whipping around, I glared at the tower, still standing in my way. From a quick glance, I combed over his high-collared, fitted black coat and matching breeches. His clothes were disheveled like he'd been out drinking all night, but the textiles were pricey, stitched with silver thread on black brocade that gleamed like the moon. He, too, had either stolen them from Gilders Eye, the wealthy quarter, or he was a Gilder himself.

There was only one reason Gilders wandered to this side of the city—to seek a mortal lover for the night. And the group of young men the tower was with looked like they were up to no good.

"Would you watch where you're going?" I growled, eyeing the mug of ale in his hand before tilting my head back to look up at him.

I didn't feel like starting a fight tonight, but I had Ma's spear shortened to a quarter of its length hiding under my fur-lined cloak. Just in case, I'd told myself when we'd left home.

My mind shifted when I looked at his smug yet hauntingly beautiful face. Colorless eyes raised from the ale sloshing over the edge of his mug and landed on me like I was little more than muck on the bottom of his boot. A thin scar snaked from his eyebrow to his jaw, and his eyebrows were unnaturally dark compared to his pure white hair, which hung in his pale face in places and swept backward in others.

"Excuse me?" he rasped out. "Do you know who you're speaking to?"

Definitely a Gilder, that was for sure.

Maybe I do want to start something tonight.

The alcohol buzzed in my veins. That, paired with the high of my hustle, was enough to set me off.

"If I knew *or* cared, I'd at least have the courtesy of using your name, you damn giant. Thanks for spilling on me. You're supposed to drink it, you know."

Ciel gripped my arm and pulled me back. "His eyes, Sersa. He's a Bonespeaker. Let's go. Now."

If that were true—and I was willing to bet it was because all Ciel did was read—we needed to get out of here. The Bonespeakers were a blood clan in the northern Soullands. Their magic flowed through their soulless kin, and they could raise the dead and control the living. The last thing we needed was a Bonespeaker having a little fun with us in one of the city's many back alleyways.

The Bonespeaker smirked and raised his mug in mock salute, but there was a dangerous twist to his scarred lips and his eyes were hard as marble. He lowered his drink and took a step toward me.

"I'm only a quarter Bonespeaker, love," he whispered, eyes locked on mine before they flickered, taking in the rest of me. "I assure you I have plenty of other tricks, but you better get going. It's almost Reaping Hour. You never know when one of the spirits might drag you into the Soullands for good."

I gritted my teeth as a cloud of red teemed in my mind. Revolted by his threats, I shoved him away and slapped the mug out of his hands. Cinnamon from the ale coiled in the air as the glass shattered between our boots.

By the time I realized what I'd done, it was too late.

I held the Bonespeaker's gaze.

"Threaten the heir of Clan Scáth again, and you'll find yourself at the bottom of the Wraithsea, *love*."

"Sersa." Ciel's grip tightened on my arm. "We need to go."

He tugged me out of the bar, the door with its little bell slamming hard on our heels, and I threw a look over my shoulder. Empty-handed, the Bonespeaker watched me through the windows, a mix of astonishment and bewilderment plastered to his face.

I grinned, basking in his reaction all the way down the street.

2

"What in Dúm's name were you thinking?" Ciel growled once we reached the next street. He looked over his shoulder to be sure the Bonespeaker wasn't following us. "I told you what he was."

I dodged his question and posed my own. "What do you think a Bonespeaker was doing there? And if he was a Bonespeaker, wouldn't that make him—"

"Royal to some presently unknown degree? Aye." Ciel walked a few steps ahead of me. "And *you* provoked him, Sersa. I didn't recognize him from Uncle Archibald's ledgers either..."

Our father's second oldest brother, Archibald, had spent his life amassing as much knowledge as he could about the Daemon King's affluent Circle of Gilders, the nobles of the Soullands.

"When I warn you about something or someone, can't you at least act accordingly?" he said.

"Good gods, you sound like Ma."

He glared at me so sternly that I swore he wanted the Bonespeaker, or a Sluagh spirit, to snatch me up. I shuddered just thinking about it. The Sluagh were the size of three men and exceptional hunters because of their powerful wings and unparalleled hearing. They flew in flocks, almost like bats, but there was nothing redeemable about them. Some bats were cute.

The Sluagh were monstrous.

The streets whipped by as Ciel moved at a feverish pace, and I jogged alongside him to keep up. He kept glancing at the dark sky, no doubt searching for the first signs of light. He was right to be worried. Immediately following sunrise, the Sluagh began their daily hunt.

Grubby street vendors standing outside the Midnight Market tried to lure us past the towering walls that hid its wares. One could buy and sell anything in there from a soul to their own body. The nobles living around Gilders Eye were said to have mortal servants aplenty in their homes. Rumor had it some also feasted on bits of their souls. A delicacy in Nos Ovscura, nicknamed the City of Soulless. The market was a despicable place, and we tried to steer clear of it at all costs.

A few minutes later, we reached a depressingly neglected betting hall on the outskirts of the city.

Ailerby was leaning against the wall beside the entrance, chatting up a young man with dark brown curls cropped shorter on the sides and deep golden skin. Ailerby looked lanky in contrast to the shorter fellow, and today, his hair was a pale shade of blond that annoyed me —his snowy skin and light eyes reminded me of the Bonespeaker. But together, I had to admit they were a handsome pair. Their bodies leaned closer as the other young man whispered in Ailerby's ear.

"Ail...?" I said, not wanting to disturb the coquetry so obviously unfolding. I could practically see the fire emanating from their bodies, and Ciel clearly could too.

My brother's eyes flickered away from the pair as if he were witnessing some hedonistic act when it was nothing more than a fling that could never be. Little more than an after-midnight distraction. The other fellow twirled a finger around one of Ailerby's curls. Their lips drew closer.

"We need to leave," Ciel gritted out, loud enough for the young man to look at us, brow furrowing in aggravation. "*Now*, Ailerby."

Ailerby waved goodbye to his new friend and barreled toward us, fists hanging at his sides. His mouth twisted into a scowl. "Just because you like to spend your days and nights with your nose in a book does *not* mean the rest of us do."

Ciel snickered. "What were you going to do—go home with a wraith?"

"Maybe I would. And he wasn't a wraith. He says he's visiting from the Western Pointe."

"For someone who's an expert on illusions, you can't see one when it's right under your nose. He probably forgot he's soulless now. Besides, it's almost Reaping Hour. The bridge is going to drop into the sea soon and I don't know about you two, but I'm not getting stuck here for the hunt."

I blocked out their bickering as we navigated the city and headed toward the ferryman. Dilapidated shops and housing poked at the horizon while the bridge stood farther in the distance, stretching for at least a mile. Dúm's Cross led to Os Íseal, our home, across the raging sea. The bridge was our only way home, and despite how many times I'd crossed it, my heart still raced as we approached.

Behind us, the Daemon King's Citadel twisted into the sky, black glass towers my mind couldn't make sense of. Obviously forged by magic, the citadel mismatched the slums on the outskirts of the city. The northernmost section of the city was the nicest—I'd never been, only glimpsed through the gates—and Gilders Eye encircled the citadel like an iris dripping with gold, bleeding into the white of the eye people so frequently overlooked.

I silently bid the city farewell again, glancing over my shoulder at the Daemon King's home. My eyes pulled toward it like a magnet. I'd always wanted to see inside. But the only thing that awaited a mortal there was death.

"Hoods up," Ciel said.

With a nod, Ailerby and I obliged. I returned my focus to the bridge and kept my eyes on my feet, despite knowing Ailerby was distorting at least some of my features with his magic. Ciel's too. If Ma discovered that we were visiting the city again…

I didn't know what she'd do, and I wasn't about to find out.

The flock of patrons leaving the city felt endless, inching forward at the pace of a snail. As our bodies crowded together, I tried not to meet the eyes of anyone around me. Any one of them could belong to

Clan Scáth. Any one of them might recognize pieces of my face or my boots or my messy braid. I tucked my dark hair inside my cloak for good measure and raised my eyes fleetingly, stealing a glance at my surroundings.

"We're not moving," I said as we took our first steps onto the bridge. My boots thunked against the thick, black stone. "Why aren't we moving?"

"We cut it too close," Ciel growled. "Ailerby, can you veil us? We need to make our way to the front."

"Sure," Ailerby said, "but I can't stop your elbows from poking at people."

"I'm not concerned about *poking* others right now. We need to get to the front." Worry wheedled its way into Ciel's expression, and under the darkness of his cloak, the bags under his eyes looked even hollower.

They'd been bickering so much lately, and I didn't understand why.

Ciel and I both clasped hands with Ailerby, standing between us. He could veil both of us without a single touch, but the crowd was so dense that the real danger was in losing one another. When Ailerby lowered the veil of his magic over our heads, I no longer saw either of them. The comfort of Ailerby's hand in mine was all I had to lead me as Ciel started making his way between groups of people.

My eyes focused on the end of the bridge.

We'd gotten stuck in the flood of people leaving the City of Soulless a few times before, and it was the one reason I often entertained the thought of never returning again.

But I, like so many others in Os Íseal, couldn't help myself. I was drawn to this city.

My palms grew sweatier by the minute, and my heart thumped in my ears, audible even over the crowd's ruckus. Every breath I took clouded in the frigid air, which was beginning to smell of sweat. People should be nervous. If we got trapped on the bridge, the Sluagh spirits would fly overhead and pluck us up one by one so our souls could be harvested. When I thought about this possibility, it seemed even more ridiculous anyone visited the Soullands.

I refocused on our trek through the crowd. The farther we got, the harder it was to push through.

"What's taking 'em so long?" a woman shouted in my ear.

"Move already! We haven't got all night," another man hollered.

"It's nearly dawn," said another.

I glanced up at the dark shore ahead where the bridge ended. A horde of people trudged up the path through the sand dunes, while others worked their way up the rocky cliff stairs leading into our elevated city. Even they stood little chance of getting to safety before the Sluagh started their hunt for souls, but there was a cave straight ahead we might be able to hide out in if it came to it.

"We're almost halfway," said Ciel.

But the bridge throbbed right then, sending my gut into the tips of my numb toes. The separation. It was a warning: *get across now*. The middle of the bridge would be dropping into the sea, cutting the city off from Os Íseal and leaving a gap that couldn't be traversed except by the Sluagh with their gargantuan wings.

As the crowd heaved forward, Ciel found an opening toward the very edge of the bridge's right side.

Ailerby dropped the veil for a moment, and I watched his chest rise and fall, mimicking both mine and my brother's. Ciel glanced down the thick, stone railing then looked back at us. Behind his black eyes were a hundred calculations.

"It's risky. But spending a night trapped in Nos Ovscura is riskier."

Others were hopping up onto the railing from the crowd now too, sensing it was their only way out of the city. Some hoisted their children onto the narrow ledge.

I couldn't believe my eyes, and I had the horrid, heart-wrenching thought that the father might have been trying to see how much he could get for his boy. My clan did what we could to ensure the people within our territory were well fed, with clothes on their backs and shelter over their heads, but there were other reasons one might try to sell another. Addictions. Ailments. Who knew what else?

Ailerby shrugged, feigning indifference, but my eyes dropped to his teeth, fumbling his lips. "Nothing left to lose at this point. Let's do it."

A familiar sensation encircled my wrists, almost like feathers tickling my skin. I refused to look at the black wisps resembling shackles that would be there.

Ciel's gaze was drawn to my magic—the manifestation of my fear. "You good?"

I gritted my teeth and nodded, trying to force the tendrils to disappear.

"Keep us veiled," Ciel said. "We don't need someone trying to knock us off into the sea below."

That was an understatement. Not only were there colossal sea serpents dwelling at the bottom of the Wraithsea but there were spirits, skeleton-like creatures, and sea daemons too.

If we fell into the sea, it might not be an immediate death, but death it would be in the arms of the dead below.

"Now," Ciel said.

Ailerby dropped the veil over Ciel's body right as my brother hopped onto the railing and started to cross the bridge, toe to heel with each step. A second later, Ailerby disappeared too. I tried to squeeze between two groups as they came between us, but at the last second, they merged with one another, cutting off my opening.

"*Dûm's piss*," I muttered under my breath.

After Ailerby disappeared, I couldn't be sure how far either he or Ciel had made it in the line of people balancing on the stone balustrades because they remained veiled.

But I heard Ailerby. "Sers? Sers!"

"Go!" I shouted over the people's heads. We'd be quicker separated anyway.

But the trouble was, Ailerby could no longer see me buried in the crowd, and I was no longer veiled. Which meant neither were my features.

"Where you think you're going, pretty? Not escaping the city when none of us will tonight, eh?" One man reached for me and ran his tongue along rotting teeth.

I shoved him.

"She's definitely a blood," he said. "Aren't you, pretty?"

To make such a comment, they were probably unbloods—magicless folk—from the mountains or Redthorne Wood. Unbloods worshipped the woods, praying to the gods that they'd give them magic.

Without a thought, I unsheathed the blade at my hip and pressed it to the man's stubbled neck, yanking him closer by the shoulder of his jacket.

His friend's eyes bulged.

"Whether I am blood or unblood is neither of your concern. Now, get up on that railing before I slit both your throats and leave your corpses behind for the Sluagh to devour. They like easy prey, but I'd keep you alive just long enough for you to feel every last *rip* into your flesh."

I couldn't stand the sight of the man's black teeth as he fumbled his lip. "Gods, you little monster! We was only jesting."

"I bet you were. It's always jesting with men like you." I wasn't afraid of them. What made my stomach toss was the thought of being caught in the city when the Sluagh descended.

I pressed the blade closer to his throat, feeling the flick of his stubble against its edge. The one with the gnarly teeth nodded, eyes darting to his friend, who hopped up first. We followed together, and I brought the blade from his neck to his back, poking it against his ribs. It could be plunging into his heart within a few seconds if he made any wrong moves.

"No fast movements," I instructed. "Otherwise, this dagger goes right where you think it will."

He nodded.

We started to cross, one foot in front of the other. I tried to stop myself from looking down, but that was impossible. Not with the sea thrashing below Dúm's Cross, licking at the bridge's curved stone supports. The bridge was steady as a healer's hand, but my legs were not.

I forced myself to take a deep breath and yanked the other dagger from my breeches' waistband, brandishing it at the crowd below, lest any of them try anything.

Several people pulled themselves up onto the railing behind us, following the line ahead of me. I didn't like having others behind me, not when both my hands were occupied. There was little I could do but focus on my steps. My breathing grew labored, and the bridge pulsed underneath me. I squeezed my thighs, rooting myself into the stone.

The middle of the bridge detached from the two ends. When it began to lower, I cussed out the gods and prodded the dagger deeper into the man's coat.

He flinched.

"Go. Faster." My eyes lifted as two figures appeared at the end of the bridge among the exodus of others.

Ciel. Ailerby. Good.

I didn't need any distractions when I was in such a precarious position.

"I said move faster," I snapped.

"Going as fast as we can, little monster..."

I veered around him. Where the middle of the bridge was lowering, forming a gap, a man was hesitating to hop onto the platform. He was at least twenty ahead of us.

I hollered, joining the other people's furious shouting.

The woman behind him wasted no time. With a shove, she sent him hurtling onto the sinking platform. But he scurried toward the edge like a rat and pulled himself over the other side at least a hundred feet away. I had a fleeting thought that he didn't deserve to make it, not when I could've reached the end by now if not for his trepidation.

The people following the coward stormed the platform while it was still high enough to reach the other side. It quickly separated, widening the gap.

Three feet. Five. Ten.

My rutted breathing sped up. There wasn't enough time. I wasn't going to reach the other side.

I'd have to climb onto someone's shoulders to get up now or rely on someone to pull me up. Ciel and Ailerby rushed forward, realizing the same thing, but others in the crowd were blocking my way as they tried to pull their own kin up. They elbowed their way through, only for the crowd to break out into a fight. The man in front of me rammed the next person in line—his *friend*, I realized with a start—and started plowing through everyone ahead of us.

I stumbled after him, seizing the path he cleared.

I dropped onto the platform a half second after him. Then I sprinted toward the wall of bodies trying not to plunge to their death between the gap while also reaching toward the people on their bellies, struggling to pull up those below.

But the ones doing the rescuing were selective.

"Let me get my son up," pleaded a man, the same one I'd suspected had brought his son to the Midnight Market. "Please. He's just a boy. Let me get him up. Then I swear I'll help you."

Lie.

Lucky for the liar, as soon as he pulled his son up, someone shoved the man he'd promised to help into the chasm below. He reached toward the sky even as he plummeted before the waves swallowed him whole.

The man with the gnarly teeth perked up. Where the platform had dropped, balustrades enclosed the sides of the bridge's other end. He eyed them, measuring the distance I guessed, before he made a jump for it. His hands gripped the balustrade tightly, though his legs swayed beneath him. He grunted as he pulled himself up. Spit flew from his mouth.

He was arguably stronger than me, but he also weighed a lot more. I eyed the balustrade as he had, readying myself. But I would have to rotate my body mid-jump. I bent my knees to fling myself. I didn't know if I was strong enough.

Regardless, not trying meant death.

With a quick prayer to the gods I didn't believe in, I pitched myself off the edge of the platform, turning my body. I scraped the stone railing but held on.

I barely got a grip.

My dagger clattered over the edge, and the gnarly-toothed man whirled around. A smile spread his lips. He knelt for my dagger, gripping it between grubby knuckles, and stalked toward me.

"Oh, you think *you* deserve to cross?" he whispered.

More than anything I wanted to claw his eyes out, but I couldn't risk losing my grip. Just when I thought he was going to pry my fingers from the stone, he brought the dagger against my pointer finger and started to saw into my flesh.

I cried out and bit down simultaneously. He chuckled, savoring every cut he made before moving onto my middle finger. Slow, taunting cuts, each one deeper than the last.

Tears sprang to my eyes. Red skirted the edges of my vision, tinting his face, while mine grew hot from the mix of terror and anger. I bit down hard, almost expecting a tooth to pop out as I tasted the metallic tinge of blood.

"Say hello to Dúm for me," he whispered as he drew the deepest cut yet across my third finger.

No longer able to fight through the pain, I lost my grip and cursed. The last thing I saw as I plummeted toward the Wraithsea was Ciel sinking a knife into the man's back.

He, too, would meet the god of death now.

Lying on his front, clawing at the air as Ailerby held him back, Ciel's scream echoed in my ears until I smacked the black waters.

3

A hundred Iarsmaí swarmed me the instant I plunged into the water.

They were the souls of mortals who'd drowned in the Wraithsea, and they longed for others to join them in death.

Since piercing the black surface hadn't killed me, I knew they were going to.

But I'm not dead yet. I steeled myself.

I ignored the ice running through my veins, freezing me to the bone, and reached for Ma's spear clipped to my hip. My motions were delayed under the water, *slow*, and no matter how hard I fought the crushing pressure, the Iarsmaí were swifter. Swarming me. Pulling my arms behind my back. Tugging at my now-loose hair, blinding me as the black strands intertwined with their rag-like clothes.

You're going to die at the bottom of the sea, said the voice in my head.

Near the surface, waning moonlight glinted off the water above. That light alone drove me—forced me to keep fighting—but my limbs moved as if coated in honey.

I shoved an Iarsmaí away, kicked at another, and reached for my hip again. My fingers brushed the spear, but another was on me in a single breath. Not that I had any right now. It clawed my arms, loosening my thick pelt, drawing tendrils of blood that curled through the water before they disappeared.

My eyes rolled back in my head, and my vision flickered as they pulled me toward the bottom of the sea. All went black before I could see again. The thought of death was certain now, but it was the thought that did it—that sent me over the edge of my fear.

All the darkness inside me punctured through my skin, shooting rays of black into the sea. My magic pierced the willowy forms of the Iarsmaí, propelling them backward like hundreds of spears.

My opening presented itself.

Widening my eyes, I pumped my arms and legs until I reached the surface. The first gasp of air was like a drug. As soon as I tasted it, I needed more. I was willing to do anything to stay above the sea raging around me.

I righted myself, seeking the nearest shore beneath the bridge, but when I realized the other side—home—was too far of a swim, something in me died.

Because I was as good as dead if I became trapped in the city during Reaping Hour.

Though the tide carried me back toward the city, I kept pumping my legs and arms at a feverish pace until I washed up on the rocky sand with a final push from the water. The sand wasn't soft like the other side, but it comforted me as I bowed my forehead to the rocks, coughing up all the water in my lungs. The sea daemons, serpents, and other creatures trapped in the Wraithsea couldn't reach me from here.

Dúm wouldn't claim me today. At least not now.

But while the Wraithsea constrained its inhabitants somehow, the Sluagh were confined by nothing.

I looked up and down the beach, searching for a way back into the city. I couldn't stay here until dusk when the bridge would rise again, reopening the city for the night. That was out of the question, when the Sluagh would be returning from Os Íseal in a bell with their harvest.

Down the shore to the left, two enormous pipes drained into the black sea from somewhere beneath the city. Even if it led me to the sewers, it was my only option. Not to mention, I would be safer beneath the city for the day.

I rose onto my hands and knees, sopping wet and freezing without the pelt I'd lost in the sea, and wrung out my tunic.

But a cloud shifted overhead, dousing me in darkness—or so I thought.

Sturdy black leather boots planted themselves in the sand right in front of me, and as I peeled my eyes from the ground, I realized my spot under the bridge was anything but safe. The tower from before—the Bonespeaker—stood over me. His white eyes weren't amused but steady. Hard. Ready to retaliate for slapping the drink out of his hands earlier.

"Hullo," he said. "We meet again."

I cursed the gods and pulled myself to standing. To my surprise, the tower yanked me up by the forearm, readjusting his gloved grip to the crook of my elbow.

"Let go of me!"

"Quiet." His voice matched his sharpened glare. "The Sluagh may not be able to see but they have impeccable hearing. We need to get off the streets."

In case he hadn't noticed, we weren't on the streets, and the only way to get up to them was the pipes.

"There's a ladder that way." He pointed to the right of the bridge. "Come on."

"I'm not going anywhere with you!"

"Did I *not* say to be quiet? I'm not exactly the Sluagh's favorite delicacy. You are. Believe me. I'm not trying to get you off the streets for my health but for your survival."

"It seems your commands don't work on me. Maybe it's the fact that you're only a quarter Bonespeaker." I sneered.

He chuckled as he dragged me under the bridge. "Hanging onto my every word, love?"

His cloak billowed, curling around his long legs as he sauntered through the sand like he owned this shore. I was reminded that he might. Ciel had said he was royal to some degree.

"Don't call me that," I growled.

He halted and turned, once more towering over me. I ran into him, my chest meeting his firm abdomen. He had to be part Colossi too. According to legend, the giant-like beings slumbered in the western part of the Wraithsea after being hexed by a great Druid.

A malicious grin curled his lips. With a smile like that, a single dimple marking his left cheek, he was likely also a direct descendant of Dúm himself.

"I am, in fact, half Colossi. I can change my form at will," he said with a wink. I pulled backward, horrified. "Care to know the rest of my ancestry, love? It will help you for what's next."

I didn't understand. What did he mean *what's next*? I also didn't bother telling him not to call me love this time, knowing he wouldn't listen. He let his leather fingers slip off my arm when I yanked it free. Imprints left behind from his skeletal fingers stung. I wondered if he had claws beneath his gloves. All the soulless had monstrous qualities. The Court of Soulless was supposedly filled with god- and daemon-like creatures, some of them deceptively beautiful and others horrifically terrifying. He seemed to be a mix of the two.

"Wait," I said. "Can you hear my thoughts?"

He smirked but didn't offer an answer. "Come."

This single word tugged on my gut as if a rope had been tied around my waist. My feet moved of their own accord now, almost flinging me after him. He didn't wait for me. No, he knew I was following.

"If I wanted you dead," he said, still not affording me the courtesy of looking at me as he spoke, "I'd have let you drown. If you're caught in the city after dawn, the Soul Guard will either take you to the Midnight Market or send you to a pleasure den—or they'll let the spirits have you. I doubt you want to experience your soul being sucked out or being sold to someone looking to have half-soulless offspring."

I shuddered. This city, especially where the Gilders were concerned, was anything but fun and games. At least as far as I'd heard. They managed to hide much of their misdeeds and dealings behind the wall encircling Gilders Eye.

My words, thankfully, were still my own, though I suspected it would be all too easy for him to control those too. To shut me up with a single word.

"But my brother and Ailerby. They'll worry about me."

Maybe worse. They might tell the entire clan. They might re-enter the city and get hurt. Taken. The thought shook me, and the tendrils of fear clawed at my skin, threatening to reveal themselves once more.

"They know how Reaping Hours work. They won't be able to enter the city again until nightfall, and they won't try if they know what's good for them. I'm sure they're safe by now, tattling to—what was it, *Clan Scáth?*—that their heir is trapped in the City of Soulless."

He had a memory like Ciel's. I despised him already.

"It seems you, too, hung onto my every word, damn giant." I grumbled the last bit under my breath when we reached the ladder.

He waved his hand and the pressing compulsion to reach for the rungs faded. "Let me go first. I need to make sure the streets are clear before you act carelessly again and go hurling yourself over the edge."

The way Nos Ovscura bustled with soulless, I highly doubted that. "And what makes you so sure I acted carelessly before? I *meant* to ruin your night."

"Oh." He chuckled darkly. "You did not ruin my night. On the contrary. You set it in a very different direction, one I pleasantly welcome. As for why I'm sure you acted so carelessly earlier? Your brother warned you I was a Bonespeaker. Yet you still provoked me."

"I did not provoke *you*—"

"Also." He paused, a grin curling one end of his scarred lips. "I'm the Daemon King's *son*, Sersa, love. Come with me willingly, or I'll throw you over my shoulder and bring you straight to the citadel."

We reached the top of the ladder after a strenuous climb. My lungs and muscles still throbbed from fighting off the Iarsmaí, but I refused the hand the nameless Bonespeaker extended to me.

The Daemon King's son. A soulless prince.

He swept his cloak off his shoulders and settled the warm, floor-length black fur around me. Though I drowned in it, I hadn't realized how cold I was until the warmth from his body enclosed mine. The cloak had only reached to his knees, but on me, it almost dragged on the ground like a train. I buried my hands against my sides, trying to hide the shivers barreling through me.

It surprised me how warm he actually was. I'd expected the soulless to be ice-cold beings made of marble, all the warmth from their souls lost long ago after entering the Soullands. That thought struck me as curious too. Had he entered the Soullands or been born here? If his father were truly the Daemon King, then surely he'd been born here.

Born soulless.

It seemed impossible, unnatural. Then again, the Daemon King was immortal, practically considered a god.

The Bonespeaker reached his arm around my shoulders. Instantly, I pulled away, horrified by the gesture.

"Stop," he said in a curt voice. It wasn't a command, and I wondered how he controlled his magic. "You need to stay close to me, or your stench will summon every last Sluagh in the city."

"*Stench?*" I wanted to retort with something about the way he smelled, but metal and evergreen clouded my senses, clinging to his cloak. The scent of fire also lingered somewhere beneath.

I liked how he smelled, and I hated myself for admitting it, albeit only in my head.

"I told you the Sluagh can hear better than anything in the Soullands. But they can also smell your soul. My scent should mask yours."

"*Should*," I repeated. We were relying on chance now. Instead of bothering to press him on how likely it was the Sluagh would find me, I cleared my throat. "What's your name?"

"Nessin," he said guardedly. "Come on."

He steered us away from the bridge, a few hundred feet to our left. I didn't dare look over my shoulder at the chasm I'd fallen into only minutes ago.

I hoped Ciel and Ailerby had made it back to House Scáth, but the thought of Reaping Hour—of the Sluagh on their heels— unsettled me.

They can handle themselves.

The empty streets summoned a chill from my head to my toes,

and my scalp prickled. Without the usual sea of bodies to wade through, the air within the city felt like ice on my skin. The wind twisted through the meandering streets, a maze of leaning buildings all holding one another up.

I was surprised when we didn't head toward Gilders Eye but wandered deeper into the slums. Part of me was a bit disappointed. I'd never been to the wealthy side of the city, the side where gold dripped off the sprawling estates that belonged to renowned Soullander artists, bards, and scholars. Favored nobles and sickeningly wealthy traders. Labor and soul dealers and the like.

We slipped down a side street then an alleyway between two decrepit high-rises with peeling shingled roofs and an unserviceable entranceway. Nessin nudged his sharp jaw at an endless metal ladder scaling a brick wall riddled with balconies. I groaned internally as he let me climb first. My callused palms tore, my thighs once again burned, and I was never more grateful I hadn't worn a dress tonight. Dresses weren't my usual attire, but I wore them when I felt like fooling others into thinking I was a lady when in reality I *was* just as much of a scoundrel as the con artist Ciel and I had met tonight.

We reached the top of the ladder, landing on the wobbly, metal grate suspended high above the ground. The landing was connected to a maze of ascending stairs. One balcony led to the next, and Nessin gripped the handrails on either side of me, his body too close for comfort. I led the way, directed only by a bony leather finger pointing this way or that every few sets of stairs.

My brow furrowed as we reached the halfway point. The ground distorted as I looked down. My gut tugged. I couldn't focus on the height.

"Where are we going?" I hissed under my breath.

He let me walk right past the window before dragging me backward by the collar of his cloak. He pried the cracked window open and nodded. "In."

Sensing I had little choice in the matter, paired with the fact that he was helping me get off the street, I slid over the wooden windowsill and turned to watch him. Nessin followed, stooping his head to fit through. His long legs resembled a spider's as he planted his feet inside the apartment and stretched to normal height.

Nessin really wasn't as tall as any normal man though. He looked like a shadow on the ground at sunset, sinister yet striking and not the type of man—*soulless*—I ought to be alone with.

I stumbled backward, fear most certainly swirling in my gaze. He seemed to like that I was afraid of him, at least of being alone with him, but at the same time, I passed him a honed glare, refusing to let that flash of a leer on his face widen.

The two-room apartment was cleaner than I expected based on the exterior. I glimpsed a bed through a half-open door, while in the main room there was only a chair and a desk in one corner. A lone candelabra sat on top of the desk, crowded with stacks of papers. A squat table and two armchairs comprised the right side of the room, and a fireplace with a tea kettle hanging on an iron arm that rotated into the flames took up the space behind the sitting area.

"This is where you live? I find that hard to believe," I added under my breath.

"No, it's where I think. Where I come when I want to be alone."

The two armchairs suggested he had company at least occasionally, and I had to wonder if he'd invited non-Soullanders over before. I had little room to question what he did and didn't do, but a certain curiosity surfaced. Many people fell into the Wraithsea, but I doubted he had time to save them all, let alone the desire to save anyone.

It hit me then. He wanted something from me.

Even worse, I suspected that if he didn't get it, he'd take it.

Nessin maintained his distance near the window. After a second, he turned to shut and bolt it before yanking the drapes closed. "I neither brought you here to frighten you nor to hurt you. I do, however, wish to speak to you about something."

4

My brow furrowed as Nessin crossed the room and unhooked the tea kettle before disappearing into the bedroom. I heard the faint pouring of water from a jug perhaps, and then he returned and immediately started boiling it for tea.

I crept over to the fire and reached my hands toward the heat. Like the flames licking at the flue, my curiosity simmered hotter, louder.

What could a Bonespeaker—a *prince,* for gods' sakes—possibly want to talk to me about?

"Please, sit," he said.

I eyed him suspiciously, reluctant to leave the fire, but the shoebox-size apartment was warm enough even in the corners. I took off his cloak, revealing my soaked clothes. The white tunic was practically see-through.

Nessin averted his eyes, telling me it *was* see-through. It surprised me. He didn't strike me as a gentleman.

"First, why don't you change? I have fresh—"

"Clothes that won't fit me, giant?"

"I'm sure you can make do for the day while yours dry by the fire."

"Dúm's piss," I cursed under my breath.

The *day*. I closed my eyes and sighed. I would be with him the entire day. Until the sun set and the city reopened.

He fished a pair of breeches, a fresh shirt, and thick, knitted socks from a wardrobe in his bedroom. He set them on the bed before finding another clean shirt. Then he shredded strips from the bottom of it and knotted them around each of my bloody knuckles and fingers. Knowing the prince's touch would give me the shivers—and not in a good way—I was grateful for his gloves. But as his white eyes locked with mine, I wondered if his touch would feel as intense as his gaze.

I raised my eyebrows. "While I realize you've likely seen every woman in the city naked, I'd appreciate some privacy."

Arrogance exuding from him as he headed for the door, Nessin said over his shoulder, "Don't be ridiculous. The city isn't large enough to encompass—"

I shut the door on his heels, rolling my eyes. I changed, drowning in his clothes as I'd expected, and hid both Ma's spear and my lone dagger under the oversize shirt. Then I found a seat in the main room. The cushions were surprisingly plush. A little worn but so comfortable I could fall asleep after the night I'd had.

The tea kettle hissed loudly, reminding me where I was.

Something about it reminded me of the bridge, of plunging into the Wraithsea, and the Iarsmaí. My memory flashed with Ciel's face as I plummeted toward the water. I could only imagine he was thinking the worst right now.

"Can you help me get word to my brother and friend?" I asked. "To tell them I'm all right? I don't want my clan trying to cross the chasm, let alone my mother trying."

"Ah, the Shadowess," he said, setting two porcelain cups and the steaming teapot on the squat table between us. "I've heard tales about your mother, that she trains warriors from all over the world, aye? Did she train you?"

I glared up at him around strips of my soaked, black hair. "Why don't you find me a spear and you can tell me yourself?"

But I froze as soon as the words tumbled from my mouth. I still had my spear. I waved my hand as he started to pour us both a cup.

"I'm not drinking your poison, my prince." I had the urge to flutter my eyelashes mockingly.

"As I said previously, if I'd wanted the Iarsmaí to kill you I wouldn't have headed to the beach. Or I'd kill you now myself." His hand grazed a short-handled scythe at his hip as if he'd again plucked the thoughts from a moment before right from my mind.

"I didn't see you rushing to help me," I accused.

"What, are you a damsel in distress? You seemed perfectly capable of handling the Iarsmaí on your own."

Steam rose from the cup of tea he'd poured me despite my declination, and I imagined it as a stream of smoke from my nostrils.

"You were watching then." I shifted in the leather chair. "You're a monster, you know that?"

"Giant. Monster. Do you have any other endearing names for me?" He nudged the teacup closer toward me.

"I don't want your gods-damned poisoned tea, I said."

"You have a real mouth on you, you know that?"

"You have no idea."

"No. But I am enjoying the learning process." Nessin traced the edge of his lip with his gloved thumb, never looking away from me. "I like sharp edges, especially people with them."

Swallowing, I leaned back in my seat.

A man had never made me feel so many mixed emotions at once. And I knew every emotion to be had.

His eyes narrowed on me. "Let me get straight to the point then. I was going for the hospitable approach—saving you from the Sluagh, fresh clothes, a bit of tea—but it appears you're more of a get-to-the-point sort of lass, aye?"

"Aye," I growled.

Nessin licked his scarred lips. "I need to present my intended to the Daemon King in three nights on Hwain. Each of my brothers is required to do so."

My eyes widened. I pushed myself farther into my seat. "Your intended?"

"My bride or groom."

"I know what 'intended' means."

"And *you*, with that foul mouth and your fitting appearance are just what I need for the Daemon King to stop questioning me." Now, his white eyes raked over me as if he were undressing me.

Gods. He was decidedly not a gentleman. "Questioning you how?"

He smirked. "That's hardly any of your concern."

"You are making it my concern." I paused. "You know what? You're right because I don't care. We just met, and you think I'd agree to...what, exactly? Pretend to be your betrothed?" I scoffed so loud I swore the neighbors through the thin walls would hear me.

"I think anyone would agree for a price, Sersa." He held my gaze for even longer than before.

Something about the way Nessin said my name—*Sayr-suh* instead of *Sir-sa*—gave me pause. I wondered where he was from. He looked relaxed with his hands on the armrests. But then he tilted his head at me. Maybe he wasn't relaxed at all.

He looked like he was trying to understand me.

"Have you ever met someone who deals in secrets, Sersa? No? Then let me enlighten you. Secrets are sort of my thing if you will. It's not uncommon along Gilders Eye, of course. Secrets are power, are they not?"

I squinted.

"If I was to say I had started gathering *your* secrets, which would you think I had garnered?"

I wanted Nessin to stop watching me now. He hadn't pulled his eyes from mine yet. *Prince Nessin.* All of this was ridiculous. Unbelievable. The thought of a prince wanting to learn my secrets at all irrationally inflated my head a bit.

But pulling the most likely secrets to the tip of my tongue wasn't difficult. They often danced in my mind with slow, taunting movements. My secrets weren't like everyone else's either. They didn't revolve around an unrequited crush or an embarrassing moment I'd experienced as a child.

My secrets could bring down my entire clan. Mine could have our allies turning on us in a heartbeat and our enemies at our throats before eventide. If the magicless unblood clans found out Clan Scáth no longer possessed their shadow magic, we were as good as dead. Or at least as good as overthrown.

But the world was less kind to young women like me. I'd be married off to another chieftain or warlord like a cow being traded. I was said to have good blood—all because magic flowed through my veins—and I would be forced to give a chieftain fifteen years my senior a dozen broods, all with magic of their own.

Or at least that was the idea.

If my clan was disbanded and stripped of their status and title, my fate would be unbearable.

"I don't pretend to know what secrets of mine you possess," I said instead of giving in.

Prince Nessin leaned forward, and it was right then, his power exuded from him. He was not a Bonespeaker or a tower. He was the Daemon King's *son*, and I was nothing in comparison. He could have me dead—either by his hand or another's—before I could leave the city.

One side of his lips quirked upwards, as did his scarred eyebrow.

"First," he said, his voice neither high-pitched nor low, "I know you have magic. I need someone who can protect themselves when necessary and contain themselves the rest of the time. And before you open that beautiful mouth of yours, let me remind you that you did daringly swat a drink out of a prince's hand this evening."

"I didn't know you were a prince."

"Something tells me you would have done it even if I were the king." Nessin leaned back in his seat and folded his hands on his abdomen. "Second, I know you're your clan's heir—thanks to that mouth again." He smirked. "Third, I know your clan has lost its magic. And *no*, not because you were so foolishly thinking of it a moment ago while looking right into my eyes."

"How—"

He lazily unfolded his hands in a silencing gesture. "My scouts are good. I've had them exploring suitable options for my betrothed for weeks. And you, love, sit at the top of my list."

My face drained of color. A wave of dizziness washed over me. What else had he seen or discovered the last few weeks? "Why me?"

"Look at you. You are rather perfect. A chieftess's daughter.

Strong for your size. Capable of escaping the Iarsmaí. Unafraid of even a *Bonespeaker*. Beautiful, especially for a mortal."

Most of the reasons he rattled off sounded like veiled insults. I worked to keep my jaw from falling. But none of them were the real reason why.

"Not to mention, you are *so* obviously attracted to me that you needn't pretend on that much. It's the small things that give you away. Your pupils. Those eyes lingering on my mouth. The way you licked your lips in the Devil's Tail when you looked up at me, probably without even realizing you had..." He reached across the space between us effortlessly and dusted a gloved finger on my bottom lip, just as he had his moments ago, before tracing it upward.

I opened my mouth to deny his claims or maybe to order him to move his thumb.

Or take it in my mouth.

Unfazed, Nessin continued over me, "Fourth, but not the last of your secrets I've gathered, is that your father Bain Scáth disappeared a year ago, never to be seen again."

Red swarmed behind my eyes. I leaped toward him, reaching for Ma's spear.

When my hand came up empty, he flashed the sheathed weapon, shortened to a quarter of its usual length in my face. Heat crept up my neck. I was practically in his lap, one knee between his legs. I lost my balance, recovering a second too late with my palms on his hard chest.

The anger faded to a paler hue of red. One I'd never seen before.

My knee had slid deeper between his long legs, right up against *him*.

With what I felt there, I would have thought any other man was aroused, but Nessin wasn't like the other men I'd fooled around with. My knee was nowhere near as sensitive as the areas I suddenly imagined him touching either, where, surely, a prince possessed the expertise of a god. Or something far wickeder in his case.

Trying to stifle my spiraling thoughts, I reminded myself Prince Nessin was not a man I was fooling around with.

"See? You prove my point," he said. I couldn't be sure whether he'd scooted forward, or I'd leaned into him. But our lips led, drawing us closer. "Already thinking about me between your—"

Fighting a blush, I reached for the hem of my shirt—for the dagger there—but the prince was swifter. He slid the dagger tucked into my waistband free and whipped it across the apartment with finesse. It landed behind his desk, upright in the wall with a thud. His fluidity hinted at great skill. Too bad there was no target there.

Nessin leaned into me, relishing our closeness, confidently thinking his presence clouded my head and my focus. He'd hardly grazed my midriff to grab my dagger. Yet my skin was on fire.

His bony hands gripped my forearms, keeping me close and my hands on him. "Your father is alive, Sersa Scáth. I saw him at the citadel a few weeks back. There are auctions every few weeks for mortals trapped in the City of Soulless, and ones the Sluagh gather in their daily hunt. He was being auctioned off, along with several dozen other mortals. I suspect his buyer was someone who belongs to the Daemon King's inner circle, but I can't be certain. Yet."

I staggered, almost falling over the little table behind me before he caught me by the wrist and my lower back, steadying me. I shoved myself free and put distance between us, stumbling toward the wall to my right. I rested against it. Sweat broke out on my forehead, and I tasted salt on my lips from the sea as I licked them and swallowed.

Gods.

He had to be lying.

I folded my arms around my waist and squeezed, hoping it would get rid of the spinning sensation in my gut.

"I don't know who he was sold to," Nessin continued, "but a powerful blood like your father—"

"He wasn't a blood. *Isn't* a blood." I shook my head. What the prince was telling me might not be true. Still, the explanation tumbled over my lips. "My pa was from the unblood lands to the east. He... He had no magic. It's why he took my mother's name when they wed."

Eyes narrowed, Nessin considered this, like it was just another secret to piece together with the rest.

"Blood or no blood, we can and will find him together. Hwain commences a whole parade of events, which my brothers and I—

along with our betrothed—will be required to attend. Some of them will be at the citadel. Others will be in Gilders Eye. If you agree to pretend to be my intended, you'll not only have access to the entire city and the Daemon King's Citadel, but you'll also be able to walk into the Gilders' mansions without standing out like a mortal in a flock of Sluagh. And when we find your father, I will help you get him out."

My voice sounded hoarse. "Sounds like a pretty big *if* to me."

"I said when, not if. I can only supply you with the facts, Sersa. Whether you want to believe them...now, *that* is up to you." He stood and plucked the cloak off the back of my empty seat, draping it around his shoulders.

"Where are we going?"

He set Ma's spear on the little table between the two chairs. Then his colorless eyes flicked to mine again.

"*We* are not going anywhere. You must stay here. I have some business to attend to. Use the time to think about my offer and don't leave the apartment. I'll be back at sunset to escort you to the bridge. We'll be less noticeable in the influx when the city reopens."

"What about my brother? Won't you send him something for me? A note. It's all I ask," I said, trying not to sound like I was begging.

"I quite *like* the sound of you begging me," he said with a haughty smirk.

"Say it again, daemon, and I won't hesitate like I did before to impale you with my spear."

Nessin glared at me for a moment before he crossed the room, fished out a clean sheet of paper, and nodded at the desk. I didn't bother sitting. My hands shook as they found the quill, dipped it in the little inkpot, and penned a quick note before signing my name.

"How will you get it to him?" I asked.

He tugged a gilded horn out from under his high-collared coat and pressed it to his lips. The balcony outside rattled under a Sluagh's taloned feet as it landed. I scrambled backward. Not bothering to hide his smirk, Nessin opened the window, slid over the windowsill, and handed the Sluagh my note.

"House Scáth," he instructed. I barely heard him over the early dawn wind coiling through the otherwise quiet city. Reaping Hour had to be finished then. "Harm no one or I'll skin your wings and wear them myself."

Before I could ask him how he'd summoned the Sluagh, Nessin disappeared.

I scurried toward the window to shut it and looked below.

The Daemon Prince was nowhere in sight.

I spent the morning trapped in the apartment, leafing through the dastardly prince's books until I fell asleep in the armchair sometime midday.

When the window creaked, I snapped my eyes open. Nessin hunched in front of it, remaining on the balcony. He wore a tattered brown cloak, the hood blowing in the wind around his high cheekbones.

"You look like you should be herding sheep," I said.

"No, only one small woman with a penchant for violence."

I ignored him. "You realize that cloak doesn't make you look shorter, right?"

"My size is out of my control. It's time. Get changed and be quick."

He extended the fur-lined cloak he'd worn earlier across the sill, and I snatched it, annoyed to the bone with him.

"No hello? No here is some supper?"

"I don't need you retching from the nerves."

"Why would I be nervous?"

"Because a Daemon Prince hid you in the City of Soulless for an entire day. If I'm seen, then you're seen, and people will question what we were doing together. Also," Nessin added, "I'd prefer if you have a day to weigh my offer. Wouldn't want you to feel like you're being forced into anything."

I rolled my eyes and retrieved my dry clothes dangling in front of the hearth. Upon further inspection inside his bedroom, my tunic had a slash across the torso. I kept Nessin's shirt on and tucked it into the waistband of my pants before finding my boots and slipping them on. They still sloshed noticeably with each step. In a cracked mirror on the wall, my appearance was unruly as all hell, my black hair still in tangles from the Wraithsea and my jaw and neck scraped from those damn Iarsmai's skeletal fingers.

I recalled Nessin's lingering gaze, the way he'd traced my silhouette through his clothes.

His thumb on my cupid's bow.

The fire I felt beneath his touch.

My lips weren't as full as his, nor the rest of my features as sharp yet perfect, but he had called me beautiful.

"For a mortal," I snapped at myself in the mirror.

Casting my folly aside, I spun the pelt around, fastening it at the neck, and entered the main room. He handed me my dagger, which he'd yanked from the wall, and I slid it back into my waistband. Then I hung my spear on my belt before following Nessin down the network of balconies until we reached solid ground. The swaying motion of their instability stayed with me.

Maybe he'd been right about the retching. Bile slid up my throat like a serpent curling around in my belly.

Nessin held me close again, and I settled into the warmth of his body more willingly as he led me through the slums toward the bridge. The fact that he was keeping me upright didn't hurt either.

Once the bridge was in sight, the influx of tourists made my head spin. We'd have to wade against the crowd this time, and it wouldn't go unnoticed by the Soul Guard standing at various points along the bridge atop the balustrades that Ciel, Ailerby, and I had balanced on the day before.

Our first step onto the bridge felt like walking on thin ice. Being that Nessin was taller than everyone—a Colossi indeed—hiding among the crowd proved near impossible, and though he stooped his head, I suspected others caught a glimpse of the white hair he'd done a poor job of hiding.

As a strand of hair fell, I reached up and hastily shoved it back under his hood.

"Thank you, love, but we've been spotted."

"Would you stop calling me 'love' already?"

"Would you do anything but make that face? You look suspicious." Then he whispered in my ear, "I can't pass the bridge's midpoint." His lips came dangerously close, burrowing themselves in my hair. That same intoxicating scent from before clouded my senses. "Look natural. I'll get you as far as I can."

"What do you mean? Why?" The immediate question in my mind was how I would reach the end without him. No one was coming this way.

I would be too obvious.

"I can only pass through the veil during Hwain, unless I want to walk around in soulform. Good news is neither can the guards."

I realized then my agape mouth and furrowed brow did little to convince anyone what Nessin was trying to: that we were together, maybe lovers, like everyone else in the crowd.

"Soulform? What does that mean?" I said through the fakest grin I'd ever forced.

"I am soulless. In your world, I would look like a spirit."

As we reached the guards, I forced a stupid fake giggle like Nessin had said something hilarious.

It didn't work.

"*Halt.*" The guard's voice reached the center of the crowd we'd been elbowing our way through, and several people glanced around before realizing who he'd spoken to. Bulged eyes darted to us. Patrons entering the city put their heads down and assumed a quicker pace like they didn't want to be associated with us, let alone seen in our proximity.

The guard hopped down from his post, thick boots landing with a dull thud, and moved across the bridge toward us. A path cleared for him. His legs moved slowly, each step deliberate and meant to frighten. He clasped gloved hands behind his back.

Nessin threw back his shoulders and turned, placing me behind him. His body eclipsed mine. "You run when I say so, aye?"

I nodded against his arm.

"Where are you lot headed so early in the night?" said the Soul Guard. Based on the pale eyes mirroring Nessin's, he had Soullander magic of some sort too.

He couldn't be a Bonespeaker.

Which left Soulreaper.

I swallowed.

"We forgot something at home," Nessin said to the guard. "We'll be back in a few."

"What could you possibly have forgotten?"

"Kofs, obviously," Nessin answered drily.

"You can take out a loan at any one of the betting halls or the pleasure dens." The guard's gaze veered around Nessin, landing on me. "Is that where you got this one?"

"Excuse—"

Nessin squeezed my wrist, silencing me.

Whereas my voice had been a cracked shout, his came out smooth. "I don't fancy the collateral. A sliver of my soul for a few thousand kofs? For a fleeting tumble in the sheets? I don't think so. And *she* doesn't belong to any of the dens, so I'd prefer if you didn't look at her that way."

The Soul Guard sucked on his teeth. His eyes narrowed as if trying to understand how Nessin knew the payment for loans in the city was nothing too painful.

Just your gods-damned soul.

I certainly hadn't known. How hadn't I recognized anyone who lived on Clan Scáth's lands since Ciel, Ailerby, and I had started visiting the city a year ago?

But that wasn't right. Nessin's eyes would have been the first thing the Soul Guard noticed. He knew he was from here.

"It's funny," the guard said, taking a step toward Nessin. "Watching you try to hide a mortal when you ought to be using her, devouring that delicious soul instead, my prince."

Without warning, Nessin shoved me to the side and shouted, "Go!"

He simultaneously commanded the Soul Guards who didn't get away to halt and shoved the guard who'd spoken off the bridge. I stared, dumbfounded for a moment as the man plummeted, stumbling over my feet as I ran.

If only the Iarsmaí thirsted for soulless like the guard as much as they had me.

Nessin's Bonespeaker command was instant, I gathered, with another quick glance over my shoulder.

The momentum of his shove had given me a good head start, but the pathway the crowd had cleared for us quickly filled with bodies again like blood gushing toward a cut, and the guards flung themselves into the sea of people after me.

I elbowed and shoved every person who got in my way.

All I needed to do was make it to the halfway point.

I rammed into a couple hanging onto one another, and they flew apart, swallowed by the crowd. Gasps rippled through the air—people leaped out of my way now, and a path cleared for me once again.

I bolted forward, paying no attention to the guards on my tail.

I pleaded with my aching thighs and calves not to let me down, not to give out now of all times, and thanked the skies for all Ma's harsh training.

When I tumbled across the midpoint, I caught myself on the stone, hands and knees first. The raw skin on my palms tore further, as did my breeches.

I looked over my shoulder at the Soul Guards trapped behind the barrier and worked to slow my breathing. Their eyes were white-hot flames, their teeth gritted, and their bodies rigid.

Nessin had not only shadowed me to the middle of the bridge to make sure I'd made it but he'd also commanded them not to run after me. Even sent a guard into the Wraithsea.

Something in me quelled. Why had he cared enough to get me home? I'd lived next to the Soullands long enough—hell, lived in Os Íseal long enough—to know that nothing came without a price.

I gathered myself off the ground and jogged to the end of the bridge until I reached the rocky sand of Os Íseal's shore. I paused and looked over my shoulder again. Nessin stood tall and hollered at the guards before turning his sights on me. The faintest leer curled his lips, but the realization of just how dangerous Nessin's world was settled at the bottom of my gut as I turned away and sprinted for home.

The night passed through blue-tinted glasses, so I decided to paint.

As I wielded the thinnest of brushes and hooked a finger through my palette with the other hand, I took a step back from the canvas and squared my shoulders. The scenery I'd painted was a motley of dark colors—a macabre city beside the sea.

My inspiration was all too obvious, and I wished I'd put my own spin on the city. But every detail felt crystalline in my mind's eye.

Painting was the sole activity that both helped get me out of my head and required me to be in it, entirely focused, so I turned to it whenever the waves of Pa's disappearance started to drown me. And Nessin had certainly stirred those feelings up. Painting wasn't exactly a cure, but when I was up for the task, it always helped reset the colors that tinted my mind, my moods.

Naturally, I couldn't stop thinking of Pa. I wanted to twirl the paintbrush in my fingers and jab him in the eye with the pointy end.

The prince, not Pa.

I pursed my lips and continued to eye the city—the prince's city—I'd created on the canvas. I was surprised I hadn't painted it every shade and hue of blue instead.

"It's superb," Ailerby said.

He sat to my left, his head and legs dangling off the leather armrests of his chair. As Ailerby sat up and turned in his seat, all the blood rushed out of his red face. He was toying with a miniature sealed pot of paint, watching the glittering black tint slide around inside like goo.

"Agreed," Ciel said. "Though I can't imagine why you'd want to paint the city that imprisoned and nearly drowned you."

"That city showed all of us mercy this morning," I said. "The Sluagh could have snatched both of you up."

"Going to set up an altar and pray to the Daemon King from now on?" Ciel asked. "Or perhaps his son?" Naturally, he ignored my second comment.

I fought the urge to turn around and flick my brush at him, splattering him with paint. Instead, I focused harder on my brushstrokes.

"How long has this painting taken you?" Ailerby's voice was a swath of curiosity with a dash of disbelief. He was also trying to smooth over the tension between Ciel and me.

"A few bells," I said with a glance at the black sky.

"Longer." Ciel's correction was harsh, though I recognized the tone beneath. Brotherly concern. "You should rest, Sersa. If only for a bell or two. You haven't since you got back, and anyone would be unsettled after the time you had."

"I'm not unsettled."

After the high of the night before, my spiraling thoughts threatened to lull me into a slump, if anything. If I stopped moving, stopped painting, I'd have to face Nessin's words repeatedly. They wouldn't stop replaying in my mind.

To say that Pa had disappeared rather than left us was a distinction I'd clung to for the last year. While my uncles believed he'd left, I knew neither my brother nor mother accepted it. Neither did I. If Pa had left, his favorite belongings would have disappeared with him. He would have said goodbye or told us where we could find him at the very least. Wouldn't he?

It was these details that kept my head above water.

Nessin had known exactly how to lure me in. Why he needed someone to pose as his betrothed, he hadn't revealed, but the thought of making it out alive from a faux engagement to him in the Court of Soulless was so preposterous.

I shouldn't be entertaining it, but a part of me was doing just that.

"What I need is to keep myself"—I threw back my shoulders, rolling out the kinks in my neck— "occupied."

Behind me, I heard the rustling of papers being gathered and pressed between a book before Ciel stood and crossed the room. He lingered beside my canvas, hands clasped behind his back. His eyes, as dark as my own, were hard as glass and so watchful I felt like they might burn through me. Ciel looked away then and reached for one of my clean brushes. He ran his finger over the tip of the brush, watching its bristles flick back and forth.

"Would you tell us what he said again?" he asked innocently.

My gaze darted to the windows beside my easel, noting a dusting of snow beginning to fall outside. The sky was heavy and dark, a silent promise that the storm would last a while. We were still in the season of Harvest, but the weather had decided to yield to the Rime early. It wasn't good news for our food stock. Watching the snow fall, I tried to recall everything Prince Nessin had said, but my memory wasn't the best. I remembered mere fragments of our conversation and how it had made me feel, but the rest felt out of reach.

"I've told you five times now, Ciel." I tapped my paintbrush in a deep rust color and went over a spot I'd already finished, not wanting to look at him. "He claimed Pa was sold to someone in Gilders Eye, okay?"

The prince's claim was a serious one, and we would have been fools to believe him. But I could see the wheels turning in my brother's mind too. He was probably entertaining the idea of posing as Prince Nessin's betrothed himself. I didn't know my brother's type exactly. He'd courted all sorts of young men, from bards to farmers to a librarian who I swore he'd never break up with for the free books, but I thought Prince Nessin was probably everyone's type, unfortunately—even my own.

Until he opens that gods-damned mouth of his.

Something about Nessin's face beckoned my irritation. I released an exasperated breath, slamming my brush down on the easel's ledge. It wobbled. With a clear of the throat, I set my palette down before swirling my brush in a jar of water. My fingers fumbled for the ties of my smock. I slipped it off my arms and draped it on a hook behind the canvas.

I put my hands on my hips. "The prince said the sale happened very recently, but he doesn't know which Gilder purchased him. That's it. Can we move on?"

"Ailerby did cover for you with Ma," Ciel said. "Perhaps entertain our curiosity a bit longer."

"Don't bring me into this!" Ailerby's mouth twisted into a scowl and his brow furrowed. Since I'd returned, he'd altered his appearance. Now his hair was red as a flame with eyes like citrine gems. He'd imitated me while I was away. They'd almost gone to Ma, but Nessin's note had arrived in the nick of time—with its messenger, the Sluagh.

"You did me a favor, Ciel," I said. "So what? If you hadn't, Ma would have marched into the City of Soulless and hunted down the Daemon King herself. She'd be dead."

"Well, she didn't, and she's not." Ciel was growing impatient—a man who rarely lost his grip on logical thought and action. Maybe I was rubbing off on him. "What did the prince want in exchange for the information? Did you believe him? Did he seem like he was lying? Also, if he was sold recently, where has he been the last year?"

I dropped my hands, balled into fists at my sides. "I don't know! You don't actually believe," I hissed under my breath, eyeing the cracked door across the chamber, "that I'd entertain it, do you?"

Ciel recognized my fury, examining my expression warily.

Sparks of red appeared in the air around me, though only I could see them.

We'd both inherited Ma's magic in theory, but the blood had never revealed itself to Ciel. As for me, the first time the magic had rushed through my veins, I'd stripped my clan members of their magic and woken up in a blackened field.

Pa and I were supposed to have finished our hunt in the woods a bell before the Hwain feast started last year when he'd just disappeared. As soon as I realized I was alone, I whirled round and round until I made myself dizzy and my throat turned hoarse from shouting for him. I searched a wide radius before running to the edge of the woods, shoving branches in my way only for them to snap backward and thwack my face. Little cuts here and there were nothing compared to the gaping hole forming in my chest.

Finally, I tumbled onto the vast fields our clan owned, stretching as far as the eye could see with crops to get us through the Rime season.

"*Pa!*"

No one answered me. Pa was gone.

I didn't remember stumbling to the feasting hall, but my memory as I arrived remained lucid. Even without closing my eyes, I remembered the hall set up for Hwain with yellow and green ribbons, wreaths of dried flowers, and enough candles to bathe the rafters crowning the lofty ceiling in bright gold. I barged through the doors, my chest heaving, my hair and dress a mess, strewn with twigs and grass stains. The entire clan—hundreds—turned to stare at me. The cheerful tune the bard played died abruptly.

My gaze found two empty seats at the head table. One on either side of Ma at the center.

The black tendrils swirled around my wrists.

"Pa is gone. Pa is gone," I whispered. Then I shouted, the words turning into a garbled shriek.

And in the blink of an eye, the tendrils had swarmed, twisting and coiling between gaps of people, stealing every last drop of magic in their blood.

It was a problem, to say the least—my inability to control my emotions. No matter how I tried, they gripped me. Controlled me.

"I'm not going to pose as the Daemon Prince's betrothed," I said finally, still with too much bite but also a hint of defeat.

Ciel followed my gaze to the door before Ailerby popped out of his seat and tiptoed across the room. His careful hands inched it shut. The small chamber was littered with my paintings from over the years, the ones I hadn't been able to part with. Luckily, the room was so packed that it didn't echo as much as the rest of House Scáth. Besides my bedroom, it was the only place—and my art the only thing—that truly belonged to me. The difference between my chambers and this room was that the servants never bothered me in here.

My brother sighed, tearing me from my thoughts. "You were there an entire day, Sersa. You must have a gut feeling about it all."

"I don't. He left shortly after bringing me to his safehouse in the middle of the slums, and we spoke nothing more of it. Now, I want *us* to never speak of it again, Ciel. I'm sure the prince was lying. I mean, why would the Sluagh keep Pa alive? If they brought him to the Daemon King, why wouldn't he harvest his soul? None of it adds up because it's all a *lie.*"

"The prince—"

"Probably wants to devour my soul too. You said so yourself at the

Devil's Tail. He's a Bonespeaker. And you heard him. He's not just a Bonespeaker, so for all we know, he could be a Soulreaper too."

"The Devil's Tail? That was him? That was the prince?" Ciel's eyes widened. "Gods. I'm surprised you're not volunteering to be his betrothed in a heartbeat."

I swatted Ciel's arm.

"Pose as his betrothed. *Pose*," Ciel corrected. But he and Ailerby grinned cheekily at one another.

I maneuvered around my stool and a cart full of painting supplies before falling back on the sofa. I did want Pa back. Our family back. Ma to return to normal.

"You want me to take him up on his offer, don't you? That's what this is all about."

Ciel took a swift step forward. He knelt in front of me, reaching for my hands and squeezing them. "You wouldn't be alone."

"I would be exposed. I'd have to be on my absolute best behavior, and we both know I've never been good at that."

Ma had done her best to keep me out of the spotlight. *At least until you learn some self-control, Sersa.*

I'd never had the heart to tell her my moods weren't something that could be controlled. They were as overpowering as the tides.

"With Ailerby's help," Ciel continued, "we could visit you every few days."

My throat caught on a swallow, and I chuckled darkly. "Oh, would that stop me from accidentally murdering a member of court? The Daemon King himself?" I didn't know whether my unpredictable magic could kill one of the soulless, but the risk was too great. "Did the two of you already discuss this behind my back?"

"No," Ciel said. "Fine, yes. But, Sersa, you know we have always been here for you. You know we *are* here for you. Please don't push us away. I thought... Since you are the one the Daemon Prince invited, I only thought you might want to do this. For Pa. Forgive me for pushing you. This is your choice and yours alone."

At that, Ciel stood.

I checked myself. I was breathing deeply, my nostrils flaring with anger and shock. Ciel had begun formulating his own plan involving me without *including* me.

"I– I only want Pa back. Please understand. I'll be here if you need to talk," Ciel added as he backed away.

He pulled Ailerby out of the room with him as something inside me cracked. Ciel said he was here for me if I started to drown again, but my own brother had to retreat when I was angry or afraid or anxious for whatever reason or no reason at all. And I wanted him to retreat. The constant nagging in the back of my mind was always there.

What if I hurt him?

Ciel hadn't been at the feast on the night I'd stolen my clan members' magic. He'd been visiting the Druids in the Blood Peaks with Ailerby. It was a fact I thanked the universe for every day. If I had taken either Ciel's nonexistent magic, or Ailerby's incredible ability to change his appearance and mirror others, I'd never forgive myself.

It could happen again.

Though I was grateful Ciel and Ailerby had left me to my thoughts, I found my mind was as cloudy as the sky.

As I studied my painting chamber, I swore it looked a little inky. A little tinged with black. Fear came in many forms, but if I wasn't entertaining the thought of agreeing to Prince Nessin's arrangement to find Pa...

Then what was I afraid of?

#

I finished the painting sometime after midnight.

My mind had finally emptied itself, replaced by a flood of exhaustion so total and complete that I knew I would be asleep as soon as my head hit the pillow. Still, I stopped in the kitchens.

Maeve, one of my mother's personal servants, offered to brew me some tea, but I insisted she head to bed. I could do it myself. At Ma's insistence, the High Druidess had looked me over the last time they'd visited my brother. She'd recommended an herbal tea, some concoction of ingredients before bed every night, but I knew Ma had been looking for something more.

After I'd accidentally rid my clan members of their magic five seasons ago, Ma wanted to know if I still possessed it, separate from mine. If I could somehow give it back. She consulted the Druids for every decision she made, be it which crops to plant or how to deal with unbloods who were plotting against Clan Scáth, but I thought she'd been too ashamed to tell them the clan now lacked magic.

I also thought the shrewd High Druidess had gathered that secret on her own.

The Druids' visit had soured my mood for other reasons. Ciel would be leaving for the Blood Peaks soon. There, the Druids learned and practiced. It was there where my brother would live for the next ten years, at least, before he could serve House Scáth—or another—as one of the sages the clan consulted. It was neither guaranteed Ciel would be placed with us, nor that Clan Scáth controlled the Northern Pointe of Clais by then.

Time was a strange concept to me. I understood the principles of it, but the practice was hard to keep up with. Imagining my brother ten years from now, me ten years from now, proved too impossible for my mind.

I supposed it was one of the reasons why I worked myself until exhaustion. It was how I managed to sleep most nights, how I managed to conquer time: I went until I couldn't think of anything else, until my thoughts became as slow as honey and I longed for sleep so badly that I didn't even know what time it was. Some days, I craved sleep so much, it was all I wanted to do. But when I was like this, set afire by some new idea, painting, or a deal as dark and risky as what the Daemon Prince had posed, rest never came easily, let alone actual sleep.

Sometimes, it never came at all.

Once Maeve had left the kitchen, I fetched a lemon from a basket of citrus fruits on the center counter and selected a clean knife from the drawer. I held it firmly against a marble cutting slab and began to slice.

By the time I found a rhythm, a voice tickled my neck.

"*Hullo, Sersa. You're up late, eh?*"

With a flinch, I fumbled the lemon, and the knife sliced my palm. Blood oozed from the cut, trickling off the counter's edge and dripping onto the floor. I reached for the nearest rag and spun in a circle, but the figure who'd spoken was nowhere to be found.

"Over here," he taunted.

I spun again, eyes landing on the shadow that seemed to materialize into existence. Prince Nessin stood in a dark corner of the kitchen. Moonlight scattered the floor before him, but only his boots were illuminated.

The rest of him remained in shadow.

"What are you doing here? How– You said you couldn't come here."

"I said nothing of the sort." His voice was hard as glass again. He was spinning something between his pointer fingers. A closer look and I realized it was an elegant dagger. "I *said*," he corrected with an air of arrogance, "that I would resemble a spirit in your world."

"Step into the light then." My voice cracked ever so slightly. I hoped he hadn't noticed, but a sliver of a smirk tainted his scarred lips.

Prince Nessin did as I requested, allowing the silvery moonlight to drench him. White eyes bit into my soul like a fisherfolk's hook. He wasn't exactly transparent, but he was luminous as the stars, every inch of his body indicating he was indeed a god of sorts from beyond the veil that separated our worlds, no matter how thin. His limbs looked longer in my world, his form stretched even further. Here, however, he seemed a shred less monstrous. More beautiful than menacing.

I wanted to reach out and swipe a hand through his silhouette.

Ma had told me stories as a child, tales about charming lurers who tempted mortals to enter their world, only to have their souls sucked out. Looking upon him, drinking in every tantalizing drop of him, I could see how he might tempt a less wary damsel than myself.

So you think, said a voice in my thoughts.

I wondered if Nessin had the ability to infiltrate my mind, to implant thoughts as well.

He leaned against the wall, folding his arms across his chest. "Have you thought about our conversation at all?"

"No," I lied. "But I suspect it's all you've done, since you're here. Couldn't last even a day."

"Time is the most precious thing we have. And the thing is, Sersa, I know you will think of me every day for the *rest* of your life if you do not agree to help me. I know you want your father back. I know how you long to reunite your broken family. But I'm here because I ran into your brother tonight at the Devil's Tail. Coincidentally," he added. His eyes dropped to my bleeding palm, which I'd forgotten about. He gestured with the dagger. "You may want to take care of that. I can't talk to you if you're unconscious."

I readjusted the rag, finding an unsoiled spot to press against my palm. Nessin took a step toward the counter's other side, spreading his arms as he leaned into it.

"*Why* did Ciel visit you?" I gritted my teeth, suddenly too aware of my throbbing wound and my fear. He'd gone behind my back, worse this time.

"He said if you won't agree to help me, he would be willing."

"You wouldn't."

"Why not? Ciel is handsome as you, and he is willing to do anything to see this plan succeed. He didn't get bogged down by the details." Nessin raised a dark eyebrow, fingers simultaneously sheathing his dagger. "He only cares about finding your father and returning him home, no matter the cost."

"The trouble is, neither he nor I know precisely what the costs are, and my suspicions tell me you're not willing to reveal all of them."

"They will be revealed in time and as needed. The king—"

"Your father."

"—will not take a deception of this nature lightly, Sersa. The less you know, the better. That way, you won't be held culpable as my accomplice if anything happens."

I scoffed. "Requesting my help to fool the Daemon King is culpability enough."

"Semantics." Nessin rolled his eyes. He didn't bother walking around the counter to halt in front of me but instead went right through it. I backed into the hard edge as he drew closer. Moonlight streamed through him, translucent and beautiful yet ominous.

"Think about it. It would be easy, love." I thought I felt his cool breath dust my cheek as he leaned toward me to murmur, but maybe that was my imagination. He pulled back, pinning my eyes with his. "I'm not asking for your body, only your camaraderie and your word of discretion—though there is the fact that I'm a Bonespeaker. Once you've agreed to enter our arrangement of your own volition, of course, I could command you to stay quiet."

"Of course." I rolled my eyes solely for the excuse to avert my gaze. The relief was fleeting, and I was drawn back to him. My head felt cloudy. Was he commanding me now? "You must forget what you are quite a lot, since you have to keep bringing it up in conversation."

Prince Nessin chuckled.

Our lips drew closer. Now I was certain I felt his hand on my waist. How could I? How could he make his hands feel solid —*tangible*—while in soulform?

"I know what I am. I saw all the fear in your eyes and your thoughts when we were alone in my apartment earlier. Deep down, you know what I am too. All mortals know what lurks in my city, my realm. So few want to face it. So few are wise enough to accept it as factual."

"If you truly wanted me to consider your offer, you'd stop insulting my kind."

"True. Forgive me. I love mortals to death."

"Mm hmm. For our souls, I'm sure."

He quirked his scarred eyebrow at me then brushed a gloved finger up my cheekbone, tracing my arched brow and pushing a black strand of hair behind my ear. I shuddered under his touch, and a whip of lightning struck the lowest part of my belly.

"You may change my mind yet, Sersa Scáth," he said, his rasped voice somehow smooth and...

Dare I say, seductive?

The thought wouldn't do.

"How are you doing that?" I asked.

"Doing what?"

"You know what. Touching me."

"Why? Do you like it?" Nessin asked.

"No."

"That's a lie."

I swallowed. "Shouldn't you be leaving?"

"Probably. Tell me one thing."

"Will you command me if I don't, Your Majesty?" I asked.

"You would call me Your Highness if I expected you to. The Daemon King is Your Majesty. But my realm will be calling me the latter soon enough."

"Cocky."

"You have no idea," he said.

I couldn't take it. Him.

I needed him to leave.

"My question. If you will. The existence of strong feelings for someone, irritation even, paves the way for passion. It stokes a fire inside us. If we had met on different terms, would you have asked me to take you home last night? Pleaded with me to touch you as you'd imagined in my apartment?"

I shoved Prince Nessin away, but my hands went through his silhouette like smoke.

He chuckled darkly as I righted myself.

"That's a yes. You're perfect—you are the one I'm in need of for this."

While I still didn't know what *this* was, I swallowed as a harsh realization burgeoned inside me. The thought of being alone with him again for any measure of time was unbearable. Tantalizing.

Daemons were meant to tempt. He was something else altogether. Born to tempt only me maybe.

At that, the prince walked through me then the counter once more and made his way back toward the windows.

"I will be waiting for you on Dúm's Cross tomorrow at sundown. Our deception will begin right away. The Daemon King knows I ushered a young woman out of Nos Ovscura last night, and it would be difficult to explain why Ciel is my choice instead of her—you." He turned for the window and winked over his shoulder. "Especially when I already told him she's my paramour."

"Wait."

Nessin had put a foot through the window, ready to stalk back toward the shore.

"Why me? I asked you before. The truth this time."

He turned. "Your magic—and your skills with a knife or three—could come in handy in the Court of Soulless, and as I said, I need someone who can protect themselves. Plus, you have a reason to agree. Don't you?"

Nessin quirked an eyebrow. Then his ethereal silhouette passed through the window before he disappeared entirely.

Someone breathing heavily entered the kitchen.

Maeve's white-knuckle hands gripped the doorframe. "Lady Sersa! Are you okay? I heard a shout."

I'd told all the maids at least a dozen times not to call me lady, but they never caught on.

"I..." I pressed the rag harder into my palm as her eyes darted to the drips of blood on the stone floor. The warmth soaked right through, staining my hands. "I startled myself is all. I was cutting lemons when the knife slipped."

Maeve's lips pursed and she swept forward, finding me a fresh rag. She walked me toward a basin on a nearby counter. Then she dipped my hand into the cold water, summoning chills on the back of my neck. The sting of tears started in my nostrils. I tried to grit my teeth so hard the tears wouldn't fall, but I knew as well as anyone that the servants had been warned about my tendency to be frightened, to see things I shouldn't—shadow people and whatnot.

The heir is mad, some said.

Maybe I was. But I was trying. To understand myself. To understand the shifts in mood that had marked my life for as long as I could remember. I'd been a temperamental child. One moment, I'd be laughing and playing. And the next, shouting at someone or shoving a playmate to the ground. It was why I kept few friends these days. The guilt and shame I'd feel after a burst made me retreat from others. Ciel and Ailerby were all I had.

And Pa.

Pa had always been there to smooth my hair. To comfort me and say he had felt like me sometimes too. *You are in control of you, Sersy. Just remember that. Always remember that. Even when it doesn't feel like it. Even when it feels like you are in control of nothing at all. The feelings are like the tide. They always reach you on the shore, but they always retreat and roll back out to sea.*

"What happened?" Maeve interrupted my thoughts. She was careful not to ask me what I'd seen. She was more perceptive than that. To be Ma's servant, she had to be.

"Nothing. I cut my hand is all," I repeated.

Maeve left me standing near the basin after knotting the ends of the fresh rag around my palm. Then she crossed the kitchen to pull the metal hook the kettle dangled from inside the fireplace. She fished a mug from a shelf and prepared my tea while I kept my eyes on the floor.

I knew she would tell Ma.

"Drink your tea. I added a splash of cold water so it cools quicker.

Then you should get some rest, Lady Sersa." Maeve set the steaming mug down in front of me. "I know you struggle to sleep, but you must try."

With a nod, I forced myself to take a sip of tea. Though it burned my tongue, I didn't let myself react or say a word. I was used to hiding my emotions in recent years—hiding *myself*—when they permitted me. And especially when a shrewd servant was ready to report me to Ma.

Maybe I was the best one to help Nessin after all. I'd become good at hiding who I was all for the benefit of others. Even at my own expense.

I didn't sleep a wink.

When the sun had barely begun to rear its head over the horizon, I threw open the door to Ciel's bedroom. It smelled faintly of liquor, almost stale, despite how tidy he kept the room to be sure he could find a specific book at all times. He was asleep face down under a pile of pillows.

I tore open the drapes hanging from the windows across from the bed then threw the pillows off him.

Ciel groaned, stretching against the mattress. He lifted his head halfway, one eye open to look at me, and then buried his face deeper into the mattress. "What do you want so early?"

"What do I want? Apparently, that does not matter because *you* went to Nos Ovscura without me last night and told a certain prince that you would replace me in his little scheme."

Ciel rolled over, head flat without a pillow, and stretched his arms out on either side of him. "He told you. That lanky Bonespeaker bastard. Did you go back to the city then?"

"He visited me," I said evenly, though my irritation hadn't yet receded.

"Look, it's nothing against you, nor is it meant to twist your arm, Sers. If anything, I want to help." He reached for the pitcher of water on his bedside table and poured himself a goblet. He drained it before pouring himself a second. His fingers paused around the stem. "But I also want Pa back, and I'm willing to do whatever is necessary. That daemon promised me he wasn't lying. He promised me access to all the inner workings of Gilders Eye. He said there'd be gatherings aplenty among the nobility's mansions and the citadel. A whole tour takes place around the betrothal, and the Gilders host the Daemon King and his kin night after night."

Nessin had told me that much too. At least his story was consistent.

"He wouldn't lie about that," Ciel added in a whisper. "He knows his fate will rest in my hands the instant he lets me into the citadel."

"Well, that's not going to happen." I steeled myself and threw back my shoulders. "I'm going. You're staying. He didn't want you to begin with."

Ciel threw the covers off his legs and over the edge of the bed. "No. I meant what I said. I'm not trying to twist your arm, Sersa. I want to do this."

"You can't lie to save your life."

"I..." He dropped his eyes and blushed. "Well, this is a good time to work on it."

"Oh, in the next day you will? You can't memorize this like one of your tomes. I hate to break it to you, but you're no master at pretending."

"And you are?" Ciel scoffed and folded his arms across his chest as he stood, wrinkling his white tunic.

"I admit I don't always succeed, but I've had enough practice with all our prying servants and Ma constantly questioning me. Watching me. Not to mention, I have magic. You do not. I can protect myself better than you," I said. Never mind that I'd stolen Nessin's reasoning.

"Fine." Ciel sat back on his bed again. "But you should know I overheard Uncle Bardic very late last night when I got in. He..." He swallowed, his chest rising on an inhale. "He said he was concerned with your recent behavior. He asked one of the servants to request a meeting with Ma and the rest of the Council today."

Uncle Bardic was a gods-damned scoundrel. The Council,

namely Uncle Bardic, had been trying to overturn my status as heir ever since I'd stolen their magic. But the funny thing was Uncle Bardic hadn't possessed magic before I'd stripped the rest of our clan. None of my uncles had.

It wasn't surprising the Council would meet with Ma. They usually did over the smallest of incidents, and with Maeve there to claim witness to the night prior, the scale wasn't tipping in my favor.

"When is the meeting?" My voice was hoarse from not sleeping.

"First thing this morning." Ciel glanced out the windows at the brightening sky. "Should be in a bell or so. What'd you do to your hand?"

"Nothing. Were you invited?"

He shook his head, long black hair falling in his eyes. "They know I can't be trusted. They know where my loyalties lie."

My brother's dark eyes held mine with a sympathetic smile.

"Good," I said, turning on my heels for the door. "Then we'll head to the oubliettes in a half bell. Don't fall back asleep."

7

The entrance to the oubliettes inside House Scáth was always guarded. Luckily, Ciel and I knew of another way.

We trudged through the tall grasses outside House Scáth, hidden in the shadows shifting along its perimeter after sunrise. As the woods drew closer and the sun higher, the shadows cast from the dark stone walls and trees waxed and waned like a dance. One partner stepping backward, the other sashaying forward.

Droplets of dew flicked onto my face, clinging to my eyelashes and braided hair as we maneuvered through the grass in a crouch.

I eyed the wall that encircled the many residences inside House Scáth, including our own.

The Dawnwatchers, guards on morning patrol, usually paced the wall overlooking House Scáth. Reaping Hour was the one time they were allowed to abandon their posts, to take shelter in the fortress away from the Sluagh who sought souls and easy prey. But with Reaping Hour over, every post was once again manned.

For a moment, I imagined the vantage point they had to the sea. The halved bridge into the City of Soulless was likely being bombarded by Sluagh tucking their enormous, veiny, white wings back against their shoulder blades as they landed. I pictured hundreds of them dragging their prey toward the Daemon King's Citadel.

The predictability of Reaping Hour afforded us the prevention of not all but some bloodshed. We knew when it was time to seek shelter, when it was time to slide iron panels over every window and door on the isle.

Reaping Hour, and our powerlessness to prevent it, felt like our entry fee into the city that provided us distraction every night. Gambling addicts and the wanton clientele who inundated the pleasure dens had no desire for the city to cut itself off from Os Íseal.

I was guilty of indulgence too.

We reached the edge of House Scáth's wall, where the trees brushed its flank. I realized I needed to stay focused and stop daydreaming about the city—and the young man who'd be waiting for me on Dúm's Cross at sundown.

Nessin.

Despite what I'd told Ciel, I hadn't truly made up my mind yet. I wanted to find Pa more than anything, but was I willing to face such a high risk of death? If the Daemon King discovered me, he'd kill me. And then where would we be?

The tree branches nearest the fortress had to be cut back each year, but right now, they formed a canopy overhead and a blind spot for the patrols above.

With another glance up the wall, I skittered forward under the canopy. Ciel clung to my heels. Hiding behind tree after tree, we played a game of silence, like we had when we were children. Both of us had worn dark clothes to blend into the woods that hid the second entry into oubliettes, and I was grateful as we moved farther inward.

We walked until we found the grate covered by a bed of dry leaves. Ciel and I brushed the ground cover away. I fished out the key hidden around my neck, hearing a click as I slid it into the sturdy lock. Then we lifted the grate together. Ciel nudged his chin at the drop, and I stepped down into the tunnel. I stooped and lowered onto hands and knees as he followed me, shutting the grate overhead.

The passageway beneath the earth smelled strongly of mildew, and slimy moss slid under my gloved palms and knees as I crawled.

After not more than a minute of crawling, the ceiling rose, and I was able to stretch out and rise to my feet. Anxiety churned in my gut. Though I wanted to hear what the Council had to say, I knew it wouldn't be positive.

Only a few steps farther and the echoing voices of the Council appeared.

"Hurry up," I hissed at Ciel.

I always forgot he was so much bigger than me, both taller and broader, and he almost couldn't fit inside this passageway anymore. It was a testament to the fact that we were no longer children, and something about it irritated me. Maybe it was the fact that, when we were young, I had no one prying about my moods or the shadows I occasionally saw. Maybe it was the weight of responsibility I felt—finding Pa, if I could, would outweigh anything I'd ever done.

I shook my head as if a single gesture might will away my thoughts. It had never worked before.

Total darkness eclipsed the passageway, save for a hint of light up ahead. The patch was faint as a star in the sky, a few hundred feet away, but we tiptoed toward it like a beacon in the night.

As we drew closer, the light spilling into the passageway beyond the lattice wall swelled. The tight-knit pattern with thousands of little apertures looked into the rectangular Council Room, splitting Ciel's face into a hundred dots of darkness and light.

Two rickety stools sat on the ground before the wooden lattice. We'd brought them into the passageway as children—back when we'd camped out behind this wall for bells on end, listening to the adults' conversations and politics we didn't understand. Dust clung to the stools, and based on the smell of rat droppings, probably those too.

I gently nudged the stools aside and grazed my palms along the lattice, feeling every groove in the pattern beneath my gloves.

Maeve stood from the rows of elevated benches near the wall we hid behind and maneuvered toward the center of the floor. She was so close that I heard her shaky breaths from here, and I hoped that didn't mean she heard mine.

The Council was comprised of thirteen members, including Ma, our chieftess. Pa's four brothers—Bardic, Archibald, Flann, and Callister—held seats on the Council, and so had Pa before he disappeared. All the members were technically considered our kin, but having our own blood on the Council ensured the Scáth line stayed in power. Now, there was little choice in the matter. I was the only one with our clan's signature shadow magic. The Council was willing to do anything to ensure the other northern clans we reigned over did not learn of it. But few of them knew my magic had taken on its own distinction. Its own mind. One might think it would be enough for the Council to afford me privacy, compassion, or even a shred of understanding, but it wasn't the case.

Instead, I was labeled the Mad Heir. Followed. Watched. Told to adapt to the world around me instead of the world understanding that I would *never* be like them. Was it so bad to be different?

All my life, I'd been told it was.

When Maeve reached the floor, her flat leather shoes softly tapped the stone. Her head remained bowed, her eyes on clasped hands hanging near her legs.

The Council adjusted in their seats, arranged in a triangle around her. Ma sat at one of the points on a throne that resembled black fire—like shadows licking at the air. She straightened, eyes scrutinizing Maeve. "You enter the Council's triangle with the knowledge that only truth is accepted here. And should you lie, may the gods strike you down, Maeve Scarbarie. Do you not?"

She dipped her head. "I do."

Uncle Bardic spoke next. "Good then. Mornin' to you, Mrs. Scarbarie."

Maeve smiled softly, a hint of sadness in her teary eyes. "Good morning, Master Bardic."

Eyes narrowed, Uncle Bardic sucked on his teeth as if he had a seed stuck between them. His graying hair curled around his temples, but unlike some of my younger uncles, it was still very full. I hated the way he leaned all the way back in his chair. I swore he'd always thought he was chief. Or he believed he deserved to be.

"Please tell them what you told me late last night, Mrs. Scarbarie," he said.

Maeve's hands shook as she licked her lips and cleared her throat. It echoed through the Council Room. Her eyes darted to each of the faces before her.

"L-Lady Sersa was talking to herself a-again." She swallowed and bobbed her head, coaxing herself through her statement. "She cut her hand nasty and was up well after midnight, closer to dawn as you know, Master Bardic, since, as you said, I came to visit you straightaway. I didn't want to bother you, Chieftess, after you dismissed me early in the night. So, I told Lady Sersa to try and get some rest, but I took care of her when she was nothing but a babe, and I worry about her as if—pardon me, Chieftess—but as if she were my own. She was talking to someone. Or *something*."

The threat of tears welled in my eyes and prickled my nostrils. I tried to rid myself of the sensation, scrunching my nose, but I wanted to scream behind the latticed panel. It was true. Many of the servants had taken care of me. My memories of them stacked against the ones I had with Ma like a tower.

Ciel squeezed my shoulder, and the desire to shove him welled inside me. How dare he see through me so easily?

I'm fine, I wanted to snap.

But I bit down, silencing myself.

"Chieftess Sorcha," Uncle Bardic began, his mustache wiggling when he smacked his lips, "you know precisely what happened the last time Sersa saw these so-called shadows, the last time she was seen talking to herself. It would only be temporary and for her own good. The Council needs more time to determine if there's a cure before we are declared an unblood clan and you are stripped of your title. We can't have another incident in the meantime, and gods only know what might happen if we let this go on."

Queen, my ma may have been called on our isle, but all the Four Pointes, the four isles, were in a deadlock to reign over Clais. The solution was that we kept our isles separate, each blood clan ruling one of the Four Pointes. Ma, known among the four isles as the Shadowess, was the most formidable of the clan's chiefs—a High Queen without question. Or she had been. She'd delayed the trials determining who would rule as High Queen or High King of Clais because of me.

We all knew she was running out of time, the Council especially.

Ma's voice and eyes were sharp. "What are you suggesting exactly, Bardic? Speak plainly."

"The tower. For a few nights at most. Simply for this episode to pass."

My throat worked in a painful swallow.

He was suggesting... My own uncle was suggesting they lock me up. Again. They'd done it before. Two seasons ago being the most recent and another time right after I stole their magic.

Ma shifted in her seat, placing her chin on her hand. Red hair flamed around her shoulders, but her eyes, like mine, were dark as night. I could never tell what she was thinking.

Neither could Uncle Bardic, I was willing to bet.

His brow furrowed as he continued, "The tower is far more comfortable than the oubliettes, and we could be sure Sersa is taken care of while she's experiencing whatever it is this time. It helped her the last time she was like *this*. We need no more rumors whirling around the clan, or beyond, about the Mad H—"

"Bardic." Ma only needed one glance to shut my uncle up. She'd dropped her hands to the armrests and straightened in her throne. "Every one of you is forbidden from calling my daughter and heir that offensive title. Ever. If you hear any clan member uttering that title, or any unblood in the city otherwise, you bring them to me. And if I hear any of you use it again, I will have one of your fingers. Or worse. We must snuff out these rumors, not fuel them like schoolboys with nothing better to do."

She paused and looked toward the windows to her left, taking a silent inhale and pausing again before she released it. When she looked back at Bardic and the rest of the Council, her eyes reflected a hint of defeat.

"But I agree that we need to protect Sersa. I..." She swallowed to hide her trembling lips. For once, Ma looked like she was in pain. "I agree that we should bring her to the tower for a few days. Ailerby, Ciel, and I will take turns visiting her every few bells so she won't ever be alone."

I staggered into the wall behind me. Red cloaked the passageway suddenly. The tint came out of nowhere, skimming the edges of my vision. When I raised my fist to punch the lattice, Ciel gripped my wrist and pushed me into the wall behind us.

"Sers," he said. "Breathe."

"Did you hear what she said? She's agreeing with him. She's agreeing to have me locked up!"

"Yes, I heard." He flattened his palms on my shoulders.

"They will never see me as their equal. They think I'm mad, and because of it..." I shook my head, swallowing.

When my magic turned red, I could bleed a person dry from the inside-out. I wanted Ciel to get away from me immediately.

He didn't. Not this time.

"Think about it for a second before you act. I can go get Ailerby. He can veil you, and we can get you into Nos Ovscura by nightfall unseen—if that is still what you want."

Now more than ever, it was. My mind was made up, I realized. The Council members were fools if they thought I'd let them lock me up. I was going to bring Pa back and show them all who I was.

"Yes," I said. "It's what I want."

"There's no sense in trying to flee right now. You must wait until sundown to move. When the city opens."

I nodded. "Ma will know where I've gone. The Council will have every patrol on the shore."

"Maybe. But what can they do if they can't see you?" Ciel raised his black eyebrows.

He was right. I knew he was. Ailerby could not only imitate others, but he could veil us yet again.

"Fine," I conceded. "I'll wait in this hell hole. But tell Ailerby to bring my nicest dress. I'll need it when I meet the Daemon King."

Something deep in my gut told me I would meet him before the night was over. I needed to look the part.

"Which is your nicest dress?" Ciel asked. He dropped his hands to his sides.

"He'll know which one to bring."

If there was one thing Ailerby knew better than anyone else, besides his magic, it was dresses.

8

Bells signaling dusk shattered the silence of the dark passageway.

For a second, I thought the bells might be signaling my disappearance. Surely, the servants or the Council had noticed my absence by now, if not to check on me then to lock me inside the windowless tower.

If anywhere, a person could go mad up there.

My limbs were cramped from sitting on the ground in a ball, and my gut was grumbling from not eating all day. When I heard the grate open followed by shuffling on the ground and later footsteps, I stood and squinted into the darkness. I couldn't see either of them, but that gave away who it was.

Ailerby dropped the veil rendering them unseen a few feet away from me and waved.

"Hi, Sers." He shifted his freckled face to mimic mine before it reverted to the original face he'd imitated today. It was a greeting customary to those with imitation magic like his, and I'd always been jealous I couldn't return the gesture.

He threw me into a hug. I hung onto him for a moment, hoping his warmth would transfer to me.

"Thank you for doing this," I said before we pulled away. I squeezed his forearm. "I have no idea what we'd do without you, you know that?"

"You'd be gorging yourself on pastries and wallowing in the tower for the next week. Doesn't sound half bad to me. I could use a break from chores and training."

I straightened the collar of his embroidered coat and ruffled his hair, a ruddy color he rarely adopted. The red was all too common among the clans, and Ailerby preferred to stand out. It always surprised me when he reflected it.

My gaze moved to the thin, long-sleeved dress draped over Ciel's arm. It was a deep nightshade blue with a form-fitting bodice and bones sewn into the inner seams. The bottom had a sheer layer of fabric on top of the others, like glittering snow coating the silky under layers. A collar encircled the neck.

I squeezed Ailerby's wrist again and winked. "I knew you'd know which to bring."

"Of course. I imitated you and tried it on myself before we came. Should fit like a glove." He handed me a pair of matching flats. It pained me to leave my thick leather boots, but I knew I had to.

After trading Ciel my gloves for the dress, he and Ailerby gave me some privacy and turned their backs as I changed under the hand of darkness the passageway dealt. Once I was decent, I called Ailerby over to button up the back. The buttons adorned my spine all the way up to the collar, making it impossible to get in and out of myself.

Unfortunately, my mind went to the thought of Prince Nessin unbuttoning it later. I quickly shooed the image away, uncertain where it came from. I refused to believe there wouldn't be maids to assist me. It was the gods-damned Daemon King's Citadel after all.

"Ready?" Ciel asked as we joined him at the end of the tunnel.

I hiked up the ends of my dress, knowing I'd have to be careful not to stain it as I crawled back through the squat passageway to reach the woods.

"Ready," I said with a firm nod.

Ailerby lowered the veil over the three of us, rendering us unseen once more for our trek to the shore.

As we shuffled in the crowd of Os Ísealns trudging toward Nos Ovscura, it proved more difficult than I'd thought. The sea of bodies got in our way, and pointy elbows nudged us like Ailerby had warned the other day. We were almost separated several times, and people threw looks left and right over their shoulders to search for us, imperceptible to their eyes.

"Drop my veil, Ail." Ciel was somewhere to my left. "Yours too. It'll be easier to focus on Sers."

"What about the patrols?" I asked.

A dozen or so Duskwatchers, the night patrols, stood at the top of the cliff.

"Even if they see us, they can't get to us in the crowd easily," said Ciel.

As Ailerby dropped his and Ciel's veils, I heard his relieved intake of breath as well as a stranger's gasp and shocked comment behind us. I could only imagine how difficult it was to veil himself, let alone three moving people.

After winding through Os Íseal's cobbled streets, past bakeries, metalsmiths, and granaries the clan taxed in exchange for protection, we reached the cliff's edge and the volatile rock stairs leading to the shore below.

Ciel and Ailerby kept close to me on either side so others wouldn't push past the gap they glimpsed. Rope and metal rails edged the stairs against the cliffside, but they did little to ease my mind as we navigated to the bottom. My lace-up leather flats didn't protect my feet, and I felt every loose stone and sharp edge I trudged over. I longed for my thick-soled boots, and without my usual wool socks or cloak, a chill crept up my spine.

Once we reached the pebbly sand, I breathed a sigh of relief. We crossed the beach, headed for Dúm's Cross, and I stood on tiptoes as the crowd lulled to a leisurely pace. At the other end of the bridge, those stepping foot in the city darted this way and that, navigating down lantern-lit streets to whatever their destination was for the night.

I wondered which of them were entering Nos Ovscura for the first time and felt a slight pang of jealousy in my gut. The city was a wonder the mind failed to wrap itself around at first. The subsequent visits were a steep slide downhill, as every besmirched crevice, corrupt daemon with their tempting looks, and desperate mortal selling pieces of themselves to a city that would never fetch an equal price revealed itself.

"Can either of you see him?" I asked.

"Regrettably, I did not have the pleasure of meeting him," said Ailerby. "But I do believe I see a bloke with white hair. You know, *I* have magic to protect myself."

"I'm well aware, Ail," I said.

"I fancy marrying a royal," he added nonchalantly. "What do you say I imitate you and take your place?"

My brother and Ailerby shared a grin.

"He's certainly the most qualified for the job," Ciel agreed.

"Nice try," I grumbled.

We reached the bridge, and my feet found swift relief on the smooth black stone. The crowd thickened before it thinned closer to the city entrance, but I, too, glimpsed a figure standing in the middle of the bridge, his hands clasped in front of him.

Nessin wore a black fur pelt over a fitted, black coat and matching pants like the day before. Only tonight, his appearance was tidier. The ends of his cheekbone-length hair blew around his face under the fingers of a soft wind. His eyes were hard, flickering across the crowd. The fact they were seeking...*me* made my gut dip into my toes.

But when he glanced over his shoulder, looking like he might leave, I told Ailerby to drop my veil. I needed Nessin to see me. If he left and headed into Gilders Eye, I couldn't follow. All chances of finding Pa would shatter.

I turned my hands over, amazed when they reappeared.

Within a minute, a shout pierced the air.

A look over my shoulder confirmed it was one of the Duskwatchers atop the cliff. Her finger pointed at the bridge, accusing me with the aim of a master archer.

"Go!" Ciel shouted.

How my raven's head of hair or my dress gave me away so quickly, I'd never understand, but I picked up my pace, leaving Ciel and Ailerby.

As black-clad figures stormed toward me, shoving through the crowd, I realized we hadn't been so clever after all. Council members worked their way through the flood of people, shoving patrons entering the city to reach me.

Nessin sensed the commotion, and from the corner of my eye, I saw him take a minuscule step forward, his brows furrowing over colorless eyes. The tips of his gloved fingers turned gossamer.

His *soulform*.

Each of my uncles closed in on me through the crowd, but they weren't as swift as they'd once been. They should've sent the agile patrols after me instead.

I slithered between groups of people, focusing ahead, always ahead, until I landed in Nessin's arms. He caught me by the shoulders, keeping me upright and away from colliding with his chest —and thank the skies he did because I didn't want to get that close to him when I knew we'd be forced to do just that soon enough.

His hands slid down my arms, grazing my palms. One gloved hand didn't let go.

Again, my gut reminded me what it felt like to be touched by another. Even an innocent touch.

Nessin stepped in front of me. My uncles and other clan members approached us, out of breath and seething, and he towered over them by at least a head, some two.

Uncle Bardic straightened his spine and threw back his shoulders, glaring into Nessin's eyes. "I'm afraid we cannot allow you to permit that young woman, Sersa Scáth, into the City of Soulless tonight. She is... She's wanted."

"Liar," I spat.

Nessin smirked. "She certainly *is* wanted. But I am afraid that Sersa Scáth is coming with me."

Uncle Bardic extended his hand benevolently to me, but behind his blue eyes was a raging sea. He could not be trusted. He wanted to lock me up and continue to conceal the fact that our clan was as good as stripped of its status, its blood. We were unbloods now.

No, *they* were.

I had matters bigger than any of them to handle. If only I could tell them Pa was alive. If only they'd believe me.

Ciel and Ailerby finally reached us and walked up behind my uncles. I wondered where Ma was. The crowd parted around us, for the scene we were making.

Uncle Bardic stamped his foot. "Sersa, obey your elder and come here. Now."

"My elder you may be, but that doesn't give you the right to treat me like I'm some mad girl unworthy of respect. I'm the clan's heir," I reminded him. "Not you. Never you, Uncle. If Ma hadn't taken you in, you'd still be rotting in the unblood lands. You're done disrespecting me because soon enough, might I remind you, I will oversee you, Clan Scáth, and the Council you believe you control."

Nessin whistled. "I believe the lady has spoken. You can tell Chieftess Scáth," he said in a thin, hypnotic voice I suspected was a Bonespeaker command, "that Sersa is a guest of the Daemon King's. She will not return for several weeks, and it would be prudent of you and your clan not to involve yourselves in Soullander affairs. Now, turn away and head back home. Do not return to the city."

My uncles were powerless. Their expressions twisted with confusion followed by compliance. Their wrinkled brows and scowls loosened. Then their tense shoulders fell, and they turned around to wade through the crowd back to the promontory.

Nessin raked a gloved hand through his hair as he looked down at me, squinting slightly.

"You know that may not keep the rest of my clan out of the city, right?" I said.

"No, but the wall surrounding Gilders Eye will."

Before I could say goodbye to Ciel or Ailerby, the Soul Guards were on us. A dozen encircled Nessin and me, their gleaming armored uniforms resembling the Daemon King's Citadel in the distance. They need not say a word for us to follow.

Nessin swept off his cloak, warm again from his body, and draped it across my shoulders as I turned to look behind.

Ciel winked.

Ailerby stood there looking empty.

"Good luck," my brother mouthed.

And then the crowd poured into every gap, every sliver, until Ciel and Ailerby disappeared from my sight altogether.

Unlike every other time I'd walked through this city, I hardly paid attention to my surroundings with Nessin steering me along. Our shoulders—or his arm and my shoulder due to the height difference—were close enough to brush, and I couldn't help but think we looked nothing like the lovers he'd told the Daemon King we were.

He cleared his throat and looped my arm through his then, inching us even closer. When he bent to brush his soft lips against my cheek, I almost tripped over my own feet.

"Are you going to read my every thought?" I asked.

Nessin steadied me. "If it helps us be more convincing, *yes*."

"*That's* convincing? My grandma used to kiss me on the cheek."

"Oh, Sersa. Next time, I will kiss you wherever you ask me to."

I held my breath. "I won't be asking."

"You tell yourself that."

As we reached the wall separating Gilders Eye from the rest of the city, my senses prickled awake, and my spine straightened. I couldn't be sure if it was Nessin's touch that did it or the fact that I was stepping foot into Gilders Eye for the first time and wanted to take it all in.

Even the wall was forged of a gold-plated stone that stung my eyes to look at. Before the gates opened to permit us, the smell of pastries and cream seeped into the air. I licked my lips.

"Have you eaten?" Nessin quirked an eyebrow at me. "You look like you're about to drool."

I glared at him, fighting the urge to stomp on his foot.

At first glance, Gilders Eye was set up much like the rest of the city. Except every visible area boasted lavish materials even the finest estates in Clais lacked. The streets formed circle after dizzying circle around the center, and on the northern edge loomed the Daemon King's Citadel.

We waited for a ritzy carriage to pass before crossing the street, arriving in a vast outdoor square. Positively everything was constructed of a rich, white marble that gleamed under the strange moons suspended above the Soullands. Their sky was different than ours—three moons rather than one. No sun. No stars. The patterns the Cradled Moons created, always conflicting, confused my mind as they cast light onto the marbled ground of the city square, like three open shutters.

On the outskirts of the Eye, two or three streets of mansions encircled the inner wall. The difference between these mansions and the middle-class and slum housing was sickening. From what I could see, the Gilders had sprawling stone courtyards out front, gabled roofs with fancily shaped shingles that gleamed, and metal gates enclosing their enormous properties.

As if the wall keeping everyone but the Gilders out was not enough.

"There will be plenty of time to see the city later," Nessin said.

I didn't remind him it wasn't the city I was hoping to see.

Pa.

A carriage arrived behind us on the circular road we'd crossed. Nessin pulled me toward it, and I breathed a sigh of relief when none of the Soul Guards who'd escorted us this far entered the carriage with us. Even the interior was fashioned in the finest fabrics, the walls a dark pattern of... I took a closer look and flinched. Hand-embroidered depictions of Sluagh dragging their prey toward the citadel.

"So?" I asked after slumping in the seat across from him. "What's next?"

"Next," Nessin said coolly, "you meet the Daemon King. I'm glad you thought to dress the part." White eyes roamed the bones of the corset sewn into my dress, and I took note of the way they lingered on my collarbone, the swell of my breasts, and my waist before meeting mine again. "I don't know that we'd have had time to stop in your rooms to change."

"Oh, do *I* look the part?" I leaned forward and simpered in his face. He managed to keep his eyes up this time. I'd give him credit for that.

"You may look the part," he said, "but you smell like...mud?"

"Mildew," I supplied, leaning back against the seat and bracing my arms on either wall as the carriage rolled over an arched bridge. I looked out the window and glimpsed a glistening pale blue lake full of tailed women.

Sirens.

For a second, I was surprised the half-naked women weren't freezing, but even the air inside Gilders Eye seemed a touch warmer.

Probably because we're a step closer to hell.

Nessin bent his knees and pushed off the walls to take the seat on the cushioned bench beside me.

"What are you doing?" I tried to scoot away, but he took up more than half the bench.

"Better get used to having me close, love. If you plan to convince the Daemon King we're in love or at least lusting after one another, you'll need to wipe that scowl off too." He turned his shoulders slightly toward me. "I don't much care what that was on Dúm's Cross earlier, what with your clan members..."

"My uncles." I chewed the inside of my cheek and folded my arms across my chest. I looked out the window. "I'm sure you've heard loads about the Mad Heir."

"I've gathered plenty of your secrets, but I haven't heard anyone call you that," he assured me.

I turned back toward him, staring in silence.

"I'm not one for gossip and rumors either," he said. "Secrets, yes. Not twisted fabrications about people. But you better get used to it. The Court of Soulless is ruthless and notorious for cheap talk. If you remember anything while you're here, be it this: you cannot trust anyone except for me. Everything you say, every time you confide in others, it will circulate around the court. And it *will* reach the Daemon King's ear eventually."

I shrugged. "Sounds easy enough."

We were so close he could have reached up to run a finger along my lips like he had at his apartment. He could've leaned forward and kissed me.

A smirk curled his lips. "There'll be plenty of time for that later, love."

This time, I didn't hold back. I slammed the heel of my foot into his toe, crying out a half second delayed. His boots were steel-toed. I cursed the gods before I cursed Nessin.

He only pulled me close. "We're here, darling. Do you like *darling* better? I haven't chosen my pet name for you yet."

"Excuse me?" I croaked.

"Fine. A term of endearment for you."

"Oh, I've got yours, all right," I growled before I listed every curse in the book.

Heel and ankle still throbbing, I let Nessin lead me out of the carriage, brandishing a hand for me to grab onto. I squeezed as hard as I could, hoping to crack at least one bone. My curses quickly faded on the wind as I raised my eyes to study the citadel's entrance.

We stopped before a garden made of arching and bisecting white paths between perfectly manicured squares of grass. It looked exceptionally clean with not a blade of grass out of line and so unlike House Scáth's vegetable gardens or the crops the unblood farmers took care of. A single etched lantern on a shepherd's hook hung at the center of each patch of grass. The flames inside flickered slowly to life as the moons darkened. The lanterns cast eerie patterns along the paths, like the shadows were greeting us.

Nessin cleared his throat. I again tightened my grip on the arm he offered, feeling him tense as my fingers slid over his upper arm and settled into the crook of his elbow. Despite the coquettish façade he'd so far displayed, I guessed he didn't like being touched. At least not by me. I didn't blame him. He was still a Bonespeaker, still a Daemon

Prince, *still* an enemy, and I reminded myself of his cold words the night we'd met inside the Devil's Tail.

I'd never been trusting before. I didn't know why I'd really believed—even for half a second—that Nessin and I were allies in this game of deception. His words, not mine. Sure, we were going to work together to fool his father.

But we were not after the same things.

Our priorities were conflicting. Whatever his were, I was sure he cared little about Pa's safe return.

We strode side by side along the paths between a row of oversized gold statues depicting Sluagh on either side. I ticked them off in my mind, thirteen on either side, each more menacing than the last as they loomed over us, much like the rest of the citadel.

It was then I realized everything about the citadel was oversized. Approaching it, I felt like a child. No, less than a child. Almost like an insect.

I tilted my head backward to assess the glittering towers. They jabbed the dark cobalt sky, the architecture somehow built to look like they were twisting vines or tentacles. Even up close, I couldn't begin to understand how such a place had been built. I reminded myself Nessin came from a line of Colossi, a bloodline that was probably as ancient as the Soullands itself. The tales said so, not that I'd read many.

When we reached the staircase stretching toward the entrance, the towers disappeared from my view. The pair of gilt doors etched with images of the Daemon King grew closer. Two Sluagh stood on either side.

"I can guess where you get your ego," I muttered under my breath.

"Please bite that tongue of yours for the next few minutes." Nessin cleared his throat as the Sluagh pushed open the doors. "Or I will be forced to find other ways to shut you up. With mine."

I hardly registered his words as I looked upon the entrance.

Beyond the threshold, everything shifted, flipped from white and gold to black and gold—heavy on the black—from the walls to the floors. There were minimal gold details here and there, like streaks in the marble floors and archways made of pure gold, and old crowns worth a fortune perched atop pedestals.

At the very end of a colossal corridor sat a man.

The Daemon King on his throne.

From so far away, he might've appeared normal in size, but my eyes didn't deceive me now. His muscular thighs were as thick as tree trunks, his shoes large enough to serve as my coffin when he devoured my soul, and his torc, a symbol of his status, was the most startling artifact, encircling his enormous neck like a collar, save for a narrow opening in the front to remove it.

But the prodigious horns protruding from his forehead were the most frightening detail.

Nessin made quick work of the corridor, my short legs struggling to keep up with him. We reached the foot of the throne after what felt like a mile of Nessin practically dragging me, and he squeezed my arm until I kneeled with him. We bowed our heads toward the floor.

"So," the Daemon King's voice boomed when he spoke, "this is the young woman you were caught sneaking out of the city a few days ago."

Nessin looked at me from his peripheral, but he didn't raise his eyes.

"Both of you may stand, Sin."

I did at once, still a few seconds behind Nessin, not wanting to make the Daemon King command us again.

"Yes," Nessin said. "This is Sersa Scáth, King Gearóid."

The king beckoned me closer with a waggle of his finger. "And what are you, my dear? Let me have a closer look."

I didn't know how I could get any closer, not with his throne as large as it was, but I obeyed and tilted my head back. It wasn't like we could ever see eye to eye, both metaphorically and physically. Still, I held his gaze. The Daemon King looked exceptionally young for a man I'd heard was a thousand years old, but his voice was rough as sand, weathered, a deep hint of age surfacing every few words. Dark hair curled at his temples and his eyes were the most startling green against his mostly unwrinkled rosy skin.

Nessin clearly took after his mother.

"I'm a painter," I said, thrown by the question. He had to know I was mortal, so what was he asking?

When the king reflected an unamused smile, a ripple of laughter echoed through the Court of Soulless. I bit my lip, realizing the throne room was filled. On either side of us stood a sea of creatures. Eerie yet beautiful wraiths wearing the finest clothes with a strange glow to their otherwise human forms. And daemons with pointy ears and teeth sharpened into daggers.

From my peripheral, Nessin stiffened, his shoulders pulling taut as he tilted his head back to watch his father.

"Then you have a bard's talent, a Gilder's beauty, and my son's heart," the king said. "That is an interesting amalgamation, dear Sersa. Where do you find your lovers, Sin? I would love to know. And that soul—my, isn't it a loud one? I see why you are enamored with this young woman."

My heartbeat thrummed. My soul was loud? Did that make it more appetizing?

When the court laughed again, the Daemon King gestured a Sluagh toward him. The solid-bodied spirit carried a bowl of sweets. Up close, the Sluagh were even larger than I'd ever believed, nearly the same size as the statues outside the citadel. Still, it looked small compared to the king. Its eyes were nothing more than gouged pits, its skin silver and slick, and its talons clacked the ground as it walked.

The Daemon King fished his hand about the bowl for a second before plucking a glowing sweet that looked miniature between his fingers. He popped it into his mouth and sucked on it for a long while, his narrowed eyes filled with curiosity as he watched me.

It was like he saw *through* me.

"We will have tea tomorrow, dear Sersa. We ought to get to know one another before you wed my son. It is standard," he added. "I'll be getting to know each of my sons' picks."

The Daemon King said the word *picks* like I was nothing more than a juicy peach plucked from a tree for his son's tasting.

Before I could get my bearings and reply, he waved his hand dismissively. Nessin hooked my arm through his and we backed out of the enormous hall together. The members of his court replaced us, flooding toward the bottom of the Daemon King's throne. Some threw looks over their shoulders at us.

At me.

Near the entrance, the corridor split left and right. I looked both ways. Nessin pulled us down the left. The citadel was a labyrinth. Everything looked identical. Every door. Every wall. Every turn.

Black. Gold. Black. Black. Gold.

I chewed the inside of my cheek, knowing I had to memorize these corridors over the next few weeks.

"You didn't tell me your father was a Colossi," I said under my breath when I was certain we were out of earshot, a few hundred feet down this new hall.

"I told you I was half Colossi," he said.

"He could crush me with a finger."

Nessin scoffed. "*I* could crush you with a finger. He'll alter his form for tea tomorrow. He simply *must* intimidate everyone he meets. It's a compulsion." He rolled his eyes, raking a hand through his hair to rid a strand in his line of sight.

I realized what his father had called him. "Do you prefer to be called Sin?"

His eyes softened before he covered it up. "Yes. Only strangers call me Nessin. Funny enough, the Daemon King usually calls me Nessin. Now, pick up your feet," he snapped, "or it'll take us ages to reach the room."

10

After climbing a few staircases, I was sure we were in one of the towers. By the third or fourth set of stairs, my breathing grew labored. After the day I'd had, I needed to eat something and fall into a comfortable bed. Yet I knew my curiosities would keep me awake tonight.

Nessin brought me into a spread of rooms that couldn't belong to me. They were too grand, too large, and the décor was a level of imperial luxury I'd never so much as dreamed of. The rooms were the size of an entire floor in House Scáth, complete with a lounge fitted with at least a few hundred books in two narrow bookcases. They'd been built into the wall next to the archway that led into the next room—the bedroom.

The focal point of this room was a black wooden bed. Four bedposts reached toward the ceiling, twisting like the citadel's towers, and the shimmering black bedding was piled with fewer pillows than I deemed appropriate for an esteemed guest of the Daemon King.

The prince's betrothed, I reminded myself, lest I forgot so easily. It wasn't like the Daemon King himself had invited me here.

Double doors sat to the left of the bed, and when I glimpsed the bathing room connected to the bedroom, I wondered where they led. The space was magnificent, but a closer look revealed that these rooms were lived in. A stack of books on the bedside table. A scythe, a rag for polishing, and a pot of wax left out on a long table near a large terrace.

I licked the front of my teeth. "Whose rooms are these?"

"Mine," Nessin said, striding toward the double doors in the middle of the back wall. He propped them open, and beyond sat another bed. A canopy of white silk draped the top and sides. "It's customary that the prince or princess's betrothed stay in the same room. This used to be my private training and weapons room, but I had it remodeled."

I gritted my teeth. "I think I would've liked it better before."

"That's one thing we can agree on."

My steps echoed as I walked through the lavish, marble bathing room, fleetingly examining the pale blue-and-white stone and the matching robes embroidered with a cursive *D* for their family name, Drumghoul. Though I'd heard the name uttered around the city, I'd never heard Nessin's. Nor had I heard his preferred name. "Sin" was quite memorable. Then again, I'd never had reason to listen or memorize details about the Soullander royals. I reached the other side of the bathing room and landed back in the room that was mine for the duration of my stay.

For only as long as it took me to find Pa.

"And we shall share a bathing room?" I asked.

"There wasn't enough room or time to add another, so yes," Nessin said. "Sorry to disappoint."

"Yes, what a disappointing state the Daemon King's Citadel has fallen to." I turned on my heel and whirled a finger in the air. "Why is this a thing?"

"A thing?"

"Why am I staying in here? Why don't I have my own room?"

"You do have your own room. And we can't have other suitors visiting your quarters at all bells of the night, now, can we? This ensures I'm the only one standing on your threshold at midnight, love."

"That door will remain shut at all times through the night," I growled.

Smirking, he folded his arms and leaned against the doorway.

"The Daemon King," he said in a silky voice, "encourages intimacy prior to our wedding night. He hopes to have a very, *very* long line of heirs bearing the Drumghoul name. It's why our betrothed stay with us."

At that, I stomped forward, shoved him out of the doorway, and slammed the doors to my room in his face. Fortunately, a lock had been placed on both doors into the bedroom.

But unfortunately, I'd forgotten that I couldn't get in and out of my dress on my own.

I tried reaching around to my back, tried fumbling for the clasps, but nothing worked. I managed to get only a few undone. Finally, I gave in with a frustrated huff. I threw open the doors and wavered on the threshold.

Nessin had already forgotten me and made himself comfortable. He sat behind the long desk in the corner nearest the terrace doors. His heavy boots rested on top of the desk, a book fanned open in his gloved hands. I wondered if I couldn't convince him to get me a pair of gloves. Though they did nothing to contain my magic, there was something about their presence that reassured me.

He didn't look up from his book.

"Come to continue our last conversation, Sersa?"

"Oh, shut up. I need help getting my dress off."

He clapped the book shut, dropped his boots firmly to the marble floor, and stood tall.

"Not from you," I said with a scoff. "Where are your servants? You must have one."

"I figured we would need extra privacy, so I excused them all. Though one is fetching us some dinner. The Daemon King is having a party tonight, but I told him we wouldn't attend."

"But that's why I'm here," I snapped, thinking only of Pa.

What if *this* was the night the Gilder who purchased him was here?

"Tonight only includes the court members who live here, not the Gilders. Trust me. You want no part of their revels. I am certain it was a Gilder who purchased your father, one of their servants, I believe."

"Do you remember what the servant looked like?"

"No."

My face fell as I sighed. "What's the difference between the Gilders and the court members?"

"Many members of the court are the Daemon King's courtesans, his entertainment and such. The Gilders are venerated members of the Court of Soulless, yes, but they are more the Daemon King's many hands than anything, responsible for controlling and running the city and the Soullands at large. The Gilders do not revel here every night but have business to attend to, unlike those who live here, whose sole purpose is to entertain the Daemon King. You need not be concerned with the courtesans and other lowly members. *Now...*" He cleared his throat and took a step out from behind the desk, extending a hand.

Part of me undoubtedly relished the invitation and that prurient look in his eye.

I stepped back. If I needed anything right now, it was separation from duty—the sole reason I was here—and desire. The latter meant a loss of focus, something I could not afford in a place so dangerous.

"Sersa. I'm sure your back is the same as the countless others I've seen."

"Oh, countless?" I raised my eyebrows and folded my arms. Heat swirled up my neck.

Nessin tilted his head and raised an eyebrow, but his face was serious. "I will look the other way, I promise."

"No, you won't."

A devilish smile curled his lips on one side. "You have my word."

"Which is about as good as believing the devil himself."

"I'm glad you think so highly of me," he said, his debonair tone sickeningly arrogant. "Please. It will look strange if I call for a servant just to unhook a few clasps and even stranger if my lover is still wearing what she came in."

"Right," I sneered. "Perhaps the servants and the *countless* others can attest that I ought to be disrobed by now—and you examining my *back*."

He flashed his palms again. "It's only my recommendation. Though I meant it. You do smell a bit. May want to bathe before tea with the Daemon King tomorrow."

"Get over here before I change my mind," I groaned, meeting him in the middle of his bedroom. My bare feet were chilled against the marble, but the plush rug beside his bed felt like it was weaved of silk. The rest of me suddenly felt hot too.

In a large mirror on the wall above the headboard, I watched him pinch the tips of his gloves and remove them with swift yet relaxed motions. His pale hands were even bonier than I'd imagined, skeletal in a way. They were an artist's hands, ever steady and made for the precise strokes of a brush.

I squeezed my toes into the rug as Nessin pocketed his gloves and reached toward me. He made quick work of the buttons I hadn't managed to reach on the back of my neck, but the way his fingers grazed my skin, especially sensitive places I could not see, made all my other senses flood with color and heat. Yet chills tickled my skin.

My eyes closed on their own, but I quickly snapped them open, remembering he was watching. I saw in the mirror a tint of color I hadn't in a long time. Not since the last time Roarke Murks's face had maneuvered under my dress in the woods near House Scáth.

I forced the color away by taking a deep breath.

It was simply the touch of another that brought chills to my entire body—not Nessin's touch, I warned myself. It turned out that stealing my clan's magic had significantly shortened my list of potential lovers. Mine at the time, Roarke, had threatened me with a blade before fleeing to the Druids who lived in the mountains, seeking other ways to regain the magic I'd stolen.

"Have you had many lovers?" Nessin asked casually. It didn't surprise me he was listening to my thoughts. "I can only hear them if I can see your eyes."

"Then I'll be sure to keep my eyes closed for the rest of our time together."

"No, you won't. You like looking at me too much. So?"

"By lovers, do you mean have I had many people examining my back?"

"Mm hmm."

"What's *your* idea of many?"

Derailing my thoughts, Nessin chuckled as he reached my shoulder blades. The middle of my spine. Lower still. His touch drew me more alert as his knuckles lingered near the base of my spine, the last buttons undone. I had the urge to squeeze the footboard in front of me.

"Don't touch me like that," I snapped. "Don't even pretend this is real, Nessin. It's not. And we don't need to pretend unless we're being watched."

"As you wish."

"*Your Highness?*" A voice and the opening of doors echoed through the lounge.

"Ah," Nessin said, striding away. "Please come in, Draea. Sersa was just changing."

I held the front and back of my dress in place, refusing to let it slip in the servant's presence but especially not in Nessin's.

"Oh, does the lady need help?" Draea was a full-figured woman wearing a plain black dress with an apron over it. She steered a wheeled metal cart into Nessin's bedroom, navigating it around the circular rug and toward the terrace doors, which Nessin propped open.

Beyond sat a breathtaking view of the Wraithsea, continuing to the north of Nos Ovscura, several isles, and a horizon so dark it concealed the rest from the naked eye.

Draea's cheeks were plump and rosy, and her red hair coiled into a low bun at the back of her head reminded me of Ma.

I refused to let myself miss my mother. Not after she'd agreed to have me locked up, even if only for a few days.

"Let me set this outside, my lady. One moment and then I'll help you dress."

"That's really not necessary," I said.

"Oh, but it is," she insisted with a bright smile. "I am here to serve you and His Highness, and I do it gladly."

"Draea has been with me since I was a child," Nessin explained. He wavered in the terrace's doorway.

She tutted. "Longer than that. Nothing but a toddler you were."

"How long ago was that?" I asked with a sharp look.

Both Nessin and Draea laughed awkwardly.

We'd both been raised by servants then. It was one thing we had in common. Though I suspected his situation had been more extreme.

Draea hobbled back into his bedroom and then into mine. Naturally, she didn't bother closing the door, even cracking it, and directed me toward an armoire of clothing for every occasion. Sleeping. Riding. Dinner parties.

She stripped me at once, revealing nothing but my little white shorts. I cupped my bare breasts, all too aware that Nessin was only a room away.

"The rest of your honeymoon clothes will be delivered in a few days, I suspect." She stopped abruptly and sniffed me. I frowned, fighting the urge to back away. "Pardon me, miss, but a– a bath may be in order."

"Told you," Nessin called.

He sounded far enough away that he couldn't see me. Playing the gentleman perhaps.

Draea blushed a feverish red before pulling me toward the bathing room. After helping me bathe and change into a set of silk pajamas with a matching robe, she left us to dine in private. Dinner started in utter silence, and Sin seemed content to let it do so. As was I.

Until I recalled I would be having tea with the king tomorrow.

"We should get to know one another a bit," I said.

He finally put his utensils down and straightened in his seat. "That seems appropriate," he said suspiciously. "If the king pries at all, you will need to be convincing."

"And you?" I challenged. "You think you know everything about me because you had your underlings follow me around?"

"I suspect you are much more complicated and difficult to get to know than the average person, Sersa."

That was a satisfactory answer.

I reached for the chalice and swirled the wine inside before taking a sip.

"Well, what should I know about you, Ne—*Sin*?"

He glanced at the Wraithsea with narrowed eyes before returning his gaze to mine. "I am the third in line of the four sons to the Daemon King's throne, but we do not follow a typical succession here. The king will choose the heir he—"

"I don't need to know about your Soullander customs. I highly doubt that will come up tomorrow."

"Then what would you propose?"

"How old are you?"

"Centuries."

"Vague."

"Indeed."

"Do you think of me as a child then, so much younger than you?"

Nessin scoffed. "You do not want to know the things I think about you."

What did that mean? Vague again, indeed. I narrowed my eyes at him now and pursed my lips as I thought about what I wanted to know.

"How did you get that scar?" I asked.

"That is a rude question even by mortal standards, I would think."

"Maybe. But I would think it's a fair one. Something that would come up between lovers."

Nessin lifted his long legs onto a nearby chair and crossed them. "The Sluagh. That's all you need to know," he said offhandedly.

"Fine."

"Why do they call you the Mad Heir?" he asked, surprising me. I'd expected to do all the talking. "You mentioned it in the carriage."

I looked away and licked my lips. What had I gotten myself into? Why had I suggested we get to know one another at all? When the black shackles appeared around my wrists, I shoved them further under the table. I wondered why they emerged when I felt filled with shame rather than fear.

Maybe I was afraid of what Nessin might think.

"May I see?" he asked flatly.

I didn't know when I might get used to him reading my thoughts, if ever.

I slid one hand out from under the table, then the other, and rested them on the edge.

Nessin didn't miss the way my hands shook, but his gaze handled the detail thoughtfully. "I don't think it's something you should be ashamed of, Sersa Scáth."

I snickered and rolled my eyes. He didn't mean it. Or he wouldn't if he'd seen how I left my clan that night.

"So." He quirked his scarred eyebrow. "The Mad Heir?"

I inhaled deeply and wet my lips. "I've seen wraiths since I was a child. Shadows. My clan, particularly my Uncle Bardic, is convinced I will bring doom to us all. I stole their magic the night my pa disappeared. I couldn't stop it. I left them all on the ground, clutching at their chests like a hole had been punctured right through each of them. It was lucky I didn't kill them."

"You see soulless outside of Hwain? That is supposed to be the only time mortals may see them, and most still don't."

I nodded slowly. "Not always. But I often see lost souls wandering around. I always figured they were beings who've pierced the veil between our lands. I like the City of Soulless because everyone sees wraiths here. Not just me."

Nessin held very still, his expression feigning nothing. "Being able to do and see and feel things others can't isn't always so terrible, is it?"

I removed my hands from the table and set them in my lap. "What would *you* think of me if I stole your magic?"

"That I might deserve it."

Chills rippled across my arms. The hairs pricked up as we stared into each other's eyes.

Nessin inhaled as if to lessen the tension either in himself or between us. "What else must my betrothed know? Most of the time, these things are about pure lust. I can't imagine anyone would question it if we didn't know one another that well."

"We don't know one another at all." I paused, studying his unnatural stillness. "I'll ask again because the last time I did you dodged the questions with insults that I think were meant to be compliments. What purpose does your betrothed fulfill?"

Finally, he shifted.

"Royals must be married. Even soulless royals. There are requirements of my brothers and me—heirs and such. You must understand. At nearly twenty, you must have been betrothed before, aye?"

"My clan knows better than to promise me to anyone. At least not while I possess all their magic."

"I don't doubt the accuracy of that. Yet they disrespect you. Their fear seems to drive them, making them want to control you."

"I am aware, thank you."

"Then we will say nothing else on the matter." Nessin dipped his head and made something of a shrug with his lips.

I pressed mine together, silencing.

At that, I tried to focus on the bustling City of Soulless below with little luck. Instead, my mind discarded the landscape for the memory of Nessin's touch, his knuckles grazing my bare skin...

I spent the rest of our dinner trying to avert my eyes from his, focusing hard on the horizon until I retired for the night and locked myself in my room as promised. Despite my exhaustion, I tossed and turned well after midnight. My mind seemed set on doing anything but sleeping and instead replayed that moment.

Our proximity. His breath. Smell. Touch.

I threw a pillow over my face and buried myself in the silk sheets. But a flutter of pastel colors dusted the skin behind my eyes as I finally started to doze off.

And my last thought before it pulled me under was, *What in Dúm's name is wrong with me?*

11

I blinked awake to a note and a bracelet with a single charm—an eye—resting on my pillow. The sharp, folded edge of the note brushed my nose. Before I read it, I rolled the bracelet between my fingers.

Burn this after you read it, the note started. *Only have one sip of tea. Druids brew it from faeleaf. A cup and you'll be so giddy, you'll say anything and everything. And no, he can't read your thoughts like I can. Also, wear the bracelet everywhere you go. It's your key in and out of Gilders Eye.*

"Some warning before the day of would have been nice," I grumbled as I threw my covers off, crumpled the note, and moved toward the dying embers in the fireplace to the right of my bed. I watched the paper ignite, the fire strengthening as it ate through Nessin's words.

Then I clasped the eye bracelet around my wrist.

A few minutes later, Draea returned to prepare me for tea with the Daemon King. She curled my hair with a metal rod she heated in the fire and pulled strands of it away from my face. The rest she arranged into a low twist, which she—to my absolute dread—adorned with little white flowers.

As I sat before the vanity in my room, watching Draea transform me, I couldn't believe I'd slept all through Reaping Hour and then some. Normally, my sleep was anything but normal. I either slept too much or too little. Either I slept through every ounce of daylight, or I roamed House Scáth at all bells—scouring the library, practicing my spear throwing in hopes of exhausting myself, exploring Nos Ovscura till dawn… It was another reason I loved the City of Soulless. I came *alive* at night, especially during the warmer seasons of the Bloom and the Heat.

I wondered if we were too far from Os Íseal to hear the screams that accompanied the Sluagh's hunt. If anything happened to Ciel or Ailerby while I was gone, I would never forgive myself.

Draea selected a white silk dress that made me look far more innocent than I was, a deception I wore proudly, for my uncles had always tutted that I was wanton for a chieftess's daughter. The dress served the start of mine and Nessin's ruse perfectly.

But I still didn't know precisely what he wanted out of this, what he got out of me being here and pretending for him. It would be short-lived, it seemed, since he knew my father was here somewhere.

I tried to quash my curiosity and convince myself that *my* reason for being here was all that mattered, but knowing Nessin's motives would help me ascertain how much or how little I could trust him.

The straps of the dress were narrow and hung off my shoulders, but Draea gave me a matching overcoat with long sleeves and a collar that clasped in front of my neck. My collarbones were bare in a scooped neckline, and the dress skimmed my waist, hips, and fleshy thighs in an eye-catching way. I didn't love the dress or even like it—I would likely spill on myself—but it achieved the look of virtue I suspected the Daemon King required for his heirs' betrothed.

When a Sluagh showed up to escort me to the Daemon King's rooms, I followed cautiously. Why or how the spirit didn't ravage my soul right then and there, I couldn't begin to understand. Magic was the only feasible answer.

Or a Bonespeaker's commands. Nessin had ordered that Sluagh

he'd summoned not to harm anyone when it'd delivered my letter to Ciel and Ailerby.

As we navigated the confusing citadel corridors, I wondered when I might meet the other princes' betrothed. Perhaps they'd be having tea with us.

Disappointment unfurled in my gut when we reached the Daemon King's tearoom. It was separate from his sleeping chambers thankfully, and I glimpsed only him at the round glass-and-metal table. The tearoom connected to a greenhouse that comprised the entire back wall with a sloped roof. Beyond the polished glass, plants and blooms of a hundred varieties twisted into the air as if stretching their necks for the Daemon King's attention. It was a rainbow of colors, though I saw mostly deep reds, bright whites, and dark, dusty pink flowers. It was a scene I'd love to paint, or I might paint every flower on a different canvas.

"Magnificent, aren't they?" the Daemon King said.

I realized I'd stopped without acknowledging him, failed to bow, and instead stood there like a fool.

"Oh, yes. Your Majesty, forgive me." I dropped into a curtsy, almost losing my balance.

The smile that curled his lips reminded me so much of Nessin, and I thought he saw my blunder for sure.

"Come here, my dear. Sit, sit." He beckoned me forward with a wave of the hand. Gold rings bejeweled almost all his knuckles, and as Nessin had predicted, he was a normal size today. He almost looked mortal, if not for his horns.

The shrewd look in his eyes provoked a strange fear that unfurled inside me like poison.

I found the cushioned metal seat across from him and noted the freshly clipped blood-red flowers at the center of the table. A servant pushed in my chair and spread a white serviette across my lap before pouring both of us a cup of tea. Miniature sweets adorned the table, arranged on various towers and elevated cake plates.

I'd never been to tea per se—I'd had tea, of course, but the clan drank their tea around a fire when the season of Rime was so cold that we could see our breaths under the starry night sky while we spun eerie tales about the Sluagh, the Soullands, and our immortal neighbors who tempted and taunted us daily.

"Help yourself," said the Daemon King, noting my eyes wandering about the field of pastries before me.

Looking for something to do with my hands, I reached for the nearest tray, plucking an iced loaf of marbled cake, and set it on my plate. A delicate fork sat beside a curved butter knife. I selected the fork and dropped my eyes, not wanting to look at the Daemon King.

"You must try the tea," he said. "It's brewed from roses cut from my very own garden."

I smiled, eyeing the pink-tinted water. A pair of rose petals floated in the cup, circling one another in hypnotic movements. I took a bite of my cake, hoping it would soak up whatever the Daemon King put in the tea, and swallowed before reaching for the dainty porcelain. The cup's exterior boasted pastel images of the Soullands, but a closer look and I glimpsed ethereal wraiths—mortals who'd died and passed into the Soullands—and horned daemons.

I lifted the cup to my lips and swallowed the tiniest sip. The hot tea coated my tongue, slid down my throat, and warmed my insides. A fluttery sensation made my head light and my stomach roil, but it was the best tea I'd ever had. Sweet but not too sweet. The subtle taste of roses and vanilla.

"It's delicious. Very hot," I lied. My excuse not to drink more.

"I thought you'd think so. And a dash of cream may do the trick." He gestured his bell-sleeved arm to a miniature carafe. Then the Daemon King leaned back in his chair and folded his hands on the table. "Do tell me, Sersa, dear."

Here we go.

"How did you and my son meet?"

"In the city," I answered. An easy truth. But the words poured off my tongue, unrestrained and without vacillation or thought. My head felt light after just one sip. I wondered what a whole cup might do to me.

"Oh? Hopefully not at one of the pleasure dens he frequents."

This comment was meant to wound me. Recognizing it for what it was, I didn't let it.

"No," I said with a light chuckle, a *boys will be boys* coyness to my voice.

If only the Daemon King knew I didn't play by those rules and expectations. Holding onto one's so-called virtue wasn't expected, not exactly, of the women in our clan because we were equals, but there were always some who didn't think so. My uncles, like the Daemon King, saw me as a trade to be made to secure more land and allies.

Though I suspected the king knew I could not offer him or his son any such things.

"We first locked eyes in a bar on the city's outskirts. I shouldn't have been there, I admit," I added, "but when I looked upon Sin, I– I couldn't explain it if I tried."

The Daemon King smiled softly. His eyes didn't soften. "Then why did you flee the city the other day, my dear? My Soul Guards told me all about it."

I bet they did.

I dropped my eyes to my plate and ran a finger along its smooth edge. "Well, I was scared for a moment. Sin asked for my hand and..."

I swallowed.

"Ah, yes. It is a shame my son didn't choose someone of noble blood. Someone already accustomed to this sort of life. You understand what I mean. Not to say that you aren't a lovely pick."

Heat rose into my cheeks. I raised my eyes slightly, hoping it passed for a blush. I also hoped it didn't mean the cloud of red might stain my vision. I checked how I was feeling and reminded myself this conversation was nothing but a dance. One meant to test me.

The Daemon King gave me little time to recover. He moved on to the next question. "And why *my* son, my dear?"

"We can give each other something no one else can," I answered, dumbfounded as to how the words tumbled from my mouth. The effects of the tea were growing stronger. I felt fluttery and light like my body was being lifted by the wind. "Your son promised me something I want very much."

"Hm." The Daemon King considered this, taking a sip of his tea, which I knew somehow wasn't laced like mine, despite that it'd come from the same teapot. Maybe the servants had lined my cup with it. "And what is it that Nessin can give you?"

"That which our hearts desire most," I answered. My voice quivered.

A pitying smile crossed his lips. "Love, then."

"Y-Yes," I stammered, hoping it passed for nerves rather than me battling the lie on the tip of my tongue.

"And what of your family? Sin tells me you come from Clan Scáth. An honorable line, no doubt."

This eased my anxiety. I could speak of my clan then. I thanked Nessin silently for setting me up. "Yes. I'm the only daughter of the Chieftess Sorcha Scáth."

His eyebrows raised with interest. "Her only daughter? Not her only child, I presume."

"No, I have a brother as well."

"Then he will carry on the line as heir. Or will the Council vote on a new line to step in following your mother?"

How did he know about the Council? My blood thrummed awake, as did the warning bells in my mind. "Truthfully, I do not know."

"Ah, yes. My daughter Niuna cares not for politics and business affairs either. And why should she? She lives life on the finer side while her brothers handle everything of duty. She is only a child after all, but she has no curiosity toward her role as princess." He folded his hands on his crossed knees. "And what of other suitors? Are there any I should be aware of?"

My next lie twisted on my tongue, the tea refusing to let me utter it. "There were...other suitors before, but they are since gone, Your Majesty."

"Good. It is important to have your fun while you are young. I know my bride did before we married, as did I. But know that there *is* a line before you, and you ought not cross it now that you are Nessin's betrothed."

My brow furrowed, uncertain what his exact warning meant.

"Let me be blunt, my dear. We must have no doubt that any heir born to you is his." The Daemon King paused. "When that time comes, of course."

My eyes widened.

"Of course," I agreed hastily.

He was discouraging anything more than stolen kisses then. No lifted skirts or midnight whispers for others to glimpse. I had the urge to scoff, but my insides burned and twisted.

Let him try to tell me what to do.

I'd never listened to a man before, let alone anyone else. Not that I'd be seeking people to lift my skirts for.

"The same rules apply to my sons, of course," he went on. "We can have no bastards ready to challenge the true line."

I fought the urge to roll my eyes. Princes did as they pleased.

"Your Majesty." I hesitated. "May I ask a silly question? I apologize for the indulgence, but I have one curiosity."

"Of course, my dear. What is it?" His eyes crinkled with a burning interest.

"Why is it that you allow your son to choose a mortal? Why not another soulless?"

The Daemon King hesitated. His eyes bored into me.

"That is a story indeed." He selected a square pastry off one of the towers nearest him and popped it in his mouth. He chewed slowly, gaze flickering across the table but never to my face. Finally, the king swallowed and dabbed the corners of his mouth with his serviette. "I killed my wife because she cursed my bloodline."

This time, I stopped my eyes from widening. I held very still, feeling my body harden into stone.

He had killed his children's mother.

"She cursed the Drumghoul line, her own children, so that they'd only be able to breed with mortals, with those who still possess at least some of their souls."

Breed. I balled my hands into fists under the table. Where I'd previously thought I was a ripe peach for plucking, I was nothing more than a bitch. A vessel to bring Nessin's half-soulless broods into this world.

I didn't have time to linger on my ignorance of how that all worked. Not the childbearing part, of course, but the state of the hypothetical children's souls.

"My late wife's goal," the Daemon King added, "was to weaken my line until one day it would die out entirely. But I have found a way around that."

Before I could ask what alternative he had found, an announcer cleared his throat to introduce a visitor. Another man wavered outside the tearoom's door.

"Ah, Claud!" The Daemon King clapped his hands and grinned as if he hadn't just told me he'd killed his wife. "You are always so punctual. Very good. I need to head to my next appointment, my dear." He stood and squeezed my hand in his claws. "Claud's very capable hands are where you want to be this morning. I assure you, Sersa, my dear, that he will make the most stunning gown for tomorrow's ceremony."

Tomorrow's ceremony.

Tomorrow.

Ceremony.

My blood went cold. I had to dissect the Daemon King's words one at a time.

"Tomorrow?" I asked innocently, trying my hand at a flutter of the eyelashes. My face felt frozen though, mimicking a smile so painful I swore I'd crack in two.

"Did my son not tell you? Oh, heavens. I must have a conversation with Nessin on proper etiquette when it comes to these matters."

I didn't think it was etiquette Nessin lacked. It was something far deeper. Engrained in him. I knew what it was.

He was a fucking liar.

"The handfasting ceremony is tomorrow at sundown," the king said. "Now, I must turn you over to Claud. He has a lot to do in so little time."

Tomorrow was Hwain.

Claud approached me. He held a leather portfolio, which he set on the table once the servants cleared away the teacups and crumb-scattered plates. Claud pulled out the empty chair next to mine and sat, straightening his spine. He set his delicate, ringed hands on the portfolio's face.

I stared at him, but I couldn't see him all that well.

Not until I forced myself to take a breath. Faint red clouded my vision. Then, it intensified, deepening to an inky black. The tint before my eyes ebbed and flowed in waves.

I couldn't believe it. And yet I did.

I was to be married to Nessin Drumghoul, the Daemon King's son, tomorrow.

"So," Claud started in a no-nonsense yet cautious tone. He squared his shoulders with mine and smiled through full lips. His deep brown skin gleamed with a sort of sparkle on his cheeks, and his many strands of braided hair were gathered into a low ponytail with a long, silver ribbon that hung over his shoulder like a tail. "Tell me what you have envisioned as your look for the big day."

"Easy. I've never imagined it."

"*Never?*" His cheery expression fell. "Not even since your engagement to Prince Nessin?"

"It's been a day. No." I stared into Claud's brown eyes.

"Oh... Okay." He pursed his lips, but amusement crossed his face now. "So, you didn't know you were marrying the prince tomorrow in a very public ceremony, and you haven't thought a shred about what you want to wear." He raised one finger and pointed toward me. "We are going to get along, you and I. I can work my magic with a blank canvas."

Claud poured himself a cup of tea, waving off the nearest servant who leaped forward to assist. He took a long sip.

"I can't imagine why the prince would keep something like this from you," he said as if remarking on the weather.

I said nothing, heeding Nessin's warning that anything I said would reach the king. Especially if Claud was his personal seamster.

"How are you going to make a dress in a single day?" I asked to change the subject.

Claud tilted his head at me and giggled. "Luckily, we have the night and tomorrow too. We have to make dresses for the other brothers' betrothed and a few suits as well, not just yours."

Then all the brothers were involved in the ceremony. That seemed strange, and I wondered what purpose it served. I didn't know much of the Soullands' customs, and why should I? They'd never affected me. Nos Ovscura opened its gates every night to let us spend all the kofs in our pockets, not to rule us. Not exactly at least. The Sluagh started our mornings, but otherwise, they didn't interfere with how our world was run—and we most certainly did not pry into theirs or try to stop them from hunting.

We had adapted instead. Sure, we lost people nearly every week. Sometimes every day. But to stand up to the Daemon King would mean death to all.

Their power far exceeded ours, and we knew it.

"I don't care what you put me in. So long as I can breathe, it's not terribly poufy, I can walk, and it comes with a sheath for either a dagger or a flask. Or both." I sighed.

"Oh." His eyes widened perceptively, and he patted my hand. "Wedding night jitters?"

I leaned forward and offered him the fakest grin I could manage. "The groom will be the one who's worrying soon enough."

Claud's brow furrowed in confusion before he replaced it with another cheery smile. "Well, I cannot promise you a sheath. But all the rest is doable. And speaking of the wedding night. May I take liberties in designing what you will wear then?"

"Absolutely." I wouldn't be caught dead in whatever Claud designed. It was going straight to the bottom of a trunk. Or in a fire.

And if Nessin failed to justify why he'd lied to me, so was *he*.

At that, I excused myself and let Claud plan whatever he wanted.

I had a soulless prince to murder.

12

"It's not like we'll be consummating our union," Nessin started when I stormed toward him on his way out of our shared rooms. He'd swiftly shut the door behind him and now towered in front of it. He backed me away, probably concerned someone would hear us.

Though I doubted any of the citadel's walls were thin, I didn't care. If they heard our argument, they'd also hear me murdering him in a few minutes, and that would be an even better show.

Nessin was dressed in a loose, white shirt that suggested he was off to train or ride. Breeches clung to his long thighs, and tall leather boots hid his calves. But those pants drew the eye to only one place, and the size of him would have made a devout Druidess blush. The idea of consummating a union with him made my head spin, and I wasn't sure the exact reason or if it was the act itself.

"You knew there would be risks in this, Sersa." Another step forward.

I moved away.

"I warned you of what I could prior."

"You never so much as hinted that I'd actually have to marry you!"

He had said *intended*. "You're aware that does follow a betrothal, aye?"

I took a step forward, daring myself to close the distance, and glared up at him through my lashes. Maybe I'd been afraid of him for a minute when we'd first met, but now I was too angry for that.

I separated each word. "You should have made it clear. Why did you lie?"

Nessin dodged my question and spun around, putting his back to me. "Why does it matter? You have my word that you *will* be rid of me once this is all over."

Unable to see his eyes, I heard alarm bells clanging in my head.

You could never trust him. Why does this surprise you?

"If you want me to continue with this absurdity, then you had better start talking. Explain why my presence here is so important to you. If we aren't just faking an engagement but a marriage, then I want to be in the know."

"So I embellished a bit to get you to agree. People have done far worse."

"You cannot embellish, Nessin. Not if I'm supposed to be able to trust you."

He spiraled on me. "Maybe I don't care if you trust me or not! Maybe you shouldn't think of consummating our future union if you aren't somewhat thrilled by what we're about to do."

"I wouldn't touch you with a ten-foot spear—"

"Sure," Nessin sneered, eyes narrowed. "You are here, and that is that. A deal is a deal. You want your father back? Then stick to the plan and play the part you agreed to play, Sersa." His voice was a lash, and his eyes were white flames before they turned black. No iris. No pupil. All black.

I'd backed away instinctively, but now I hated myself for doing so. I wished I'd stood my ground. Thrown back my shoulders. Raised my chin in defiance.

"Let me remind you, you are here of your own accord," he said. "Are you not?"

For a moment, all I saw was a daemon, a monster with its fangs bared and talons ready to strike. After I'd convinced myself that

Nessin wasn't going to rip me to shreds right then and there—he needed me, and that was a form of power—I took a step closer.

He needed a reminder of just what our deal meant.

"You want to see me play a part?" I brought my hips as close to his as possible and ran my hands up his arms, pausing on his biceps, hardened in anticipation of my touch. My fingers traveled to his chest, and I raised on my tiptoes.

His eyes dropped to my lips. I leaned forward. My breath dusted his neck, hot between us.

The feel of his groin against my waist distracted me for a second, but I didn't let myself lose focus or falter. I took another breath against his skin before planting a kiss on the base of his neck, uncertain whether I wanted to do it out of curiosity or to prove a point.

"Then *you* ought to remember that nothing is stopping me from going straight to the Daemon King, Nessin. Yes, what was it you said? You needed the king to stop questioning you. I wonder what that means exactly. I think you are sly as you look, and you fear the king finding out about whatever it is you're up to."

Pulling back, I glared deep into his eyes. They might've returned to their colorless state—I didn't know why or how—but they burned like a flame.

Shocking me, Nessin picked me up with one arm under my rear, his strong hand gripping my hip. My mouth fell open, and I only grew more stunned when he dropped me onto a leather armchair so large it practically swallowed me. The slit in my dress revealed my bare thigh.

His fingertips brushed the armrests as he leaned forward at the waist. As his gloved hand reached under my chin to pull me close, my back arched against the leather.

"Prove to me how convincingly you can play this part, Sersa Scáth. How convincing you are willing to be."

Time moved slowly, locking us in the moment.

Nessin's fingers traced my knee, trailing upward. I held my breath, knowing a soft moan would roll through me any second.

"You've dreamed of this since we met. Me. Touching you.

Pleasuring you. Don't lie." He raised his eyebrows. "You know I'll see through it."

My hips slid forward an inch, now on the edge of my seat. He drew back to bite the tips of his glove and tugged it off. Then he turned his head and let it fall to the floor.

Our gazes hadn't left one another. His had refused to let me go.

When his fingers resumed their position on my thigh, my eyes fluttered closed.

"Let's hear it," he said, his voice low and sensual. "Tell me this *isn't* what you want."

I forced my eyes open and swallowed.

"I wonder," Nessin said with a pause, "if you are as responsive to my touch as I think, Sersa. Shall I find out?" He teased the seam of my dainty silk shorts, wiggling an inch beneath.

The moan won.

"Exactly as I thought," he said against my lips but not quite on them. I felt the curve of his.

A deep chuckle filled the room as he walked away. It wasn't the restrained sound I'd heard up until now. My breaths came in short bursts that I attempted, but failed, to silence. I squeezed my thighs together, feeling what Nessin had done to me. He was right. One touch.

Just one.

"I hate you," I snarled.

His hands were in his pockets. He rested against the bookcases. "Hate is the love language of my family. You're doing marvelously. So convincing, even *I'm* convinced no one would ever believe you're faking it. I certainly don't."

Standing, I balled my hands into fists at my sides. My head spun though. "We were talking about trust, thank you. If I can't trust you, then what reason do I have to believe that my father is truly here in the city? I've lost everything I have to lose. But you?" I snickered. "Your luxurious life as a Daemon Prince also rests in my hands. Two can play this game, and I think you'll be surprised to see just how good at games I am."

He gritted his teeth. I turned on my heel and stormed out, utterly surprised the devil didn't follow. He didn't even shout after me. The silence that ensued gnawed at me until it was replaced by the red-tinted vision I knew all too well.

Even through my infuriation, that gods-damned hue of pastel pink made itself known again.

Fleeing the argument had been necessary.

I worked to calm the fury rising up inside me as I walked at a feverish pace. But more bothersome was the confusion I felt and the question seizing my thoughts. The encounter had left me with mixed emotions, anger being one. But which part was I actually mad about —the fact that we were to be wed tomorrow, or the way he'd halted the moment in an instant?

Eventually, I managed to find my way onto an open-air terrace. I breathed in the fresh air, closing my eyes for a second as the red swath behind my eyes faded.

The terrace overlooked the back of the citadel, leaving the city nowhere in sight. Lush, green lands stretched to the horizon amid the other isles in a vast, gray sea. Until last night, I hadn't known there were other isles in the Soullands, in truth, and I hadn't known the Wraithsea kept going past the divide between Os Íseal and Nos Ovscura.

Back home, the world seemed to end with my isle and begin again with the City of Soulless. But I'd never known what lay beyond the city itself. Now, I almost wished I'd never entered the Soullands at all. Never agreed to Nessin's ruse.

How I had managed not to bleed him dry moments ago was surprising. But not as surprising as a woman I didn't recognize flagging me down.

"Sersa, come sit with us!"

I peeled my eyes from the horizon, squinting at the two young women basking in the sun near the far wall. A quick glance reminded me the sun was absent. The Cradled Moons ruled this sky. How they were so bright defied science.

These were the other betrothed. They had to be.

A stone path divided eight large patches of grass in the center of the terrace. Around those patches, the stone continued to the balustrades, where guards stood every few feet. The terrace's size surprised me for a construction suspended so high up, seemingly dangling off the side of the tower.

I headed toward them reluctantly.

The woman who'd spoken was the most beautiful person I'd ever seen, with dark auburn ringlets and brown skin riddled with freckles. Her eyes were the dark blue of the lochs back home and shimmered just like their surface. A basket bursting with flowers sat in front of her, and she was absentmindedly twirling a firebloom.

Pa had bought me one before. The bright orange flowers were native to the Soullands, and I wondered if these were from the Daemon King's greenhouse.

"Sersa, I'm Stellera." She gestured to her friend, who paled a bit in comparison with plain features and stringy blonde hair. Both wore the most lavish clothes that made up for it. "This is Helde. We're Prince Lochlainn and Prince Jestin's betrothed. Won't you join us?"

I awkwardly lifted my white skirt and lowered onto the grass beside them, draping it around my legs bent beneath me.

Helde beamed at me as she ran her fingers along the silk. "How lovely. Did Claud make this garment for you?"

I shrugged. "It was in my wardrobe when I arrived."

"Did you meet the Daemon King in this? When I met the king, Claud dressed me in white too," Helde said brightly.

I wondered if she spent a lot of time with Claud based on their matched jollity.

"Yes, this morning." I hated meeting new people. The questions required to get to know someone were often akin to having a rotten tooth pulled.

"And how did you like the Daemon King?" Helde pressed.

"Oh, he's the Daemon King," Stellera said, "and she's marrying his son. The answer is always the same." She continued to roll the firebloom in her thin fingers and aimed it at the grass every time the bud spat minuscule sparks of fire. The tiniest hint of amusement formed a dimple in her cheek when the grass turned black with char.

I knew there was a fourth Drumghoul brother, and based on my conversation with Claud earlier, all the brothers were partaking in tomorrow's ceremony.

My brow furrowed as I looked around, scanning the terrace perimeter. There were the guards here and there, but no one else who looked like they might be betrothed to a prince. Not that I knew what that looked like.

"Isn't there a fourth brother?" I asked. I hadn't paid attention to my Uncle Archibald's ledgers, not like Ciel.

Helde perked up while Stellera continued to char the grass near her feet.

"Yes," Stellera answered in a monotonous tone. "There's Devlin and Lochlainn, the eldest."

"Twins," Helde added.

"Then Nessin and Jestin," Stellera continued.

"I'm marrying Prince Jestin. He feels almost younger than me somehow." Helde sighed. She looked lost in thought for a moment as if their age difference was the worst thing that could have happened to her.

I didn't bother reminding her they were all immortal.

When Helde snapped out of it, her green eyes, already too large for her face, widened. "How old are you, Sersa?"

"I turned nineteen a few weeks ago."

"Ah, that's nice. I bet you're excited for Nessin's birthday coming up. The first day of the Dark season—what a day to be born on."

His birth season explained some of his grimmer personality traits. The way they called him Nessin, I assumed neither had met him.

"Yes," Stellera said, "I suppose it's why everyone calls him Your Darkness behind his back instead of Your Highness."

I held back a snort. Unsurprisingly, he graced everyone with his bright and shiny personality, not just me.

I assumed he tried to seduce everyone too. The heat in my cheeks from our encounter did not abate.

"And the other brother," I said. "Where is his betrothed?"

"Rumor has it," Helde said, whispering behind her hand as if it did anything to mask her high-pitched voice, "that Prince Devlin and his bride haven't left their rooms since she got here. The prince sent away all servants, can you believe it?" She grinned toothily. "What do you suppose they're doing?"

I adjusted my palm against the plush grass.

"We haven't the faintest, Helde." Stellera's sarcasm made me chuckle.

"Do either of you know who Prince Devlin's betrothed is, then?" I assumed not, but I asked like I knew who Devlin was. "And why do all the brothers get married on the same day?"

"The Daemon King hasn't chosen his heir," said Stellera.

In a tone that sounded like she was reading from a book, Helde added, "To rule, the law is that each potential heir must be wed. When the Daemon King is ready, a set of trials will ensue and culminate in a death fight. That's how he'll choose his heir."

"And when does that take place?"

"You have so many questions," Helde remarked, pursing her lips and tilting her head at me.

"Yes." I dropped my eyes, pretending I was embarrassed. Or maybe that Nessin and I *had* only been fucking up until this point. "I just don't know how any of this works."

That was an understatement.

"Let her ask her questions, Helde." Stellera leaned forward and touched a warm hand to mine. "Ignore her. We grew up steeped in all this." She shot her friend an irritated look. "The trials will take place probably in the next few moons, though I suspect the Daemon King will delay as long as he can. His health," she whispered, leaning forward again, "has been..." She shook her head, not daring to speak of it.

"As for who Prince Devlin's bride is, neither of us knows. My servant hasn't seen her either. I've asked around," Helde said with no shame.

I wondered how she'd broached the topic or why she was so comfortable with servants she'd met not a day ago. Unless they'd been staying in the citadel much longer.

"Probably some girl who's only got a sliver of mortal blood," Helde said, a hint of envy there.

From my conversation with the king and with what I knew about the Soullands' view of us, those with souls, it wasn't difficult to work out what that meant.

The less mortal blood, the better.

"Prince Devlin is most likely to be the next Daemon King. He's the eldest, so it only makes sense his betrothed would be from one of the High Houses of Gilders Eye."

"What do you have against Gilders Eye?" Helde asked. "Do you believe you're not a Gilder yourself?"

Stellera rolled her eyes, but I couldn't follow the conversation.

"I'm sorry," I said. "What are the High Houses?"

"Those from the High Houses make it their sole purpose to limit the drops of mortal blood among their kin," Stellera said. "All so the Daemon King will choose from their houses for the next betrothed. We periodically induct those born in your world, high-born individuals, into our families for new blood. The head of our houses try to place their children as future Daemon Kings and Daemon Queens of the Soullands. Almost all Gilders are part mortal these days. We all have fractured souls. Pieces missing," she clarified.

"But this is a new custom, to my understanding," I added. "Because the Daemon Queen cursed their blood."

"We are *forbidden* from speaking of it, Sersa." Stellera reached forward and squeezed my wrist then looked around before continuing. "But yes. The High Houses are not new, but their purpose following the late Daemon Queen's death is."

I swallowed, and she released my hand. Why had the Daemon King told me about it if I wasn't to speak of it?

Probably so he could have my head. Or my soul, more like.

Stellera tossed the firebloom back in the basket and rubbed her sooty hands together. "The king wasn't pleased with Prince Nessin, you know. He passed up all the High Houses that weren't already chosen from."

I recalled our earlier conversation. The king hadn't expressed any real disappointment in me being Nessin's choice, besides his one comment that I wasn't used to this life. Then again, why would he tell me to my face?

"Then the two of you..." I narrowed my eyes.

"I'm from the House of Hellick," Helde said.

"The House of Caise," said Stellera.

"I'm from the House of Scáth. Of Os Íseal."

"No kidding. You smell like all pure mortals." Helde wrinkled her nose, and I had the urge to sniff the lavender soap Draea had washed my hair with last night.

"Anyway," Helde said excitedly, "we'll know which house Prince Devlin chose from tomorrow, won't we?"

The thought that I would be married off at sundown the following day tightened my gut. My stomach roiled, and I tried to distract myself with another question. I sat a little straighter, trying to look casual as I twirled a blade of grass around my finger. "Did both of you know we'd be wed tomorrow? I only found out this morning."

Helde giggled behind her hand.

Stellera's eyebrows knitted together. "Your prince did not tell you?"

Biting my lip, I shook my head.

I had hoped to find Pa before any of this could unfold, but I was beginning to accept that this would have to be a part of the plan if I truly wanted to have a chance at finding him.

Neither Stellera nor Helde had anything to say to this apparently because they both looked away. I could practically hear the thoughts running through their heads.

Good luck in that marriage.

Clearly not a love match.

I'd hate to be her.

I doubted any of the princes had attained love matches. Not to mention, trustworthiness wasn't exactly a common attribute of royals. Deceit ran through their blood. It didn't matter whether they were love matches or not.

Stellera fluffed up the ends of her steely blue dress before raising her eyes to mine. "Anyway, we deserve a night out before tomorrow. What do you say, Sersa? I bribed one of the servants already. She'll sneak us out after midnight tonight."

Helde revealed a smile dripping in mischief. "Where will we go? Which pleasure den do you think is best, Stell?"

I blinked several times. "A pleasure den?"

"Don't tell me you're a prude," Helde said. "Stellera's father owns half the pleasure dens in the city. She knows the best ones."

"I'm not," I replied.

"It's not like your prince won't be doing the same thing," Stellera said, trying to reel me in. "They'll all be dipping their swords in anything that will have them tonight, I bet." She released a lofty chuckle, but it was hard as glass. Fragile too. I supposed her family was forcing her to marry Prince Lochlainn. "But we won't be going to one of my family's establishments. Too risky."

"I mean, there are... Mortals are forced to work in the pleasure dens." It was the sole reason I'd never visited one and had no desire to.

"Oh, no. I wouldn't dream of going to one of those horrendous places," Stellera said. "Forgive me, Sersa. My father is a quarter mortal. Some of us Gilders believe we're above you, but not my house, I swear."

Helde put her nose up to this. "Some blood runs thinner than others," she said in a quiet, high-pitched voice.

I fought the urge to glare at this stupid girl. She ought to keep her tongue up Prince Jestin's—or the king's—ass, where it clearly was.

"The White Plume is different," Stellera explained. "The Plume only employs willing soulless. No mortals. Lucky for us, I find we Soullanders know a body and its pleasures best. Especially daemons." The dimple appeared in her brown cheek again as she grinned. "Plus, there's entertainment. Not everything is purely pleasure—unless you want it to be."

Helde giggled behind her hand again, like she couldn't stand the scandal.

"I'm in," I said with a smug smile. I could stick to the entertainment, but either way, I would enjoy my final night of freedom.

"Good," Stellera said with a small clap. "We'll have to be sure no one knows it's us."

"How?" I asked.

Helde grinned. "They pass out masks there. Ones created by *Mindbloods*. Illusions."

My heart ached. I already missed Ailerby dearly.

"No one will be able to tell who we are, and *what* we do will remain a secret," Helde continued.

Maybe she wasn't so obedient to her prince.

A hundred questions ran through my mind. "But your rooms are both attached to the princes' too, aren't they?"

"With the questions again, Sersa." Helde gave me a pitying smile that said *poor mortal,* restoring my belief that she was a snob. She evidently thought I lived an incredibly sheltered life.

"The princes won't be staying with us before the ceremony. It's the perfect night—the only one—to sneak out and have a bit of fun for ourselves." Stellera winked.

"Good to know."

After my argument with Nessin, his outburst, and his attempt to rile or seduce me—maybe both—the anticipation of the evening's distraction was the only thing I concentrated on for the rest of the day. Despite circumstances and despite the task I was here to accomplish, I deserved a bit of fun too.

13

We slipped out of the Daemon King's Citadel after midnight.

All of it was exhilarating. Even just being out of the citadel when I knew I shouldn't be thrust a rush of adrenaline through me. Escorted by one of the servants, it was all too easy. The woman knew every twist and turn, every passage dotted with Soul Guards and Sluagh, and where they'd be when.

By the time we were outside, my breath felt hot, and my palms had turned clammy with sweat. I was glad I'd selected one of the thinner dresses to wear tonight. Midnight-blue silk with a slit halfway up the thigh.

No carriage awaited us. Instead, the servant directed us around the back of the citadel and through a hidden door along the thick wall surrounding it. We clung to the shadows as Sluagh patrolled the perimeter. Then we slipped away from the wall, spilling out into Gilders Eye on light feet.

The white stone streets were far tamer than anywhere I'd been within Nos Ovscura at this time of night, and it was a little unsettling at first. Neither Helde nor Stellera seemed fazed, so I used the walk to calm my nerves.

Tonight, I would chase amusement, fun, distraction, and nothing more.

Triple moonlight bounced off the cobbled roads like a snowy river, and every shop was lit up tonight. The nocturnal city boasted dressmakers, haberdasheries, and jewelers aplenty on one side, and the many pleasure dens were scattered throughout the city. Outside, workers luring in clients gave the dens away.

We wore hooded cloaks so we wouldn't be recognized, but the crowd was bustling tonight. Finely dressed Gilders perused the dens and betting halls at a leisurely pace, and I wondered if any of them belonged to the Circle of Gilders, if any of them were responsible for trading a heap of gold for my father.

Rather, likely not a heap but an absurdly low sum.

Before I knew it, we had arrived at a palatial exterior forged of white stone, complete with marble feathers jutting from the top of the building like a peacock's tail.

Stellera looked over her shoulder at me, swinging a little beaded handbag around her wrist. "Welcome to the White Plume, Sersa."

A burly worker wearing a white cloak that resembled a swan stood out front. He wasn't letting everyone enter, and I craned my neck when Stellera flashed some gold token. I couldn't see what it was.

"Welcome to the White Plume," the worker said like Stellera before him, brandishing three masks from his costume.

Chills curled over my skin as he opened one of two doors for us, and I followed Helde and Stellera's lead as they slipped on the masks and threw back their hoods.

"Don't remove it," Stellera said over her shoulder. Her features had distorted but not so much that I wouldn't be able to recognize her in the crowd. "The illusion will break when you do. It'll poof into feathers. They're only good once."

I nodded as we crossed the threshold, and someone took our cloaks. My gut unfurled with a dozen mixed emotions, every shade of excitement and nervousness. The White Plume wasn't decorated in a drop of white inside. Everything was black or silver, so unlike the rest of Gilders Eye—at least what I'd seen from outside the gates. The sudden contrast reminded me, in a way, of the citadel.

A long corridor unfolded before us, bracketed by columns on either side. I caught glimpses of people between gaps in the cloisters. Their bodies intertwined with one another, and while some clutched frosted glasses or pipes in their hands, most had their hands on another's body. It was the hidden hands that caught my gaze. Most were fully clothed. Others were not. Many wore skimpy little robes or dresses, lingerie peeking out, or fancy, unbuttoned coats with nothing underneath.

I wasn't prudish by any means, yet I still felt like I was invading their privacy.

"You're blushing again, Sersa. The folks out here are the ones who love for others to watch," Helde whispered in a playful voice.

"There are private rooms upstairs," Stellera said over her shoulder. "A drink first?"

I nodded eagerly, and Stellera grinned wide.

Tantalizing music, unlike anything I'd ever heard before, played from somewhere farther inside the pleasure den. During the bards' stories in the great hall of House Scáth, the same instruments played in the background. But the pleasure den's musicians managed to elicit the desire to entangle my body with those in the entrance, to drop all inhibitions for once and focus only on the hedonistic, delicious moment unfolding inside the White Plume.

The beat thrummed in my chest and in my blood, and all my senses came alive as we moved deeper into the den.

We reached an open area, a circular parlor with a domed roof, enclosed by the columns that had continued from the entranceway. Stellera moved through the sea of bodies toward a bar at the back and returned with three drinks a few moments later.

I glimpsed my reflection in the glass. My lips were fuller than normal, my nose more delicate, and my eyes unnaturally green instead of almost black. Something else was different about my face, but I couldn't put my finger on it, and my hair had turned to a shade of brown like I'd spent years in the sun.

Among the teeming crowd, the soulless wraiths weren't distinguishable from mortals. The faint glow of their skin had been disguised, but the daemons retained their horns, pointed teeth, and beady eyes. Some of them were downright striking. I wasn't surprised Stellera took an interest in them.

After a few minutes, a daemon with greenish skin the color of a seasick mortal and short horns presented himself to Stellera. He bowed his head, and she threw hers back in a laugh. Then she strode toward a young woman standing at a little round table by herself. They laced their fingers, the woman abandoning her full drink as she led Stellera away.

I watched them climb a staircase before disappearing to the second floor.

Helde waggled her eyebrows at the daemon and handed me her drink as he swept her onto the floor of dancing people.

I nursed my own drink first. When I finished, I set the empty glass on a waitron's tray. Watching the sea of bodies moving as one, I quickly moved onto Helde's.

"Mortals should take heed when drinking soulless alcohol."

Mid-sip, I turned toward the voice to my left.

A man with dark brown eyes stood beside me. He wasn't looking at me though. He, too, watched the dancing patrons. A faint smell of sweat lingered in the stale air of the White Plume, and the ensemble playing music in the corner suddenly felt louder as I looked upon his face. I tasted salt and citrus in the air, not just from the sweet-and-sour drink I sipped on but something more. Like the pleasure den was pumping fumes all around us.

A smile curled one end of the stranger's lips, and he turned slightly, looking at me from his peripheral.

I realized I hadn't said a word.

I said the first thing that came to mind. "Thank you for your concern, but maybe I'm no mortal."

He leaned forward, his hands clasped behind his back. "Your perfume had me fooled," he said, barely loud enough for me to hear over the musicians. "Be careful. A few of those and you'll do whatever you desire most."

A flush warmed my cheeks, and I couldn't be sure whether it was the balmy air inside the White Plume that did it—or him.

I studied him for a long second. His hooked nose fit his face, almost dangerous but enticing. His clothes were modest with a sharp edge, and a trio of dainty, sheathed daggers dangled from his belt like he made his living as a bounty hunter or a thief.

He certainly wasn't a Gilder.

"Care to dance?" he said, looking from me to the center of the floor.

I grinned. As a waitron passed us, the man set my drink on their tray. He took my hand without hesitation, and likewise, I felt none. I was here to have a good time. I was here to let down my walls, to shove away the colors always flooding my mind, and live—truly live—before I married Nessin Drumghoul.

Even if it was all a ruse.

But the thought of Nessin sent me down a dangerous path.

I wondered what *his* bare hand would feel like in mine rather than this man's. I'd felt Nessin's knuckles brush against my spine when he'd helped me out of my dress yesterday, and today when he'd traced my thigh in what I'd hoped would culminate in nothing short of utter satisfaction, but as far as I searched my memory, he'd otherwise always worn gloves since I'd met him.

My memory was fickle. The thought of Nessin's hands on me again presented itself as both desirable and confusing. Because it was only my body that wanted him. Not my mind.

No, *not* my mind.

Gods. Admitting that to myself made me shudder.

I shoved those thoughts aside as the man spun me into his arms. His presence had caused the others dancing nearby to clear a space, a barrier separating us from them and placing us in our own world.

Our bodies skimmed one another, his hips close to mine, my leg elevated around his upper thigh. I fought a grin as the heat between us built. His hand traced my wrist, summoning tingles on my skin where his touch set me afire, but he never actually held onto it or my hand. The arm wrapped around my waist, however, was firm with a yearning to keep us close. Never more than an inch apart while we circled the floor.

When the music peaked on a crescendo, the stranger dipped me backward and buried his face in my neck, right above my chest. My dress left little to the imagination, a purposeful choice in the throng of dresses Draea or Claud had procured me. When I'd dressed earlier, I imagined Draea warning me with a shake of the finger —*Wear that one for your husband*—and defiance had surged inside me.

It surged inside me now too, louder, both refusing to think of Nessin and drowning in thoughts of him.

The music slowed, and the stranger spun me so my back faced his front. I lost myself in the movement of his hips, guiding mine... I looked over my shoulder. His face was there, cheek pressed to mine. Our breaths uneven.

"Shall we go somewhere private?" I asked, breathless.

"There is only us here. Do you see anyone else?"

My heart leaped when I looked all around us. We were alone, the den empty.

He was a Mindblood then. I worked to keep my jaw from dropping by biting my lip. The stranger's finger traced it.

"I'm afraid I can't let you do *that*." His voice was almost a rumble. "I think we shall find somewhere private. I want to show you something."

His whisper against my neck ignited every eager nerve in my body. The scent emanating from him, sweet and musky yet minty, clouded my every sense until I no longer cared what I was feeling or hearing or seeing. Chills unfurled across my entire body from my arms to my scalp to my toes and then along every point where we touched.

Before I knew it, I was following him upstairs.

The stranger guided me not up a single flight of stairs but toward a second stairwell too. A short, white rope with a sign dangling from it blocked off the narrow stairs, enclosed on either side by papered walls.

Restricted. Staff of the White Plume Only, the sign read.

He lifted one leg over the rope then the other, and I gasped when he lifted me effortlessly, setting me in front of him. Hands gripping the railings, he walked behind me closely. His chest brushed my bare shoulder blades. His lungs and heart had evidently stopped racing, or maybe they'd never started, while mine echoed in my ears.

Halfway up the stairs on a step above him, I turned and crushed my lips against his. He pulled me close, parting my lips with his tongue, and I tangled my hands in his hair. The strands were longer than the illusion showed, and it was the strangest sensation imaginable.

When I pictured Nessin's hair in my hands, I wondered if the liquor had me imagining it all.

I pulled away, and he turned me back around, chuckling to himself as I restarted our march up the steps.

We reached the next landing. Silver doors sat on either side of a straight, narrow corridor. Yet another staircase and we reached what I suspected was the top floor. At the end of a long corridor sat the only double doors in the entire pleasure den. At least from what I'd seen of the second floor on our way up.

"Where are we?" I asked.

"That's the penthouse. It's where I'm staying." The stranger took the lead, whisking me toward the end of the hall at a quickened pace.

He didn't want the heat to cool, the rush to lull, or the attraction to fade. Neither did I. I knew all too well that too many flings fizzled this way. So few preserved their spark.

I didn't care to look around the penthouse as we swept inside, and it was so dark that, even if I'd wanted to see what it looked like, I couldn't.

Our lips locked again, my hands skimming his body, his keeping me torturously close. His hands otherwise kept to himself as he maneuvered me around the furniture.

We halted in front of a terrace, where moonlight dusted the floor.

The taste of him was indescribable. Likewise, little justice could be done to express the feel of him through his clothes. When he spun me around as he had on the dance floor, his lips moved from mine to my neck. He masterfully tickled my skin with his tongue.

A sofa faced away from us with a little table behind it. I peeled my hands from his body and rested my palms on the table to stop myself from swaying with the waves of elation that overtook me. Our eyes locked in the mirror across from the sofa. Mine dropped to the thumb running circles on the silk against my thigh, then my hip, higher and higher when I wanted his touch lower.

I watched him caress my neck with his tongue.

"Hmm?" he pressed, the noise somehow dripping with lust. I swore I detected restraint too. "You say the word, and I'll stop."

Smiling, I took the hand on my stomach and led it downward, positioning his splayed fingers on my hip bone. Further still, letting him feel the warmth through the lacy shorts I wore beneath my dress.

Fingers pausing between my legs, he chuckled in my ear. "Then this is what you want."

What I wanted was for those fingers to be *Nessin's*.

I watched my chest rise and fall in the mirror before us. His brown eyes locked with mine, never blinking, never looking away. I felt every solid plane of his body, the hardness of his thighs, and his arousal against my back. Holding his eyes, I knew what I wanted.

I reached behind me, feeling his face—and found purchase.

The edges of the mask he wore.

I pulled it free. He didn't stop me.

But as it fell, my whole body went rigid. The mask twirled to the floor in a heap of feathers, the one-time illusion shattering like glass.

My stranger wasn't a stranger at all.

Nessin.

"So responsive," he whispered. "As I suspected, love."

14

My first thought—my only thought presently—was that I'd gotten what I'd wanted. A taste of Sin.

He continued to stare back at me in the mirror, our bodies locked against one another for a few seconds that felt like minutes. White strips of hair fell in his devilish eyes.

The illusion now ruined, I shoved free from Nessin's arms and spun. He didn't fight me, but the dark chuckle that started from deep in his chest was enough to set me aflame, reminding me of our prior argument. I ripped my mask free and whipped it at the ground, leaving a second heap of white feathers at my feet.

His lanky form had returned, no longer the bulky stranger I'd thought I was kissing. Even still, my hands hadn't expected what they'd felt. He was all lean muscle beneath those clothes.

Gods. Damn. Him.

I wanted him. I'd wanted *him* the entire time.

My gut dipped into my toes like it, too, had realized.

"*You*. You! You scoundrel!"

"Is that the best you've got, love?" He crossed the room and lit a single lantern. That single lantern ignited all the rest around the room, one after the other.

Magic. They must've been hexed. They illuminated the miniature bar he stood before.

Unexpected fear replaced my anger. The room suddenly tinted black around us, all the lanterns darkening. When Nessin looked around, eyes narrowing, I thought for sure he saw it too. Was I darkening the room, dowsing the flames? If so, I needed to cool my fear. *Fast.* But what was I afraid of exactly—how badly I wanted the Daemon Prince?

Another part of me wanted to hurt him right now. He'd let me follow along this path of illusion. He'd known I wanted him. I needed to say something, to explain that I was attracted to him, yes. But it was nothing more.

It *wasn't* anything more.

"I hate you."

It was the second time I'd said so, hoping it would dull the ache between my thighs.

Nessin selected two glasses and picked up a carafe. "Oh, please. What you're feeling right now is dissatisfaction, an ascent without reaching the peak, Sersa."

"I am well aware of what I'm feeling," I growled. I balled my hands into fists at my sides.

"Plus, I heard your every thought when we were dancing. *Oh, I wish he were Nessin. Oh, I wonder what Nessin feels like...* I told you —I would prefer if you called me Sin. And as I've said before, your obvious attraction to me definitely helps our situation." He smirked as he turned around, holding two glasses filled with a pale red liquor. Petals floated inside the glasses, reminding me of the Daemon King's tea. "What was I to do but grant a lady—my betrothed—her every desire?"

"I will show you my every desire if you give me one of your daggers, *Sin*," I growled, balling my hands into fists. My eyes dropped to the trio hanging from his belt.

"Oh, your mind says differently. If you want me so badly, if your body aches so tenderly for mine, you need only ask, love."

"Stop calling me that!" I rubbed my temples. The liquor had gotten to my head, and so was the weight of our...newest entanglement.

I closed my eyes, trying to slow my breaths. The worst part was that he was right. I couldn't look at him right now. I had wanted him. Still did. Not the stranger. Nessin. My body had taken over, allowing no input from the rationality I ought to have but didn't.

Sin. Sin. Sin. I tried to hammer it into my head. Though I had to admit, it fit him better than Nessin.

He handed me the glass, and I fought the urge to smack it from his hands like the night we'd met.

"It's rose water," he said.

I took it and downed the cool liquid, feeling a small piece of myself ease. I closed my eyes and took three deep breaths before opening them again. "What are you doing here? Did you follow us?"

"No, I didn't follow you, Sersa. I'm many things but not a stalker. You have free rein, and you will maintain that, with a few guards to keep you safe, after our engagement ends."

Ends. I scoffed. That was a circuitous way of saying *when we're married*.

"I know what it's like to be smothered, and I will never do that to you," he added. "You know... If you prefer illusion to the real thing, I can put another mask on," he offered with another chuckle.

I set my empty glass down in his palm with a sneer, noting his gloveless hands, and turned my back on him to shield my thoughts. I'd changed my mind. I wouldn't dare admit aloud that he was insufferably handsome.

He already knew it.

Sin had an air to him, and I was drawn to it like a bee to honey. Except I knew once he lured me in, it'd be like landing on a spider's web instead. It wasn't even the way he looked that did me in. It was puzzlingly deeper than that, and I refused to give in. I refused to let it cloud my head. I couldn't afford distractions and what they might mean.

Remember why you're here. Pa.

I wrapped my arms around my middle and took a deep breath. "Then you knew it was me all along?"

Sin set the empty glasses on the bar before taking a seat on the end of a colossal bed. I kept my back to him.

"Yes," he said. "Though I wasn't going to touch you until I heard your most intriguing thoughts when we were dancing. No need for embarrassment though. People fall for my good looks all the time. Or it's the gold in my family's coffers. Maybe both."

"I suspect it's your overdone charm that deters them as soon as you open your mouth. Your father told me to have my fun, you know. I came here for that tonight, not this."

"I won't stop you from going back out there. Get another disguise and go." He nodded at a collection of masks hanging on the wall near the doors.

He knew he'd spoiled that.

But had he actually? I'd gotten what I wanted, yes. A taste of Sin to get me through, even if I hadn't known in the moment that it was him.

Now, we could face the fact that we *were* attracted to one another and move on. He was right. A bit of lust couldn't hurt us when we were playing this game anyway. We didn't need to convince the Daemon King we were in love exactly. I didn't think the Daemon King believed in love to begin with. Not the man who'd killed his own wife.

A shudder rippled up my spine.

But with my curiosities now out of the way, I could focus better.

When Sin cleared his throat, I looked over my shoulder.

"Between you and me, I came here tonight because I own the White Plume," he said. "No one knows that, so you'd do well to keep it to yourself."

"How would your father not know? Your money is his."

"I have...let us call them investors." His expression was flat as a board. "For safety, my crew sees through every mask. We only let patrons in who've been granted a token."

He turned something over in his hand, and my curiosity got the best of me. With narrowed eyes, I crossed the room. He extended his hand, and I took the token, weighing it in my palm.

A metal feather.

"Grab another mask just in case," Sin said abruptly. "I want to show you something."

"Ah, then that part wasn't a lie. What you said when we finished dancing," I reminded him.

Sin winked at me. "None of it was a lie, Sersa. You aren't the only one who wanted a little... What was it? *Taste.*"

My mouth fell open, but I snapped it closed. His eyes were filled with mischief, and something about the look made my irritation thaw.

"The fact that the so-called gods gave you the ability to hear thoughts is mind-blowing," I said. "One would think you'd keep it a secret."

The realization hit me abruptly. Sin wasn't just Colossi or Bonespeaker... He was a Mindblood too. It was how he heard my thoughts and how he'd made the White Plume appear empty when we were dancing.

"The gods had nothing to do with my creation. It was the devil himself who gave me that. Along with many other traits and skills, love."

"Yes, maybe it was the devil. No one deserves that many gifts."

"As you are aware, our gifts can also be curses," he said quietly.

Sin strode toward a narrow mirror on the far wall behind the bed, pulled it open to reveal a dark passage, and turned on his heels.

He extended his hand. "I promise it will be worth it. You want to trust me, so I am going to share a secret with you. This is how it starts, Sersa. *Trust.*"

Though I didn't take his hand, I entered ahead of him, and he pulled the mirror closed behind us.

The dark passageway reminded me of the one beneath House Scáth. The last two days, I'd managed to keep thoughts of Ciel, Ailerby, and the rest of Clan Scáth from my mind. But now there was nowhere to turn.

I hoped I might find a way to meet them somewhere on the less glitzy side of the city after the wedding.

Gods.

The very idea of the wedding, that we'd take part in the handfasting ceremony tomorrow, made my head whirl. It certainly helped sweep aside all thoughts of my clan.

The passageway split left and right as soon as we entered, and it was so narrow we couldn't walk beside one another. I followed Sin as he took a sharp left and listened to the echo of our footsteps, scarcely able to see a few inches in front of my nose.

I grazed the walls on either side and halted when my fingers ran into a tiny metal latch and a...

A *peephole*?

I took a sharp intake of breath. "Good gods, Sin. Do you *spy* on your pleasure workers?"

I only saw his white eyes and the tip of his nose as he turned.

"Despite appearances, this isn't a pleasure den at all. You'll see in a second. Trust me." He extended his gloved hand again, and despite my reservations, I took it this time.

I wondered how I'd missed him slipping gloves back on.

Nessin guided me forward a little farther and then halted, sweeping me in front of him so I faced the wall. The motion reminded me of the dance we'd shared downstairs. Standing behind me in the narrow space, he rested his other hand on the wall.

"You say it's not that sort of pleasure den," I whispered. "But what about in the entranceway?"

"All illusions," Sin said. He reached around me for the peephole's handle, hesitating. "I have a dozen Mindbloods on staff cultivating the ambiance in here. The patrons that the *real* patrons see change every night so that they don't catch on. But if any one of the real patrons goes up to them, the bloods give them a good time. In their minds at least."

"Genius."

The chuckle he released told me he was wearing a wicked grin. "I like to think so too."

His fingers hesitated further, hovering over the peephole.

"Sersa, I need to apologize for my behavior earlier." He exhaled like he'd been holding these words and his breath in for some time. "I was worse than uncouth. I was a real foul-mouthed bastard, and then on the chair, I was partially deflecting."

"Partially?" I echoed.

"Yes, *partially*, because I liked seeing you angry with me."

"You are a sadist."

"Only partially," he said sardonically. "Please believe me when I say I want to be able to tell you things. I want you to trust me, but it's not wise. Just know that I am playing a dangerous game, I don't want you involved more than you already are, and I *do* have fears. About things not working out."

"What things?"

"I'm apologizing, which is already difficult for me. Please don't make me say more than I have to. I only want to say that you didn't deserve to be spoken to that way. And the chair," he repeated.

I wondered how long he'd been thinking about that moment. It thrilled me.

"I should have told you about our union," he continued, "and I promise you it will be annulled the second we both have what we need. I won't touch you with a ten-foot spear either. Unless you beg me. Should you desire a little fun since you are so attracted to me."

I shook my head. "You almost made it through that entire speech without telling me what I think of you."

"It wasn't a speech. I mean every word. Furthermore..." Sin leaned forward, lips near my ear. "How many times must I remind you that I know exactly what you think about me, love?"

He lifted the peephole, giving me no chance to reply.

A thin swath of fabric or wallpaper lay in front of the peephole. I couldn't be totally sure what the other side looked like, but an opaque design covered it, concealing us.

Two alleged pleasure workers—both daemons, by the looks of their barbed tails—wore skimpy outfits. But as they walked in a circle around their client, a middle-aged man with a drooping white mustache, I saw the illusion for what it was. Their outfits were only costumes.

The client's full head of hair had a stiff quality to it, the front swept backward like a frozen whitecap.

Sin adjusted his palm against the wall and shifted his weight behind me. He stooped forward, bending his neck to look through the peephole as I did.

"She's a Mindblood," he whispered in my ear, nodding at the petite woman on the right. "She specializes in searching memories." He took a breath that seemed too deep to fit inside the narrow, unlit passageway, and his inner thigh brushed against my hip. "And the other girl—her too, only she is best at crafting illusions of the mind."

"Speaking of, that trick you pulled before we went upstairs—you're a Mindblood too. So, do you have blood from every Soullander clan or just every useful one?"

"I'll let you wonder if my trick was the moment that got to your head or magic."

I groaned internally, finally realizing everything that had happened. Everything I'd done. *I'd* kissed *him*. "If this is no real pleasure den, why is the client in his skivvies?"

"That's not any client. That's Daigh Hellick. Before Lord Hellick lost his soul, he lived in Djelsa across your eastern sea."

"Hellick, as in Helde's father?"

"Ah. You've had a chance to meet the others. Good. That should make the revelries following our wedding more tolerable."

"Ha. How far away is Djelsa? I've never heard of it."

"Even if you sailed east for an entire moon, you wouldn't reach it."

My brow furrowed as I recalled all of Ciel's history books. I tried to wrap my mind around the thought of there being more than the Four Pointes of Clais. On all the maps Pa had garnered over the years and ones he'd had before I could remember, the cartographers had always put The Distant Lands or The End. With a dozen or more clans scattering the Northern Pointe and then dozens more on each of the other three pointes, my world had always felt big enough.

Cutting off any further questions, Sin nodded his chin at the peephole.

We returned our attention to the room beyond.

"Tell me, Daigh," the first Mindblood said, "and I hope it's all right I call you *Daigh*."

Though I'd never met any Mindbloods before, her voice was the sort of melodic, hypnotic tune I expected from someone with the ability to slip into another's mind, to manipulate and pluck whatever memories they wished.

Fleetingly, I wondered if Nessin had been commanding me to feel certain things for him, while enjoying the sight of them whelming my mind.

Together, the Mindbloods halted their circling, and the first leaned forward, pressing her palms to her knees. "Is that all right, Daigh?"

"Y-Yes," he stammered. But his lips told a different story. They pulled into a sleepy grin, and his rosy cheeks plumped further. "Please. Do call me Daigh."

Sin's voice brushed my ear again. "It's the Mindblood on the left that's doing it. It'll pass as soon as she releases the magic, but for now it's like a drug. Hellick's high on it, only seeing what she wants him to see."

I nodded in understanding.

"*Daigh*," the woman purred once more, "did you look for the name I asked you to in your ledgers?"

Hellick nodded fervently like he'd been waiting for her to ask.

"Oh, yes. Oh, yes. I most certainly did. *Bain Scáth*."

My body went rigid, my knees buckled, and Sin squeezed my arm to steady me.

"And?" asked the first woman.

Hellick fumbled his trembling lip, worry sewing his forehead into deep lines. His cheeks wobbled. "I-I did not purchase a servant by that name. It isn't in my records."

"Are you absolutely certain, Daigh? Look upon Bain Scáth's face again. *Allow me.*"

I couldn't see the illusion the woman wove, but I blinked tears from my eyes, wishing I could. Pa's face felt so far. I hadn't seen him in so long, and I couldn't remember every detail like I wanted to. Black hair like mine. Green eyes with little crow's feet.

But what else?

I pressed my lips into a thin line, holding my breath.

"No," Hellick said. "No, never seen him. I'm certain."

The other Mindblood frowned and lifted her hands. She started swiping them left and right as if she were swatting at superfluous memories before settling on one. Her eyes narrowed, and her head tilted as she studied the empty air—or so it appeared.

I dug my fingers into the stone wall, feeling the bones of a corset I wasn't wearing digging into my ribs, constricting my breath.

Finally, the Mindblood blinked and stood tall. Her eyes found the peephole, and she shook her head once as if Sin had warned them he'd be watching.

Either that or he was always watching.

Hellick had never seen Pa. Hellick wasn't the one.

With an exhale, I deflated. Though my hands slid down the wall in defeat, I wanted to claw my way through the stone separating us.

The magic faded when both Mindbloods waved their hands in a dismissive gesture. Then the expert of weaving illusions leaned forward and swept a finger under Hellick's chin, eyeing him like a doting lover.

"How was that?" she asked.

Hellick was panting. He pressed his palms to the ground, a deep belly chuckle echoing through the room. "Oh, *yes*. Excellent!"

I couldn't believe Sin ran this operation. The Daemon Prince had been forthcoming that he dealt in secrets. But an entire house of secrets? He could gather whatever information he wanted.

How had Sin built this place right under his father's nose?

He shut the peephole slowly, silently. I rested my elbows and head against the wall next to it.

"He's not the only one." His voice rasped the silence. "Hellick is only the first. There are seven more High Houses, and tomorrow they'll all be at the citadel. I'm sorry."

I turned slowly then threw my arms around his waist because I couldn't find his neck in the darkness. Sin barely moved as our bodies collided.

"You kept your word," I said. "You're helping me look for my pa."

"Of course," Sin said, surprise lacing his voice as his hands slid to my back. "I wouldn't lie about that, Sersa."

A shiver rattled down my spine as I understood his words for what they were. Maybe Sin wouldn't lie about this.

But he'd lie to me about plenty of other things.

15

The next morning, the feeling of nausea yanked me awake. My gut spun with acidic liquid that burned in my throat as I threw the covers off me and skittered into the bathing room. I spilled the contents of my stomach into an empty marble basin, barely making it there on time.

Once the feeling subsided, I pressed my palms into the counter and hung my head. It wasn't the two drinks I'd had. It hadn't been enough to make my stomach spin like *this*.

"I was sick on the morning of my wedding too," Draea said from the doorway. She hobbled forward and handed me a towel. I used my sleeve to wipe my mouth instead. "I didn't meet him beforehand though. And he wasn't a prince. Seems you're ahead of the curve already, Lady Sersa."

I chuckled just to avoid crying.

She disposed of my vomit by tossing it in the fire behind the grate, and I almost gagged again. Then she craned her neck out of the doorway connected to Sin's room. "Innes, can you take this and fetch us a fresh basin? We're going to need it."

Fighting the nausea still spinning in my gut, I moved back into my room and shoved open the doors between mine and Sin's rooms.

Servants were everywhere. Bustling left and right. Draping a veil on a cloth-covered mannequin. Inspecting a pair of pointy-toed satin shoes. Studying the sketches Claud had evidently drawn up for my hair.

Right on cue, Claud entered the room and swept past me, carrying an enormous bag that required another set of hands to keep it from dragging on the ground.

My dress.

"Hello, Sersa," he said. "Goodbye, Sersa. I've given them everything they need to make you look perfect."

"What time is it?" I asked Draea.

"Almost midday. I suspect *someone* hit the bottle last night." She leaned forward and sniffed me. "As suspected. My instincts are always correct. Though I'll bet Sin and his brothers are in far worse of a state. Women need not be convinced to marry. Men, on the other hand... Up until the very last minute."

"That's a generalization," I said under my breath. "I could use more than some convincing right now."

"The prince has waited centuries to get married, Sersa Scáth. It's how I know he's ready. You will be just fine. Now, get in the bath," Draea snapped.

And it was the first of many commands over the next few bells.

The four betrotheds stood in a line.

I was the third, for Nessin, the third oldest brother.

Each of us wore a beaded, opaque veil that fell to our shoulders. Draea had explained the custom right before we'd left Sin's rooms, but I'd tuned it out, not caring in the least why the Soullander princes wanted their betrothed unable to see on their wedding day.

Probably so we couldn't run away.

Draea had all but grappled me to get the suffocating veil over my head. The fabric blinded me, and it didn't help my shallow breaths. I could only look down at my feet, at the pointed shoes I wore, poking out from the front of my dress and pinching my toes.

I had two Gilders on either side of me, ready to walk me to Sin as soon as the terrace doors opened. I only knew we were headed onto a terrace because we'd been told. My hands shook at the thought that either of these Gilders might have purchased my father to work in their High Houses. Or worse. If Stellera's family ran numerous pleasure dens, then what places of iniquity did the others own? Where had they sent Pa?

When the Gilder to my left warned me that it was almost time, I recognized the voice.

One of my escorts was Daigh Hellick.

Bile crept up my throat. The nausea hadn't gone away since this morning. Not since I'd been shuffled from servant to servant. Bathed. Groomed from head to toe. Carefully coiffed and disguised with honey blotted on my lips. Berry stain added to my cheeks. Kohl smudged around my eyes. And a collar around my neck that displayed the Drumghoul signet.

The sour state of my gut worsened as I recalled the way the Mindbloods had fooled and controlled Lord Hellick the night before.

The dress was another thing altogether. While it wasn't a complete pouf, it was made of hundreds of feather-like strips of fabric sewn to look utterly realistic. The sleeves, while long, were sheer and hung off my shoulders. The neckline dipped into a sweetheart shape.

I wondered if Sin hadn't slipped a hint to Claud to fashion my dress of feathers, secretly paying homage to the White Plume.

He owned the pleasure den, and now he was about to own *me*.

I blew a shaky breath through my lips, reminding myself that this was all a means to an end. Sin wasn't my owner. He wasn't going to *be* my owner. He was going to be my husband—my *fake* husband—and only for a few weeks until I was free of him for good like he'd promised.

But I couldn't stop my mind from turning over the fact that women were so frequently treated like livestock for trading. No, we mortals were treated as such in the City of Soulless and the Soullands beyond. I blamed myself for every time I'd traded a kof in the city for entertainment, a watery drink, or another distraction.

That was what Nos Ovscura was for all of us—a glimmer of distraction to forget our sad, mundane lives beyond the bridge.

I closed my eyes as the doors swept open, propelling a gust of wind through the hall where we waited. My knees buckled, but the Gilders on either side of me kept me steady. They held my hands in theirs, straightening my arms like I was on a tightrope. I'd probably have been more comfortable on one than where I was right now.

We started for the doors. I looked down at my feet the entire time.

As soon as we reached the terrace, the air turned crisp, and the salty taste of the Wraithsea mixed with the honey on my lips. But as soon as I stepped over the threshold, the Cradled Moons warmed me.

Before I knew it, the Gilders deposited me into Sin's bare hands. They looked so pale in the light. So wrong.

He adjusted his grip on mine, and I focused on a long scar that was somehow whiter than his skin. Though they looked unnatural without his gloves, they were steady enough to stop mine from shaking.

The cheering from the crowd below reached a crescendo before silencing altogether. With my thoughts booming around my skull, I almost didn't notice the sound at all.

If not for the veil, Sin would have seen how quickly my chest was rising and falling. I tried to slow my breaths, but the air burned in my lungs.

"Breathe," he whispered.

Gods. Then he did see.

"Your veil will be removed after my older brothers are bound. *Breathe*," he repeated.

I licked my lips again, unable to bring myself to acknowledge him. Still as stone, I closed my eyes and focused on my breath. I squeezed his hands, and he squeezed back in answer.

It struck me odd how...here for me Sin was.

But with the air whipping around me and the intermittent cheering of the crowd below us and my spiraling thoughts, I couldn't focus well enough to truly calm myself. I looked down continuously, waiting for the black shackles to enclose my wrists.

Minutes passed, turning into moments that blurred together.

My thoughts went off on a tangent as I wondered how high up we were. But right then, a Druid priest of the High Triad finally approached.

Oh, gods.

"Nessin Drumghoul," he said. "You may lift Sersa Scáth's veil."

Sin released my clammy hands and lifted the veil at once. The Druid took it from him and handed it off to another, maybe a fellow Druid. I didn't care who.

All my cares were swept aside.

I looked upon Sin, and my heart beat faster. His colorless eyes never left mine. The black coat and pants he wore contrasted me in all ways, save for silver-and-mauve stitching. Even his hair, perfectly styled out of his eyes for once, contrasted against my black strands intricately braided, looped, and adorned with flowers.

I couldn't read his expression as he studied me.

We stared at one another for a moment. Then the Druid began.

He said very little during the ceremony, save for our names and a few words about being bound to one another. Likewise, we said nothing. We agreed to nothing aloud.

The silence between us stretched on and on.

Neither of us smiled or moved or even shifted.

The handfasting began before I knew it. The Druid wound a cord of three intertwined colors around our hands—silver, lavender, and gray—and coiled our wrists and hands tighter with each circle and knot he made. I knew what the colors meant because the clans practiced handfasting on all the Four Pointes of Clais too.

Lavender for spiritual healing and to cleanse the soul.

Silver so that we would make wise decisions.

And gray so that our union would weather the storms ahead.

I realized his coat's embroidery matched our handfasting cords. Part of me wished I had been there to help choose the colors, but I thought Sin had made a wise choice with these. We needed everything to go right to find Pa. I hoped there were no storms ahead, but something about his choices made my gut spin faster.

He'd chosen them because he knew.

He knew something, many things, that I did not.

The Druid's next words stunned me. "I present to you, Prince Nessin and Princess Sersa Drumghoul."

Sin reached forward, sliding a hand along my jaw as he leaned into me. Unlike the night before, I froze as his lips neared mine. But then he veered to the right and pressed a gentle kiss against my cheek. His hands were neither cold nor warm, neither soft nor rough.

Either that or I was so desensitized, shocked by the moment as reality swarmed me. So did a sea of colors when Sin pulled away. Mixed emotion after mixed emotion. Not for the first time, colors I had rarely seen before appeared. Pastels like watercolors. Pale yet vibrant all the same and utterly breathtaking. I didn't know what they meant.

But one thing I knew for sure.

Daemon Prince Nessin Drumghoul and I were bound.

The last ceremony—Helde and Jestin's—passed so quickly that it felt like I had blinked.

It was the only one that I'd been able to watch, but still, I felt nothing. My emotions had flattened when I should've felt everything.

As my body fell into a state of shock, I held onto the fact that Sin and I were not truly bound.

Fake, fake, fake, I chanted in my mind.

The terrace on which we stood was suspended high enough over the crowd of Gilders and their families below that I could see the slums and Dúm's Cross in the distance. I realized only now I hadn't peeled my eyes from Sin since my veil had been lifted except to watch Helde and Jestin's handfasting.

Maybe it made me look like the lovestruck bride I was supposed to be playing.

Devlin and his betrothed—now his husband—were directed toward the double doors we'd come through. Over the crowd's cheering, I could scarcely hear the relieved chatter between the two of them.

I caught the first glimpse of Devlin's husband without his veil.

Both were tall, a few inches apart, and utterly picturesque together. Unlike Sin, Devlin's hair was cropped close to his head. But like Sin, he wore black, while his partner wore a blinding white coat and matching pants with silver stitching on the cuffs and down the legs. Black hair in a ponytail secured with a silver ribbon. And black eyes that pierced my soul as he looked over his shoulder.

Ciel.

My brother looked right at me as he and Devlin moved across the threshold. It was a look that spanned no more than a few seconds, but it felt like a hundred years.

I halfway believed my mind was playing tricks on me. Of all days, today was fitting for it to do so. But Ciel had always rooted me in reality.

Tears welled in my eyes as I studied the back of his head. My lips trembled, and I bit down on the bottom one to stop them. My breath caught in my chest as the Daemon King halted in front of Sin and me. His whitish horns caught the light as they poked the air. A little girl in a buttercup-shaped dress with a full head of white curls beamed up at me beside him. She was holding her father's hand, oblivious to my reaction. Maybe she mistook the tears in my eyes for tears of joy at having married her older brother.

"It's so wonderful both you and your brother can be here together," the king said, "experiencing this *together*. Don't you think?"

The Daemon King didn't wait for my answer. He took the liberty of cutting off Lochlainn and Stellera to exit the terrace and never looked back, equally without a care as his daughter bouncing beside him.

While Ciel had all but told my uncles to piss off when they'd expressed disapproval of me and provided a list of qualms pertaining to me succeeding my mother as heir, he'd already renounced the role of chief. I had no idea what the clan knew—probably nothing yet—and no idea how they'd act.

My hands burned.

"Sersa," Sin said quietly.

I dropped my eyes. The tiniest hint of grayish-black tendrils coiled around my wrist like our handfasting cords had earlier. I didn't know what I was feeling. Fear. Hatred. Nothing. Emptiness. Everything all at once.

"Sersa, breathe," he said, not for the first time today. "Breathe. Think about your father. Think about him."

I pictured Pa's face, and suddenly his features were much clearer. Not just his black hair, like Ciel's and mine, or his green eyes but the warmth of his smile and the scar on his cheek that always looked like a dimple.

Pa. Pa. Pa.

I was here to find Pa.

But Ciel... Ciel was too. And this detour was already taking too long and causing too much chaos. Each of us was bound to a Daemon Prince.

Not to mention, Ciel hadn't warned me. What was he thinking? Clearly, he wasn't at all. My gut threatened to empty itself again. This time on the floor.

It was our turn to walk. I managed to smother my feelings long enough for us to reach the corridor and file in behind the first two couples. The walk helped my head significantly, and so did the fact that Ciel didn't look at me again.

But the moment we halted, the fury returned, surging deeper, redder.

From my peripheral, I saw Sin glance my way and then—

His bare hand slid under my jaw and pulled me close. The other found my waist, spinning me toward him to palm the small of my back. Under Sin's touch, an irrepressible shudder whipped up my spine. My height required Sin to bend forward, but his lips found mine fluently. They were soft, save for the finest white stubble around his mouth, the kiss also soft, unlike the ravenous ones we'd shared the night before. He opened my mouth with his, making way for his tongue to swirl around mine. His taste—maybe a pre-ceremony drink or two—and his scent like flames doused me, intoxicating my every sense.

I thought of how badly I wished his hands had finished what I'd started last night.

Reflexively, I reached for his shoulder. With my eyes closed, it was hard to tell how far I needed to extend. I found his neck instead and ran my fingers along the nape, now lifted onto my tiptoes.

"Good gods," Jestin huffed behind us with a heavy scoff. "Didn't you kiss your bride ten minutes ago, Sin?"

Nessin pulled his face back, but his gaze pierced me to the core.

The devil himself couldn't have imitated Sin's smile. I studied the jagged scar traversing the left side of his face, a break in his eyebrow, and the slice through his full lips. My hand remained around his neck, his around my waist. His lips were red, which meant mine were doubly red, and those lips curled into a smile as he said over his shoulder, "Didn't want to upset the High Druid with our passion."

"Save your passion for later," Jestin replied.

"For someone hundreds of years old, Jest, you think you'd be comfortable witnessing such encounters by now. Since you're offended so easily, you ought to steer clear of Sersa and me for a while." Sin winked, and we pulled apart, facing forward.

I blinked slowly, focusing on a spot along the gilded wall as I emerged from my shock and the head rush I felt.

Sin's lips were shining now too. Honey.

He squeezed my hand and looped my arm through his.

"You are doing well. Keep breathing."

I nodded dumbfoundedly and licked my lips, tasting him a second time. It was worse than the first—and by worse, I meant better. Far too satisfying and tantalizing all at once, making me crave more.

Sin snickered under his breath. "Oh, Sersa. How am I to focus with that inner monologue?" He chuckled. "You taste all right too, I suppose. For a mortal. Then again, never kissed one before you."

Though I elbowed him in the ribs, I laughed. A feverish flush had risen into my cheeks.

But his voice lulled me. I couldn't begin to understand how or why, especially with his flippant insults, but I told him to keep talking. I focused on his soothing words the entire walk to the grand ballroom, uncertain whether it was his words or a Bonespeaker's commands keeping me from bursting with rage and fear.

Or the kiss itself.

16

Each prince was presented with a moon cycle's worth of mead from the eight High Houses, and the newlyweds were invited to toast.

Newlyweds.

That word made a lightheaded feeling wash over me before I'd even had a taste of mead. Atop the dais elevating a long, wooden table, Sin and I stood across from one another as we clinked our chalices together. The bite of mead on my tongue quickly slinked to my head, worsening the sensation. All the Daemon Princes, plus their father, remained on the table's other side, a strange distinction for the occasion. As if it were a reminder that we would never sit on the thrones they did.

Before I could take another sip of mead, it was time to receive our wedding gifts. Like everything else, the princes went from oldest to youngest, starting with Devlin and Ciel.

My brother stood tall but red-faced in front of Devlin, sitting on his throne with his chin resting in his hand. Ciel fumbled his own hands in front of him as he awaited the gift. Everyone was looking at my brother, and standing in front of Sin's throne, even I was guilty of staring. I couldn't look away from Ciel.

I couldn't believe he was here.

Two servants carrying a gilded chest navigated onto the dais. They set the chest on the table between Ciel and Devlin with a thud. Ciel looked to Devlin then to the chest and back again. My brother's eyes widened as the blush in his cheeks deepened.

Never in my life had I seen Ciel blush. He may have been quiet, but he'd always had unwavering confidence when it came to men.

"Go on," Devlin encouraged.

It was the first time I'd heard the eldest prince speak, and I prayed to *all* the damn gods Devlin was as kind as he sounded. I even bargained with the gods that I'd finally believe in them if that initial impression proved correct.

I didn't care about myself. Only Ciel.

He took a step toward the chest as the servants propped it open. With a gasp, Ciel's fingers shot forward. He pulled a tome with gilded edges from the chest and gasped again, hands shaking as he carefully flipped it open. He turned the first page like he was handling an infant.

I couldn't read the title of the book from here, but the collection looked priceless, the illustrations inside all hand painted. If Devlin knew my brother's favorite thing in the world, had they talked at length the last few days?

Regardless of how valuable or rare they were, who wanted books as their wedding gift? Devlin must have put a lot of thought into it.

Closing the tome and pressing it to his chest, Ciel bowed to the Daemon King then Prince Devlin. His eyes raised an inch, catching Devlin's, who smiled demurely at my brother.

Gods.

Ciel was in trouble. Devlin was already infatuated with him based on that look. And why wouldn't he be? My sweet yet strong, intelligent brother. But if Devlin harmed even a hair on Ciel's head, I would murder him with my bare hands.

Our gazes caught, and Devlin offered me a small smile.

Next was Stellera and Prince Lochlainn. He gestured to the outskirts of the room. A single servant carried a bassinette toward Stellera and set it on the table between them. All the Gilders and the Court of Soulless erupted with laughter.

The Daemon King hid a smile behind his bejeweled hand. "Very inventive, Lochlainn."

"Thank you, Father! I always am with my gifts. What better wedding present than the Daemon Line's seed?"

All the blood drained from my face as I watched Stellera receive the gift with tact. She ran a finger along the little silver stitching and smiled without showing teeth. But beneath that façade—beneath it, a phoenix blazed, and her teeth were sharp as a wolf's when her mouth finally opened. I knew she'd have his head. Maybe not today, not tonight, but one day.

The look behind her dark blue eyes sent chills up and down my spine. It reminded me that she'd been born in Gilders Eye, grown up here. Stellera knew how to play Prince Lochlainn's games.

At least I hoped.

After a final laugh, the crowd turned their sights to Sin and me. Without warning, another servant came barreling through the crowd, chasing something. The crowd cleared a path, some gasping, others tittering.

A little beast with black fur and red eyes settled at Sin's feet.

"No, no." He prodded it under the table toward me. Bent over to redirect the little beast, Sin looked up between a strand of fallen hair. "She's a hellhound."

I knew what it was. The pup skittered and splat on the marble at my feet with a tired sigh. It seemed we'd had quite similar days. I scooped her up and held her against my chest, studying her furry face and wet nose.

Sin straightened behind the table separating us and watched me.

The Daemon King's chortle cut through my momentary joy. "Ah. One of my sons gifts the prompt promise of an heir and the other, a beast that will put his bride off having broods for years." His eyes left the crowd and landed on me. "Well, at least until the bitch is trained."

Unsmiling, I discarded the Daemon King's gaze. Which bitch he meant was clear.

I pressed a kiss to the hellhound pup's head and whispered, "He means me, not you. Never you, precious girl." I turned to Sin and projected my voice. "She is perfect. Truly."

He nodded, feigning no emotion. I'd always loved animals, so it was a thoughtful gift. But I also wondered if he'd gathered this information about me on Os Íseal, well before we'd ever met. The pup yawned, releasing a little squeal, and I laughed. It felt strange to think a hellhound was adorable, but she was.

As I rocked the pup in my arms, I tried to think of a name for her. Nothing came to me as I watched Jestin present his gift to Helde, a collection of jewelry in a chest like Ciel's. It summoned a gasp of glee from her, and she pressed a flattered hand to her chest. I wondered how often she'd received jewelry growing up. Being a Gilder, it seemed unlikely she wasn't used to gems set in precious metals. Jestin looked quite bored with it all. Though I highly doubted it, I wondered if he'd had any interest in getting married.

That made me wonder. Had Sin?

I didn't wonder if he'd wanted to marry me. That was preposterous when we didn't know one another, but still, the thought stayed with me as the crowd applauded the conclusion of the gifting.

With a groan, probably due to the noise, the pup burrowed her face into the crook of my arm. As my eyes flicked upward, Sin was still watching me.

I offered him a smile, but inside my gut writhed. Our kiss remained top of mind.

When a servant tried to take my hellhound away for the night, she growled at him.

"*Dúm's piss,* what a frightening little thing!" he exclaimed before he cupped a hand over his mouth. "Excuse me, Princess."

"Huh. That's an excellent name," I said, looking into her vibrant eyes. "Hello, Dúma. I'm Sersa. I'll keep you safe from now on."

None of the princes danced.

Instead, I was passed from daemon to daemon and, to my chagrin, the occasional Gilder, all boys at least a few years younger. I doubted they had bought Pa. After eating a heavy dinner, I almost hoped I'd get sick and be able to leave my own wedding early.

Thankfully, Sin had volunteered to hold Dúma in his lap after she'd snapped at another servant. I didn't know if the no dancing thing was a custom, but I looked in his direction every time I faced him amid the twirling. I couldn't give a damn about Sin, but my pup looked content enough, sleeping as he absentmindedly stroked her black fur.

The people I suspected belonged to the Circle of Gilders did not dance either. Each of them wore long gold necklaces that resembled leaves and vines, and their clothes paralleled the Daemon King's brocade finery. Leather shoes so polished I had to squint every time the firelight caught on their toes. And noses that always pointed at the air.

By the time I finally caught a break, I made a beeline for the refreshments. The table was near the thrones where the brothers sat alongside their father. I tried not to let my eyes flicker that way and failed.

Four lines, mostly young women, extended all the way to the dance floor in front of each throne. My gaze darted to Sin. A young woman with strawberry blonde curls piled on her head leaned across the table between them, whispering what I suspected were sweet nothings only for him to hear.

Unfortunately for her, Dúma sprang awake and yipped in her high-pitched bark.

The young woman stumbled backward, caught by another behind her.

"The night has hardly begun, and yet they're already being propositioned with Gilders wanting to be their lovers or ready to let them feast on bits of their incomplete souls. I don't know whether to blame the ones throwing themselves at them or the princes."

I turned.

Stellera downed a glass of water before grabbing another champagne. Tendrils of deep red-brown hair draped her collarbones while the rest was pulled off her face. She looked hot and flustered. She'd been forced to dance for the last two bells too.

"All right," said a loud voice. "Enough, *enough*."

We both turned to see the Daemon King waving off the swarm of shameless guests surrounding his sons' thrones.

"Hello, Sersa," said a calm voice behind me.

"*No.* No, I am done dancing," I replied, whirling around.

Prince Devlin had somehow made his way across the floor in the blink of an eye. Or at least in the time it'd taken me to grab a chalice and down the liquid.

"Oh." My eyes widened. "Prince Devlin."

Stellera patted my hand and excused herself without another word. Evidently, she'd heard the news that my brother was Devlin's betrothed.

His husband.

"I wanted to introduce myself now that we are family by marriage," Devlin said. "Ciel has not stopped talking about you in two days."

The way he said *two days* reminded me just how little time they'd known one another.

"Care to take a turn around the hall?" he asked.

"Uh, sure."

He offered his arm, and I took it. Devlin was a little leaner than Sin, though nearly the same height and build. His hair was cropped close to his head, and while he and his brothers shared those white eyes, his had no sharp edge to them. Not like Sin. His porcelain face was unmarked too.

"Ciel tells me you are a year younger than him."

"That's right. And you are...how much older than him?"

Devlin laughed. "We can't speak to mortal time that well here. I'm sure you understand."

"I'm beginning to."

"How did you like your wedding gift? Sin has been racking his brain for weeks on what to get you."

Weeks. My eyebrows rose. "That can't be. He only asked me for my hand a few days ago."

"He said you've known one another a while. He must have known you'd say yes. Cocky bastard, aye?"

"Aye," I agreed, half lying but fully suspicious.

The lanterns and torchlight in the hall gleamed overhead, catching the dark blue thread of Devlin's coat. I noted little green leaves and yellow flowers stitched into the black fabric too. The colors stood for truth and faithfulness. Good health and happiness. Warmth and luck, among other things.

All the opposite of what Sin had chosen.

Devlin caught me looking and smiled. Guests bowed to him as we passed groups of them. He nodded graciously every time. "We chose the colors together, Ciel and I."

I bit my tongue when the only reply that came to me was, *Oh, when? The day you met or yesterday?*

I didn't need to piss off my in-law so soon, fake or not.

We reached the back of the ballroom and continued to weave around the rectangular tables festooned with center displays of white runners, arrangements of greenery and hawthorn flowers, and long candles. Many Soullander eyes traced us, a mixture of curiosity, judgment, even disdain.

I cleared my throat. "Stellera tells me you're the most likely to succeed the king, being the oldest son."

Devlin smiled politely. "Pardon me for refuting her, but Stellera would be wrong." He swallowed and licked his lips. "I told the king I do not want it. Ciel tells me he and I share that outlook, what with him wanting to study with the Druids. The king was also blunt about the fact that Ciel and I will provide no legitimate heirs, but many children in the Soullands need homes. And hellhounds, I suppose. Should Ciel want children," he added hastily. "I thought it rude to ask so soon, and I've gone so long without children, it would be up to him."

I didn't bother noting that they were married now. No conversation would be considered too soon. In fact, most were probably too late. The topic of children included.

"Ciel does want children," I said. "But first, a very large collection of books. Your gift to him was spot-on."

Devlin glanced at me with a broad grin. "I realized when we passed the library the night he arrived. I've never seen someone stand that still for so long before I asked if he wanted to go inside."

I laughed, imagining my brother like a mouse skittering through a maze.

Devlin's throat bobbed in another swallow as his eyes searched the crowd. I suspected it was to find my brother. "I very much meant the vows I made to Ciel today, Sersa."

I hesitated.

How easy would it be for Devlin to lie to me, to falsely reassure me he'd keep Ciel in his care? I withdrew into my thoughts until we reached the front of the room and the thrones again. We pulled apart, facing one another.

"You certainly exceed expectations of what I had imagined a Daemon Prince to be like, but words don't mean much until actions confirm them. Also..." I leaned forward. "If you harm my brother or treat him any less than he deserves, I will not hesitate on the fact that you're a prince, a daemon, or turned into a god before my eyes, Prince Devlin."

The threat was brazen and stupid on my part, but despite how angry I was with Ciel, I saw the underlying dangers of his decision bright as a beacon.

Devlin threw his head back and laughed, catching me off guard. "Now there is the spitfire Ciel told me you were. I hoped to see her. My brother, the ass, needs it thrown back at him. Daily."

I tilted my head.

His gaze found Sin, still petting Dúma absentmindedly.

Devlin straightened and dipped his head in a chivalrous bow. "I plan on exceeding every single one of Ciel's expectations too. I promise you my intentions are pure." He leaned forward and pitched his voice low. "As are Sin's—"

"Sersa?"

Ciel. I closed my eyes at the sound of his hesitant voice.

Devlin touched a hand to Ciel's abdomen as they shared a chaste kiss before he excused himself.

I faced my brother and glared up at him. His cheeks were flushed from dancing, and his lips were swollen like he'd already managed to steal some time in a shadowy corridor with Devlin between songs. After meeting Devlin, I wouldn't be surprised. Though I hoped what Helde had said—that Devlin and his betrothed hadn't left their rooms since he'd arrived—wasn't true. And yet, seeing the way they looked at one another, I'd bet a hundred kofs it was.

"I don't want to talk to you," I said through gritted teeth.

My feet moved instinctively toward the doors. The heavy, feathery dress I wore made it difficult to maneuver through all the guests. But I needed to get out of the hall before I exploded.

Seeing Ciel's face had done it. Pushed me over the edge.

I felt him on my heels, but with my blood already thrumming from the hot anger I felt, I didn't let myself look at him again.

We reached the corridor. Away from all the guests, it was easier to breathe.

Ciel spun me around.

"Sers, talk to me!" he hiss-whispered.

"I have nothing to say to you right now." My vision darkened as it had on the terrace earlier. Then it reddened. I had every reason to be angry, but I was afraid too because of the dangers awaiting my brother here. "You just had to come here, didn't you?"

Ciel's voice shook as he whispered, "I want Pa back as much as you do. Can you imagine what he or Ma would say if I didn't follow you here?"

"And yet you were not invited here, Ciel."

"Yes, I was." His eyes twisted from my provocation. "Prince Devlin chose me just as Prince Nessin chose you."

Speak of the devil. Sin entered the corridor and got between us. I hadn't realized until now we were in each other's faces.

"You." I shoved Sin. "You did this then, didn't you?"

Sin flashed his gloved palms. "It's true I introduced them at the Devil's Tail when your brother found me the day after we met, but I had nothing to do with Ciel coming here. I swear on my life. He didn't tell Devlin a thing—I checked my brother's mind—but Ciel and he started talking and I could not tear them apart that night, Sersa."

Ciel took a step toward Sin, still standing between us. "He's telling the truth."

"Ciel." Sin waited to speak until he looked at him. "You must know that while I understand your decision to accept Devlin's proposal, you endanger all of us—my brother too—and what we're trying to do here."

My brother gave a firm shake of the head. His eyes hardened, as did his jaw. "That isn't true. I can help."

"So, what?" I asked. "You have just given up studying with the Druids? Just like that?"

"Is there any better reason to do so than to find Pa?"

The Soullands offered more hidden knowledge than studying with the Druids ever could, but I couldn't believe he'd given that up so easily.

"And what of Devlin?" I asked, voice shaking. "You realize you're married, don't you?"

"Do you?" he countered.

"You will break Devlin's heart," I snapped.

"I will do no such thing," Ciel said. "You don't know him, Sers. He's kindhearted."

"Exactly! I'm not disparaging any developing feelings you may be having, though I highly doubt any of it is real in the last three days. I am asking what you will do, what you will tell your prince who knows nothing of this, when it's time to leave with Pa." I raised my eyebrows, leaning farther over Sin's arm trying to hold me back or together or both. "Hmm? By then, leaving here will break him if whatever you feel for one another is or does become real."

"And you? Are you having no real feelings for your prince?" Ciel looked Sin up and down before turning his black gaze back to me.

Sin stiffened in my peripheral.

"Or are your moods too fleeting to tell?" Ciel continued. "One day you're captivated by him. The next you're telling him you hate him. And the next you'll be throwing yourself at him. Has it started yet, Sersa? If anyone shouldn't be here, it's *you*. You pretend to be able to hide yourself, to hide what you're feeling, but we all see through it."

As I raised my hand to slap him, Sin grabbed my wrist.

I backed away. I didn't know what level of hurt flashed in my eyes, but my jaw tightened as Ciel's face flickered with regret. He closed his eyes and took a deep breath. When he finally opened them again, he shook his head. Loose strands of black hair that'd fallen from his ponytail framed his face.

"I didn't mean that," he said quietly.

I snickered. "Oh, but you did. You're as bad as Ma and Uncle Bardic. Stay out of my way. I came here for both of us. You came here because you wanted not to feel useless for once. I hope the prince thrusts you aside so you don't have to."

"Sersa. Come to bed."

Dúma, that gods-damned traitor, had already chosen her spot. In Sin's bed. He stood outside the doors to my room, waiting for me to cave. I patted the sheets on my own bed enthusiastically, hoping my hellhound would join me.

"Absolutely not. The last thing I need tonight is Your Highness—"

"You have my word that I will sleep straight as a board, and I expect you to do the same. I will not so much as breathe on you. You have my word," he repeated. "We cannot have Draea entering *our* bedroom and seeing you in a separate bed on our wedding night."

"Normal couples do it all the time."

I closed my eyes, gnawing on my lip. While I'd touched my fair share of men the last few years, and had been touched in return, I'd always halted things before giving myself away completely. Nothing had ever felt right, especially not with Roarke. Warlords visiting from other isles had been desperate for wives too. Giving them my body would have likely culminated in a rushed proposal, and one I didn't want, at that.

The thought of sleeping in the same bed as Sin felt far too intimate.

Not to mention, on our wedding night.

While he had been clear we wouldn't consummate our marriage, my body had already proven that it had a mind of its own. Desires that ran deep.

"Your furniture will be removed tomorrow," Sin added. "That room will be made into a parlor for you. You will have to get used to this. I would offer to sleep on the settee, but that doesn't quite solve our problem of Draea walking in on us separate."

"What was the point in turning this room into a bedroom for three days?" I snapped.

He snickered. "Come to bed, please. We don't need our ruse—"

I threw off my covers and whipped a pillow across the threshold at him. I brought another pillow, dragged a blanket behind me, and stomped toward the settee. "Oh, shut up. And don't say 'come to bed' like it's a normal thing to say."

Dúma didn't care. She stretched out on her side, her little round belly so cute I wanted to forget everything I was mad about and hug her.

I'd had enough talk about mine and Sin's ruse, let alone the one Ciel was trying to pull off by himself.

Sin laid down and propped himself up on his pillow. In my mind, he seemed like the sort of man who slept shirtless just to have the sunshine dust him in the morning so he could bask in his own ego. I was glad he'd at least opted for a tunic and loose, thin pants.

"Fine." He pinched the bridge of his nose. "Switch."

He threw the covers off his feet and stood.

I crawled over the footboard. Sin fell back on the settee and stretched out, trying to get comfortable on my pillow. His legs hung off the edge.

"Do you want to talk about today?" he asked.

"No. I was fine. You didn't need to kiss me."

"Oh, I wasn't talking about the kiss. But if you'd like to—"

"I want to talk about your magic, Nessin. I've been thinking, and we need to test it after what happened on the terrace."

When mine had appeared, swirling around our entwined hands, I could have stolen his magic.

Sin was staring up at the ceiling, hands on his abdomen. "Why?"

Dúma sighed loudly in her sleep.

I faced him and leaned over the footboard. My loose dark hair fell around my face and shoulders. "Our hands were bound. We were so close I heard your breath. You might have no magic left."

"You think I'm so easy to steal from?" Sin burst into laughter. "How insulting."

I swallowed. "I told you I stole my clan's magic."

He propped himself up on one elbow again and found a loose thread on the settee. He twirled it around his thin finger. "What'll it be then? Shall I give you a command?"

"Or use your other magic, whatever that may be. I'm willing to bet you're part daemon as well. Why else is your father called the Daemon King?"

"Maybe I am. Maybe I'm not. But he's called the Daemon King because the Soullands used to be nothing but daemons. They say a drop still runs through our blood, despite that no daemons have been in our line for centuries." He dropped his eyes to the settee, running a bare hand along the velvet. "The king used to tell my brothers and me when we were children that whichever of us inherits the throne will sprout horns the instant we slip his torc around our neck."

"Do you believe that?"

"I believe that I will be Daemon King. I don't much care if I sprout a tail or horns or the whole lot."

I rolled my eyes and straightened my legs in front of me, pressing my palms into the mattress behind me. I reached a hand toward Dúma and scratched her belly. Her feet kicked as she dreamed deeply. "Devlin told me he relinquished his right to the Daemon Throne. Why did he marry at all?"

Sin sighed and waved his hand. "The king is preposterous. There are rules. Devlin is getting old. The usual reasons parents believe they can involve themselves in these sorts of life decisions that ought to be entirely up to their children."

"I'm sorry."

He raised an eyebrow, eyes flicking up to mine.

"That you had to marry me, I mean."

"I didn't *have* to marry you. I could have chosen a dozen others."

"As you like to remind me, thank you."

"So. A command then?"

"Nothing that involves kissing you or—"

"I would never." Sin scoffed, and his face scrunched with offense. "I have no need to make others kiss me, Sersa. It just happens on its own. As you're well aware after last night."

I hummed. "Well? What will it be?"

"Tell me..." The rasp in his voice retreated, revealing all velvet. "What do you desire most, love?"

"To reunite my family. To make us as we once were. To help my mother feel again." The words tumbled over my lips.

He was still a Bonespeaker bastard then.

"You know a thing or two about feeling," he noted.

I averted my eyes to the silvery rug. "Even with as much as I feel, how deeply and oftentimes unexpected and inebriating, I wouldn't give it up. My mother's lost that. She can't feel since Pa was taken from us."

"In my experience, it's usually that people can feel but don't want to." Sin rubbed his fingers together to release the thread. "But it looks like I have my magic still. I am untouchable."

"You are *something*, Nessin Drumghoul."

"I like when you say my name, Sersa Dru—Scáth."

My mouth fell open an inch before I recovered and snapped, "Then I will be sure not to say your name. Why don't you avoid saying mine too in case you get it wrong?"

Sin hummed as I had a moment ago. "Is there anything else you'd like to do tonight?"

"Excuse me?"

"We could stargaze, get to know one another more, play a game perhaps."

"I'm sure you have loads of energy, don't you? You didn't partake in a single dance tonight. My feet are killing me, my legs haven't burned that much since the last time I trained, and I have an entire millennia's worth of history on the various battles at Falness thanks to a few Gilders, which I now must try to sleep out of my head. Playing a game, whatever that means, is not on tonight's agenda, thank you very much. Goodnight, you damn giant."

Smiling, Sin shook his head. "Whatever you say, love. Oh, and don't be surprised when I climb up there after you fall asleep. We have pretenses to uphold."

I blew out the candelabras on both nightstands before settling into the middle of the bed. Sin's side was still warm from his body, and mine was cold as ice. Under the haze of sleep, I couldn't be sure if it was a dream or not, but I vaguely recalled rolling over in the middle of the night and reaching for something to hold onto.

Or *someone*.

17

The next night arrived before I knew it.

The Daemon King was hosting the House of Hellick and the House of Caise for dinner and entertainment, and naturally, the newlyweds were expected to attend.

For me, and maybe even Ciel, it was an expectation. But for Stellera and Helde, it was a delight. Their families had been invited to celebrate with them, while ours remained across the Wraithsea, uninvited even for the night. Of course, even if they had been, I wouldn't want them here among the Court of Soulless or the Gilders.

I was bathed and preened much like the night before. It was all very tedious, and I'd already had enough. Even back home, I wasn't subjected to this level of preparation for special occasions, let alone every day.

Draea fished the midnight-blue dress I'd shoved back into my wardrobe after the other night at the White Plume. Scooping the end of the dress with her forearm so it wouldn't touch the ground, she held it in the air. "How 'bout this one for tonight, Princess?"

"Please never call me princess again."

"I love that one," Sin cut in. Mischief laced his voice. "Sharp eye, Draea."

I turned to see him, also wearing a midnight-blue coat and fitted pants. The coat had a tall collar, while his dark boots were short with a slight heel and pointed toe. The trio of dainty daggers he'd had at the White Plume hung near his hip, and his white hair was slicked backward. I'd only seen him with his hair out of his eyes a few times, but a defiant strand always fell over his unscarred eyebrow.

Draea dipped her head. "Hello, Your Highness."

"I hardly think it's appropriate for a husband to choose his wife's clothes, let alone have any say in what she ought to wear." I spiraled to face the mirror again. "Also, I'm not matching you." I dropped my voice into a mumble. *Even if my life depends on it.*

"Then you choose, darling." Sin looked far less agreeable than he sounded. "Whatever makes your heart croon."

"It's lovely to see a bit of true love in this citadel after so many years," Draea said with a pleased sigh. She tucked the blue dress back into the wardrobe and touched a hand to her chest. "What a lovely occurrence it is the Daemon King allowed you to choose your beloved."

I rolled my eyes as she offered to show me a few more dresses.

"Actually, Draea, I can help Sersa dress if you wouldn't mind," Sin said. "I need to speak with her about a few things."

Before I could protest, she stepped away from the wardrobe.

"Oh." Her eyes softened. "Of course. Though I hope you will still need my services, Prin—Sersa. It's been so long since I've gotten to, well…" She rolled her wrist at the dresses, the honey she'd placed on my lips, and the plait she'd created with my long hair.

"She will definitely still require your services," Sin said. "As will I."

I passed him a glare, unsure whether that was a dig at me. Not noticing, Draea beamed as she excused herself.

I kept my back to Nessin as I leafed through the dresses.

I couldn't look at him.

I'd dreamed of him last night. Not him. Us.

My fingers had tangled in mussed strands of white hair, soft against my skin without it slicked and styled. Pale fingers had bunched the end of my silk nightgown up near my waist, pinning my hip to the mattress to keep me from writhing, while the other fingers moved in and out of me, creating an inebriating rhythm with his tongue. The moans his tongue elicited from me had forced me to wake in a cold sweat, and I'd wondered, to my sheer horror, if they hadn't been confined to my dream.

If I'd been moaning aloud in my sleep.

Sin cleared his throat. "Did you not hear what I said?"

I flinched. "Huh? What did you say?"

"That I need to talk to you."

"Look, I didn't mean to hold you last night. If I actually did. It won't happen again."

Sin chuckled. "Not about that, love."

I had done it then. Lovely.

I recalled breathing in his scent, that intoxicating fire emanating from him, and the honed hardness of every muscle beneath my fingers. Apparently, my desire for him remained even in sleep.

"I am very sorry. For whatever I did or said in my sleep."

As soon as the words tumbled over my lips, I recalled Sin's knuckles brushing my spine the other night. The feel of his hand splayed on my hip at the White Plume before I'd led his fingers where I really wanted. Or almost. His lips on my neck. His arm coiling around my waist when he'd kissed me after the handfasting.

The memories unraveled me. A chill rolled down my entire body.

Why? Why had his touch stayed with me?

"I'm not sorry. Frankly, I would've welcomed more from those hands, love. Had you not been half asleep. Though I will keep your delightful commentary, among other things, to myself."

My eyes widened, and I leaned my forehead against the wardrobe.

Thank the gods my back still faced him. But also, damn the gods.

How many times would I humiliate myself in front of Sin?

Memories of the kisses and every touch we'd shared refused to leave me alone. It was bad enough my unconscious mind had allowed me to sidle up to him. Dealing with my dreams would send me over the edge.

I closed my eyes, practically feeling his breath behind me at the White Plume again...

I snapped my eyes open, focusing harder on the wardrobe. "Well, please accept my apology. I am horrified I touched you at all."

"Let's leave at this. You have my permission, Mrs. Drumghoul."

"Ha." I didn't think it appropriate to correct him after what I'd done. I'd give him one free pass. "So? Talk." I cleared my throat. "I need to find a dress myself since you sent Draea away."

I slid hangers left and right, running my fingers down the bodices and lengths to assess the scratchiness of beading and embroidery. After a few, I thankfully found a gold dress that laced up in the front. It had built-in bones shaping the bodice, unfortunately, and the skirt fanned outward into a fuller look than I was used to, but it would have to do. The beaded straps shimmered in the firelight.

Sin remained silent, so I headed into the bathing room, where I stuffed myself into the dress alone. I cursed Claud as I lifted my breasts into the cups above the bones of the bodice before lacing myself up and tying the ends into a dangling bow.

I re-entered the bedroom. Then I slipped into the matching flat gold shoes.

"Well?" I asked.

"You look—"

"I was not asking how I look. My breasts are an inch away from falling out of this dress, I can barely breathe after wearing it for less than a minute, and I doubt anyone has ever mastered walking in something with so many layers. Don't get me started on dancing in this." I tried to gather the ends and free my feet. "So, of course, you'd say I look ravishing, Nessin. I was asking what you wanted to talk about."

"You sure are something, Mrs. *Drumghoul*." The amusement had returned to his expression.

"Never again." I held up a finger in warning. This time, he needed a warning.

"Are we going to be all right tonight?" he asked with an eyebrow raise. "Or are you really that embarrassed you cuddled me almost as much as Dúma?"

Still beside myself, I shielded my eyes with a hand. "Can you just get to what you wanted to talk about already?"

"Certainly. I wanted to warn you that I'm not on the best terms with the Hellicks currently."

"Is that supposed to surprise me?" I pulled up the bust of my dress and cussed, certain I'd be doing this all night long. "Did they—oh, I don't know—find out what you regularly do to Lord Hellick at the White Plume?"

"It's not what I did. It's what Hellick did." Sin took a lazy lap around the room, absentmindedly fingering the knickknacks atop the fireplace mantle. "He tried to bribe me into taking one of his daughters as my bride before Jestin chose Helde." He selected an egg-looking trinket, shuffling it between his hands before he rested against the edge of his desk beside the terrace doors. "The young woman in question, Aislinn Hellick, approached me last night."

He paused.

I didn't know if it was for effect, to gauge my reaction, or simply to collect his thoughts. "And? Is there a point to this admission?"

"She asked if I would visit the House of Hellick for tea sometime after our honeymoon."

Never mind the fact that this was the first I'd heard of a honeymoon. Maybe someone had mentioned it, and I'd ignored it.

"Is tea code for something?" I asked, careful not to let an edge sharpen my voice.

"It's probably code for a lot of things. Aislinn hinted that her father has offered to discreetly advocate for me among the Circle of Gilders. He wants to see me—of all my brothers—sit upon the Daemon Throne."

I dug my palms harder into my sides, the dress's bones undoubtedly leaving their mark. "Why you?"

"Remember how I told you I am half Colossi?"

"How could I forget you supposedly transform into a literal giant?"

Sin stared at me, unsmiling. "My mother was half Bonespeaker, half Soulreaper. We don't know how the Mindblood trickled in. But do you know what this means?"

I nodded as those intense white eyes burned into me.

"Tell me what you know."

I hesitated, trying to recall the stories Ma and Pa had told Ciel and me. They were lodged in the deepest part of my memories, the crevices in which I'd tried to hide them.

My memories that included Pa.

"Bonespeakers can control the living and the dead. Soulreapers are as they sound. They steal souls."

He nodded, set the egg down on the desk behind him, and crossed one leg behind the other. Then he folded his arms across his chest. "I am the only one of my brothers to have inherited all three. I can alter my form like the king. I can control the living and the dead. And I can reap souls."

A shudder crept up my spine.

I had already witnessed his ability to control the living firsthand, but I wondered about his other magic. I wasn't sure which was more frightening: the thought of him taking on an enormous form or taking my soul from my body in one fell swoop.

"A lot of the Gilders believe this makes me—and me alone—fit to rule the Soullands Realm next."

My voice emerged scratchy. "What can your brothers do?"

Sin shifted back on the desk, letting one leg dangle. With his legs spread, I tried not to let my eyes fall to the protruding fabric there. I also tried not to think of him parting my legs, positioned between them.

I failed and looked away fleetingly when Sin caught me feasting my eyes upon him.

Fuck.

"Despite all your denials lately, you certainly look like you want to right now. Feel free to look *all* you want, love, and you need only tell me if looking doesn't satisfy you." Smirking now, he steered the subject back to what we'd been discussing. "Lochlainn can also alter his form, Devlin is a frighteningly skilled Soulreaper, and Jestin is the other Bonespeaker of the family."

As I managed to clamp my hanging jaw shut at the insinuation that I wanted to take Sin for a tumble in the sheets, I diverted my gaze from his. We both knew what I wanted.

My body wanted, I reminded myself. *Only my body.*

I recouped enough of my composure to speak. "And your little sister? That was her yesterday, right?" I recalled the girl with white curls, who looked so much like Sin and his brothers.

"Yes, Niuna. Named for our mother. But we're not sure what her magic is yet. Maybe something to do with foresight, undoubtedly a recessive trait like my Mindblood if our speculations are correct." Sin untucked one hand and waved it. "The point is, I want you to steer clear of the Hellicks tonight if you can. There are times when I won't be by your side, but they will try to fill your head with nonsense. They believe I am the sole heir, the True Heir to the Daemon Throne, and Hellick is a dogged bastard if I'm being forthright. He wants to see his daughter Aislinn become Daemon Queen, no matter the cost."

18

I had been placed between an Elittes and a Caise by the name of Thane and Gildie, respectively.

"I'm technically a Hellick-Elittes," Thane explained. "My mother, a Hellick, initiated a nasty divorce with my father that ended with me straddling the lines of the two High Houses. Lucky for me, it means I have two inheritances."

"Good for you," I said against my chalice as I took a swig of wine.

While Thane claimed to be a Gilder, I swore he had the sharpened teeth of a daemon. I tried to get a better look without being obvious.

Gildie Caise, who I assumed had been named after the Gilders, had sleek black hair to her shoulders, a pointy chin, and full lips. She was about my age by appearance and had a curvaceous body, her black dress fitting her with utter precision. Specks in the glimmering fabric brought out the pink undertones of her porcelain skin.

Naturally, Sin had been placed across the table between Aislinn Hellick and another nameless Caise. He was speaking with the woman to his left, and by the look of the Gilders' necklace dangling against her chest, she was part of the Circle. When Sin served himself seconds of the boar crowding the center of the table with an apple in its mouth, he waved off the servant who jumped forward with a polite nod. Sin graciously offered to serve the ladies on either side of him. Aislinn declined with a broad smile Sin ignored, but the nameless Gilder obliged.

I felt Aislinn's eyes darting to me and away but didn't dare afford myself a proper glance. Still, from my peripheral, I recognized her as the girl I'd seen talking to Sin the day before when all the guests had crowded the four brothers' thrones. She wore a dress that was red as a rose, drawing the eyes of everyone in the room, and her strawberry blonde hair was once more piled on her head, leaving her collarbones fully exposed. Though her faintly gold-tinted complexion spoke of trips to the Western Pointe, basking beneath the powerful sun and clear skies there, I knew it couldn't be. These Soullanders couldn't travel beyond the veil into Clais, to the home I found myself missing.

Gildie leaned forward. "Thane, how is business?"

He veered around me in answer, and I pressed my back as far as I could into my seat.

"Flourishing. I opened a new pleasure den, the Crescendo."

She snorted. "Don't tell me you came up with the name yourself."

As I took another sip of wine, I chuckled into the glass. I would have said the same.

Thane turned, passing me a pointed look. "What do *you* think of the name, Princess?"

I turned to look at him. His brown eyes glinted with a hint of mischief. His curly, shoulder-length hair was a tawny color. He'd slicked it back for the occasion, and his deep bronze skin had the faintest pink to his cheeks like he spent his days lounging under the Cradled Moons. The slicked hair had to be the style here in the Soullands. It reminded me of Sin's.

"I only hope it lives up to the name," I replied.

Thane leaned forward and said just for me, "Why don't you come and find out? It's outside Gilders Eye. Open to anyone."

"Why don't *you* keep those questions to yourself?" I turned back to my meal, taking my knife and fork back up.

"I only meant you and your husband might come visit together. Some find that sort of thing, if I may, arousing."

"You may not. But thank you for the unsolicited suggestion," I said without looking at him.

This time, I didn't bother moving out of Thane or Gildie's way for them to chat. The conversation quickly ended, and tension swirled in the air on either side of me.

The rest of dinner passed slowly, and I was glad I couldn't see Ciel from where I sat. He was on the same side of the table, several seats away. When we were finally released to the attached parlor, he didn't approach me. But Sin did.

"Hate these dinners," he growled.

"Same."

"You hardly ate anything. Why?"

"The *whole* boar staring at me made me lose my appetite," I said.

"What do you like to eat then?"

"Potatoes and cabbage with lots of salt. Oh, and cheese."

Sin laughed.

I dropped my eyes to his chalice. "And copious amounts of ale. Wine will do."

"*Copious amounts.* Sounds healthy," he said sarcastically before handing me his drink.

Inside the parlor, a group of performers were balancing on one another to form a growing tower.

"Let's walk." Sin's hand hovered in the middle of my back as we circulated the room together at a leisurely pace. He leaned in close. "How was sitting next to Thane?"

"You should have warned me about him instead of his stepfather or Aislinn. Naturally, you were seated next to one another."

"Do I detect a hint of jealousy, wife?" Before I could answer, he asked, "What did Thane say?"

"There's a new pleasure den called the Crescendo in the slums."

"And?"

"He invited me," I said smugly.

Sin's hand firmed against my spine.

"Fine. He corrected himself and invited *us* after I set him straight. Said we might like to visit together to ignite the passions of our marriage bed."

"And did you also set him straight on the fact that we have no issues igniting the passions of our marriage bed *alone*?"

"No," I said as we turned the corner of the room. "But feel free to go tell him yourself. Embellish on your wildest dreams all you like."

He chuckled. "I think I'm rubbing off on you, and I'm not sure whether that's good or bad."

"Bad," I said hastily.

"Also, don't you mean *your* dreams, Sersa?"

I should have known he knew. If we were alone, I would have swatted him.

We passed a table filled with sweets, and he stopped to select one then stood in front of me.

"You must try this one with that wine." He held the brown pastry over his open palm. He also held my eyes with his, piercing white. "Take a sip. Oh, come on. *Pretenses*, love."

As I licked my lips, I noted the way his eyes dropped, watching me take a swig of his wine. Sin took a step closer, so close we drew eyes all around us, and I took a bite of the pastry. Chocolate. Caramel. Tart berries.

I moaned as he fed himself the rest.

I raised my eyebrow and said through a mouthful, "Is that enough pretense for you?"

"That followed by a long, slow kiss would be better."

I swallowed, running my tongue along my teeth to be sure there wasn't chocolate in them. "Stop saying stuff like that."

"I'll stop when you don't bury your head in my chest in your sleep. I wasn't going to tell you this, but those hands also found themselves creeping up my shirt last night."

I swallowed, feeling my eyes widen.

"Prince Nessin?" a voice interrupted. One of the Gilders. An older woman with short gray hair in a long-sleeved, deep red dress stood a few feet away. "The Daemon King has requested you. *Only* you."

Like I didn't exist, her eyes didn't even flicker to me. But she'd clearly acknowledged that I did exist but was not invited.

"Of course, Lady Hellick." Sin squeezed my waist to pull me toward him and pressed a kiss to my cheek. His lips summoned heat where they'd touched, but he was moving through the crowd before he noticed.

I helped myself to another chocolate pastry. Without Sin to feed me it, it didn't taste quite the same. Even when I prefaced with another sip of wine.

"They're excellent, no?"

Thane. I squeezed my eyes shut as I was caught trying a different pastry. I set my drink down on the table and turned. Before I could reply, he smiled warmly. His teeth were impossibly white, almost sparkling against his skin. That smile drew my eyes to the tips of his teeth again. He had to be a daemon.

"I hope you'll forgive me—for what I said earlier, Princess."

"Drop it."

"I meant no offense."

I looked toward the floor of twirling bodies ahead, couples sharing a tantalizing dance that was difficult to look away from.

Thane cleared his throat. "Would you care to dance? A gesture to smooth things over?"

My stomach clenched. How did one say no to a Gilder? Back home, I'd have spat in his face. But this place was all refined manners and veiled insults.

I licked the front of my teeth again and grunted. "Sure."

Unlike his abrasive personality, Thane was a gentle lead. He chose a spot on the floor surrounded by the rest of the couples. When he spun me around, I realized just how deliberate the spot was.

Ciel and his husband danced next to us. They were close enough that I could hear their laughter and see the lowering hand of not just my brother but also Prince Devlin. Those hands were evidently in a race down one another's lower backs. I still couldn't believe how comfortable they seemed to be with one another after only a few days.

Then again, I'd allegedly nestled Sin in my sleep. And felt him up.

Gods, strike me down now.

Ciel had been right about one thing. My feelings for Sin were dithering back and forth. One minute I couldn't stop thinking of his lips, and the next, I was utterly annoyed with his boldness.

Fighting a grimace, I turned my head away from Devlin and my brother.

"It must be strange having your brother here with you." Thane's voice was steady, confident.

"Not at all," I lied.

"It's a shame, really. I wonder about the strategy behind their choices. Both Prince Devlin and Nessin chose their betrothed so hastily. I can understand why Nessin chose you—perhaps you're already with child—but as far as I've heard, Devlin hasn't been with anyone in only the gods know how long."

I snapped my head back to stare at him, trying to loosen my hands from his grip. "What did you just say?"

"It's a shame," he repeated. "They could have chosen others."

"What, like Gilders? Your sister perhaps?" My blood boiled.

"Aislinn is my half-sister. I like to think I got the better genes from the Elittes on my father's side."

"I highly doubt you got anything good from either side, except maybe a deceptively handsome face."

"Deceptively handsome? I can deal with that."

His quips suggested he hung out with Sin too much.

"You don't know the first thing about Ciel and Devlin's relationship," I said.

"Relationship?" Thane scoffed. "That is called an acquaintance, Princess, and don't even get me started on *love*. There is no love in marriages like these." He gestured to the room around us, still holding my hand in his viper's grip. "I think you'll be hard pressed to find it in yours."

I tried to pull away again, but he held me tighter. Through the fabric of my dress, his fingers dug in between my shoulder blades. At least they weren't creeping down my back.

The music faded as the orchestra prepared for their next song, but a single drop of blood dripped from Thane's nose.

I hadn't realized the red tint to my vision, to the room.

I looked around. Everything was red. My eyes blurred like blood coated them too.

No, no, no. Not here. This couldn't happen here.

Ridding my clan of their magic was one thing. Releasing my

magic in front of a room of Soullanders, and the Daemon King, would mean death.

Thane abruptly pulled away to catch the next few drops in his palm. The red deepened behind my eyes. I needed to get out of here before I killed him. Though it might be what Thane deserved presently, I couldn't let the entire court and all the Gilders see. Had we been somewhere private, I doubted I'd hold back.

I turned on my heels to go, but Thane thrust his other hand out and squeezed my wrist. He smiled with bloody teeth. "Oh, and Sersa? Prince Nessin asked me to tell you he's waiting for you in the hall."

I didn't care about finding Sin. That was the last thing I cared about. Rage pooled in my fingertips. I needed to get away from everyone before I lost control.

Before I ran Thane's body dry.

I stumbled out into the hall. The fresh air hit my face, and I gasped feverishly until the crispness eased my lungs.

The doors to the terrace ahead were open, the sheer curtains blowing in the night wind. And there beneath the moonlight, Aislinn Hellick saw me, closed the distance between her and Sin, and pressed her lips to his.

19

Sin freed himself from Aislinn's grip and, in an instant, snapped his head in my direction.

How had he known I was there? How had he sensed me? I needed to get away from them immediately, to pretend I hadn't seen when we all knew I had, and yet part of me wanted to see whether they continued. I hurried down the corridor, lifting the ends of my dress and holding up the front.

Not a moment later, Sin caught up to me as I reached the end of the hall. He grabbed my hand and pulled me toward him in a dark crook beside a sprawling staircase.

"Sersa," he said, low and edged with warning.

"Let go of me, Nessin."

"No." He gripped my shoulders. "*Pretenses*."

There was no one around.

"Screw pretenses. You were the one kissing someone other than your blushing bride not a moment before. Did you tell me to stay away from the Hellicks because she'll be joining us on our honeymoon?"

"Her father must have told her to do it, Sersa. I promise I did no such thing."

I replayed the image of her leaping forward to find his lips.

I folded my arms tighter.

"Wait." The word seemed to be a light in Sin's mind. Holding up a gloved palm, his eyes livened, and that notorious smirk reappeared. "Why do you care, Sersa?"

"I don't."

"You answered awfully quick."

"I *don't*," I said, slower this time. My thoughts echoed that I was a liar. "What I care about is if our pretenses fail. What would that mean for my father?"

"It means nothing. Even if Aislinn tells all the Gilders she kissed me, you and I are bound."

I couldn't face the fact that we were bound, and my wrist still felt like the handfasting ropes were cutting off my circulation.

My breathing slowed as my thoughts pieced together. Thane Elittes had obviously wanted me to dance with him to give his sister and Sin a moment alone. It made sense. Thane's last words to me did too.

"Did the king even summon you?" I asked.

"No. That was Aislinn's mother who interrupted us. They're all in on it. When I went out there, she was alone."

"Tell the king."

He scoffed, finally releasing me. "He would not believe it, nor would he care. I tell you what. Why don't you kiss any bloke you like? But just once. My only condition is that you let me watch."

"Pervert. A Daemon King ought to do something in these instances."

"You're right. Stay here. I'll be back."

"What? Where—"

Before I finished my thought, Sin had stormed back down the hall the way we'd come. I picked up my feet to follow as he strode through the ballroom with fire on his heels and in his eyes. I wavered in the doorway for a moment.

Until he lifted something from his belt.

A dagger.

What was he going to do?

I snaked my way through the crowd, trying not to look like my movements were urgent when they were. Would Sin kill a Gilder out in the open?

He halted before Daigh Hellick. For tonight's occasion, the Gilder wore a pale blue suit in the high-collared style that matched Sin's but was decidedly less lavish. That was saying something, when Daigh's attire sparkled under the firelight.

Without warning, Sin held the dagger between Daigh's legs.

My eyes widened.

Sin's voice was so low it was almost a growl. "If you ever disrespect me or my family again, either in private or public as you and your wife just did, I will cut off the very things that allow you to continue your line, Hellick. Then, I will strip your house of its reputation, followed by its title. Do you understand?"

People around us were watching now.

My eyes darted left and right.

I touched a hand to Sin's back, and he stiffened. Though I couldn't find words, I meant to pull him away.

"I did noth—"

Sin pressed the blade closer to the seam of Hellick's pants. "Apologize to my wife. Now."

"Prin-Princess Sersa, you must forgive me for any behavior that may have offended you tonight. I apologize sincerely."

With nothing to say to Daigh Hellick, I curled my hand around Sin's bicep, hooking my arm through his. Surprisingly, he followed my lead. Before anyone noticed, he'd sheathed the dagger once more.

"You did not have to do that," I whispered.

"They needed to know how serious I am. I wanted you to know how serious I am. Especially because it upset you."

"I'm not upset."

"You were," he said, voice like steel.

Finally, we reached the corridor. I steered Sin to the left, and he took over, arm tugging me in the opposite direction.

"That's the wrong way," he said. "Let's head upstairs. You can shred a down pillow if you like."

I scowled at him. "The only thing I'd like to shred right now—"

"I get it, I get it," Sin said. "My face, presumably."

"Don't think so highly of yourself. I was going to say that I want to shred this dress. You are free to kiss whoever your lips—or other parts of you—desire."

"As are you," Sin whispered, holding my gaze. His eyes seemed to darken, to focus harder, while I could barely bring myself to look at him.

No one had ever elicited this reaction in me before, this need to look away as if I were some pure lady.

"But..." Leaning toward me, he buried his lips in my hair, an inch from my neck. "My offer still stands if you do want my lips on yours again, love."

As we headed back down the hall, the beat of my heart posed a hundred questions, one the loudest of them all.

Why *did* I care someone had kissed Sin?

Things had been so hectic the last few days that I hadn't even stopped to think about the gift we'd received. A moon cycle's worth of mead. It was the traditional gift for a wedding.

Rather, for the post-wedding trip.

Sin or Draea or both had mentioned a honeymoon, and I didn't want to face the word any more than I wanted to face the occurrence of it.

Our night with the Houses of Hellick and Caise had felt like enough of a revel, almost more eventful than the wedding itself, but when I woke to leather luggage being taken out of the rooms the next morning, I groaned.

We didn't have time to go away.

Dúma heard me stir and toddled over to me. She plopped on my chest, dragging her tongue across the tip of my nose.

I chuckled. "Ew."

Directly across from the bed, Sin sat on the terrace with his legs on the table and his gloved hands folded on his abdomen. He was basking in the light of the Cradled Moons.

"About time," he called.

I threw myself back against the pillows and cocooned Dúma

under the covers with me. I needed to face the day, only because I knew Dúma needed care. But maybe I could strike a bargain with Sin. Surely, we didn't have to leave the City of Soulless.

After a few more minutes, I threw off the covers and stood with Dúma cuddled against my chest, realizing instantly how translucent my pale nightgown was—far less scandalous than the lingerie Claud had made me—but still.

I moved toward the terrace, keeping my distance from the bizarre moonlight. Or sunlight. I was too tired to ponder what I ought to call it.

"Don't tell me you're a morning person," I said. "You seem all...chipper."

Sin lifted his head and squinted one eye at me. "I'm more interested in what you are, Sersa. You don't strike me as a night owl based on the way you fell asleep as soon as your head hit the pillow last night, and you're definitely not a morning person based on *this*." He circled a finger at me. "So, what does that leave?"

"I have one good bell a day," I growled. "You'll be lucky if you manage to catch it."

"At least you have one."

He set his boots on the ground and took a deep breath with a sip of coffee. The aroma carried through the air, and I had the urge to sit and drink cup after cup. Dúma sniffed out the other scents. Eggs. Griddlecakes. Syrup. *Butter*. My mouth salivated.

"With you," I added, "that one bell might be reduced to a half."

"Well, can you put that half bell to good use right now? You need to get ready so we can leave. I already took care of Dúma for you. Fed her and everything. After how repulsed you looked by last night's menu, I figured feeding her freshly hunted animals probably wouldn't sit well with you."

That was...thoughtful. He'd let me sleep.

"Where are we going?" I asked instead of thanking him.

"To one of the nearby isles, Nos Nua. It's tradition. Each of us goes to one of the Soullands' four main isles. To the west, there's many more, but the ones on the Soullands' border are the closest."

I wavered on the terrace threshold. "For how long?"

Sin shifted. "I'm sure you're well aware the moon cycle's worth of mead gifted to us is supposed to last the honeymoon."

"An entire moon cycle." I groaned, looking over my shoulder when I heard how loud it came out.

"We can cut it short, but the Gilders are taking their own holiday right now. It's tradition after the Daemon King's children are wed."

"Then we..." I dropped my eyes to my bare feet.

We could make no progress for the next four weeks. The realization made me feel useless, and the thought of stalling felt unbearable. Pa could be chained up right now, serving only the gods knew who.

"We will use the time to prepare, Sersa. It won't be in vain. Then it will be Gilder party after Gilder party once everyone returns. I swear. Plus, I'll have my associates at the White Plume working the entire time."

"Pretenses."

"Yes."

I sighed loudly as I walked away, but I could already feel a grayish-blue tint settling over me. Pa felt farther away than ever.

20

It was well after dusk by the time our ship arrived on Nos Nua. Along with a few too many suitcases, Draea, her daughter Innes, and a trainer for Dúma had accompanied us. To my chagrin, Nos Nua was exceptionally cold, the northernmost of the isles like Os Íseal, and covered in snow. I had expected a fortress by the sea, but instead, the carriage brought us to one that was nestled between a lake and a mountain. Halfway built into the mountain, the aged stone structure was unlike anything that still existed in Nos Ovscura, and it further reminded me of Os Íseal with its traditional architecture. I felt more at home than I had in days.

As our carriage came to a halt at the end of a short bridge crossing one of the lake's arms, Sin studied the surrounding woods through the window. Today he wore a neck ring like his father's, though thinner and less showy. Wolves adorned the open ends of the torc that rested against the front of his neck.

A closer look and I wondered if they were hellhounds.

He interrupted my line of thought. "According to Soullander folklore, those woods house the entrance to the Otherworld."

I looked away from the window to him. His brow furrowed as he stared into the woods like he saw into the depths I couldn't.

"I thought this was the Otherworld."

"Oh, no." He chuckled. "We may be beyond your world but make no mistake, this is closer to hell than any heaven you've ever read about."

Sin exited the carriage first and turned to offer me a hand. With a row of servants waiting to greet us at the end of the bridge, I obliged. Before I could scoop Dúma up, she bolted down the steps and rushed toward the snow. She ran circles for a few minutes before relieving herself behind a nearby tree, panting happily.

I continued to stare into the snowy woods as we walked along the bridge.

"It's been said that those who venture into these woods have glimpsed the gods between the trees," Sin said. "Many have disappeared over the years."

"The gods." I snickered. "I'd have thought you and your kin were something of gods if I didn't know any better."

He looked down at me before returning his gaze to the servants we approached. He whistled between his teeth for Dúma to come, and she did. Then he released another chuckle, this one darker.

"I would expect you to realize my kin and I are more like devils."

"But you are immortal," I said.

"We pay a price to remain immortal. The gods do not."

"And what is that price?" I snapped, growing more impatient by the second. He was being very elusive, and I found myself turning more and more irritable as the distance to Nos Ovscura—where Pa was, where I'd left behind every chance of finding him—widened drastically.

Until the next moon.

Dúma reached us and trotted alongside my feet.

"We consume souls. The Sluagh are our hunters. They gather our soulstock, our harvest, every dawn during Reaping Hour."

"And you…" I wet my lips, feeling his eyes flickering repeatedly to me in his peripheral. I couldn't bring myself to look at him. I focused on the servants ahead, some of them appearing more wraithlike than I was used to. "You have consumed souls?"

"I am still young, unlike the Daemon King, so I have little need for souls. But I never claimed to be innocent, Sersa."

"No, you didn't."

When I tried to pull away, Sin gently pinned my arm against his waist. "Pretenses." His voice changed to a growl in a matter of seconds. "You knew I was a monster. I warned you. If you're looking for gods and pretty things, I suggest you head into the woods tonight."

"Maybe I will," I muttered under my breath. Maybe I would dance naked beneath the moonlight and beg the gods to take me away.

I doubted they would, damn scoundrels.

But Sin had no reason to be so upset over any of this. This ploy, his motives for helping me find Pa, was temporary. It hardly mattered what I thought of him, or what he thought of me.

Draea and Innes hugged each of the staff. I welcomed the servants' greetings as they swept aside mine and Sin's conversation, but I still looked at him a little differently. I thought he *wanted* to be monstrous. A daemon. A devil. And maybe he was. I knew he was, but even the devils had lived in the Otherworld once.

Hadn't they?

After we settled into Sin's family estate, my mind refused to quiet.

I tried every distraction I could to stop thinking of Ciel and what he'd done. His lie. His lack of faith in me that I could do this. Though I knew he'd been telling the truth, that he'd acted to keep me safe, I wasn't confident in how capable he might be at doing that, let alone protecting himself. I had warned Devlin, yes, but what if his intentions weren't as pure as he'd claimed? What if he was as cruel as his father beneath that kind façade?

The inability to make any progress finding Pa made me feel a bit hopeless—stuck—and I didn't know how to shake the feeling. I only knew I needed to. There was no leaving Nos Nua until our honeymoon was over.

Already, I felt so depleted. Yet I knew I would be forced to do nothing, to try to relax, until the next moon.

The thought alone made my mind race.

Luckily, neither Draea nor the fortress's head caretaker had coordinated any romantic activities for our first week on Nos Nua. As our luggage was brought to our room so that we could rest for the night after the journey, I was both relieved and genuinely surprised. The whole point of a honeymoon was beaten into the heads of all girls of marrying age years before they *were* of marrying age. I'd never had any desire to be wed, at least not with the sole aim of pleasing my hypothetical husband, and especially not so young.

But alas, here I was. Minus the pleasing Nessin part.

Pretending to be happy might drain everything I had, but I had to try. Still, the distractions of activities would have been welcome.

Inside our rooms, Sin shucked off his coat to reveal a loose, deep red shirt. The torc around his neck caught the firelight already budding in the hearth as a servant stirred it with a poker. With a wave at the intimate table in the corner, filled with platters of food, she quickly excused herself.

Well, here was one romantic activity—a dinner for two.

Dúma flopped on the ground right beside the hearth with a huff, and the heated room paired with all Sin's rustling made me want to change out of my dress too. I twisted my arms behind my back, reaching for the ties. Though my hands found purchase, undoing the laces was easier said than done.

"Is Draea not... Never mind," I said with a sigh.

Instantly irritated, I tapped my foot and dug my hands into my waist. The bones sewn into the dress I wore made it hard to breathe, and the lace-up back ensured Sin and I would share yet another intimate moment tonight—a repeat of our first night. Why did every dress Claud design have to be so constricting?

"Would you..."

After a moment's hesitation, Sin crossed the room on light feet. With a glance behind, I realized he was not only barefoot but also shirtless. I caught a glimpse of scars raking their way down his bone-white chest.

"Sluagh," he said before the question rolled off my tongue.

"That's all I need to know," I said, repeating what he'd said a few days ago.

"For now, yes."

I wasn't sure whether he meant it about his scars or our arrangement. Maybe both.

I held my wrists against my chest to stop the dress from falling. A single tendril of black snaked around my wrist like a garden snake. I had no reason to be afraid with Sin so close, his hands on me, but the unease in my gut said otherwise.

I'd never wanted a man so much, while also wanting to resist the pull. Our arrangement was temporary.

He loosed the final crisscrossing ties and hesitated. "It seems there are marks on you as well. I had Claud make you more comfortable garments for our stay here. Pants too, since I assumed you fancy them. You were wearing them when we met."

My eyes flickered to the side wall, searching as if they might find the true meaning of his words somewhere along the patterned upholstery.

"I was. I mean, I do prefer them. Where are they?"

Sin moved to the armoire where the servants had hung our clothes. He returned with a pair of pants and a soft, long-sleeved shirt. Gold seams adorned both.

"Change in the bathing room," he said as if I were going to do anything else.

I made my way into the dark room through a carved archway without a door, slipped off my dress, and changed. The entire time, I envisioned Sin walking in on me. And if he did, where might it lead?

As I sat down at the table a moment after clearing my head of that thought, my stomach growled. Sin had filled my plate with potatoes, cabbage, and cheese. "As you like."

"I was kidding about the cabbage. I actually hate it." It reeked too.

"Then potatoes and cheese it is."

I noted his empty plate.

Instantly, I recalled our conversation earlier.

Souls. Sin consumed souls.

My body reacted before I could restrain myself. I shoved my seat backward, raising on unwavering limbs. But the black tendrils swarmed, licking their way across the table, around my seat.

"Now that we're on a gods-damned isolated isle all alone, I suppose it's time for a Soullander delicacy, aye?" I snarled.

Nessin matched me and stood, studying me closely. I searched his body for the daggers he always carried. They weren't at his hip though.

As shock twisted his face, one eyebrow raised, he lowered back into his seat.

"You think I'm going to feast on your soul while we're here?" He scoffed, but the sound was more offended than anything. "Now you see me for a monster. Good. As you should." With a scowl, he found a sharpened meat knife and stabbed a block of cheese with it. "There's your weapon, love, though you have plenty of your own." His eyes drank in my magic, still curling over the table like Os Íseal's ever-present mist. "How many times must I remind you that if I wanted to feast on your soul, I would have done so the night we met. I would have done so while you slept last night. Or the night before. Or at our wedding for every Gilder and wraith in Nos Ovscura to see. Other royals have done far worse to their mortal brides. So, sit. Eat."

Going against my gut, I retook my seat. "Forgive me. I don't actually think you're a monster—"

"Mm hmm."

"I only assumed. There are stands in the Midnight Market selling souls."

"You've gone there?" He snickered. "Who am I kidding? Of course, you have. You're about as reckless as you are stubborn."

"I haven't been inside. But they set the stands up right near the entrance. You can see them when you walk past. I suppose yours are delivered to the citadel. Do they taste good?" I blurted.

"*Dúm's piss*, Sersa." Sin pinched the bridge of his nose.

"It's a fair question!" To avoid saying anything else, I speared a sliced potato and shoved it in my mouth. They didn't have nearly enough salt. Sin nudged the shaker toward me then, and I sprinkled my plate, scowling.

"Souls don't taste like anything. But," he added before my face reflected any assurance I felt, "they are satiating."

A shudder passed through me.

His hand shot out to squeeze mine.

"Believe this one thing I say if you will believe nothing else. I'm not interested in stealing your soul, Sersa. The Sluagh steal too many as it is."

I dropped my eyes to his hand and licked my lips. "Okay. What are you interested in, Nessin?"

A muscle in his jaw twitched. "Finding your father as was promised and returning you to where you came from."

At that, he stood and whistled through his teeth, grabbing a platter off the table. Dúma bolted upright, her head bobbling like she was still at sea until he set the platter piled with slabs of meat on the ground. It took no more than a minute for her to devour it. I continued to eat too, both amused and irritated by the metal clanging against the stone floor as Dúma licked the platter clean.

Sin returned to the table and took a long swig of his ale. I traced his gaze to the windows on either side of the enormous bed, wondering what he was thinking.

When I finally finished, he stacked the platters on top of the cart and rolled it into the corridor. Then he shut the door and locked it. Seeing him perform such menial tasks, ones I imagined a prince would never do, was unexpected. Even back home, we had servants, though Ma had always told us to leave the area around our plates as clean as it'd been when we sat down.

Sin collected a few books off a desk in the corner near the bathing room before settling onto one of the settees near the hearth.

"You aren't going to sleep?" I asked as I peeled back the thick covers and slid under.

"Not yet."

I supposed it was still early, but I felt exhausted. I blew out the candles on the bedside table and laid back, not expecting him to say anything else.

"You could," he started with a lilt to his voice, "come sit over here with me."

"And you could..." I didn't want to say he could lay down with me. "Uh, you could come sit over *here*. With me."

"I can't read in bed. I find I fall asleep too easily."

"Maybe that's your body's way of telling you what it needs."

Sin chuckled.

"What?" I asked.

"Nothing."

"*What?*" I snapped, sitting up.

He draped one arm on the back of the settee, twisting at the waist to study me. Firelight flickered in his white eyes, tinting them ocher as he pointed toward his empty spot. "If I come over there, I suspect *your* body will be telling you it needs quite the opposite of sleep, Sersa. Especially after your little handsy mishap. Is that what you want?"

I warred against the urge to bite my lip. Heat flooded my body, and even before I spoke, I knew my voice was going to shake.

"No, Nessin. It's not what I want."

I couldn't be sure from afar, but I swore Sin's nostrils flared.

"Then we can safely drop our pretenses a bit while we're here. We will sleep in the same bed and share meals, of course, but we can do the bare minimum to ensure the servants don't talk. You'll stay on your side, and I'll stay on mine."

I laid back down and hid my hands beneath the covers. Then I pulled them past my shoulders as I rolled to put my back to Sin. "That's a relief," I whispered.

"Glad you think so too. Goodnight, Sersa."

I swallowed, squeezing my hands into fists beneath the sheets.

"Goodnight, Nessin."

Both of us had managed to keep our voices even. Especially Sin. Always Sin. But I fell asleep wondering if that was what either of us wanted.

21

Dúma finished her first training session the following afternoon under a heavy, slate-gray sky. Her obedience under Era's guidance was impressive, miles better than I could have done, and based on her recent behavior—having chewed one of Sin's torcs last night while we'd slept—I wondered if she would ever calm enough to listen to me.

"I think we worked her mind enough for the day," Era said, handing Dúma off to me. The pup had plopped her butt on the snow, paws sliding until she was lying down, sprawled out. "She did well today, and I can see the prince chose well. She's smart. She is showing a little aggression, however, but that is to be expected from a hellhound. Even a pup as young as her." Era cleared her throat and lowered her chin cautiously, but her mouth shut as Sin approached.

She bowed.

"Good to see you, Era. How did Dúma do?" His breath clouded in the air before him. His nose and cheeks were red like he'd been outside a while.

Era smiled, and a breath of air fogged around her face too. Her light brown hair was shaved close to her scalp and traditional Claisin designs of swirls and coils carved paths through it. "Good to see you too, Your Highness. I was just telling your wife that Dúma did very well. She's an impressive hound."

"Excellent." Sin looked at me then back to Era.

"She'll sit, stay, come, lay down, howl, silence," Era said. "All of the basic ones."

"I meant to ask," I said. "Is howl a basic command?"

Era's smile was cautious. "Not really, but Prince Nessin insisted. I was also saying that I do worry with a hellhound," she started, eyes flickering from Sin to me, "about the aggression. I can work to train it out of her, but her nature will play a role in the success of it. She could be a dangerous pet to keep in the Court of Soulless."

"That is what we want," Sin said with a curt nod. "Dúma should protect Sersa. Always."

Era licked her lips and nodded. "As was promised."

He took a step forward and pitched his voice low. "And the discretion that was promised?"

"I assure you, Prince Nessin. You forget I trained all of Queen Niuna's animals."

Sin stepped back, stood tall, and nodded. His eyes were surprisingly trusting of Era.

She turned to me, folding her hands in front of her. "I'll need you present for our training sessions over the next few weeks. I can tell you what to do, but you must be the one to guide and command Dúma. You must teach her you're in charge. Hellhounds are pack animals. She..." Era tossed her head side to side and scrunched her face. "She may need a mate in the future, or she could slump a little. We'll deal with that when the time comes."

I understood that. Maybe not the part about needing a partner to be happy. That was ridiculous, and my parents had always told Ciel and me that being happy with yourself came first. But Dúma was an animal. Whatever needs she had, we would see to them.

I would.

But what was I to do with a hellhound back in Os Íseal?

"I can do that," I said.

"Good. I'll see you tomorrow, Princess. Nine o'clock sharp."

"I told you not to call me princess," I called.

"If I tell you to call me princess, will you?"

I laughed. At that, Era stalked inside.

As my smile faded, Sin and I shared a knowing look. He'd procured Dúma for a reason.

"I thought you said I could protect myself." I allowed accusation to lace my voice.

"There's nothing wrong with a little extra protection."

A thought clicked into place like lock and key.

Was he afraid of the Hellicks, of what they might do to see another in my place? One thing I didn't understand was Sin's deep-rooted desire to protect me. He'd told me the night we met that he'd chosen me because I could protect myself, but I wondered if he really believed that. What was it exactly he feared might happen?

Later that night, we left the dining hall together after we finished eating. As Sin had watched, probably slightly horrified by my ravenous state, I'd gorged myself on every delicacy presented—ones he had requested especially for me. I felt like I hadn't eaten in days.

We walked in step with one another under the domed ceiling, Sin's gloved fingers intertwined behind his back, while mine, clasped, hung in front of me. Our leisurely pace made me face reality. This was what we'd be doing for an entire moon cycle. Nothing. No progress.

Sin had shed his typical black coat for a black shirt tucked into dark green pants. The sleeves were ruffled and bell shaped, fashionable for the City of Soulless, I supposed, but then again, the Gilders and Daemon Princes probably steered all the latest fashions thanks to Claud.

After Dúma's training session, Draea had helped me clean up and change into a dress—again, courtesy of Claud—with a bodice that was adorned with at least a hundred hand-sewn flowers. The connected skirt flowed outward, and the strapless heart-shaped neckline left nothing to the imagination, my breasts nearly spilling over the top. The way Draea had cheekily smiled at me as she pulled it from my trunk, I knew it was another dress meant to tempt my *husband*.

I had to admit it was comfortable though.

"I want to show you something I think you'll find humorous," Sin said, his rasped yet smooth voice cutting through the silence.

"Oh?"

He offered a gloved hand, and I thought of declining it before something in me cracked. I slid mine into his, a smirk playing at his lips. He guided me through several torchlit corridors with stone floors and upholstered walls boasting impressive paintings of Soullander landscapes.

Finally, we halted in front of a set of double doors.

"Close your eyes." He waved a hand when I didn't immediately obey.

I sighed and did as he said for what I told myself was the first and last time. The doors swept open. Sin directed me forward, holding me by the elbows.

"A bit farther..."

Our steps echoed through the room as we walked in a straight line. At least, I thought we were. "All right. Open them."

Sin stood tall in front of me and a little closer than expected. My eyes flicked up to his before I veered around him, curious as to where he'd brought me.

We were in a gallery filled with paintings. But not any old paintings.

Portraits.

It wasn't lost on me that the white-haired woman I'd expected to see, his mother, was absent from every painting.

As I wandered to the edges of the room, I couldn't hold back the smile curling my lips. Some were family portraits, while others were individual paintings of Sin. I focused on the latter. Crossed swords, gilded spears, and other priceless objects like torcs hung between nearly every painting.

I paused in front of a canvas that was unmistakably Sin, despite the lack of the scar that snaked from his left eyebrow to his jaw. He had no front teeth either.

His hands were once more clasped behind his back, and he was following me at a distance. "Soullander children, soulless, grow the same way as mortals. We're born the same, only it takes us far longer to mature. As I said earlier, we stay 'young' at least to the eye by consuming souls."

I reached out to trace the smile on his little face. That carefree boy was gone. I swallowed. "How has the king aged then? He looks quite a bit older than you, though still eerily young."

"My mother's curse."

"Ah." I nodded to myself as I continued around the perimeter of the room. I sensed he didn't want to talk about it by the curtness of his tone.

While there were several portraits from Sin's childhood, there were dozens in which he looked the same as he did now, an entire corner of the room with him crowding the walls.

In every portrait, Nessin stood proud, shoulders back and chin raised, his eyes devoid of any softness.

He looked like a king.

Suddenly, he was behind me, so close I heard his breath. His chest had to be mere inches away. I wanted to test the accuracy of my senses, to let myself lean back slightly.

"That was a hundred years ago," he whispered smoothly. Too smooth. Some of the ladies in my clan had issued us younger women warnings.

A man who speaks like velvet will cut your heart like glass.

Heeding warnings wasn't my specialty. In fact, warnings made me want the thing more.

Unable to stop myself, I glanced over my shoulder. Sin was right there. Any closer and he'd be on top of me. One hand hovered near my shoulder.

Facing forward, I reached out and touched the portrait in front of us. My fingers trailed over the brushstrokes of Sin's hip, down his thigh clad in dark blue fabric that had been painted to look like silk. Those brushstrokes were hard yet smooth, the rich colors perfectly preserved like they'd been painted only years ago rather than a century. I let my hand drop before it reached the gilded frame.

We walked to the next portrait, taking the slowest of steps.

"And that one two hundred years..." Sin said, quieter still.

Again, I trailed my fingers along the second canvas, uncertain whether I deliberately slid them across his painted groin or not. I heard no reaction from him, no intake of breath or chuckle. As his fresh yet fiery scent clouded my head, I inhaled. Stopping myself —*trying*—was futile. He smelled like what I imagined hell would. But in the best of ways.

We reached the next painting, and I interrupted him as he took a breath to speak. "Let me guess, three hundred years ago?"

"Mm hmm," he hummed in my ear, and he sounded somehow closer. Impossible. "Care to take a stab at the next, love?"

"Ooh, I'm not sure. I can only count to three, Nessin."

Understanding my sarcasm, I practically heard the smirk on his lips as an amused laugh escaped him. He reached forward, placing his right hand over mine to guide it over the next painting.

"I'd be happy to teach you. To count, that is." Sin's voice echoed between us. We ambled on. "Four hundred. Five…"

Every few steps, I felt his hip brush my rear or back. I eyed the portraits ahead without counting them. I was too distracted for that. We passed several more portraits this way, his hand on top of mine, lacing our fingers. While Sin hadn't danced at the wedding whatsoever, this *felt* like a dance.

His other hand brushed mine as we walked on. It would be so easy to take it, to position him how I wanted. No, this wasn't in my head. Maybe he was already bored in the fortress, sure, but he'd hinted before that my attraction to him wasn't one-sided.

Don't even. No, no, no. Stop. Turn away. Do anything but this.

I swallowed to clear my throat, hoping my voice came out even.

"You're extremely old, Nessin. How many more are there?"

"That's extremely offensive, Sersa. Why? Are you uncomfortable like this?"

I swallowed again, trying to ignore my racing heart as the lie tumbled from my lips.

"Not at all. Are you?"

"No." His voice was pure confidence, an effortless reply.

I knew, with him behind me, that he couldn't hear my thoughts presently, but it did little to console me.

In the next portrait, Sin was shirtless, a spear aimed at the verdant ground by his side.

I sighed, and Sin laughed.

"What was that for?" he asked.

"Your ego is showing in this one."

"It's from the Battle of Dánlin. Although I wasn't shirtless there. Good artists take...creative liberties. The spear is real, of course. You alluded before that you're good with spears, no? I'd love to see your skills."

Our touching hands roved over the canvas before finding a pair of crossed spears. I paused, examining the jeweled handles. They were identical to the one he held in the portrait.

I swore he was getting closer with each step we took. Finally, the hand that hovered near my side made contact, his thumb tracing deep circles on my shoulder.

Knowing I couldn't take this proximity any longer, I pushed away and spun around. I clasped my hands behind my back to stop myself from using them and stared up at him. Sin stood with one knee bent, his hands now low on his hips. His chin always tilted downward when he looked at me, and mine upward, trying to accommodate our height difference.

I grinned and raised an eyebrow in challenge. "I would like to see *you* use one."

His gaze darted to the etched iron spears behind me.

"I am not fighting you, Sersa."

"It's just for fun."

"I don't care what it is. I'm still not fighting you. Especially in that dress."

"You could only be so lucky to duel me in the nude."

"That's not what I meant."

I ignored him, reaching for the first spear. I tossed it, not bothering to confirm he'd caught it. Then I grabbed the second and faced him. I kicked off my slipper-like shoes and squeezed my toes into the icy stone.

Sin kept his spear hand dangling beside his leg, a perfect imitation of his shirtless portrait. If only he lost his shirt.

"Oh, come on," I said. "How else will we entertain ourselves for an entire moon cycle?"

"Not this way."

I lunged, aiming right above his hips. He blocked with zero effort.

"Sersa. I am more than a foot taller than you. My arms are almost as long as your legs. I've been practicing, training, killing with a blade, spear, scythe—you name it—in my hand, or using my bare hands, for hundreds of years. I will not insult you by saying you're no match for me—"

Another lunge and he swept to the side, our spears skimming one another with a hollow knock of metal on metal. I threw a glare in his direction, but where he'd turned serious I was already having fun with him.

He really didn't want to fight me.

"You might as well say I'm no match for you if you won't fight back."

"I think you should be more concerned about the front of your dress falling down, Sersa."

The second I glanced at my cleavage—breasts covered, my dress in place—Sin disarmed me. He didn't catch the spear that flew through the air over our heads. It landed upright in a groove between stone slabs behind him. The force and speed he moved with astonished me, and now he stood right in front of me.

"I hate to be right about everything, but..." Arrogance dripped from his voice. He tossed his spear to the far side of the room, and it went soaring with a clatter.

Sin got so close, kept getting closer, that I was forced to walk backward.

"What are you doing?"

"Hand-to-hand combat next? Grappling?" His eyes were wild, his teeth showing in a grin.

"Hilarious."

"Knife throwing? Brass knuckles? Archery? What'll it be, love?"

It hadn't been a fair fight. I knew my skill with a spear, both in throwing them and using them as close-contact weapons. He'd distracted me. With a laugh, I shoved Sin. He barely moved, and the inch he did was likely only to make me feel less pathetic. I fell back on my rear as I tripped on the end of my dress.

"Ow." I tilted my head to stare at his monumental frame from the ground. "Now that was offensive."

"Sorry. You don't strike me as the type of woman who likes being saved."

"At least you know that much about me."

Sin raked a hand through his white hair. Then he lowered to the ground and stretched his impossibly long legs out in front of him. He laid back, head resting on his hands. His eyes moved along the ceiling.

"This is what we'll do for the duration of our time here. Rest. Prepare. Try not to impale one another with spears."

"What is there to prepare for?"

Turning silent, he licked his top lip as he adjusted against the floor. It was just the right distraction to halt my curiosity. After the way he'd kissed me following our handfasting, his lips called to me. It was a line not to be crossed though, one that would only lead us down a dangerous path.

"Is it actually dangerous though?" Sin challenged.

"Gods! Would you stop intruding on my private thoughts?"

"I literally cannot help it. Your mind is the most fucking distracting thing I have ever heard. You know," he added, propping himself up on his elbows, "if you want something so bad, you need not restrain yourself. This life is yours for the taking. To do with it as you please."

"Thank you for that. But I won't be seduced by a Daemon Prince."

"What about when I'm the Daemon King?"

I closed my eyes and shook my head, trying not to smile. "If I had something to throw at you right now, I would. Also, we're having a rematch soon."

"Fine. But I told you at the White Plume, love. Beg me—"

I rammed my heel into his shin. Sin bolted upright so quick, hand sliding under my dress to yank me by the ankle, that I didn't even have time to react.

I squealed as I landed and blinked him into clarity.

"Oh, gods. It's not like I'm going to hurt you. But *you* are always trying to hurt me. You should stop that."

I was straddling him, my skirt an utter mess as it rode up my thighs, and I had absolutely no idea how I'd fallen into this position. The hand that'd gripped my ankle rested on my knee.

Under my dress.

Sin took notice too, pulling it out from under the tangled fabric.

"Pardon my hand. And other things."

Through the thin, silk shorts I wore under my dress, I felt all of him between my legs. The low neckline of my dress betrayed me as my chest started rising and falling at a feverish pace. I hated myself for reacting physically, but I pressed my lips together to shut myself up. My mind had to be saying enough.

"It is, love." Those white eyes flickered around my face, taking in every inch.

Likewise, I studied his scar up close. The silver flecks in his irises. The sheen to his white hair and full lips he'd just licked.

"Do you want me—to touch you?"

I refused to let my mouth fall open, but my mind screamed.

Yes.

"You may stop this whenever, Sersa."

"I know."

Seduction laced his reply. "Tell me to stop."

That would imply I wanted him to stop. I didn't know what he was going to do. But *no* part of me wanted a cessation to whatever this was.

Expression darkening with temptation, a look I'd seen in one too many daemon's eyes before, Sin's hand slid under my jaw. As his fingers trailed down to feel my pulse with his thumb, he leaned forward until our chests touched. The hand on my back made me arch as his lips came close to my neck without making contact.

"Beg me, Sersa. Succumb to the Underworld." His whisper both set my body afire and sent shivers rippling through me.

If Sin Drumghoul was sin personified, I wanted to commit every single one with him. But they wouldn't be sins at all. Even if we hadn't been bound, I wouldn't believe they would be.

But we were bound. Technically.

The single protest in my mind was the fact that we'd known one another for days. *Days!* Not even a week. Then again, I'd done more in one night with strangers than sit in their lap.

This was innocent. Enough.

Sin's breath dusted my skin. My hips moved reflexively, noting his matched lust for me through his thin pants. Definitely not thin enough.

Finally, his mouth found my skin, and his tongue traced a path to my collarbone. Yet again, my hips twitched of their own accord. The hand on my back lowered to my hip, and he guided me to grind against him. All the blood rushed into my cheeks. Trying to bite back my gasp twisted it into a moan.

"Aye, love? That?"

I rolled my hips against his. My hands gripped his arms like he might get away from me. I felt him watching me—somehow, I did—but I couldn't drop my eyes to watch him.

What were we doing? What was *I* doing?

Sin laid back again, gently lowering us both, and positioned me right where he wanted me. Our chests touched. His bony hand gathered my hair off my neck and out of his lips' way, the other still guiding my hips against his. The feeling between my legs swelled until the moans couldn't be helped.

He was going to send me over the edge.

He should stop, *we* should, but neither of us was going to.

We focused on one another's bodies. As I tracked his movements, they were almost as intense as the feeling building inside me. The hand that fisted my dress slid back under to grip my thigh as I took over. Teeth softly scraped my jaw.

I pressed against Sin harder, and he answered by putting even more pressure on my hip as if he could meld us together through our clothes. I couldn't contain myself. I didn't want to think about whether I'd regret this because of how it felt.

I bit back a final moan as heat rolled through me like a wave. Every muscle in my body loosened and contracted, pulsing uncontrollably.

Trying to slow my breathing was hopeless.

I didn't want to see the lascivious look on his face, but our gazes locked instinctively. Mine widened with recognition.

Gods. What. Had. I. Done?

Sin peeled off the ground an inch to whisper in my ear, "Imagine what I could do to you with nothing between us, Sersa. *Imagine.*"

My heart raced, and surely, he felt it in his own chest.

"I—"

The illusion shattered as quickly as it'd started.

"Oh, *my! Oh!*" came a jarring voice in the doorway.

Still straddling Sin, I snapped upright. My fingers slid down his chest, and his head whipped in the corridor's direction.

Draea and several servants stood outside the gallery, their mouths open, eyes roaming over the sight of us. They studied my dress cloaking our hips, seemingly locked together, his hands still on me with one under my skirt, and my rutted breaths.

"So sorry, Your Highness! Er, Your Highnesses!" said one of the servants.

At once, the others backed away while Draea, shaking her head either at us or them, swept the doors shut.

The second they left, my cheeks burned. Reality took root inside me. I couldn't believe myself, and yet I could. Reckless as all hell. Acting on fleeting emotions. Had I really allowed myself this indulgence? Now, I'd never hear the end of it.

Mortified—I was mortified!

Closing my eyes to avoid looking at Sin, I pressed the back of my hand to my lips, the other on my stomach, and stood. My dress trundled down my legs and around my bare feet, dusting his body before I focused on the swish of the fabric against the stone as I headed for the door, unable to look at him.

"What about your shoes?" Sin called after me, still lying on the floor.

Though I picked up my pace, I couldn't escape the diabolic laughter that filled the corridor I fled from.

22

I hadn't realized an activity was scheduled for the second night. If I'd known, maybe I wouldn't have found myself unabashedly grinding against Sin in the gallery. Well, unabashedly until the servants walked past and saw. While I definitely hadn't expected our activity to include visiting a Druids' parish, Sin insisted he'd planned this one.

It was Hwain, and we needed to honor the High Triad.

"Are you going to look at me?" Sin asked.

We were on our way to the barn at half-past eighth bell. The Cradled Moons were high in the dark sky beyond the windowed corridor. I'd thrown an overcoat on top of my flowery dress to fend off the chill tonight, but I already felt it in the air as we neared the fortress's edges.

"I'm sure you're aware that *no*, I won't be looking at you ever again."

"Oh, come on. It was harmless. It's not like either of us will let it slip any further."

Slip. Knowing Sin, albeit how little I did, that had to be a euphemism.

"I was only jesting, what I said about what I could do to—"

Halting abruptly, I held up my hand to shut him up. "I don't need you to repeat the exact words, Nessin."

"Remember them just fine on your own, aye?"

"Don't think I'm so easy to please," I snapped.

"I never said you were. I only implied that I'm that good, love."

I had no doubt of that.

"Well, it was exactly as you said. Harmless fun. Don't think about it in your free time."

"You either. But what happened was perfectly natural, Sersa. We are wed."

I spiraled on him again. Thank Dúm we were unaccompanied.

"We are not actually..." I raised my eyebrows, hands balling into fists.

Sin leaned toward me, taunting me with his lips. "In the eyes of the gods we are. Besides, why shouldn't you reap the benefits of our union?"

With a wink, he moved around me to keep walking.

As we entered the barn and the smell of hay and dung assaulted my nose, I welcomed it. The scent was so strong I couldn't think straight. There were a dozen cows in a pen, a few horses, and some chickens and goats near the entrance. Carriages that were as ostentatious as Sin's attire with gilded details and swirling designs sat on the far side. Four Soul Guards sat atop their horses waiting for us. One of five carriages had been loaded with a hefty cauldron filled with berries, nuts, bread, and cheese, and an enormous carafe of wine—our offerings to the High Triad.

Regretting that I hadn't exchanged my flowery dress for something thicker, I shuddered even in my fur-lined cloak and matching gloves as I stepped into the carriage, navigating around the cauldron. But when Sin didn't follow, I popped my head over the little half door.

"Am I to go alone?" I asked.

Sin mounted a black steed and turned to look over his shoulder. He was mid-smile, talking to the guards and looking far too pleased with himself.

"I'm going to ride tonight, love. Care to join me?" An impish look crossed his face as he extended his hand to me.

One of the Soul Guards snickered. "If the princess rides this mount, my prince, she'll be too tired to ride your cock later."

All the blood drained from my face. Had the servants– Had they said something? Or was the guard simply a vile bastard?

"I assure you I have far better stamina than that. A pathetic man like yourself could only dream of finding out, I'm sure." My words flew like an arrow, but I heard the shake in my voice.

The guard's lips pursed. "I didn't know mortal men allowed their ladies to speak that way these days," he retorted. "What has happened since I crossed over?"

None of the other guards laughed as the one who'd slighted me led the way out of the barn.

While Sin went very still, his eyes twisted with murder, and he slowly turned to look at the guard's back.

"Ass," I muttered under my breath, gesturing obscenely out the window. As I fell back against my seat, blowing out a heavy breath, I wondered whether Sin had brought those dainty daggers of his.

"*Daris?*" Sin's voice was almost saccharine.

I poked my head out the window again. Sin's teeth were bared in a demented expression, his eyes wide.

The guard turned, pulling back on his horse's reins. "Yes, my prince?"

"If I so much as hear a single, half-formed thought of that nature regarding my wife in your grain-size brain again or if you ever so much as think of speaking to her that way..." With each word, Sin's threat grew louder, sharper, until his voice was thunder striking. "I will personally skin you alive and feed what's left of you to the princess's hellhound. That clear?"

Without waiting for an answer, Sin turned his horse around and trotted into the snowy woods. I didn't need him to defend me, not like he had against Daigh Hellick the other night, but it sure felt good to have him on my side.

We reached our destination a half bell later.

The frozen sea was closer than expected, and the Druids' parish perched at the very edge of a rocky shore. Or so I thought until the carriage halted right beside the sea where the grass met the coastline.

My brow furrowed as Sin approached the carriage and took my hand, leading me toward a line of three beehive-shaped huts. The tension between his brows hadn't dispelled on the ride, and I didn't miss the glares he cast in Daris's direction.

"Thank you," I said, for more than one reason.

The huts sat far enough from the tide that they wouldn't be washed away but close enough that I wondered how they'd weathered the furious tempests during the wettest and stormiest season, the Haze. There was no sand this far north but pebbles galore that made it difficult for me to walk in my slightly heeled shoes as we approached the huts.

Two of the Soul Guards carried the cauldron where Sin directed them. The wind whipped my loose hair across my face, and I tucked it inside the back of my cloak. I tasted the salt in the air and closed my eyes for a second, reminded of home.

"What is this place?" I didn't ask if we'd fit in the huts, surely our aim, but the wide-eyed looks of the guards suggested they were thinking it too.

"My childhood." Sin rapped on one of the hut's doors in a deliberate pattern.

After a full minute, it opened to reveal a little Druid wearing a set of white robes in the sliver. Sin waved his hand at the cauldron and the carafe of wine. The Druid looked him up and down then at the offerings. After a pause, he gestured for us to enter. When the Soul Guards moved forward, the Druid thrust his hand out. He wagged his pointer finger at them in warning.

They set the cauldron down, which Sin took up, and I carried the carafe over the threshold. Then the Druid slammed the door in their faces and took the carafe of wine from me.

Good. I didn't want to be crammed in here with them and the Druid.

A single look allowed me to take in every detail inside the hut. No bed. No lantern for light or warmth. Really nothing at all. I looked around, certain this could not be all there was. What were we going to do, sit on the floor and stare at one another?

I whirled around at the sound of something opening. The Druid had lifted a trap door for Sin to set the cauldron inside. He placed the carafe beside it.

At once, our offerings disappeared.

I moved too slowly. By the time I reached the trap door, the Druid slammed it shut and wagged his finger at me now.

"Oh. Sorry," I said.

He crossed the hut and opened another trap door, standing aside for us to go first.

"I—"

But I had no words.

Enormous stone stairs unfolded underground. Sin took the first step before offering me his hand to lead me below.

"Are you about to sacrifice me to some underground fiend?" I asked.

"*I'm* the only fiend in your life presently, love."

The Druid followed a few steps behind us after shutting the trap door and latching it from the inside.

"What did you mean this place is your childhood?" I asked.

The staircase unfurled into an underground network of staircases, walkways, and stone chambers. There were no railings on either side of the stone steps, and the fall would be endless.

I shuddered, my feet pausing without my input. My body grew rigid. "Where are we?"

"All Druids live here after death," Sin explained. "I lived here with them for a while."

"What? Why?"

He shifted, molding me against his body as I clung to him. We walked on together, but I couldn't look to either side of the stairs. I focused straight ahead.

"My face," he said. "You've thought about it, no doubt."

"Which part are you referring to?"

"My scar."

"Oh."

"I'm not ashamed of it. Some say it makes me even more devilishly handsome."

They'd be right.

I looked up at him as we continued down the stairs.

"My brothers and I learned when we were very young what being sons of the Daemon King meant for us. Our tutors told us we'd be pitted against one another when the king's rule ended. So, Lochlainn tried to convince our brothers to take care of the competition before we grew up." Sin's throat bobbed as he swallowed. "I was six. Lochlainn and Devlin were seven. Dev told on Lochlainn, but my mother came too late. Lochlainn had thrown me into a circle of Sluagh. He'd ordered Jestin, four at the time and terrified of our older brother, to set them on me."

I held my breath.

"Luckily, I have no soul for them to steal. But the wounds they left on my body were ghastly. When my mother got to me and ordered them off, I was a bloody mess. She summoned the best Bonemender in the realm. They healed me, but the scars remained. Obviously. After that, my mother didn't feel she could protect me. My magic was delayed, unlike all my brothers', so she sent me away. Here."

We reached the end of the steps. Only then did I release my breath.

"What about Jestin?" I asked. "Why didn't she send him away?"

"As I said, he had magic very young. He could protect himself well enough, and for some reason Lochlainn didn't see him as a threat." Sin did not smile as he looked at me.

"How long were you here for?"

"I returned to Nos Ovscura a few years ago. Most of those portraits you saw were done here actually. The Druids always stressed over getting the background right for the painter who visited us."

"You lived here that long?"

"Longer than you've been alive." He chanced a fleeting look at me, but his face was indecipherable. "Druids in the Soullands are Soulsmiths. They create new souls. I've always been fascinated by it and didn't really have a desire to return to the Court of Soulless."

I didn't blame him. "Sin, what happened to your mother? Why did she curse you?"

He focused ahead. "I tease you about being mortal, but the Daemon King truly hates the living, Sersa. He believes all mortals should have their souls sucked out. That all souls should either satiate or serve him. I don't know how my mother did it, but she was clever. She wanted to ensure his line, ours, slowly dwindled until we were mortal too, until we became the very thing he hates. When she did it... I remember it so clearly. She was on the ground in the throne room. She laughed in his face, and then he killed her in front of me, and Devlin. It's why Devlin wants nothing to do with the throne. He lives his life exactly how he wants—traveling, indulging, always contented—and I must admit I am envious at times."

"This life is yours for the taking," I mocked. But I couldn't stop myself from grabbing his hand and squeezing.

"How very wise for one so young." Sin squeezed my hand back, and something—some emotion I couldn't read and desperately wanted to be able to—affected his white eyes.

"I'm an old soul, thank you."

Sin's lips curled with amusement but faded equally as quick.

"You were saying," I said.

He didn't let go of my hand.

"After my mother cursed our line, we all started to catch ailments common to mortals. The king grew very sick at times, but souls had always kept this sort of thing at bay, aging too, so he forced us to devour them night after night and day after day."

The Druid had already disappeared by the time Sin's story released me from its hooks, but the Daemon Prince knew every inch of the confusing passages under the hut. Everything was made of stone, and runes I couldn't read etched long stretches of the walls.

"Come," Sin said. "The temple is this way."

This place, home of the Druids, made me think of Ciel more than I cared to. Our fight still weighed on me.

We reached a doorway framed by two enormous standing stones with one stretched across them. A dark tunnel loomed ahead, and an elevated basin filled with blood rested beside the doorway. The liquid glowed, highlighting the bare skin of my chest. Even before Sin pinched the tip of his glove and removed it, I knew what to do. These were the practices of the High Triad—the three gods known as Aon, Dúm, and Nev. It was the prevailing religion in Clais, and Druids worshipped devoutly.

Aon was the goddess of life, birth, love, and all things light.

Dúm was the god of death, war, lust, and darkness.

Nev, neither god nor goddess, was known simply as the Balance. They sought to achieve equilibrium between light and dark.

Pinching the tips of my own gloves to remove them, I dipped my fingers in the blood. Then I dotted one speck on my forehead and under both my eyes. I didn't replace my gloves and neither did Sin. We took the second ones off in unison as he led the way into the tunnel. Though we'd unwound our bodies since the terrifying stairs, I kept close to him.

After a minute, the temple revealed itself.

An enormous chamber lit by blue torchlight unfolded. Sin's pale skin and hair tinted as he moved toward the back of the chamber, or I supposed it was the front where the stone altar stood. Hundreds of candles covered the altar, their little flames swaying softly on an invisible wind.

I moved between two sides of curved stone benches. Behind the altar sat three archways.

"Which god do you honor this Hwain?" said a Druidess who stood before me.

I flinched. She'd appeared practically out of nowhere, holding a stone dish that had been split into three parts. The symbol of the High Triad: three drops of blood, all connected in a triangle.

Three different objects filled each of the bowls.

Sunstones for Aon.

Teeth for Dúm.

And hawthorn flowers for Nev.

Though I had little faith in the gods, the Balance had always seemed the most reasonable. I chose one of the pungent-smelling hawthorn flowers before I changed my mind. When the Druidess directed me toward the archways with an unreadable expression, I entered the middle passage.

Sin was headed down the left-side corridor.

Then he'd chosen a tooth. *Dúm*, naturally.

I met an empty chamber at the end of the passage where a single dagger laid on a plinth. Firelight bounced off the gleaming hilt, inlaid with jewels. Because of our many sacraments back home, I knew what to do. But I hated doing it. Not just because I had to drag the dagger across my own palm and feel the bite of the blade but because others in my clan claimed the gods spoke to them when they drew a rune on the wall and pressed their palm against it.

I, on the other hand, had always pretended to draw some rune I'd memorized from one of Ciel's tomes the day of. Then I'd close my eyes for a full minute and pretend the gods came to me, telling me which rune to draw and what my destiny was.

"Ridiculous." I snickered under my breath. "Absolutely ridiculous."

I sighed, wondering if I could wait a few minutes, slip my gloves back on, and then go back the way I'd come.

Instead, I decided to get it over with.

I picked up the dagger, drew it across my palm, and bit back a cuss. The least I could do was avoid swearing in this place of gods. After dipping two fingers in my blood, I touched the wall.

My head snapped backward. I gasped.

I couldn't see a thing. I was lost in a sea of white like Sin's eyes. A voice hissed at me. It was all around me, both filling the chamber and my head.

You seek balance, do you? Balance? Balance? Balance...

I gritted my teeth, clawing my fingers against the wall.

You wish to have control over yourself, no? No? No... The gods can give you what you wish...if you only give something in return.

I forced a word out, choking on my own breath. "No."

Your soul. Soul. Soul... It will not be yours much longer. What you desire requires sacrifice. Sacrifice. Sacrifice...

Beware. Beware. Beware...

Finally, the white vision released me. The voice faded, and I dropped to my knees, wheezing. The blade stained with my blood clattered to the sooty ground. I didn't care. I refused to touch the walls for support as I struggled to my feet, but when I finally did, I ran back the way I'd come.

I ran and ran and ran.

Someone caught me under the archway, halting me before I rammed into the altar of candles.

"Sersa?"

Sin.

I gasped as he held my shoulders, steadying me.

"What happened?" he asked. "Are you okay?"

I shook my head and licked my lips, unable to form words. "No... *No.*"

"We made our offering," he reassured me. He had put his gloves back on, and the cool leather grazed my face as he cupped my cheek. "We can leave now."

Sweat beaded at my temples, but the breath in my chest felt as cold as ice.

"Okay?"

Still breathless, I nodded.

But the Druidess from before approached us. Her eyes said a thousand things. Loudest of all was the fact that she knew I'd heard something in Nev's passage. I didn't want to believe it. I never had before.

The Balance had spoken to me. But what was the meaning?

The Druidess circled us at a leisurely pace, her hands clasped behind her back and hidden by the bell-sleeved robe. A glint in her eye brightened when she stopped in front of us beside the altar. Blue shadows danced across her face.

"It seems the lady heard the voice of the gods tonight," she said carefully. "Even great queens and kings have been frightened by what they've heard in those passages, by the warnings they've received."

Her smooth voice sounded like nails against stone to my ears. Delayed chills rippled up my forearms, raising every hair on end.

"I had wanted to warn you about your choices beforehand," she continued. "But the gods look down on that. You cannot change what you choose once you choose it."

The Druidess looked between us, and I had the urge to let my hawthorn flower fall to the ground and stomp on it. I hadn't realized I still had it. It clung to my sweaty palm.

"A new union, no?" she asked, gesturing between us.

Sin nodded curtly. His jaw was firm, and his hand tightened around mine.

"I thought as much. The gods smile on this night, but as they look upon you, their smile turns wary. Cautionary. As does mine."

I studied her face, both losing my patience and consumed by what she had to say.

"I noticed one of you chose darkness, and the other the Balance. But without light *and* dark... The union without balance always fails us. Only light can bring balance to something utterly dark. Only darkness can bring balance to the blinding light. Nev may work miracles, but they don't always wish to."

"And if we had both chosen the Balance?" I asked. "Or both of us Dúm?"

The Druidess only smiled.

Sin stood a little straighter. He glared down at her. "Then what do *they* ask of us?"

He cared what the gods thought?

The Druidess's eyes gleamed under the flickering light. "Sacrifice. Always sacrifice, Prince Nessin."

My eyes dropped to Sin's fingers, tapping the dainty daggers at his waist. He didn't look my way before he turned on his heels.

"Sin—"

His eyes were murderous again. "I will be back. Stay put. Please."

It wasn't a command, and I knew he'd be back. He wouldn't leave me down here forever.

But where was he going in the first place?

"We're missing Daris," said one of the Soul Guards.

Sin had returned to the temple a few minutes before, and he'd made swift work of guiding us back to the world above.

Atop his horse together, I felt Sin's body tense around me. He gripped the reins tighter as his thighs squeezed my hips. He'd insisted I ride with him despite that the carriage would be warmer.

"Daris is not missing," Sin said coldly. He turned our horse toward the road, facing the Soul Guards. "I know exactly where he is. And if anyone else wants to make a comment about my wife, what we do in private or otherwise, please, I invite you to do so now. I'd be glad to chaperone you to the bottom of the sea next."

Then...

My thoughts spiraled.

"No? Didn't think so," Sin growled.

He steered the horse away from the rocky shore and clicked his teeth. Two Soul Guards rode on horseback behind us while another drove the carriage. I didn't offer to ride Daris's horse. Instead, I allowed it to trot alongside us. The midnight air was sharper than when we'd arrived, and halfway home, Sin wrapped one end of his fur cloak across my body.

"We'll be home soon."

With my back pressed against his chest, I nodded.

When we reached our rooms a half bell later, I couldn't bring myself to shed my cloak or clothes. I sat by the fire, shaking, determined to toast my feet and hands until I thawed. Sin stood near the wardrobe between the fireplace and the door. He pulled his white tunic over his head, mussing his hair before finding another shirt for sleeping.

My eyes were drawn to the bare muscles of his back, lean but corded—until his gaze caught mine in the mirror right in front of him. Down his chest and honed stomach were those scars I'd glimpsed before, where the Sluagh had dragged their talons through his flesh.

Sin discarded my gaze as he kicked off his boots, and I looked away just as quickly. Still, my mind swarmed with thoughts I tried to bury inside the deepest part of myself. I wanted to touch his skin, to feel those scars—and other places—against me. Again and again.

It wouldn't do. He had to be listening to my thoughts, and it was probably better he was ignoring them.

I cleared my hoarse throat. "You didn't drown that guard. Not really, right?"

He looked at me for a long time, standing next to the glowing light of the hearth with an impenetrable expression. He didn't move for a few moments until finally he grabbed a leather-bound book off the fireplace mantle.

"Get some sleep, Sersa."

"What? Wait. I asked you a question, Nessin." I took a step away from the fireplace. "If the Druidess hadn't asked for a sacrifice, would you still have done it?"

"Yes," he said. No hesitation. "Do you think I've not killed a thousand men before him? Do you think I won't kill a thousand men after him?"

"No. But you didn't kill for yourself tonight." He'd killed for me. Killed one of his own guards.

"It probably won't surprise you to know that I happen to like killing men like that, Sersa. I *enjoyed* watching the light fade behind his eyes. He insulted a Daemon Princess, he was undressing you in his mind, and if you only knew the rest of what he'd been thinking about—" Sin halted himself from saying anything further.

"And what do you believe that sacrifice achieved?" I pressed. My wind-chapped cheeks flooded with heat.

"I do not know." His eyes were unwavering. "But when it comes to the gods and you, I'd rather not take any chances. Now go to sleep."

"I need help with my dress," I blurted.

"I'll send for Draea."

"No pretenses?"

Lips closed, Sin sucked the front of his teeth silently. After a moment's hesitation, he strode toward me, sliding his book under his armpit. He unhooked my cloak at the front, pulled it off my shoulders, and draped it over the back of the settee before rotating me. Then he worked on the laces down my back.

As my dress started to go slack, I didn't bother holding it up. It slid down my hips without snagging on my curves and pooled at my feet.

Sin took the deepest of breaths behind me. His exhale was a growl.

I remained facing the fireplace, nearly naked save for pale blue silk shorts Claud had fashioned me.

Sin's thumbs traced circles on my shoulders, and he was so much taller that I knew he saw every inch of bare skin down my body from his aerial view. My collarbones. The swell of my breasts. My navel.

One gentle but firm hand slowly curled around the front of my neck. He tipped my head backward until it touched his chest. My eyes closed and lips parted in a gasp, waiting...

"*Do not tempt me tonight, Sersa Scáth.*" Sin's voice was a low rumble.

His words made my mouth hang agape, and my eyes snapped open.

I knew instantly that it was a command. A Bonespeaker command!

"Nessin! How dare—"

At that, he released me and left the room with heavy steps. I stared into the fire for a long time before sliding into bed shirtless.

Let that daemon command *me*.

My last thought before I fell asleep was what a pair we were because I wished he hadn't drowned the guard.

I wished he'd let me do it.

And I wished he'd given into his other impulses, the ones I *knew* for certain that we shared.

23

The first few days passed quickly, but I still found I needed regular distractions outside of chasing Dúma around to stop myself from unraveling. The seclusion of the fortress in the mountains reminded me of the tower Uncle Bardic—and Ma—had threatened to lock me up in.

For almost a week straight, Sin woke up well before the diurnal moonrise. I stirred every morning only to find his side of the bed empty before I drifted back to sleep. I didn't try sleeping shirtless again and felt the tiniest twinge of embarrassment I'd done so. A far larger part of me wondered how Sin had reacted that morning when he'd roused and seen me.

While he left me a note on his pillow each morning to say he'd taken care of Dúma's needs and fed her, we hadn't spoken more than a few words since returning from the Druids' parish.

My days quickly fell into a routine.

After training with Era, Dúma snoozed at my feet for a few bells while I sketched in an empty journal I'd found until her energy returned in quick bursts. There was no paint in the fortress, but I didn't mind other mediums of art. Especially after so many days without any creative outlet. When my hand finally tired, we walked through the woods—me cautiously and Dúma sniffing everything—

until she exhausted herself again. Though the woods surrounding the fortress troubled me, I couldn't avoid them. To ease my mind, Dúma and I stayed in sight of the fortress.

A thick swath of heavy clouds had settled overhead sometime after breakfast a week into our stay. I glimpsed the sky through gaps in the canopy and knew that a blizzard loomed as the squalls picked up and the temperature dropped. The bad weather hovered overhead readily, an omen that reflected my dipping mood.

Though the passing days allowed me to count down the time until we returned to the City of Soulless, they also meant more time had passed since I'd made any progress finding Pa.

Instead, I'd married a prince, ground against that gods-damned daemon in a moment of weakness and desire, then all but offered myself and my body up to him that night, and worst of all, allowed my mind to become clouded with thoughts of him day after day.

I supposed it was good Sin and I spoke so little. I had failed one too many times since then to so much as look him in the eye at breakfast, lunch, and dinner.

I wanted him to hear my thoughts, and yet I also wanted to guard them adamantly.

At the edge of the woods, I threw a handmade leather ball Innes had sewn for Dúma. It rolled between two evergreen trees that were almost as tall as the fortress behind us. We walked like this for several minutes, me throwing, Dúma fetching and carrying it back to me in her little razor-sharp teeth.

But on the dozenth throw, she darted ahead without retrieving or returning.

My brow furrowed as I craned my neck around the trees, trying to see what had caught her attention. Hopefully a rabbit or something harmless—but my thoughts went straight to all the potential predators in these woods.

I tried to catch up with Dúma, but she skittered forward before taking off at a run. I was never more grateful for a pair of thick boots and breeches as I chased after her between the trees.

"Dúma!"

She'd halted in a clearing. I shoved through face-height branches in my way and halted at the edge. A stranger knelt to pet Dúma at their bare feet. Her paws climbed bony knees, clad in long robes of the richest green. The color was reserved for royalty and...

The gods were always described as wearing the rich hue.

Brown curls touched the stranger's dark cheekbones, stirred by a gust of wind. They almost reminded me of that pompous Thane Elittes in a way, but there was no arrogance in the stranger's face. The trees answered the haunting whoosh of wind that curled through the woods by shaking their branches. Snow coiled in the air, clinging to my lashes, dusting my lips, and settling on my hair.

The stranger straightened to full height, and I staggered backward. Their figure was stretched and thin, as tall as Sin but more willowy and utterly ethereal.

As the stranger looked upon me and I upon them, I examined eyes that were neither sharp nor gentle and facial features that bore the same neutrality. No hard or soft lines. Almost celestial bone structure.

No, it *was* celestial. They were. My breath caught in my throat.

It was a deity, one of three in the High Triad, who had visited me at the temple the other night, and the Balance had returned.

"Nev."

"I did not think you would recognize me," Nev said.

Dúma ran toward me, and I scooped her up in my arms. Her little paws had to be freezing from the snow by now, though I wondered fleetingly if hellhounds got cold. Her downy fur and blazing body temperature warmed me.

"I'm as surprised as you," I admitted. "Then it's true. The entrance to the Otherworld is in these woods."

Nev chuckled. "Mortals and soulless alike cling to their folktales like a baby to its mother's breast. The gods reveal one bit of information, and you take every word literally."

I wanted to argue that I wasn't the one who'd said it—I hadn't believed in the gods until the Druids' temple and even then, I remained skeptical—but I suspected, like Sin, that Nev could infiltrate my thoughts if they wanted.

"Then it's not true. About the entrance," I said. Dúma licked my chin once before burrowing back into my cloak.

"Oh, no, it is true. There are entrances to the Otherworld in just about every forest." Nev's lips spread into a smile, revealing blindingly white teeth. "But I am not here to talk about folktales, Sersa."

Nev paused. So did I. I allowed myself a glance to assess Nev further, but my eyes weren't like theirs. Not so perceptive, unable to see through their expression like they saw through mine.

"Then what are you here to talk about?" I asked.

"My visit to you the other night."

I hadn't realized until now that Nev was circling me. I also hadn't realized we'd switched spots. I was in the middle of the clearing. I swallowed, knowing Nev had moved me here somehow. I turned to watch them, but their form had shifted in the second my eyes lost them.

A woman with loose red hair like my mother's had replaced Nev, but she wore the same green robes. This was *Aon* herself. The god of light, birth, and love.

My heart beat faster. Nervous, I licked my lips.

"You did not seem at all happy I spoke to you the other night." Though Aon's voice was as smooth as silk, the gods were known for their sharper edges, and I detected the glass behind her words.

"You presented me with a riddle."

"Was it really a riddle?" Her tone was almost punitive. She was the mother goddess. "I thought it was quite clear."

I held her gaze, but in a single blink, her form shifted. To Dúm.

The god of death wore a smirk like Sin's. He also wore green robes, but his hair dusted dark eyes that reflected my own like a mirror. His stubbled, pale face might have fooled me into disbelieving he was a god if not for the glowing quality of his skin.

Dúm said nothing, only watching me, studying me, eyes roving with unbridled curiosity.

Another blink, and Nev returned.

They halted in front of me, squaring their shoulders with mine.

"We can give you what you desire, Sersa Scáth. *Balance.*" The last word echoed through the clearing as it had in the Druids' temple.

I focused harder on Nev's face, trying to detect Dúm and Aon within it futilely.

"For a price, I'm sure." I stood taller, nudging my heels deeper in the snow. Shivering now, I held Dúma closer.

"Everything has a cost. We can take away your ability to feel at all. No pain. No anger. No sadness. No fear." Nev grinned, and I assumed they knew the last had always been the hardest to navigate for me. "We warned you about your soul. Will you take our warning or thwart it?"

"Haven't you heard the old adage?"

Nev tilted their head at me. Every detail of their appearance remained faultless. Their hair was not mussed from the wind, nor their robes wet from the snow.

"Without pain, there is no pleasure," I said.

Nev's expression wiped clean, striking a perfect balance like their namesake.

"I see some light in you after all but with a glint of darkness too. Then again, there is dark and light in everyone, is there not? I hope you find what you are looking for here in the Soullands."

"Can you tell me one thing? Will I find that which I'm here for?"

"You are here for one thing, Sersa Drumghoul, but I believe you'll find another thing entirely. Call on us if you change your mind."

"How? How do I call on you?"

Without another word, Nev slid away, leaving no tracks in the snow. They disappeared as if they'd stepped through a veil between worlds that only they could see.

And they had.

I didn't have the chance to snarl that the gods had never been here for me. The chain of events that had led me here—losing Pa, stealing my clan's magic, being labeled mad—proved their neglect.

I rushed back to the fortress, both Dúma and me now freezing, and didn't say a word to anyone about what I'd seen. For the rest of the night, I wondered if my mind had fabricated the entire thing, and I tried to understand what Nev's message meant, if it had been real at all.

24

At the start of our second week on Nos Nua, I woke to a book on my nightstand.

The title assured me it hadn't been misplaced there because Nessin never came within an arm's length of my side of the bed. When he was forced to pass it to reach the bathing room, he steered clear like the air I breathed was tainted.

After Dúma's training, I spent my morning reading *The High Houses of Gilders Eye*, gathering whatever bits of information might aid me for when we returned to Nos Ovscura.

My patience grew thin. It always had with reading—with anything that required me to be still—but it was different here. The inaction of the last few days alone tortured me until I was so irritable that I could no longer read, sketch, or think straight.

To busy my thoughts and exhaust my body, Dúma and I walked laps around the fortress at all bells, day and night. Inside laps. I only ventured outside when necessary. At first, Dúma enjoyed it, but after a few circles, she, too, looked at me like I was mad. Luckily, the fortress wasn't so big that I got lost every time I walked around alone, but it was big enough that I didn't run into Sin at every turn.

But he was there, always, in my mind.

I'd barely seen him in days except for mealtimes, and even then, we carried on in silence. I wondered if this was intentional on his part. I wondered if what had happened in the gallery suddenly bothered him. Our inadequate affection had to be rousing talk among the servants. Draea, the most perceptive of them all because she knew Sin the best, often passed me regretful looks with downturned lips she tried to force into a soft smile. I might've felt bad for myself. If this was a real union.

Whether the servants were talking about us or not, they didn't pry, not like mine had back home, and Sin didn't insist on upholding our pretenses any longer.

But what troubled me most was that I wanted to understand why he'd changed. It couldn't have been the gallery or the evening to follow. He'd been all too smug with himself after the gallery and then instantly flipped when he'd undressed me.

Unless he regretted that time together. Probably. His reaction to the latter had been peculiar.

The following day at breakfast, Sin sat across from me, eating nothing for what felt like the fifth or sixth day in a row. I wondered if he had to eat or if he could get away with only consuming souls.

A shudder rippled up my spine. Hopefully, he hadn't brought any soulstock with him here.

"Have you been reading?" he asked. I nodded in silence. "Good. Name the High Houses."

I glared over the top of my coffee cup as I took a generous sip and swallowed. It was much too hot, the first taste too sweet, until it turned bitter on my tongue.

"Is that a command?" I replied.

The days that'd passed hadn't helped me get over the fact that he had, in fact, commanded me.

Do not tempt me tonight, Sersa Scáth.

"Indulge me," he said lightly.

"You don't speak to me for days, and *this* is the first thing you wish to say?"

"I have been busy. My apologies. I was under the impression you did not want to talk either."

"*My apologies?*" I echoed with a scoff. I was ready to whip something across the room. With a clear of the throat, I set my cup down. "You owed me an apology days ago. A far more sincere one than that."

My patience had worn thinner and thinner the longer he'd disregarded me, threatening to snap like an unraveling rope.

"For what, Sersa? For stopping us from doing something we would regret?"

Regret. Then that settled it. He had regretted it.

I inhaled sharply. "The House of Alders. Berell. Caise and Hellick." These two were easy to recall since I had Stellera and Helde's faces to tie the houses to. "Drichte. Ó Laighin." Another easy one because the Ó Laighins of the Western Pointe ruled the wealthiest of the four isles of Clais. "And..."

Sin sighed when I couldn't name the others. "The last two are the House of Turrian and the House of Elittes."

Right. Thane Elittes.

He seemed all too content resuming our meal in silence, so I pushed back from my seat and stormed out. He didn't follow or react, and it was probably better that way.

Regret. Sin would have regretted something happening between us. I snickered under my breath, smiling despite how rattled and furious I felt.

Now I was the one who regretted reality, real moments, rather than mere possibilities. The White Plume. The gallery. My dreams.

My fixation with Sin.

Guilt flooded me as I again took to the corridors, taking lap after lap to calm my mind.

Nothing worked. Finally, I returned to our room and succumbed to my exhaustion. It was the only thing I wanted to do—pass the time by avoiding reality.

The sky finally burst sometime after dinner, and in a matter of a few bells, the snowfall hastened until it was so thick it made it difficult to see through gaps in the trees. I stood near a window in a parlor, which I'd taken up as my own. A knitted shawl wrapped my shoulders as I stared into the woods ahead. The flakes were enormous, and I could see their little sparkling forms as they twirled to the ground, coating everything in sight. The window's exterior was caked in ice and crusting snow too. I touched a curious hand to the glass, and the wind coiled through it, summoning a chill from my scalp to my toes.

Draea's voice startled me. "Oh, move away from the windows, Prin—Sersa. You'll freeze!"

I did as she asked but only because my nap had left me even more exhausted. I wanted to sit. Even sketching sounded like too much for my heavy mind. "Is there wine, Draea?"

"How 'bout some mead instead? It'll keep you warm. And where is the prince?" she asked, trying to make light of the situation. "Where has that boy been the last few days?"

Boy. He was immortal, not a boy.

Sin entered a moment later as if he'd heard us. He clutched a book in one hand, the other twisted behind his back.

"There you are, Your Highness," Draea said. "It's too cold and the roads likely too dangerous to go anywhere tonight, so how 'bout a game of cards with your wife?"

Wife.

A shudder rippled down my forearms, raising the little hairs, and I convinced myself it was the chill in the room. So few people had used that word since our handfasting, and I certainly didn't think of myself as such.

Before I could say that he didn't have to play, he set his book on the table in the center of the room and nodded. His eyes cut to me, and I swore I saw the reflection of the crackling fire in them.

"Seven Daggers it is," he said. "Do you know how to play?"

"You insult me."

Seven Daggers was the most popular game in Clais. Clan members of mine had secured ladies' hands in marriage against the reluctance of their fathers by winning a game of Seven Daggers.

Sin took the seat next to the head of the table and gestured for me to have it instead. Though I didn't miss the way Draea's eyes narrowed, I obliged and sat. She scurried toward us and set the Seven Daggers deck on the table.

"Oh, and don't forget the mead," she said before jabbing a finger at a carafe she'd poured in the corner of the room. Then she excused herself, beckoning Innes to follow. One might have thought Draea believed we'd be making love on the table in the next five minutes with how quickly they scurried out.

I sighed loudly. Sin crossed the room, carried the carafe and chalices toward us, and poured both of us a serving.

"Do you think anyone actually finishes the barrel of mead?" I asked.

Sin retook his seat and focused on the cards as he cut and shuffled the deck, never looking at me. He dealt with adept fingers. Seven cards for both of us.

"Probably," he said. "I was thinking we might roll it into town tomorrow and give it to a local tavern. But I'm not sure that will be possible with the storm." His eyes flickered toward the windows to his left. But again, they didn't find me even for a second.

I watched him. "You want to give it away."

"I want to gift it," he corrected. "We're not going to drink it. We're not going to make a dent in it."

I laughed. Sin did not crack. I took a swig of the mead.

"How 'bout we tell the servants to have some? After I kick your ass in a game of Seven Daggers, we can bring them each a goblet."

In a single, fluid motion, Sin slid his cards off the table, fanned them in his hand, and leaned back in his seat.

I did the same and stole another look at his face. "You know what they say about a player who wears gloves?"

His reply was dry as fallen leaves. "Never trust a player who wears gloves."

I narrowed my eyes at him. "Shall we set the stakes?"

"Sure."

I was certain something was wrong. He was acting colder than usual. Being short with me. "If I win, you tell me why I am here. Explain to me what you're doing, what you're planning all alone in the dark corners of this place, why you really needed me."

"No."

"What—"

"I said *no*, Sersa."

"At the White Plume, you said we would start to build trust, Nessin."

"I reveal what is needed when it is needed. You need to know nothing at this time. Choose different stakes."

I slammed my fist and my cards on the table as I stood, kneading my palms into the table. The cards scattered face-up, my hand exposed. It didn't matter.

I leaned toward him, glaring.

Now, Sin looked at me.

"Withholding the truth from me does neither of us good. And it's all you seem to know how to do. You won't even talk to me."

"Sersa—"

"Quit saying my name like I'm a child."

"Then quit shouting like a child."

I scoffed and removed my hands from the table. I dropped them at my sides, and they reflexively curled into fists.

"Excuse me for wanting to know if all this"—I gestured to the room around us, implying our fake union—"still has a purpose. Spending our time holding up pretenses. Then not speaking a word to one another for days. You knew we'd be here for an entire moon cycle, yet you didn't warn me beforehand. You knew this would be a painfully slow dance, yet you did not tell me. You can continue to keep everything to yourself, but I think I know *something*." I leaned forward again, planting my palms on the edge of the table as I dropped my voice into a whisper. "I can walk away from all this and not lose anything I hadn't already lost. You, however…your stakes. I think yours are so enormous that you're terrified of losing, Nessin."

When I tried to head for the door, Sin thrust his hand forward and held my wrist in place.

His biting eyes flicked up to mine. Even sitting, he was almost as tall as me.

"You're right, Sersa. And you know what else? You want to know my stakes? You are here so that I can become the next Daemon King. You are *nothing more* than a tick off one little box in a list of ridiculous requirements. Failing is not an option for me as much as it isn't for you. You came here knowing the stakes already. Pretend to be my wife—"

"I recall the word *intended*."

He continued right over me. "—and I help you find your father when we get back to Nos Ovscura. I have held up my end of the deal so far, despite the delay of being here. Keep holding up your end until we can part ways for good."

"I can't wait for that day," I snarled as I yanked my hand away and stormed toward the door, Dúma on my heels.

25

Voices trickled out of the dining hall the next morning.

The pair was so boisterous, howling with laughter, that I heard them at the top of the stairs outside mine and Nessin's rooms.

I descended the steps and maneuvered through the archway that connected to the dining hall. I hadn't thought to change out of my nightgown and housecoat, but I pulled the velvet ribbons tighter as I entered the hall and grimaced.

Thane Elittes was here.

Thane, who'd said Devlin and Nessin should have chosen betrothed from the High Houses.

I gritted my teeth.

"Good morning, love," Nessin said in the expertly fake tone of a lovesick man. "You remember my friend Thane, no?"

Thane smirked at me, daring me to tell Nessin that he'd asked me to dance with him all so his half-sister could kiss my husband.

Fake husband, I reminded myself.

"How could I forget?" I said aloud.

"I certainly haven't forgotten," Thane replied. His brown eyes glimmered like when we'd met. "I never got to apologize for that random nosebleed when we were dancing. I assure you, Princess, it will never happen again."

He was right on that much because I'd never dance with him again.

"My nose doesn't even bleed during fights," he continued, "let alone while dancing. My opponent can hit me a dozen times, I swear it, and I will not shed one drop."

"I'll take you up on that challenge," I said sweetly. I threw in a wink for good measure as I sat across the table from him.

Nessin sat at the head again.

I knew Thane understood my intentions. A threat.

"Aye," Nessin said with a chuckle. "I will take you up on that as well."

"Or I *would* take you up on it," I started, wrinkling my brow with mock concern. "If only I weren't feeling *so* nauseous the last few weeks. And terribly hungry at the same time," I added theatrically. "Oh, perhaps I should have a healer confirm whether I'm with child, Lord Thane. You did mention it when we were dancing. Maybe you're right. You men are so intuitive when it comes to women's bodies, no? What do you think, my prince? Might the Daemon Line's seed be as powerful as Prince Lochlainn claimed?"

As I cut Nessin a deadpan stare, he choked against the lip of his chalice.

Thane grinned, flashing his palms as if he were conceding and agreeing to shut up. "You and the prince would know best." He leaned forward then, stretching his fist onto the table. "Have you been training for the fights?"

Sin recovered in time to scoff. "Train. I don't need to train."

"Says the man I beat not a moon ago."

"Oh, shut up. Archery does not count, and aren't trusty friends of the prince supposed to let said prince win every time?"

"Still beat you. And what kind of friend would I be if I went easy on you? Your ego needs to be checked every now and again. Maybe when you're king."

I quirked a brow as I grabbed two pieces of toast and started to slather them in butter. Butter would solve my problems. "What fights are we referring to?" I asked.

"The week we return to Nos Ovscura, three fights between my brothers and me will take place."

"Think of it as a prelude to the upcoming…" Thane trailed off under Sin's cautionary look.

"Trials are held in Clais to determine the High Queen or King too," I said, pinning Sin with my gaze.

Stellera and Helde had told me about the trials already. Why didn't he want to talk about them?

Eyes narrowed, Sin cleared his throat. "The winner of the fights will inherit the estate of their choosing, excluding the Daemon King's Citadel."

"And which will you choose?" I asked, reaching for the jam.

"Whichever my wife wants. Though I'm partial to this one."

Thane looked between us. "Oh, don't make me sick. I don't want to hear about all the memories the two of you are making."

Sin rolled his eyes. "Anyway, I'm glad you came." He pushed out his chair and stood. "Let's head upstairs. I've been meaning to talk to you about a few things. We need to catch up."

When my gaze lifted to Sin's again, his reflected no guilt. I glared at him, wanting to smack the two tittering boys who'd woken me up with all their laughing and reminiscing.

Sin could confide in his ass hat of a friend but not me.

I hated him. I hated them both.

After they left, I took a massive bite of my toast and reached for the steaming plate of hotcakes.

Dúma and I headed to her training session a few minutes after breakfast, but Era was blocking the doors that led outside.

"Today is a difficult lesson for some," she said.

I slid my fur-lined cloak over my shoulders, securing it at the front, and then put on my gloves. "What's the lesson?"

Era raised a cage dangling near her hip. Inside was a hare. "Tracking and hunting."

"Dúm's piss." I swallowed and shook my head.

"Aye."

"Dúma's ready to hunt?" I'd fed her whatever animal had been caught and skinned each day over the last week, but they'd never been whole, let alone alive. My gut roiled at the thought.

"She was born ready to hunt," Era said. "I understand if you want me to handle this lesson on my own. I wouldn't have you watch something like this if you can't stomach it, Princess. But this is a vital part of Dúma's training."

My brow furrowed. "No, no. I know it is."

"She deserves to hunt her own meals. Dúma is not a house pet, and we must remember that."

"Of course." I nodded at the door and pushed it open for Era.

She looked over her shoulder at me and grinned. "We can have her sniff you out a loose potato under the fresh layer of snow if you like."

I snorted and followed her outside, Dúma sticking close to my flank. As soon as her paws hit the snow, she bounded ahead of us.

"Dúma, heel!" I called.

She halted, plopped her bottom on the ground, and waited for me to catch up before continuing. She tilted her snout up at me, red eyes darting across my face.

We didn't need her finding another deity. Who knew which we'd get this time?

"Good girl," I said. She wagged.

Era squinted at Dúma. "She's certainly gotten the hang of that. And she's grown. We'll have to weigh her today."

Her black fur had grown a bit since Sin had given me her, but I couldn't see any difference in her size. "How much should she weigh?"

"Her dam was five hundred and twenty pounds. Her sire was almost six hundred."

I blinked in disbelief at the thought of the little pup next to me growing that much. "Then she'll be hunting a lot."

"Indeed, she will, Princess."

Draea and Innes were waiting outside around the corner for us in a patch of faint diurnal moonlight. The Cradled Moons still confused me when I looked at the sky, but I ignored them and approached the others.

Draea rubbed my shoulder. "We figured you could use a little moral support today."

I pressed my lips into a thin line.

"It's one hare," I said.

"Regrettably, the hare is the warm-up," Era called over her shoulder.

I urged Dúma to go on, and she padded over to her. All her instincts drew her to the cage Era set on the ground. Dúma sniffed it fiercely, tail stiff and hackles raised. When Era commanded her to stay, she reached for the cage door and released the hare. It bolted through the trees. Impressively, Dúma obeyed. But her bright eyes widened, and her snout reeled left and right, keeping track of the hare's path. Her nose worked, twitching impatiently.

"Go," Era said calmly.

Dúma darted between the trees on powerful legs, and it was then I saw her change in size. Her legs were no longer the cute little knobs they'd been. That explained why holding her was beginning to hurt my arms. Soon, I wouldn't be able to pick her up at all.

I turned away, unable to look.

But I heard it all.

I squeezed my eyes shut, and Draea patted my back. "There, there, dear. It's nature."

Something told me I was being watched. I looked up, meeting Thane's gaze from a third-floor window. I glared at him over Draea's shoulder, and he looked at me until Sin appeared beside him.

I spent the next day trying to eavesdrop on Sin and Thane's conversations, but they took strolls in the snow and whispered when they were inside. Gone was the rowdiness they'd woken me with the day before.

When they excused themselves to take a walk after dinner, I decided to take matters into my own hands. I had asked Innes to watch Dúma earlier. She'd agreed eagerly and called my hellhound *cute*. I wondered if she'd still think that in a few moons. Sin and Thane gathered their cloaks—always handy and draped on the back of an armchair near the fireplace in the dining hall—and navigated toward the nearest exit.

I didn't have time to run upstairs and grab a cloak, but after two nights of the same thing, I'd dressed as warm as I could without giving myself away. My dress had a fur collar and pockets, from which I fished a pair of mittens I'd hidden. I slipped them on and tiptoed after them.

But as soon as I was outside, I realized they were heading into the woods.

I bit back my superstitions and my fears of seeing the High Triad again and skittered toward the first layer of trees. I hid behind an evergreen that served as a good vantage point, its thick, drooping branches weighed down and caked with ice.

But while I could see Sin and Thane well enough, they were far enough that the howling wind concealed every few words.

I closed my eyes and focused, trying not to think about my body shuddering from the cold, my lips growing more chapped by the second, or my dainty shoes soaked all the way through.

"—will act soon," Thane said. He hammered his fist into his palm as if trying to get past Sin's thick skull and prove his point. *"Trust me when I say the rest of the Elittes back Lochlainn with every beat of their cold hearts. They do not want to see you on the throne, Sin. They would rather die trying to prevent it. I would know better than anyone."*

I veered an inch around the tree's edge. Snow clung to my eyelashes. I blinked the icy flakes away and hid myself again.

Elittes. The House of Elittes. Thane's family.

Another stolen glance told me Sin didn't want to hear it. He scowled between the trees, eyes fixed on something.

"The Daemon King has decreed a search for Sersa's father, Sin. He knows he was taken by the Sluagh a year ago. He knows he was serving a High House in Gilders Eye and recently resold."

All the blood drained from my face, and I almost lost my balance.

"You're certain?"

"Yes. Soon enough, he will figure out which servant of which High House bought Bain Scáth. The Daemon King will close in on Sersa's father before we know it. I promise you that. His decree means he suspects something—and his eyes will land on her."

I shifted one foot on top of the other. My entire body was mere minutes from turning to ice—from dropping to the snow and giving up. The bite of the wind through my dress stung every inch of my skin. I wrapped my arms around my middle and tried to shield my face from the snow against the tree.

Sin said something I couldn't hear as the wind cried again.

Thane interrupted. "*Your father has visited mine at the Crescendo a dozen times since you left. They are handling their dealings right under my nose. I swear to you. You're not safe, and neither is she. They know what she is to you.*"

Though I didn't understand everything, I'd been convinced of one thing the first time I'd met Thane. He could *not* be trusted.

But now—now, my mind was racing. The Daemon King suspected I was here to find my father. How had he caught on so quickly, and worse, what moves had he made since we'd been away?

I furrowed my brow, suddenly more alert. Less cold. More focused.

"*They mean to deteriorate you bit by bit,*" Thane continued. "*You know that, and you don't want to put a target on her back.*"

Sin needed me to become Daemon King. Rather, he needed *a* Daemon Queen—not necessarily me. It didn't much matter to him if I became a target or if I was a target already. He'd told me from the start. He'd chosen me because I could protect myself, and I didn't expect or want him to protect me.

Sin scoffed. "*They won't do anything. Bluffs.*"

"*Won't they? I know you would protect her at all costs. No matter what it costs you. You may fool others. But never me.*" Thane shook his head of pale brown curls. "*All I'm saying is you need to be mindful. You don't want the Daemon King setting his daemons on you, Sin. Or her.*"

"I need to think. I– I need the night. I'll have my answer to you before you leave in the morning."

Thane nodded but didn't follow Sin as he strode toward me. Panicked, I dropped behind the foliage. But the snow was icy, and I was forced to kick my foot out to catch my balance.

I heard the side door into the fortress slam shut.

Then a clear of the throat.

"He's gone. You can come out, Princess."

It wasn't just the cold that froze me to the bone.

"You could die out here tonight, you know."

I uncoiled my shaking limbs and pulled myself to standing.

Thane was in front of my tree. He wrapped his cloak around me, and I sighed at the warmth. "If Sin sees us, he'll kill me. Come on."

"If it's so cold, then why were you two out here?" I growled.

He didn't answer. My legs protested when I tried to follow him. With a sigh, he picked me up. The points along my legs, my back, and my arms where he held me stung with pain from the bite of the wind.

Thane brought me somewhere unexpected. The barn.

He set me down on a barrel of hay before turning on his heels and shutting the enormous doors to ward off the chill. I huddled in his cloak, pulling my legs to my chest. My teeth chattered, vibrating my entire face, and my nostrils and lashes were frozen.

"Are you always this reckless?" he asked, surprisingly gentle.

"I didn't think it was this cold."

"I'm not talking about the weather. Sin doesn't want you involved in any of this."

"I know." Blood was beginning to return to my limbs. "But my father—tell me what you know about him."

Thane held my gaze for a long time. "How much did you hear?"

"What is there to hear?" I countered.

"The Daemon King has clearly had his spies doing their research on you and your brother. This is speculation, but perhaps he found his sons choosing non-Gilder siblings for their betrothed too coincidental."

"Then Ciel is in danger too."

"Oddly enough, my father and the king only spoke of *you*. Do you have any idea why?"

"N-No. Will you tell me why Sin doesn't want me involved? I also want to know why you helped your sister Aislinn kiss him," I growled.

"Because I want my family to believe I am loyal. The more people you play in the game, the better your odds of success."

"Does that mean you're playing Sin?" I snapped.

Thane held my gaze for a long time. "You're in love with him."

"*Excuse me?*" I choked on a laugh.

"You heard me."

"Love doesn't exist, according to you."

"That isn't what I said."

Thane sat on the hay barrel in front of me. His arms hung between his legs, and he hunched slightly as he tore a piece of hay free. He straightened and started twirling it around his pointer finger.

"And you were a first-rate gentleman when we met, were you now?"

He shrugged. "I was wrong about the two of you. A gentleman can admit when he's wrong."

"Well, there is nothing going on between Sin and me, so you're half-right because you're still wrong."

Thane hummed annoyingly.

"I won't tell him a thing," I said. "I only want to know why I'm here. That's it."

His brown eyes narrowed. "You say that like this is a temporary arrangement, Princess."

"I—"

Thane grinned. He was messing with me. He knew about mine and Sin's agreement. "Is it really all that difficult to put together yourself, Princess?"

I glared at him. "If I had worked it out myself, I wouldn't be asking."

"Let's work through it, shall we?" he said in an even voice. "That way, I didn't tell you."

I sat up straighter. Warmth seeped back into my hands and face. The trembling lessened, and I became painfully aware of my other senses. The barn *reeked*.

"Start with what you know," he said.

"I know I'm here to..." I didn't trust him enough to say it aloud.

"Act as Sin's temporary betrothed," he finished for me, waving his hand to reel it out of me. "Well, his wife."

"Yes," I grumbled.

"And you want to find your father, Bain Scáth."

He knew everything. How much did Sin trust Thane?

I gritted my teeth.

"And Sin wants to be Daemon King," I added.

"To be Daemon King, he needs…"

"Me."

"Not necessarily you. Any old—"

I tore a fist of hay free and chucked it at him. "What, has Sin given you a set of responses that will piss me off too?"

His dark bronze face twisted up as he spit out a piece that'd gotten in his mouth. "Yes, this is the script where I purposely help an ungrateful mortal, all while earning the wrath of Dúm's less cheerful cousin."

We glared at one another for a long moment.

Thane looked around before he continued. "For Sin to become the Daemon King, Princess, what needs to happen?"

The king needed to die.

The realization hit me like a battering ram.

Sin was going to murder the Daemon King and take his place.

His own father.

My mouth hung open in silence and disbelief, and Thane leaned forward to wink at me.

"There you are, Princess."

26

Thane left the next day.

I didn't say goodbye or thank you, and I didn't think I owed him that. If anything, I was entitled to the information he'd provided. But now, the thought of spending an additional two and a half weeks alone with Sin was inconceivable. Especially when he might be planning something he couldn't return from.

Patricide. Regicide. A dozen other crimes, surely.

I recalled what he'd told me weeks ago.

The less you know, the better. That way, you won't be held culpable as my accomplice if anything happens.

With this information turning over and over in my mind, I found myself restless and distracted, my appetite for Sin subsiding—and thank the skies it had. Trapped in a snowy mountain fortress for four weeks was enough of a challenge. I didn't need to be trapped with Sin indoors *and* fighting off cravings for him. Though I knew what would preoccupy the other couples' minds and bodies, working them toward exhaustion each day and night, that was not an option for us.

Part of me still wished we'd never ventured into that territory at all.

Sin had grown quieter by the day, more focused, and he had retreated to the point that I knew what he was doing—plotting.

During the day, he locked himself in a study on the third floor. At night, he hardly slept. Meanwhile, my sleep deepened, dragging me under, night and day. After Dúma and Era's daily training sessions, it was all I wanted.

As I noted the shift in Sin's mood, mine started to shift too. I'd unconsciously sponged others' emotions since I was a child. By no means was it Sin's fault, but the lack of banter, the lack of danger from being in the Daemon King's presence, or the descent from all that had happened the last couple of weeks urged the spiral.

I didn't know what day it was, and I could barely get out of bed. The only thing that got me up was Dúma's needs, but even Innes insisted she take care of her after I'd worried her, as she kindly put it.

The next day, I couldn't be bothered to let Draea brush my hair, even when she warned me it would only get more tangled, and she'd have to rip out the knots. The comment made me snicker under my breath. I rolled my back to her. It was funny she thought I cared. Dúma coiled next to me for days on end, staring at me when I managed to open my eyes. On Sin's pillow, she laid her snout on my arm and blinked behind long black lashes. I stroked her fur until I fell asleep again.

It was more than a lack of desire to get out of bed. I *couldn't*. My body felt so heavy, every joint ached, and my mind moved from racing to slower than dripping honey. My fears made it race, and the feeling of fragility, my inability to save Pa, made it slow.

The two extremes warred with one another, ridding me of any opinion or say of which I wanted to win.

Then there was Ciel. I couldn't protect him now, and not when we returned to the City of Soulless. Not *ever*. He was in Devlin's hands, and who knew whether that was a good or a bad thing?

I'd agreed to Sin's deal knowing precisely what I was getting. *Who* I was getting.

But Ciel—Ciel had not thought any of it through. He'd leaped without a net. I didn't know what to do for him, for myself, for anyone. I was going to fail in saving Pa. We both were, and I didn't think I could live through such a failure, through dealing with Pa's absence again.

I buried my face in the pillows and sobbed until I was sure I'd run myself dry. Dúma licked my salty tears, but it didn't make me laugh.

Days passed this way.

I didn't know how many days had gone by as they all blurred together, the drowning waves merging one after another, but I heard fragments of whispers, which I discarded until a Druidess showed up in mine and Sin's rooms.

"*She is unwell, I think. Please help,*" said a rasped voice filled with concern.

Sin.

The Druidess checked me over, asking me questions about how I felt, but I couldn't begin to describe the blueness swathing my eyes. Sin had stood in the corner watching me, his arms crossed and face expressionless as ever.

"*She must rest,*" was all the Druidess said as she helped me lower back onto the plush covers.

So, rest I did when they all finally left me alone.

"*Sersa?*"

Ciel's voice stirred me. A weight tipped the bed.

My eyes fluttered open and landed on my brother. I blinked several times, certain I was dreaming.

I was on my side, hands tucked under my head. The shoulder I laid on ached from being in one position too long. Inhaling deeply, the mingled but faint scents of sweet orange and lavender coiled under my nose. I noted the jar of oils next to my bed.

Ciel and his Druidry.

I definitely wasn't dreaming.

He looked over his shoulder. His husband stood before the doorway near a display table with an enormous bouquet in a crystalline vase. The prince wore a pale blue ensemble that looked so wrong in the darkness of the castle, while Ciel wore an off-white tunic tucked into dark blue pants. A fur-lined cloak draped his shoulders. It was dusted in melting snow, but both their cheeks had color to them that they hadn't weeks before.

"We brought you some flowers from Fient, Sersa," said Devlin. "I'm afraid they wilted a bit on the ship and in the cold. But we thought you might like them nonetheless."

For the first time in days, I smiled softly. Something about his calm tone of voice and thoughtfulness did it. "Thank you, Prince Devlin. That was very kind of you."

"Devlin, may I have a moment alone with my sister?"

Devlin bowed his head at Ciel like their roles were reversed, and I squinted to be sure I'd seen what I had. He left the room, shutting the door on his way out. My raw eyes stung as I tried to focus on Ciel's face.

Dúma had draped herself across his lap.

"I hear you named her after the god of death," he said as I watched her. "I must say she is quite the ham. I love her already."

"Me too."

Ciel studied me for a long moment. "How do you feel? Prince Nessin sent for us. He said you were unwell. Said he couldn't hear your thoughts because you wouldn't get up or open your eyes long enough to do so either."

After so many days of crying and sleeping, I was surprised these words didn't make me cry.

I forced another smile as I sat up in bed and played with the knitted blanket twisted around my legs, restricting my movement.

My brother had uprooted his own honeymoon for me. I was ashamed. Ashamed I needed help. Ashamed I couldn't get out of bed. Ashamed I wasn't strong enough to fend off the darkness alone.

As a gods-damned surprise tear slid down my cheek, I licked my lips and tasted salt. My vision tinted blue, bluer than it'd been in over a year, and Ciel frowned.

"I can feel it, Sersa. What you feel. I'm so sorry." He pressed a hand to his chest, and I panicked. I tried to pull back, pried mentally at the air, but he squeezed my hand. "It's okay. I'm here for you. You're never alone in this." Through glazed eyes, Ciel added, "Is it cruel I'd rather you be sad than angry? I'd rather not have my eyes bleed."

I laughed through my tears, making a horrible sound. It was gruesome I laughed at all, but then Ciel and I turned hysterical, laughing until my gut hurt. My magic when I was enraged *was* the worst of them all, but it shouldn't have been funny.

Still, it was much needed.

I was glad he was here.

He hugged me tightly, and the blueness faded to a paler tint that reminded me of Devlin's clothes. Dúma stretched out onto my legs and yawned. She was definitely heavier. I could barely breathe with her dead weight on me.

"Do you think you'd like to eat something?" he asked. "And maybe take a walk?"

Pressing my lips together, I nodded and wiped away the leftover tears. "That sounds nice. I can try to eat."

"Wonderful. Because I asked the kitchen to start on your favorite. Fresh bread, Pa's vegetable stew, and hard cheese. I jotted down the soup recipe for them."

"Leave it to you to remember it by heart."

As Dúma jumped down, Ciel helped untangle me from the blankets. Draea was there to help brush the knots from my hair—and knots there were—but she was gentle. She didn't say she'd told me so, and I squeezed her hand in thanks.

Ciel waited outside while I bathed and got dressed.

The warmth of the lavender water brought me back to life, and while the low hadn't passed, I realized that Ciel and I hadn't made up after our last fight. It was all I wanted to do presently.

That and see Sin.

Ciel's presence might help my head level out, and I needed to keep a level head if we were going to find Pa together.

Draea selected a deep red velvet dress with a sweetheart neckline, and long sleeves made of lace. As I stood in front of the mirror, examining the person who had been a husk of nothing but desolation just this morning, I looked almost revived.

Draea's expression betrayed nothing as she stood behind me and squeezed my shoulder.

"Sometimes when I feel at my worst, looking my best helps

convince me that I will not feel this way forever, that I am not defined by what I feel, Sersa."

She was right. I wouldn't feel how I had forever, but the waves would always come and go, and despite myself, I was beginning to understand that controlling the boat that rocked me, that threatened to throw me overboard at times, wasn't always going to work.

Maybe I would have to learn to wait out the storms as they came, to learn simply how to stay afloat.

27

At dinner that night, Sin reiterated the folkloric beliefs about the woods—the ones he'd told me weeks ago. I tried to focus on the tales, many of them familiar, but I couldn't stop thinking about the way he'd held me against his chest when I came down the stairs earlier. He hadn't met my eyes for more than a second, and even when he'd squeezed my hand and led me to my seat at the table, he'd been gentle and unsmiling. Not the Sin I knew.

"We used to come up here and hunt," Devlin said, spinning the wine in his chalice. "Our mother would always tell us the stories. She said the gods were watching us from the woods. Jestin insists he saw a goddess. A beautiful maiden who told him he'd be Daemon King one day."

I set my serviette on the table and leaned back in my seat. After eating nothing for a few days, I had eaten so little but felt stuffed. The vegetable stew had taken ages, and I'd spoiled my appetite on the hard cheese and bread. By the time the soup was done, I'd only taken a few sips to warm me up.

Sin chuckled. "I remember that trip. Jestin couldn't have been more than four. He wasn't allowed to hunt yet, but he was already stubborn as any Drumghoul."

"We haven't stopped mocking him to this day," Devlin said.

"Maybe he *will* be Daemon King one day," Ciel said, hiding a grin behind his chalice as he took a sip. "The gods do lurk in forests."

Of course Ciel knew that.

Devlin pressed a hand to his heart. "Well, because *I'd* rather be taken into the Faerie Forest for a hundred years than be king, all the gold in my vault is on Sin."

"Naturally, you'd rather the Fae whisk you away and fondle you for a hundred years." A lazy grin pulled at Ciel's lips, and Devlin shook his head, taking a generous sip of wine.

"I will drink to that," said Sin.

Ciel and Devlin raised their chalices in a toast. My eyes didn't deceive me as they shared a glance. It was demure still but crystal clear. My brother and Devlin were besotted with one another. Part of me was relieved Devlin was capable of kindness as my brother had said, affection even, and that he'd kept up what I'd witnessed at our wedding.

Another part of me still feared what would happen in the coming weeks and how the situation would unravel.

Sin and I shared a look.

"Here, here," said Devlin.

"I believe it," I said. "About the gods lurking in the woods. Nev came to me."

"When we were children?" Ciel asked, brow furrowing. A hint of his smile remained but slowly faded. His lips were berry red from the wine.

"A few days..." I blushed. I'd laid in bed for more than a few days. "A week or so ago. Dúma found them. Though I doubt it was a coincidence." I didn't know the risks in admitting this aloud, but I wanted to see what they thought. "Nev also presented themselves to me when we visited the Druids' parish."

"What did they say?" Devlin asked, shocked.

Sin's eyes narrowed.

"They wanted to strike a stupid bargain was all."

"You did not take it," Sin said. It wasn't a question.

Still, I shook my head. "I may be reckless at times, but I'm no fool."

"What was the bargain?" Ciel pressed.

They all believed me. I had barely believed it when Nev appeared.

"That is between me and the High Triad," I said with a weak laugh.

"A little more wine and you may spill yet," Ciel said.

Devlin cleared his throat, eyeing the last sip in his glass before thinking and setting it down. "After tonight, I think none of us will crave wine for at least a year."

"Aye," Ciel said, downing the rest of his chalice. "We already finished our barrel of mead. How 'bout you two?"

I shook my head.

"We should be headed to bed before a century's worth of secrets start to spill," said Devlin. "My brother has no mercy in the art of embarrassing his own flesh and blood. Also, the journey back to Fient will be long and rocky. The Wraithsea was angrier than most days when we came here. *Oh.*" He turned his eyes to me, nudging his chalice toward the top of his placemat. "Sersa, are you sure you're feeling better? How rude of me. We can absolutely spare a few more days. Whatever you need. And the offer still stands. The two of you are more than welcome to join us in Fient for the next week. The constant Bloom-like weather, the endless light, and the flowers alone would do anyone some good."

"Does the Dark not reach Fient?" I asked.

"No, it's the only isle in the Soullands that doesn't succumb to the total darkness," Devlin explained. "I always go there during the season. Ciel and I were talking, and we will likely vacation there when it strikes."

The Dark was the upcoming season following the Rime. The Bloom wouldn't actually start for several more moons.

"Thank you again for the offer," I said, "but I'm not really up for a trip right now. Unless Sin wants to."

Finally, he met my gaze and held it.

Sin waved his fingers but didn't look away from me. "I'm more the frigid and dark type. Climate, that is. You two deserve to get back to your honeymoon."

Ciel and Devlin both grinned distractedly.

Before they excused themselves and ducked out of the dining hall, I stood. "Ciel?"

Devlin kept walking and lingered down the hall, giving us another moment of privacy in the doorway. Undoubtedly, Sin was listening, but it hardly mattered. He'd witnessed our fight after all.

I stammered on my words. "I wanted to say I'm sorry for yelling at you—"

Ciel pulled me into an instant hug, crushing me against his chest. "I already forgave you. And a lot of what you said... You were right. Please forgive me, and *please* take care of yourself."

"I forgive you, and I will. I meant to ask about Devlin—he's been taking care of you, right? Treating you right, I mean."

"He's been nothing shy of a gentleman," Ciel said with a glint in his eyes. "Except when I ask him not to be."

A snort escaped me, and I cupped a hand over my mouth.

"I'll see you back in Nos Ovscura." I veered around Ciel to see Devlin grinning at his back. "Have *fun*."

"What is life without a little fun, Sers?" Ciel winked then met Devlin at the end of the hall. They intertwined their arms, and I watched them leave with a smile on my face.

After I returned to the dining hall, I retook my seat and stared into the fire, feeling light for the first time in days. "Well, our brothers are definitely in love, and I think that's the best thing to come from this so far. Until one of them rips the other's heart out."

"Why must it end badly?" Sin asked.

My eyes slid to his. "We know how this is going to end, don't we?"

"Do we?" He stood, tossing his serviette onto the table. "Would you like to go to bed as well then?" His eyes were still cold but thawing.

"I've slept so much the last few days. I wonder if the kitchen has any lemon balm tea. The Druids recommended it for when I'm feeling restless."

"Why don't we go check together?"

I nodded and followed him through the dark corridors.

There were a hundred jars on a shelf in the shadowy kitchen, and none of them were labeled. We stood side by side, sniffing each of the spices and herbs until we located some dried lavender. It took us a few minutes more to find orange peels and the lemon balm.

"Aha," Sin said.

I went to unscrew the jars and gather the tea kettle beside the fireplace, but he waved his hand, pointing me toward two armchairs.

"You sit. I will prepare it. It's the least I can do."

I nodded, watching him work with curiosity for a few minutes. He finished quickly and grabbed the hissing tea kettle with a towel. "We'll have to let it steep and cool for a few."

"How did a prince learn to brew tea?" I asked as he joined me in the armchairs by the fire.

"My mother was a heavy tea drinker."

"I'm sorry for what your father did," I blurted. "I don't know if I told you before."

Pain crossed his face but only for a second as he stared into the hypnotically twisting flames. "Yes. Devils, all of us, as I said."

"A devil wouldn't know how to help me. Sending for Ciel—it was the best thing you could have done when I was like that. Thank you."

"I have motives for wanting you to be well, Sersa. I had no idea what to do for you. It..." Sin swallowed and shook his head.

"What, so you can enjoy your Soullander delicacy?"

The glower on Sin's face told me he didn't appreciate my attempt to cut the tension. He cleared his throat to steer the subject back on track. "Ciel told me you can make others feel what you feel, apart from some other useful gifts."

"Dúm's piss," I cursed. "Then he told you about the bleeding incident."

Sin narrowed his eyes, fighting a smile. "He may have alluded to it."

"It isn't funny."

"Not at all," he said, "but it's wicked good magic to have."

Indeed, it was.

"The man was fine," I said. "But Ma sent me with Ciel to the Druids for a week to learn to clear my mind."

"Did it help?"

"No. I have to be alone when I'm enraged. It's all that works."

"Maybe you simply haven't found the right person to have around during those times."

I considered this then said, "I made Thane bleed when we danced the night after the wedding. It was why I ran into the hall in the first place."

"I put it together at breakfast the other day."

"Right."

Sin's eyes grew thoughtful. "I wish I could feel what you were feeling the last week. I failed you. I should have realized something was wrong, but it was Draea and Era who came to get me. I didn't know what to do when the Druidess had no real advice, so I sent a letter to Ciel and Devlin. I had no idea what you needed," he repeated.

"You don't want to feel what I was feeling. And even if you did, I can't summon it at random."

"I can't imagine if you could make others feel what you're feeling. People might reveal their darkest secrets to you if you could make them feel fear or even at ease around you." He looked at me through a penumbra of black lashes as he tilted his chin down. "You could bend a person to your will. It would almost be the equivalent of a Bonespeaker's magic: the ability to influence people. But influencing others' emotions seems even more powerful than my commands."

"I can't control my own emotions, Sin, let alone other people."

"Understood." He flashed his palms, withdrawing his previous comment. "Can you feel emotions whenever you wish? Mine, for example."

"Do you have any of those?" I asked.

We both laughed. He stretched his long leg across the space between us to impishly nudge my foot.

"But no, I can't. I've only made a few people, those closest to me, feel things before and only when I'm..." I didn't want to call it *blue* aloud. I'd never told anyone about the colors. "Have you seen them before? The colors I see. Since you can see my thoughts."

Sin nodded, his expression soft. "Once or twice."

"Hm. That's embarrassing," I muttered.

"I don't want you to be embarrassed around me."

Silence stretched between us for a few moments. Finally, he

stood to pour us two cups of tea and then returned, handing me one. It warmed my hands, and I immediately took a sip to savor the heat.

"May I ask a question?" I asked.

Sin looked over the top of his cup. "I've never known you not to ask anyway."

Unease swirled in my gut. "You were avoiding me the last few weeks. Weren't you?"

Sin shifted in his seat, looking more uncomfortable than I'd ever seen him. He set his cup on the table beside him. Then he slid his hands onto his thighs, tapping his fingers in slow motion, thinking. His eyes shifted to mine, my lips, the rest of my face.

"Well?" I pressed.

"Being alone with you has made things difficult for me."

I didn't recognize the undertones in Sin's voice. It was flat, and yet... He sounded like he might be fighting the words.

"Because you want to eat my soul?" I offered again.

His eyes grew darker as the moment grew heavier. Each second he stayed quiet weighed on me.

"No, Sersa. Not because I want your soul. But we have been over this." He dropped his voice to a whisper as he leaned forward in his seat. "I am a monster."

"I think you want to convince yourself of that fact. I think that you think to rule a realm, you must be."

"Mustn't I? The Soullands aren't exactly a place of peace and happiness. It's a place of death, a place that exploits the living, those with souls, and thrives on depravity. Hell, I thrive on it. I *crave* it."

I wasn't sure what he was getting at.

Nessin planted gloved hands on the armrests as he stood. He took a step toward me then another.

My mind raced.

What was he doing?

He halted an arm's length away. Either he'd read my thoughts or... He looked as though he were stopping himself from prowling any closer. His eyelashes cast shadows onto his bony cheeks again, and his eyes turned dark in the dim light.

"I have found it difficult to be here with you because I find myself fixating on our time at the White Plume and in the gallery together.

Those memories circle my thoughts. They chase me. They devour me, Sersa."

Sin stood his ground, but I found myself leaning forward, eager to hear the rest of what he had to say.

"I've imagined you begging me," he said. "Oh, the things I've imagined. If you only knew, Sersa. I find myself wanting you more and more with each passing bell, and *that* is not what we agreed to. It's unexpected, and I know it cannot happen. Still, convincing myself..." Sin snickered, but it had to be forced because his nostrils flared, body stiffened, and hands flexed from the fists they'd made a second ago.

His reaction, his method to do away with these feelings, was to avoid me at all costs?

He held very still as he studied me. "Keeping my distance has not done away with any feelings I have for you. But lucky for us, I am an expert when it comes to curbing my desires."

My throat caught on a swallow.

I'm not.

"The choices we make will mark our success or our failure. Focus on our days ahead as we enter the Gilders' world is paramount. Above all else," he finished.

"Good to know," I whispered. It was all I could manage in my shock.

But inside...inside my heart raced fiercely, and I tried not to let my reaction show. Heat crept into my cheeks. I fisted my crimson skirt, and I gnawed on the inside of my lip.

"Anyway," Sin said, voice mastered once more. "We should get to bed. It's well after midnight, and I want us to have a productive day tomorrow."

Once we'd changed—him in the bedroom, me in the bathing room—I returned to our room and slid into bed beside Sin in utter silence. Blankets draped his legs. He held a book in his bare hands, his gloves on the nightstand.

Tonight, of all nights, he'd chosen to sleep shirtless.

I turned the opposite way and curled my hands under my head. Neither of us uttered a word. The minutes passed, and I heard no turning of the pages either. He took a breath. I matched him, trying to silence mine.

Then Sin shut his book, set it on the bedside table, and blew out the candles.

In the darkness, my mind wandered to every territory I hoped it wouldn't. I didn't sleep a wink, but I was almost back to normal.

And my appetite, my desire for Sin, had returned with a vengeance.

28

We spent the last few days of our honeymoon in a dance of politely rigid dialogues.

It was one we danced on our toes. Never looking each other in the eye. Never brushing our hands against one another's, even if we were close enough to touch.

Never uttering a word about what Sin had confessed over tea that night.

We pretended the conversation hadn't happened, and yet I knew neither of us had forgotten. How could he? How could I?

How would I *ever*?

Tension swirled in the air whenever we were near. I wondered if his thoughts were as occupied with it as mine were.

In the mornings, I found myself pathetically spending extra time dusting a bit of perfume on the crook of my neck. I told myself I was simply taking care of myself after the low I'd experienced or trying the expensive assortment because we'd never carry a scent so luxurious in Os Íseal.

Draea didn't question my sudden receptiveness to the dressing table in our room. Scattered with cosmetics and metal hair rods, gilded mirrors, and lace bralettes hidden in the drawers. She trimmed my hair and braided it into a crown one day, leaving my collarbones and shoulders exposed. She blotted my lips with berry stain the next day and pulled from the back of the wardrobe the dresses I'd been rolling my eyes at for weeks.

I swore even Dúma shook her head at me.

But I caught Nessin's gaze when we passed one another in the corridors—once—and that single look had me touching myself in the bath later, when he was off in some other corner of the fortress.

I didn't know what I was trying to do. Rather, I tried to deny myself the reasoning when secretly I loved torturing Sin. Didn't I? The stark shift from the darkness that had consumed me days before to thinking only of his confession, that I had left such a mark on his mind too, felt good. I had to admit it did.

Then, on the last day, I entered the dining hall to find a palette of watercolors and brushes beside my breakfast.

"What are these?" I sat down skeptically.

Sin raised his eyes from the large book he held for a second. "I found them lying around."

When our gazes met, his moved toward the snowy landscape beyond the windows. Never in a million years had I expected him to act timid, to fold as I looked at him.

I pushed my metal plate to the side and asked a servant if they had any paper. Before they could answer me, Sin rose from his seat and surprised me, taking the chair to my right. As he flipped his book open again and tore a blank sheet from the front, I couldn't help but laugh.

"Ciel would murder you for doing that."

Sin set the sheet in front of me. "Then it's a good thing we're alone."

I ran my fingers over the paintbrushes' stiff bristles, allowing them to scratch my skin. I selected a thin one. Leaning forward, I swirled it in my chalice of water and dipped it into the black circle. As my brush swished around, it created little paths of bubbles in its wake.

"What will you create?" he asked.

"Why don't you try some patience and wait to find out?"

Sin's lips twitched, but he didn't smile or even smirk.

I started with broad strokes, outlining distinct features I'd memorized. It shocked me how many details I managed to recall without ever looking at Sin.

A few minutes passed in silence. I knew the second he realized I was painting him. Whereas his gloved hands had been relaxed on the table before, his fingers curled under. My eyes flicked upward for the first time since I'd started.

"Did my brother tell you?" I asked.

"Tell you what?"

"That I like to paint. Or did you learn of it while visiting Os Íseal? I don't remember telling you if I did."

"When you met the king, you told him you were a painter. Why else would I have brought you to the gallery?" There was the slightest hesitation in his voice as he brought up our encounter there.

I kept my focus on the paper, on the lines I was touching up. "I did, didn't I?"

"Yes, and it appears you're quite talented." Sin reached for me unexpectedly and tucked a strand of hair behind my ear. His leather fingers grazed my cheek. My jaw.

I watched him, speechless. We sat close enough that either of us could reduce the distance to nothing in a heartbeat.

"Your hair was getting in the paint." He grabbed the strand, flipping it upside down. The black paint was hardly noticeable against my hair color.

He straightened in his seat, pulling away, and I added the finishing touches to his hair and scar before spinning the sheet of paper around and giving it a final tap.

"You're a good subject to paint. Very still. Plus, you have one expression—maybe two—so that part was easy."

"And what are my two expressions?" He pulled the paper toward him, eyes scanning it.

"Glaring and smirking. Though I suspect both have a thousand different meanings."

Finally, his lips quirked upwards. "You see me quite clearly."

Now, I was the one to laugh. "I highly doubt that. But if there's one thing I don't see in you, it's a monster. Maybe I did before."

Sin abruptly slid the paper back toward me before he stood and crossed the room, leaving the book on my side too. "You should keep it. Something to remember me by. A self-portrait of you would be a better gift to me."

Heat crept up my neck and into my cheeks. "It'd be difficult to paint myself."

Sin nodded curtly. "I suppose you're right. My memory will serve me fine when you return to Os Íseal."

We finished eating in silence, and I kept my eyes down in fear that he'd be watching me. But I couldn't stop looking at the painting of him.

A bell later, I focused on the book that identified the many Gilder families—the members of the Circle, mainly—in the library. Sin periodically directed me to a page with a folded ear, another offense in my avid reader brother's eyes. Sometimes he leaned over me, as close as was reasonable, to point out the passage he meant me to read. When he stayed in his seat, usually across the table that we'd taken over in the library, Sin would watch me leaf through the book for the next marked passage. But a few times I saw his gloved hands grip his own book tighter, like he wanted to get up as he had at breakfast to be next to me.

At least I told myself this.

I was testing myself on the names and faces of the Circle when Sin cleared his throat.

"There is a hot spring in the fortress cellar." He shut his book slowly as if trying to slow his next words down too. "It's not really in the cellar. The fortress was built into the mountain, and it's hidden in a cavern burrowing through it. You ought to go there before we leave. Not with me. Alone," he added. "It's quite peaceful."

He'd rushed to say we didn't have to go together. Maybe we *shouldn't* go together.

"You can show me if you like," I said.

Sin schooled his expression deftly. "Sure. We can go there after dinner. Night is when the water is at its most temperate."

29

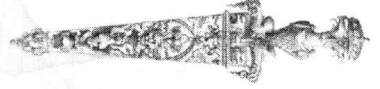

Neither of us ate a thing.

We picked at our food like fussy children, pushing it around on our plates for minutes at a time before taking a single bite. I didn't have a taste or a stomach for mead, and neither did Sin apparently, because we wasted the jugs the servants had set out, one on both ends of the table that felt like it was a hundred paces instead of barely five.

Sin rose from his seat in silence, and I followed to our rooms, heart pounding so loud, so fast, I swore he heard it too. There, Draea had left us two robes as plush as clouds. She ushered Dúma away and told us to enjoy ourselves. Her simple gesture made my gut flip.

I went into the bathing room to strip off my clothes, *agonizingly* aware that I would be nude in a spring of steaming water with Sin in minutes. I abandoned my clothes in a heap, gathered my hair off my neck with a ribbon, and met him in the corridor. His robe parted in a V down his chest, the tie at his waist loose.

A key looped around his finger. "Ready?"

I nodded.

Though I didn't know where we were going, we walked in step with one another as we descended into the crypts. The stone corkscrew stairs had no railing, but they were wide enough for us to walk with space between. Sin took the outside. Torchlight flickered across his high cheekbones, arched brows, and scarred lip.

"Have you always been afraid of heights?" he asked.

"Only since I fell off Dúm's Cross."

We retreated into silence until we reached the bottom of the stairs and a wooden door. Sin slid the key into the lock and jiggled the rickety handle to push it open.

The sparsely lit cavern ahead stole my breath. Pale blue water shimmered in several pools, each separated by a rocky ledge that looked like they'd been sanded down smooth. Steam coiled in tendrils above the water, and the air was so thick it offered privacy between each separate pool.

"It's not as hot as it looks. Please." Sin gestured to the pools, and I headed toward the furthest.

He hung back and turned away from me. I realized he was being a gentleman, allowing me to get in the water first. I dipped my toe in and sighed with pleasure before peeling off my robe and lowering myself into the hot water. It eased every lingering ache from the days I'd spent in bed without moving. I bent my knees to stay covered by the shallow water and pulled the ribbon from my hair before dipping my head backward.

Water reached up to my cheekbones. I closed my eyes and breathed deep, but they reflexively snapped open when I heard Sin lower himself into the water.

He didn't quicken his movement. My gaze landed below his navel then lower still, all of him bared to me. And what a sight it was. The gods had not been stingy with him.

My gut dipped into my toes, and I scrunched up my face, closing my eyes again. If not for the heat, the certain blush in my cheeks would be undeniable.

"Sorry."

"No need for apologies, Sersa," Sin said flatly.

By the time I opened my eyes again, the water covered him. He sat on the step encircling the pool's edge.

Too bad because I wanted another look to assure my unraveling mind of the perfection that was Nessin Drumghoul.

"So." I attempted to sound normal. "Which Gilders' residence will we visit first?"

"The House of Alders," he said in a pragmatic voice. "Followed by the House of Berell."

"And what will we do there? Dinner, I presume."

"Always. Now that I think of it, we may need to conduct a lesson on table manners."

"Hilarious. I'll have you know that Pa taught us how to be proper, if ever necessary. I won't embarrass you or the Daemon King, I swear." I splashed him.

"Did you *splash* me?" His eyes widened, showing teeth in an expression that wasn't quite a smile as he raked his hair backward and straightened off the step. The shallow water barely touched his hips, leaving little to the imagination once again.

His muscles tightened. Taut, incredibly corded muscles that looked almost unnatural.

The water was steaming, but a chill raised the hair on my forearms.

As he swept forward and splashed me back, I moved out of range. I tried to keep my eyes up, away from his torso that seemed to draw my eye lower. He halted in the middle of the pool and bent his knees again, so the steamy water reached up to his shoulders.

"I was *going* to say that there will be a very competitive game of Seven Daggers at the House of Alders before you so rudely interrupted me." Sin swirled his bare hands in the water absentmindedly, but he kept his eyes locked on mine.

I wondered if he found himself trying not to look down too. He didn't strike me as the type to hide it though.

"It's a shame we didn't get to practice the other night then. I bet I would have beat you. My clan plays Seven Daggers like we drink ale. Every night."

"Is that so?" He raised an eyebrow.

My eyes dropped to his lips, curved into that notorious smirk.

One more taste won't kill me.

Sin's nostrils flared. My gods-damned thoughts again. I couldn't control them any more than I could control my magic.

Damn it all.

I moved closer and hooked one arm around his neck, allowing my hand to graze the scar just above his collarbone. The skin was surprisingly smooth.

I wrapped my legs around his waist under the water, and he coiled one arm around me, pulling me ever closer as if he'd been waiting for me to close the distance forever. As I became acutely aware of our bare chests pressed against one another, I wondered which part of our bodies he was focusing on right now.

I leaned forward and licked his lips, begging them to open for me. They did. *Oh*, they did.

He slid his hand under my jaw, fingers grazing my ear. Those small touches made my head spin in the most intoxicating way. His grip was firm yet gentle, keeping me close but giving me the chance to pull away first if I so desired. Our tongues moved slowly at first.

"Is this okay?" he whispered. "Tell me if it's not."

My kisses became more desperate, needing to shut him up, and he followed my urgency. He sensed how badly I needed him. This.

Us.

Sin buried his face in my neck, tracing soft kisses up and down my skin. Then he lowered his lips to my collarbone, the top of my breast.

"Is—"

"Ask me one more time, Sin."

He chuckled, working his way back up my neck until he locked our lips and tongues once more.

Sin braced one hand on my fleshy thigh under the water as he pulled away. He stared into my eyes. "What do you want, Sersa?"

Our gazes locked, and I had a single thought.

Everything. I wanted everything from him.

With a sound that was almost a growl, Sin closed the distance and again pried my lips open with his. I ran my fingers through his hair. He pulled away and found the top of my breast, sucking on the skin there. I gasped and arched my back, telling him where to go. His other hand trailed down my spine, raising chills along my entire body. Then he took my nipple in his mouth, curling his tongue around it with torturous slowness.

He moved again, leaving me breathless, guessing, the heat climbing in my body.

"You have *no idea* the things I want to do to you, Sersa." His whisper in my ear made me shudder. "I want to hear you cry out my name."

The hand on my thigh trailed up to my groin. His other hand coiled tighter around my waist as he found my center, drawing circles there.

I said his name.

He grinned against my lips, working me toward the peak before he halted. When he slid a finger inside me, my hips instinctively pressed into it.

I didn't expect his touches to be tender, but they were—mixed with potent desire. My moans grew louder, and I was certain the servants would hear me if Sin continued.

I didn't know exactly what I said next, but Sin lifted me out of the water and onto the step at the pool's edge. He spread my legs, his palms on my knees as he knelt on the top step before me.

Then he leaned forward, finding my center with his arousal.

The feeling ignited my body, sending pulses up my legs.

I waited and waited for both the pressure and the pleasure, but it never came.

As I lifted my head to look, Sin hung his. He'd halted. He'd gone from hot to cold all in the space of a breath. His fingers still gripped my thighs.

Startled by the sudden shift I felt in the air between us, my voice emerged shaky.

"Is– Are you okay?"

His entire body quivered. He released a vicious growl from deep in his chest.

"We—*can't*. Gods. We can't." Despite the strangled words, he schooled his expression as he pushed away from me, and I slid further back on the stone.

He pulled away so quickly, it was like we'd never been touching in the first place. Still lying flat on my back, I watched my belly fill with astonished breaths. My heart pattered in confusion and exasperation. Standing now in the center of the pool, Sin turned his back to me. I was forced to watch the expansion of each breath between his shoulder blades and the lean muscles there.

"I do not have as much control over myself as I'd hoped. For that, I am sorry," he said.

His prior words still drowned me, so much so I barely registered these.

We can't.

We can't.

We can't?

"This wouldn't change anything, Nessin... I mean, the gallery."

As soon as I uttered the words, I knew they were a lie. One of the best and worst I'd ever told.

"It would change everything for—" Sin paused and took another breath. "It would change everything," he repeated.

My face grew hotter and not from the balmy air rising up from the pool. Again, I felt mortified. I'd become so used to setting my sights on whoever I wanted back home. My infatuations were always more than willing.

But Nessin. He'd refused me.

No.

No, he'd restrained himself. I didn't understand why.

After I composed myself, I turned on the slippery step and out of the pool, yanking my robe off the ground. I didn't care in the least that he could see all of me now too.

Headed for the door without looking back, my wet feet slapped the stone.

As I put distance between us, I saw those pastels in place of deep red, and the exasperation was replaced by something else. Something I didn't recognize—or did not *want* to recognize.

This was more than lust.

Sure, every part of me wanted Sin. But this was something altogether much more potent.

This was innate. Unable to be undone by either of us.

I wouldn't allow myself to fall into this position again until he was crowned Daemon King, until I could watch him lower onto his knees to beg *me* with the Daemon King's torc around his neck.

Until Nessin wanted me so badly, he couldn't stand it.

30

The following day, we arrived in Nos Ovscura around midday. I was immediately rushed into preparing for the Alders' dinner party. I asked Draea to let me bathe alone, and as the steam filled mine and Sin's shared bathing room, I somehow managed to release some of my anger and fear as if the heat were extracting it from my pores.

Sin's words had stung.

We can't.

More than that, they'd confused me beyond belief.

But tonight, my sole purpose eclipsed all of it. If anything, Sin's demand to focus on our objectives propelled me into the state of mind I needed to get me through this.

It was time. But finding Pa would only muddle the waters for us. Last night, I'd wanted nothing more than for Sin to have and take me—even vowed that I would have him when he was Daemon King. I'd almost forgotten about his plots—or I no longer cared because of how badly I wanted him.

But how were *we* possible with my impending departure? It had always been the plan.

Find Pa. Leave.

A few bells later, Sin and I loaded into our private carriage as the others did the same. The Daemon King and Niuna shared the first carriage in the procession.

I hadn't said a word to Sin all day. He sat stiff as a board across from me, white eyes tracing the streets we passed. He hadn't made a sound, not even to breathe, until we reached the edge of Gilders Eye furthest from the Daemon King's Citadel.

"We need to be convincing tonight," he said abruptly. "We cannot raise any flags. Can you do that?"

I cut him a glare. He was staring out the little window, refusing to look at me.

"You asked me to do this for a reason, did you not?" I asked.

"Many reasons."

When the carriage halted, I exited first. I plastered a smile on my face as Sin caught up to me and hooked my arm through his. I didn't want to feel his skin on mine or the fire his touch left behind. Any reminder of last night might unravel me with fury or desire. I tried repeatedly to shove aside those thoughts, burying them with any feelings I had, but I looked down and saw a coil of black smoke curling around my wrist like a snake. I slid my hand into the folds of my dress as if I were adjusting it.

Sin took note, and unlike when my magic had appeared on our wedding day, he didn't pull me into a kiss to distract me.

"Do you need a moment?" he asked.

"If I need one, I will tell you."

"Your curtness with me is probably deserved."

"You think?" I snapped.

"I did not mean to put you in that position," he whispered. "I mean, I did—"

"*You* did not put me in that position, Nessin. I started it because I wanted it." *You.* I scoffed, shaking my head. "Why don't we focus," I mocked, "on having a good night?"

He hesitated. Silence.

"As you wish, Sersa," he finally said.

We followed the Daemon King beyond the gilded gates of the mansion, striding through a cobbled courtyard dotted with lanterns. A statue of the king loomed near the gold fence surrounding their property. Lanterns encircled it. It looked like a shrine, and I wondered if the Alders worshipped it.

Three marble steps led us into the entranceway. The mansion was as palatial as the Daemon King's Citadel, on a smaller scale, with gleaming cream-colored floors, papered walls in bold patterns, and enormous windows dressed in garish drapes. A little table sat in the middle of the grand foyer with the largest bouquet of red flowers I'd ever seen. The mansion's décor came from another time, far beyond the one in which House Scáth was trapped.

The Alders stood under an archway that connected the foyer to a vast parlor filled with Gilders. The Circle members wore the same gold necklaces they had at the wedding. Some boasted dangling pearl brooches, while others wore simpler jewels.

I thanked the skies they wore those gaudy necklaces. It was easy to identify them.

But now I needed an excuse to get close to them.

"I'll be searching their minds," Sin whispered in my ear. "Stay away."

At once, the lady of the house swept forward to greet Stellera, Helde, Ciel, and me. She gasped, pulling Ciel close to kiss him on both cheeks.

"I can see the resemblance between you two! Everyone, *everyone*, is chatting about Ciel and Sersa Scáth, the siblings from little ol' dingy Os Iseal, who have captivated the Daemon King's line. Pardon me! Ciel and Sersa *Drumghoul*." Lady Alders winked at Sin as he moved to shake hands with Lord Alders.

He, his brothers, and the Daemon King formed a circle. Their chatter was low, contained unlike the ladies' voices, and I hated how stratified these parties felt compared to back home. Here, I didn't feel like I could walk up to anyone and strike up a conversation. Here, I suspected I would be watched like a hawk. It was something in the air, something unseen yet *felt*. Judgment sparkled in the guests' eyes, waiting for someone to make a wrong move.

And I was an expert at it.

"And *you*." Lady Alders turned to face me as Devlin saved Ciel, pulling him into the circle of men beside us. "It is lovely to meet you, Princess Sersa."

Based on the way she greeted me, a tight hug like we were old friends rather than two kisses on the cheek, I wondered if the House of Alders supported Nessin's claim to the Daemon Throne too. Before I could sort through my suspicions, she titled her chin and full, red lips toward Stellera.

"The servants tell me your cycle is late, Princess." Lady Alders gave her a pointed look, and the feather in her hair only made her look more pretentious like she was entitled to this information.

Stellera's mouth opened an inch before she snapped it shut.

"I have ears everywhere," Lady Alders said with a wink, patting Stellera's hand.

Pale red, irritated shock flashed behind my eyes. "I hardly think that's your—"

Stellera cut me off. "If you must know, Lady Alders, my cycles are frequently late."

Lady Alders's eyes widened. "O-Oh." She turned to look at me. Again, pointedly. "And you, Princess?" She raised her brows at me with a gleam in her eye. "Have you started your cycle yet?"

I didn't miss the way Sin perked up, still standing in the next circle over.

"When was your last cycle, Lady Alders?" She wrinkled her nose at me, and I added, "Privacy is of the utmost importance, especially for princesses. Maybe you should have been a healer if you think yourself entitled to the status of other people's bodies and wombs."

Lady Alders smacked her painted lips but recovered quickly. "These things do take time. Well, not always. I was with child not a week after returning from my honeymoon. As was my daughter." She gestured to a young woman who looked just like her father, her belly swollen with child. "Not all of us can be so fertile. I told the Daemon King this when his sons passed up my third youngest daughter."

At that, she spiraled, her long dress swishing the polished floors as she strode away.

"Does everyone treat the princes' spouses with such contempt?" I growled as I turned to Stellera. "I think I hate that woman."

I was angrier tonight than I'd thought, the night before having triggered a feeling I couldn't allow to overwhelm me in public.

"I don't think I do," Stellera said. "I *know*, and I should have known she'd pry into our business. But this? Even the citadel's servants act as her ears."

I shuddered as we made our way into the parlor for drinks.

But Nessin looked over his shoulder as he grabbed my arm. He pressed a kiss to my cheek and whispered, "Are you okay?"

Trying to keep a neutral expression, I tugged my arm as discreetly as I could manage. "I'll be fine so long as you don't touch me for the rest of the night."

I made my way through the crowd and felt his eyes following. When I requested water instead of wine or ale, Lady Alders whispered something to her daughter. I rolled my eyes and looked away, not caring in the least what she was gossiping about now.

I craned my neck every time a new servant entered the room. There were a few daemons who curled their short tails tight against their bodies as they carried trays of finger foods, but most were mortals. Neither their skin nor their eyes glowed. Instead, they had deep purple bags under their eyes from exhaustion and a slump in their posture.

Stellera widened her eyes at the room then me, like she couldn't stand the crowd we stood among. "How are you by the way? I feel like I haven't seen you in ages."

"That's because you haven't," I said. "But I'm well. And you?"

A dimple appeared in her cheek. "That was the fakest answer I've ever heard, and I know fake. I've lived among these people my entire life."

I laughed a little too loudly. "If you must know, I was ill on Nos Nua for a few days. I guess I'm still recovering a bit." I knew I shouldn't tell her about my week spent in bed. Saying it aloud oddly released a sliver of the burden I felt.

"Oh, no. I didn't hear."

"Good. I don't want anyone to hear about any of my business," I said, letting my eyes drift from Gilder to Gilder.

"Agreed. But I'm afraid it's a little late to hope for that." Stellera looked through a pair of open pocket doors attached to the far end of the large room. Inside sat a spacious table for seven players.

She pointed to the game room. "Have you played Seven Daggers before?"

I nodded as I sipped my water. "My whole life."

"I haven't."

I flashed a mischievous grin. "All the easier to beat you then. Though I doubt I'll play the first game."

I didn't actually want to play at all tonight. I needed to stay on the outskirts of the room so I could slip away instead of focusing on a silly game.

"There are twenty-eight daggers in a Seven Daggers deck. Seven players, each starting with seven cards in their hand," I said. "Seven dagger cards, one of each, are needed to win."

"This game hinges on lying, no?" Stellera understood the basics then.

"Essentially." Much of the game revolved around lying. At least, the strongest players were the best liars. "A good player memorizes the face cards the other players hold and reveal."

She matched my grin. "Shouldn't that be considered cheating?"

"In some games," I said. "Not in Seven Daggers."

"This sounds thrilling! Cutthroat but thrilling," Stellera said.

"You should play. It's the best way to learn the rules."

As Stellera studied the table, fascination shone in her dark blue eyes.

"Any other rules I ought to know?"

"Too many. You have to be holding a dagger at all times. If you're ever caught without one, you're out of the game. Again, you can lie. But if the controlling player chooses you for a card check during their turn, you're done. The players can single one another out at any time and have the dealer verify cards. If a player is correct, the dealer steals all but one face card from the liar, including the Seventh."

"Then it would return to the deck," Stellera said.

I smiled, thinking of all the nights my clan ended up shouting at one another over a game.

"Few players claim another has the Seventh Dagger, because once your hand is down to a single face card, the other players close in."

When a dealer in a gold-and-black uniform entered the attached room and started to unlock the deck of Seven Daggers from a box, all the guests took notice. The dealer's hands were mesmerizing. He cut the deck, shuffling and fanning them across the table as two bosses watched. I wondered which betting hall they'd come from. I could be impulsive at times. I knew this about myself all too well, so I avoided the halls at all costs.

It was difficult to procure a hand of Seven Daggers but not impossible. The game took patience. Luck. An ability to lie. Two players nearly always had the same dagger in their hands, so it was the lying that made it both fun and challenging. Most of the game was based on luck alone, but there were also the odds of how many of the daggers existed in the deck. Each was rarer than the last, the seventh being the least prevalent with only one in the whole deck, while the first dagger had seven cards.

The objective was to get the Seventh Dagger early in the game.

At least, that was always my objective.

At the same time, it was easy to lose that prized Seventh Dagger, and the game often went on for a couple bells at least.

A pang in my chest reminded me of Pa. He'd taught Ciel and me everything we knew about how to play the game.

The dealer gestured to the seven seats around the table then, signaling that it was time to fill in. The Daemon King waved his hand and hung back to chat with a few Gilders, even when offered the first seat.

Sin and his brothers took four of the seven seats. Naturally, Lord and Lady Alders took the fifth and sixth seats.

Ciel and I made eye contact in the crowd. A knowing look. With the players and the crowd distracted, looking for Pa wouldn't be easy but doable. I tried to shrink myself, hiding behind Stellera without being obvious. The game was an excellent distraction for our hosts and fellow guests.

Stellera, surprisingly, raised her hand for the final seat.

"Maybe I'll have some beginner's luck," she said over her shoulder, slinking away. She winked at me as she slid into her seat across from Lady Alders.

Then the dealer started to dole out the cards to each player.

Sin had taken a seat against the far wall inside the grand gaming parlor, as had Stellera and Lochlainn. As they rearranged their hands, strategically or out of habit I wondered, their eyes slowly raised to signal that they were ready to begin.

The person to the left of the dealer always went first: Lord Alders. He hid a devious smile behind his cards, and I knew right then and there he wasn't going to win if he was that bad at concealing his expression. The players' faces, Lady Alders's especially, gave nothing away as they waited for the lord to begin.

Lord Alders's eyes roved around the table before he halted. "*Prince Devlin.*"

At once, Devlin hovered his fingers over the cards he'd gotten in the deal. His eyes were methodical yet calm. If either of them had received no daggers in the deal, they would have three turns to procure them. But it would have to be through catching the others lying. They couldn't throw down any cards.

Devlin, thankfully, had a few. He clicked the cards against the mahogany table in the order of the daggers he'd received.

The first dagger.

The third dagger.

He paused, and I couldn't tell whether he was holding any others back or this was indeed all he had. He sat perfectly still in his seat before raising his eyebrows at the cards and looking at Lord Alders, who wiggled his greedy fingers and plucked the third dagger off the table.

"I'll take that!"

The game continued this way for the first twenty minutes. Players stealing from one another's hands, carefully staring over the top of their cards, and plotting left and right.

I needed to slip away while the early game hypnotized the guests. As the first of lies and retaliation spread around the table like wildfire, I moved through the crowd. Ciel, too, had settled on the outskirts of the room to watch my back. He folded his hands in front of him, pretending the game had absorbed him like everyone else.

Maybe my brother had learned a thing or two in the last few weeks. Maybe he could give even Ailerby a run for his money now.

31

Alders Manor was strewn with couples hiding in the shadows. For a second, I thought I'd stepped into the White Plume again. At least a handful were bickering under their breath, and they bowed their heads and dropped their eyes as I passed them, imitating polite but thin smiles. I pretended not to notice, but as soon as I passed them, the hiss-whispering resumed.

Others were lost in lustful interactions, however, their backs pressed against a wall or an archway or hiding under a staircase where they assumed their midnight whispers and kisses went unnoticed.

As a young man caught between a tall, slender woman and one of those archways under the carved wood stairs caught my eye, a smile curled his lips. The woman traced his gaze to mine and beckoned me toward them. I nodded hello and kept walking, but I flinched when the man looked up again.

Thane Elittes.

His eyes narrowed before he resumed his activities, pulling the woman closer to bunch up her dress near her hip. Thane deliberately flicked his gaze toward the archway's other side, signaling for me to move on.

I wondered whether his presence was coincidental. Could Sin have put him up to this?

Losing focus wasn't part of the plan tonight. I needed to find the kitchen. On a night like this, I couldn't imagine any other place the mansion's staff might be, so I followed my nose. The thick smell of honeyed, roasted meat trickled into the air. It grew stronger as I walked, and I took that as a sign I was moving in the right direction.

The clack of a boot appeared on my heels. I whipped my head around, realizing a second too late how suspicious it looked.

Ciel.

I released a heavy breath, pressing a hand to my heart, then stalked on. I assumed he was there to distract anyone who came up behind me. I whispered *thank you* under my breath, knowing he couldn't hear, yet I felt better voicing my appreciation.

We were in this together, no matter how much I wished he'd stayed in Os Íseal.

Relief settled my tossing gut when the enormous kitchen seemed to unfold out of nowhere beyond another archway. Only one girl occupied the wide room. With a flinch, she immediately looked up from her mixing bowl and spatula. She was pouring batter into a buttered pan.

"Oh, good evening. Are you lost? I can lead you back to the party, Lady..." Her eyes enlarged. "*Princess.*"

At once, she set the bowl down and dropped into a curtsy.

"Please, no." I swept forward, almost tripping on my dress. But I caught myself against the counter, damning my stupid feet. "I– I was looking for the kitchen. We had the most marvelous sweets out there, and I wanted to see if I could snag a recipe for a party!"

If Ciel was eavesdropping outside, he'd be rolling his eyes or cupping a hand over his mouth to stop from laughing. I couldn't cook or bake to save my life and had no desire to learn anything remotely domestic, lest I ended up being forced to marry some unblood chieftain after all.

The girl's brow furrowed. Strands of dark hair poked out from under her cap, gleaming under the golden torchlight. She was pretty and petite. Couldn't be older than sixteen.

"Are you the one who makes the pastries?" I asked.

She nodded, dropping her eyes.

"Well, they're very tasty." It wasn't a lie. I just hadn't had the chance to try one yet. I was sure they were scrumptious. "What's your secret ingredient?"

"It–um, it depends on which you liked." Her eyes widened again. "Would the princess like to try one that hasn't been set out yet? The servers will be delivering them to the parlor soon. They're always gobbled in minutes."

Shoot. That meant the others would be back soon.

"I'd love to."

She set down her spatula, wiping her hands on her apron. Then she walked over to a little cart beside the counter and gestured for me to follow. She fished a plate from the stack on the cart's lower shelf and used tongs to set the pastry on it. I took it eagerly, wanting to eat quickly, and popped it in my mouth.

"Delicious," I said through a mouthful, covering my lips as I chewed and swallowed.

She blushed again. "Thank you, Princess."

"Call me Sersa."

"Ser–Sersa," she croaked.

"I thought I might trouble you with a question as well."

She looked up, blinking.

"It's all right. Just between us," I reassured. "Do you know the other servants in the house? Are you friends with any of them?"

She hesitated, then nodded. "Nearly all of them."

"And is there anyone by the name of Bain Scáth here?"

She searched her thoughts for a moment before her brow furrowed. Her clasped hands shook.

"No, I know no Bain Scáth." The tone of her voice, low and knowing, told me she remembered my family name.

"Are you sure? Or do you know of any other servants in other houses by that name?"

"I never leave the House of Alders," she said. "The servants who've been here longest, those the Lady and Lord Alders t-trust, are the ones who run errands and do the shopping."

I sensed her loyalty to the Lady and Lord of the house wasn't as strong as those tenured servants. But she stammered over the word *trust*, like talking to me wasn't something she should be doing if she wanted to earn their trust one day. I could only imagine the treatment she received. Either it was harsher than the others or she was ignored altogether, unrecognized for her talents. I wished I could help but had no authority, even as a false princess.

"All right. Well, thank you anyway. You've been very helpful."

"If I hear that name," she blurted when I turned away, "I will be sure to get a letter to you at the Daemon King's Citadel. I hope you find him. Your…"

Father. Hearing her say the word aloud might shatter me.

I turned back and reached forward to gently squeeze her wrist. As I did, the blue depths of the sea that'd drowned me only weeks ago, the one Ciel had said he felt, lurked at the edges of my vision.

Curious after the conversation with Nessin, I tried harder to reach it.

The lack of information I'd gathered about Pa didn't exactly make it easy to tap into, but with the faint wisps of blue still painting the edges of my mind, it felt in reach.

Every part of me protested when I washed us both in the blue, but I focused on the fact that I needed her silence. While I didn't think she'd talk, Sin had warned me everything got back to the Daemon King. I couldn't have her telling a soul that one of the princes' spouses was lurking and questioning servants.

Especially after the snippets of conversation I'd heard in the woods on Nos Nua. Might the king be looking for Pa too?

"You won't tell anyone. You understand, right?" I said quickly.

I pushed the blue tendrils forward—at least I tried—and almost choked on my breath when her eyes changed from dark brown to the deepest shade of indigo.

It worked.

She tilted her head and frowned at me.

I trembled, wondering if she was in pain. If I'd inflicted pain upon another, I couldn't forgive myself. I knew the sadness didn't steal magic like my fear, but what if I couldn't pull her out of the depths? I prayed to Nev they wouldn't let her become trapped in the sadness…

After a second, the pinched expression passed, her eyes returned to their shade of brown, and she nodded with a gentle smile. I hid my relieved breath.

"Of course," she said. "It's our secret, Sersa. I'll send a few recipes to the citadel."

When I returned to the parlor, the game of Seven Daggers was concluding, Sin extending his hand to Stellera in congratulations.

"Well done," he said.

"I taught her everything she knows," Lochlainn said, leaning back in his seat. I suspected he couldn't help himself, and I couldn't help but roll my eyes as the crowd cackled.

But I wasn't looking at Lochlainn or even Sin as they swept past me, laughing and recounting highlights of the game, to leave the room. I was looking at Stellera, who'd fooled me. All of us. Even Lochlainn, no matter what he claimed.

She wasn't just a good player but an expert.

I wished I'd been here to see her fool everyone, including me. When she caught my eye in the crowd, she winked, and I thought for sure—only for a second—that she might be on my side too. On Sin's side. Had she seen me slip away? Had she purposely given them a good show to cover for us?

As Stellera stood, she lifted her dress and approached the doorway I occupied. Without pausing, she too swept past me and whispered in a sly tone, "Find what you were looking for, *love?*"

"Tomorrow is what really matters," Sin said when we entered the carriage to head home a few bells later.

Based on the brightening sky, it was almost Reaping Hour. I hoped we'd make it home before. I couldn't bear to listen to the shrieks. It'd been weeks since I'd been subjected to them, and I was guilty of forgetting the way we'd always had to rush inside at sunrise.

"If I win my fights, I win an estate for us." He waggled his eyebrows at me, and I thought for sure it was the honey mead talking. "It would be advantageous to have another location for..." He waved his hand, rolling his wrist.

I tilted my head. "Oh? There is an *us* now."

"There has always been an *us*," he slurred, shaking the hair from his eyes.

This statement ignited me in so many ways, so many mixed emotions, but I tried to shove them all down. I only succeeded when Sin leaned toward me. Crowded on the bench together, his breath was warm and even smelled of honey.

"I mean it, Sersa. I want to prove it to you. I'm going to show you something the night after next at the White Plume."

"Why not tomorrow?" My nerves buzzed with thoughts of Pa. Maybe Sin had another Gilder to interrogate.

"Because tomorrow we'll be with the Berells, and as I previously mentioned, it's fight night." He slipped a gloved hand through my hair, cupping my jaw as he whispered in my ear, "Thane will be there to help us again."

Sin was only touching me because he was intoxicated, and though I wanted to be as cold to him as he'd been to me the night before, I didn't want him to stop.

No part of me wanted him to release me.

I was weak when it came to him.

He took a deep breath against my neck, distracting me.

"Yes," I whispered and then cleared my throat, returning my voice to normal. "I thought I saw Thane tonight. Why didn't you warn me he was here? Surely, he wasn't invited to the Alders' party. Stellera too. She called me *love*, so I know the two of you are co-conspirators or something."

I stiffened as Sin's gloved thumb drew circles down my neck, no doubt feeling my racing pulse.

"No, Thane wasn't invited. He has a string of lovers in every High House though. He and his dalliances make him highly useful. The man can charm his way into anyone's heart. And other places. As for my co-conspirators, they are everywhere," he whispered. "Becoming king is no easy feat, love."

His breath dusted my neck, his lips hovering against my skin. The proximity summoned a chill all over my body.

"What happened to *we can't?*" I growled, shoving him away. I wasn't strong enough to let him continue. Even after I'd vowed that I wouldn't give myself over so easily, I was one touch away from letting him have me in this very carriage. "Changing your mind after one day isn't a good look, Nessin. Especially coming from the man who told me life is mine for the taking when it comes to the things I want. *Hypocrite.*"

With a chuckle, Sin dropped his hand and pulled away. He tipped his head back against the carriage wall and closed his eyes. "Technically, Sersa, we can do anything we want. But we shouldn't. *Shouldn't* is what I meant last night."

"You're drunk."

"I am, indeed," he agreed with a hiccup. "It's helping right now."

"Helping what?"

"You know," he said furtively.

I hadn't the faintest idea what he meant.

"Well, whatever it's helping you with, I'm sure tomorrow you'll think differently when you lose your fight from a hangover."

"I'm a daemon. Soon to be Daemon King," he slurred proudly. "I won't lose. I could win my fight blindfolded and bound and…"

We reached home a few minutes later, and the second Sin hit the bed, still fully dressed, he was asleep. I tried to remove his boots, but he rolled onto his side, sending me stumbling onto my knees at his bedside. I cursed him. He couldn't be comfortable in his coat. His pants—I wasn't about to remove those.

After I managed to pry his boots off, I rolled him onto his side.

"Gods-damned Colossi." I grunted.

He was heavier than a fallen log and sleeping as heavy as one.

I tried to remove his coat. With one arm finally free a few minutes later, I panted. When I tried to roll him to the other side, he threw his arm around me, pulling me into the sea of sheets with him. His enormous body eclipsed mine, and I was forced to press my head to his warm chest. To my surprise, I heard the soft beats of his heart. The sound comforted me in a way I'd never expected, especially after he'd refused me.

Damn Sin.

I was content with where I'd ended up and followed quickly into sleep right beside him.

32

The following night, a strange feeling settled over me.

I felt like I'd been doing the same thing night after night, despite that we'd only been back two days. All the High Houses' mansions were the same, their parties likely all shades and hues of one another. Sure, it was fight night and Sin seemed excited for once, but I missed the nights I'd spent looking up at the stars under Os Íseal's sky, sitting around a bonfire with my clan, or training with my Uncle Flann and Ciel.

There was another feeling too. A hunch. I'd woken that morning with caution in my blood. My dreams were usually hazy, but I swore I'd seen Nev's face in them. I'd heard their words. A warning.

Beware.

I threw my bare foot up on the settee at the end of our bed and reached for the hem of my dress with one hand, the other holding a dagger and sheath.

Sin perked up in the doorway to the lounge, sweeping the white hair from his eyes to get a better look. "What is that for?"

He hadn't woken with so much as a *hint* of a hangover. Nothing. He was perfectly fine.

I mimicked the smirk he was always giving me. Right now, however, his eyes were locked on my exposed thigh as I bunched the end of my skirt up to slide the sheath on. I slipped it over my toes, up my ankle and knee, until it finally rested where it needed to.

"You never know when a Gilder might be in the wrong place at the wrong time," I said, a little too satisfied with myself and his reaction.

I wiggled the sheath to be sure it was secure.

Sin recovered, his tone flattening. "Don't you mean when *you* might be in the wrong place?"

"You know what I mean. I need to be able to protect myself."

"And your magic? Have you disregarded that protection? Or Dúma?" He gestured to her, asleep in the corner.

Dúma had already more than tripled in size over the last few weeks, and while she was growing at an impressive rate, she was still a pup. Not a protector. I saw her as a life I needed to protect, not the other way around. I wasn't sure I'd ever see her that way, regardless of what she'd been bred for.

I sighed. "Until she's too heavy to sleep in the bed with us, she's a baby to me."

"I think she'll be trying to sleep in bed with us for the rest of our lives."

I froze, fighting an internal flinch. The thought of being here with Sin forever... I didn't know what I felt about it, and when those pale colors danced at the edges of my vision, I shoved them away. I couldn't think of any future with Sin.

He cleared his throat, and I changed the subject.

"Speaking of my magic, you'll be happy to know I used it last night on a servant in the kitchen. You were too drunk for me to tell you afterward," I said, releasing my dress and letting it fall back around me, "but I...somehow projected my feeling."

Sin's eyes lit up before they darkened. "Yes. I apologize for anything I may have said. That will *not* happen again. As for the magic, I don't want to say I told you so..."

"But you can't resist."

"And what happened?"

"I told her not to tell anyone I asked about my father."

"You asked directly?" Sin pinched the bridge of his nose. "*Sersa*."

"What was I to do?" I growled. "I've been here for over a moon and have nothing." All thanks to the unspeakable weeks we'd spent on Nos Nua. "My father could be in danger, or worse, so I'm done sitting back and playing by the rules. No more trips to remote isles and dawdling. Pa is counting on me."

I thought again about the warning Thane had given Sin in the woods.

Every day I spent in the Soullands—and every day Ciel spent here—brought us closer to the Daemon King coming for one of us, maybe both of us.

Fight night, hosted by the Berells, wasn't at Berell Manor.

It was the first time I'd been outside Gilders Eye in weeks, besides our trip to Nos Nua, and we weren't just outside Gilders Eye.

We were in the slums near Dúm's Cross.

As the royal carriages halted in front of the Crescendo, I groaned. I'd already snapped at Sin for not mentioning that I wouldn't be able to search Berell Manor. The thought that we would be stuck inside Thane Elittes's pleasure den tonight was my tipping point.

My mood shifted when we arrived, my thoughts laced with irritation as thick as ice. I didn't know why, but the thought of seeing Thane irked me. Probably because I didn't feel like I could trust him. I didn't know why Sin did. Though he'd told me Sin planned to kill his father, I hadn't forgiven his callousness the day after the wedding.

While there would be a party at Berell Manor afterward, I was feeling more impatient, more impulsive than normal. The days felt never ending, while the nights felt pressured. I only had so long to search for Pa.

But Sin insisted the Berells' after-party would be the perfect opportunity to search, so I fought the urge to order the carriage back to Gilders Eye.

"No one will be able to walk straight, let alone see straight by the time we all get back to their mansion. Fight night is a rowdy one," said Sin under his breath. "And we'll use it to our advantage."

"Are *you* going to be able to walk straight later?" I asked as we stepped out of the carriage.

"They have healers on hand in case anything serious happens," Sin assured me.

"I was alluding to last night again."

"I knew. I decided to spin it another way. Also, I am disturbed that I allowed myself to get that drunk. After the last few weeks, I suppose I needed a distraction. Sorry," he added flatly.

I folded my arms across my chest, ignoring everything else he'd said. What did he need distraction from? Me? His feelings?

"Soulless can be healed, then? That doesn't make sense."

"In this world, we're still attached to our earthly bodies in a way. It's just that we're trapped without our souls, unable to cross into your world. If we couldn't be healed, most of us would be walking around looking like the Iarsmaí, skin hanging off us, bones exposed. A lovely thought, aye?"

Lacking the energy to analyze his logic, I focused on the Crescendo.

It looked nothing like the White Plume. The exterior didn't stand out along the street. Rather, the entrance was wedged between two enormous buildings, set back a hundred feet. Iron gates bracketed the narrow courtyard between the two buildings out front. We were forced to file into two lines, following the Daemon King as guest after guest greeted and bowed to him.

Booming music trickled through the courtyard.

Thane, wearing a red-and-black jacket, stood in the doorway at the end of the courtyard. He slid to the side when we reached him, permitting us to pass. He winked at Sin and nodded at me before we descended a shadowy staircase.

The pleasure den was underground then. Interesting.

A circular landing at the bottom of the stairs connected to a narrow hall that curled and curled, leaving me lightheaded. We walked through the papered halls with dark, treble-clef patterns and black doors on either side. Little fires behind glass shades illuminated the way.

Eventually, we reached the center of the den.

A sunken sandpit sat in the middle of the large space, the walls rough stone like it'd been hulled from a colossal boulder. Though it was dimly lit and smelled strongly of sweat, I welcomed the ambiance of the slums, albeit an elevated one. Blood spattered the sand in the pit like a dozen people had taken red paint and flicked it this way and that. A daemon in a cap that covered his horns was raking the pit, stirring it around to hide any remnants of the fights before. The sections of seats were separated by High Houses. There were also sections designated for non-Gilders, though significantly fewer for this event. I wondered what the tickets cost and craned my neck, looking for anyone I might know. Scattered along the elevated stone benches were daemons and wraiths ready to bet on the four princes. But no one I recognized.

There'd be three fights.

Devlin against Lochlainn.

Sin against Jestin.

Then the winners of both fights would go against each other.

Though I knew Lochlainn could change his form like the Daemon King, I couldn't imagine him standing a chance against Devlin. Sin had said that Devlin was an exceptional Soulreaper, but I didn't know if that meant anything other than being capable of stealing souls. Their bodies resembled one another in almost all ways, but where Devlin's hair was cropped cleanly, Lochlainn's hung in a ponytail down his back.

The Daemon King had a dozen Soul Guards surrounding him and his Circle of Gilders. The king's servants had brought little silk cushions to sit on. Niuna sat beside him, swinging her legs against the bench.

Sin left me within the area surrounded by Soul Guards then headed to the roped-off area outside the sandpit. He and Jestin took seats on the lowest stone step, watching their brothers warm up inside the pit.

To my surprise, Thane stole a seat two over from the Daemon King. Next to me.

He turned his head to the pit and, without looking at me, said, "Evening, Princess Sersa."

"Evening." I eyed the arches on either side of the far wall to my left, past the crowd standing on the floor.

There was a bar on the pit's other side. Glimpses through the arches told me that it was where the rest of the *entertainment* was. Scantily clad performers hung from the ceiling on thick strips of silk, twirling in slow, hypnotic circles. Long corridors stretched beyond the main area with many doors on either side.

"I didn't know how close you were to the royal family," I said.

From my peripheral, Stellera beside me turned her attention to us. Ciel sat beside her, and next to him, Helde.

Still, Thane said nothing.

"The Crescendo is not at all what I expected," I added.

"And why is that?" He didn't bother peeling his eyes from the pit to speak. His voice was hardly audible over the noise inside the pleasure den.

"I don't know. I just pictured something different."

"There are crescendos in everything. In music. In life. In love. Lust. When the crowd roars—and they will in a moment—when the first fight starts, their applause reaches a crescendo before the excitement falls. That fall is when you notice your heartbeat most. When you realize how alive you are. As it slows and slows and slows, and you hear it in your ears." Thane's words were enthralling in a way.

My eyes dreamily traced Devlin and Lochlainn's movements before they fell upon the back of Sin's head.

He was like a crescendo. He made me feel alive.

But he also irritated me to no end.

The hypnotism ended the second Niuna Drumghoul shimmied past peoples' knees to get to us. She slid onto Thane's knee and threw an arm around him, narrowing her eyes like he was a business partner she was about to deliver a new proposition. "I didn't know you'd be here, Lord Thane."

"And I didn't know you'd be here, Princess Niuna. What a lovely surprise this is. I didn't think you were allowed out so late. You and..." He thumbed the stuffed daemon toy she held. "Who is this?"

"Lacha. He eats hearts."

Thane widened his dark eyes. "Excellent. He and I have that in common."

Niuna grinned. Some of her teeth were missing. "Father allowed

Lacha and me to come tonight. Draea will be taking us home straight after the fights. I'm not allowed to go to the Berells' afterward."

Hearing her call the king *Father*, when Sin only ever called him by his title, sounded wrong.

"I must side with the Daemon King, I'm afraid. That's definitely a good decision on his part," Thane agreed, a fleeting look finding me. Evidently, both our minds had gone to the compromising position he'd been in the night before. "A princess needs her sleep."

Niuna's eyes slid to me. "Hello, Sersa."

I smiled. "Hello, Princess Niuna."

Through the crowd, Sin looked over his shoulder at us from the bench.

"I suppose you are a princess too now. Excuse me." Her manners were that of the Gilders already but not in a fake way.

"Not at all. Call me Sersa."

"And Lacha?" Niuna held up the little wyvern-like stuffed daemon by the legs.

"He may also call me Sersa."

Niuna leaned forward then, meaning for only me to hear, but Thane's eyes flicked up to mine as she whispered.

"One day soon, we'll call you Daemon Queen. But it won't be for long."

Niuna's white eyes held a warning within them. Then she slid off Thane's leg and skipped past the few seats between us and the Daemon King. In my shock, I failed to ask her what she meant.

Thane held my gaze, but before either of us could say anything, a horn scratched the air.

The fights were starting.

Niuna's warning pooled in my gut like poison. If I understood it correctly, I might sit on the throne beside Sin, but I'd be removed even swifter.

Either I was returning home to Os Íseal, or I'd be dead.

33

To my great surprise, the first two fights were decisive wins.

Lochlainn beat Devlin effortlessly, and Stellera explained that none of the brothers were allowed to use magic tonight. That made sense, but I wondered if Lochlainn could hide the incredible strength that surely came with his Colossi form. The fact that both Lochlainn and Sin could shift like their father meant the fight between them would be equal. At least I hoped.

As for Jestin, he never stood a chance. Helde ran down to the pit immediately following the fight against Sin to check on him. Jestin didn't look upset. Instead, he smiled through a bloody lip as Sin gave him a final playful shove as if they'd both known who would win.

Both Sin and Lochlainn stood near the pit, shirtless and corded with muscle. Whereas Sin was taller and leaner, almost lanky, Lochlainn was broader shouldered, and more built. I tried to guess who was faster, but as the horn sounded again, I realized I'd find out in a second.

The two brothers stepped up to their marks in the sandpit across from one another. As Stellera squeezed my hand and grinned, I wondered who she rooted for tonight. Both Sin and Lochlainn were only marginally scathed from their first fights—little cuts and bruises here or there. After this one, I didn't doubt they'd both be a wreck, no matter who won.

The daemon referee took a step back and sliced his hand through the air between them, grunting to signal the start of the fight.

Sin moved first, catching Lochlainn off guard by slamming a fist into his nose. I tried not to cheer, still uncertain whether Stellera cared for Lochlainn, but sweet satisfaction rippled through my body.

A single drop of blood trickled from one of Lochlainn's nostrils.

He grinned at the challenge and leaped across the sand to shove Sin.

Sin rolled backward and recovered, balancing on his toes in a crouch. When he rose again, he gave Lochlainn no time to plan his next attack.

Sin threw an uppercut to his brother's ribs then his side then under his chin. Lochlainn staggered, gritting his teeth.

All brotherly play faded between the two of them.

Lochlainn caught Sin off guard and flipped him over his shoulder like he weighed no more than a feather. But Sin didn't fall like a feather. He slammed the sandy floor face first, a cloud of it flying up everywhere.

Sin rolled over, grunting.

Then Lochlainn was on him.

Before Lochlainn managed to pin him, Sin rammed his knee right into the middle of Lochlainn's back. He rolled as Sin sprang to his feet, putting his guard back up. Between strenuous breaths, Sin tilted his chin down, staring at Lochlainn with sharp eyes.

The crowd roared, and I knew it wasn't the first time, but all my senses had narrowed, focusing solely on Sin.

His unscarred eyebrow was bleeding now, dripping into his eye and tracing a path down his cheek like a mirror of the scarred side.

I hadn't even seen Lochlainn strike him to draw blood.

Both their chests were heaving now.

What happened next was so unexpected, the crowd silenced as they watched it unfold.

Sin hooked his leg around Lochlainn's when he lunged for him. Lochlainn recovered, but Sin slammed a hand into his ribs again, this time summoning a terrible crack, the sound rippling through the crowd.

He had to have summoned Colossi strength.

There was no way he hadn't.

My eyes enlarged, devouring the scene as I held my breath.

Sin spun Lochlainn around his back, bent his knee, and slammed Lochlainn down onto it. Like he was going to snap him in half. A second blow struck the same side where Lochlainn's ribs had cracked a second before. Lochlainn rolled back onto his head and landed on his face. His arms splayed. Blood dribbled from his mouth. His hands fisted the sand, but he didn't get up. Lochlainn lifted his head before it fell again.

Then the crowd roared.

I shouted so loud, clapping and bouncing on my toes, that Sin's eyes found me in the crowd with the tiniest hint of a curl to his lips.

As I looked to my left, I realized Thane was gone, and the Daemon King's assessing eyes also drifted to me, wearing an almost imperceptible smile. Though it was nearly the same smile as Sin's, it wasn't filled with joy. Not at all. Palms frozen in a clap and sweat prickling on the back of my neck, I bowed my head at him.

The Daemon King turned his gaze back to the sandpit below before touching a hand to his daughter's shoulder. The second the fight was called, he led Niuna, his courtesans, and Gilder friends out of the Crescendo. The Soul Guards followed.

Chills rippled up my spine and along my scalp as I relived the way the king's eyes had discarded me. Then I recalled Niuna's warning. Maybe it was the Daemon King who'd told her to threaten me. Maybe he planned to kill me, but that didn't make sense. Not if Sin needed to kill his father to take his throne. Not if her warning had been correct.

I'd sit on the Daemon Throne beside Sin but only briefly. That would mean his father was already dead. Wouldn't it?

I shuddered again. All my elation had vanished in the space of a breath.

I looked at Ciel, sitting next to Helde. He narrowed his eyes at me in question. I couldn't look away, but I hardly focused on his face.

Another fact dragged me under a flood of colors. Blue. Red.

Black. Sadness. Anger. And horrible, gut-wrenching fear.

We needed to find Pa before the Daemon King could hurt me. But more than that, if he did have plans to hurt me, there was one way he knew—better than any other—that would shatter me to pieces, leaving me irreparable.

Harming Ciel first.

After a celebratory drink, we loaded into the carriages outside the Crescendo. A Bonemender had tended to the brothers' wounds, but Sin still looked a little drained. He was saying something, the carriages rolling down the street when my eyes locked on a man lingering in the crowd along the first street we passed.

He looked over his shoulder—right at me.

My gut dipped into my toes.

My mouth ran dry.

Unmistakable was the scar right where a dimple should have been. Though his head had been shaved, his black hair was the same shade as mine. But his eyes—his eyes were the same deep green in my memories, his skin still tan from the sun.

During the season of Heat, the sun had always burned mine and my brother's skin while it bronzed Pa's. He'd taught Ciel and me how to plant and which to use for different ailments. We'd had to wear long sleeves and pants to avoid the tender, splotchy red skin we'd gotten every time before.

Pa.

The second was over before I knew it, but it felt like an eternity.

I shoved open the carriage door and tumbled onto the cobbles, Sin calling after me. My palms scraped and bled as I tripped and landed on my front. The throbbing in my knees told me they would be a bloody mess too.

The endless sea of patrons roaming the slums tonight made my head spin. I used my elbows to shove past people, earning glares and cusses as I went. But I didn't care. Nothing mattered except for Pa.

"Bain," I called, not wanting to call him Pa in so public a place.

"Bain!"

At a fork in the road, surrounded by towering buildings all teetering together, I spun in a circle.

I didn't see him.

I grew dizzier by the second as I reeled and reeled, searching.

Then, I glimpsed a shaved head moving through the crowd. Again, I picked up my feet and ran. He'd paused before turning down another street.

He wanted me to follow.

"I'm following, Pa. I'm following," I said under my breath, panting.

Surely, someone would recognize me. But that didn't matter either. When I reached Pa, we would get Ciel and go home. All of us together. My heart raced. My knees wobbled. I lifted my skirts as I ran.

Pa darted down another street, at least I thought, but I froze the instant I reached it, stumbling over my feet tangled in the ends of my dress. I spun in a circle to be certain.

He was *gone*. Nowhere to be seen, not so much as a hint as to where he'd fled.

He...

I shook my head, lips now trembling. "No. *No!*"

Fury surged through me like a wildfire. I slammed my fists against the stone wall and shrieked in frustration. I knew if anyone was around me, I'd bleed them dry. Dropping my fists to my sides, my chest couldn't contain my heart as I took heaving breaths, and tears threatened to fall.

Had my mind chosen tonight to play tricks on me? It couldn't have. His shaved head—that *had* been him. That detail, that change, meant it had to be. I'd never seen his shaggy hair so short. My memory wouldn't change that.

But my memories vanished from importance when two clicks followed by another two, quicker in succession, skittered on the cobblestones behind me.

The hairs on the back of my neck prickled as a breath dusted the nape.

All my senses jolted, I turned slowly.

A wyvern-like daemon blocked the alley's entrance.

Before I could take in any other details, it spun around, its tail throwing me into a wall. I cried out as I crashed into it, slid down, and rolled. As my surroundings spun, blood dribbled onto the cobblestones beneath me. I touched a finger to my brow. My fingers came away stained crimson.

Fighting the pain now racking my entire body, I lifted the end of my dress and reached for the dagger along my thigh, unsheathing it. How coincidental I'd had the urge to arm myself tonight of all nights.

I thanked Nev.

This daemon looked exactly like the plush wyvern Niuna Drumghoul had been carrying. It prowled the edge of the street on its four taloned feet, eyes glowing red as my hellhound's. It was completely unlike the two-legged, human-like daemons that frequented the City of Soulless.

This was ferocious, animal-like.

No, this beast was straight from the Underworld. All instinct. No humanness behind its eyes. Its teeth bared in a snarl, and saliva dripped onto the cobblestones like my blood.

Pulling myself to standing on weak limbs, I held the dagger close to me, ready to strike when it charged. It was going to. There was no question.

The Daemon King had sent this beast to finish me.

His plan then wasn't to hurt my clan or Ciel at all. He wanted to go straight to the source.

Me.

"Come on," I growled at the daemon, gritting my teeth, bending my knees, readying myself for its attack.

The daemon obliged, scampering forward on its clacking talons. It scaled the wall it had thrown me into. I whirled around as it swiped its front talons at me. I slashed my dagger, finding purchase against its scaly flesh. The daemon cried out, a torturously high-pitched noise, but its eyes twisted with renewed rage.

It spun again and whacked me with its tail. This time, the barbed extremity coiled around my waist and shoved me beneath its belly.

I screamed as the spikes dug into my waist and back.

But shoving me beneath it was the beast's first mistake.

As it raised another talon to strike, I spun the dagger in my hand and plunged it as deep as I could.

When it slumped on the ground, I crawled between its legs.

I knew I hadn't struck the heart though. The beast was whimpering now, and I almost felt bad as it raised to standing again. The blade remained in its chest.

I had nothing to protect myself.

Nothing.

Nothing.

Sin's voice rang in my ears.

And your magic? Have you disregarded that protection?

I closed my eyes for a second, allowing myself to feel everything. Every emotion I was terrified of. Every emotion that had ever steered me wrong. Even the one that had stolen my clan's magic.

The black-and-gray tendrils crept at the edges of my vision. Fear swarmed me.

I didn't want to die. I didn't want to lose Ciel, Pa, my clan.

Nessin.

I was afraid of all of these things, so many things. Yet my fears did not make me weak. They bolstered me. At least now they did.

The tendrils of my fear started from my fingertips, snaking along the ground slowly. When the daemon noticed, it skittered backward. Simultaneously, dark blood began to ooze from its eyes.

This fear was powerful.

This fear could do more than steal from others, I knew. It could do more than numb and control me. I'd always known.

It could kill. And as if this fear were from the deepest, darkest depths of me, the worst parts, it *wanted* to kill.

As the tendrils surrounded the daemon on all sides, it had nowhere to run. My magic coiled up its nostrils, seeping through its scaly skin, and burst from its body like a thousand daggers.

The magic couldn't hurt me, but the daemon stood no chance against it. The tendrils gouged its eyes, turning them into black pits. It slumped onto its belly a final time, legs splayed out to its sides.

While I had won, I, too, faltered. I barely caught myself as I fell, and as if my own fear had consumed me, the tendrils of black and gray pulled me under until I saw nothing at all.

34

Aches and pains rattled up and down my body, each making a ruckus and trying to outdo the last as I shifted in mine and Sin's bed.

"Easy, *easy*." It took a moment for Ciel to come into focus.

My blurred eyesight slowly retreated until I saw my brother and Sin at my bedside. Ciel sat off the edge, petting Dúma. Sin stood at the foot, scowling.

"Thank the gods you're up," Ciel said, breathless.

"Ha. The gods." The pain I felt either meant the gods decidedly did not exist or they were punishing me for every time I'd doubted them. But as soon as I thought it, I recalled Nev's warning in my dreams the night before. They had been right. They hadn't steered me afoul.

"A Bonemender tended to you," Ciel said. "But they said your wounds were rather serious, Sers."

Arms folded over his chest, Sin kept silent and stared at me. I peeled my eyes from his.

"That explains why I feel like I was hit by a carriage."

From the corner of my eye, Sin's scowl grew more pronounced. He folded his arms. "You did *throw* yourself from a carriage while it was moving. Close enough."

Ciel nodded in agreement. "What were you thinking? You could have died."

I opened my mouth to protest, but Ciel cut me off.

"And the prince already told me about the daemon," my brother said, "so don't bother trying to lie."

"I wasn't going to. I'm going to say something, and you're going to believe me. Okay?"

Ciel sighed before he nodded again.

"I saw Pa last night. I know it was him because his head was shaved. He'd never shave his head. I remember how Ma and the uncles used to tease him, saying he'd be balding soon enough." I took a deep breath. "The Gilder he was sold to must have done it. Maybe they're particular about their servants' appearances. I don't know, and it hardly matters, but I saw what I saw."

Ciel didn't question me. His eyes darted back and forth along the covers, working through the information in his mind. He helped me sit up when I grunted, trying to do so alone. At the end of the bed, Sin stiffened as if I'd screamed instead. Dúma tilted her head at me, red eyes enlarged with concern.

Sin blew a heavy sigh through his nose and put his back to me.

"What is your problem?" I snapped at him.

He whirled back around. Irritation lit his colorless eyes. "The Bonemender said you need to rest. To move *as little* as possible. Though I understand you are wholly incapable of following even the most basic instructions," he said, "perhaps you ought to listen to this one."

"Not after what I saw." With a grumble, I turned back to Ciel. "It was him," I repeated. "I promise my eyes didn't deceive me."

Ciel nodded. "Then we know he's alive. Did he look all right?"

"From what I could see. He looked healthier than I would've expected. Though I can't begin to understand why he'd be out in the city alone at night and why he wouldn't be with a Gilder or running straight to Os Íseal while the bridge is open."

"Some Gilders take a sliver of their mortal servants' souls so they can never leave the Soullands," Sin cut in. "Once a sliver is taken, the mortal is trapped. It's unlikely to get it back, but perhaps with a skilled Soulreaper..."

It explained why so many clan members and unbloods who owed Ma their weight in gold had simply disappeared over the years.

They'd traded a piece of their soul.

"You—you're a Soulreaper," I said, trying not to let myself unravel any further.

"We'd have to retrieve the sliver of his soul that was taken," Sin said, gaze sliding cautiously to Ciel, "from the Gilder who took it. If anyone did."

My brow furrowed. "Are all Gilders also Soulreapers?"

He pursed his lips. "No. The Daemon King keeps reapers on hand. All Gilders can request their services. Some High Houses keep them on staff, but they're rare. It's a simple task, taking a soul. Retrieving it, on the other hand, would require a willing participant."

"Or an unconscious Gilder. Is death an option?"

Sin clasped his hands behind his back. "The sliver the person possesses, in this case almost certainly a Gilder, would stay with them in death, so no."

Ciel was holding his breath. "Then all we have to do is make sure we have a Soulreaper with us when we find Pa," he said. "Both Devlin and Sin—"

I sat up further and groaned again when a pain in my side reared its head, reminding me of the daemon's barbed tail digging into my flesh. "Don't tell me you told Devlin?"

"No!" Ciel waved his hands. "I promise I didn't. I wouldn't. But he..." My brother dropped his eyes, pink rising into his cheeks. "Devlin truly loves me, Sersa. He would—he would help Pa for me, no matter the cost, and he would keep our secret."

My gaze flickered to Sin as he sighed, raising his chin with narrowed eyes. "I believe that. My brother's told me he's never been happier in his life. He admitted he can't imagine it without you, Ciel."

My brother blushed deeper. "We love one another."

I swore I saw an emotional glaze over Ciel's eyes. I reached forward and squeezed his hand. "I'm happy for you. You deserve the world. But what about the Druids? Your training? Ma, Pa?"

"We'll both have heavy decisions to make soon, Sers." The bed evened when he stood. "I'll visit you later, I promise. I have tea with Devlin and some Gilders."

Ciel excused himself, and Sin took his spot on the bed. He absentmindedly ran his fingers through Dúma's thick fur. "You killed a daemon yesterday."

"Yes, and my positively throbbing body reminds me every time I move."

"I told you not to." When Sin reached forward to cup my face, I froze. I wanted to touch his hand, to keep him close. My breath hitched and my nerves got the best of me. I buried my hands under the covers to stop myself from using them. From doing something I'd later regret.

At the same time, my soul was screaming, *Fuck regret.*

But Sin's hand fell away, and strain crossed his face. "Thank the gods I didn't have to fight you last night."

"I forgot all about your win. How are you feeling? Did you choose your estate?"

"Feeling better than you, and yes. I selected the fortress on Nos Nua. The documents were drawn up in our names this morning."

"Ours?"

"We're married. What's mine is yours. It is *our* estate."

"Ah."

He nodded, but there was something else behind his colorless stare.

Silence stretched between us. We stared into one another's eyes, neither of us moving, breathing, looking away.

"I meant to tell you last night," I finally said with a clear of the throat. I had to drop my eyes to say what I wanted. "Watching you, I realized how clever you are. You seemed to anticipate his moves. You are stronger too. More resilient. I was impressed."

With a curious tilt of the head, Sin narrowed his eyes. "You think I am clever, strong, and resilient? After what I saw last night, that describes my wife more than anyone else I've ever met."

"That's quite the compliment. Seeing as you've been around for ages." I bit the inside of my cheek to hold back a smile.

Sin rolled his eyes exaggeratedly. When he refocused on me, his seriousness had returned. "I didn't actually see you slay the daemon, but I saw how you left it. I won't be getting on your bad side anytime soon."

I felt everything all at once, a swarm of colors. Some I'd never seen, at least not before meeting Sin. But others—others terrified me more than the rage, the sadness, or even the fear I'd allowed to consume me in order to summon my magic last night.

I tried to tamp those feelings down, but they whirled around my head like will-o'-wisps. I couldn't catch them in my fist. Instead, the feelings swarmed faster, more steadfast, when I looked away from Sin.

I couldn't let him see my thoughts.

I can't. I can't. I can't.

Sin shifted on the bed. He had such control of his body that it hardly moved. "By the way, I have something for you. I know you are no damsel in distress, but I want you to have something to protect yourself. Or in this case, three somethings, in case you lose your first in a daemon's chest. Especially while Dúma is still a pup."

He fumbled at his hip, loosening the three dainty daggers.

"I'm sure you have many more daggers back home in Os Íseal since you use one so well." His throat worked as he swallowed. "But I figure these may come in handy here. Hopefully not, but you never know. They're souldaggers and should be used on soulless wisely. They bring true death to one of my kind."

Sin sounded circumspect. I couldn't bring myself to tell him what Niuna had said or that I suspected his father had sent that daemon after me. Unless...

Unless he knows.

"I also wanted you to have something to remember me by. For when you leave the Soullands." He handed me the daggers.

I pulled my hands out from under the covers and turned the glossy blue sheaths over and over.

I snickered, keeping my eyes down again. "I'm not sure you're so easy to forget, Sin."

"I hoped you might say something to that effect."

I thought about what he'd said in his dingy apartment in the slums the day we met. That I'd think of him every day for the rest of my life if I didn't agree to help him—to take the leap in trying to find

Pa. But as I focused on the daggers in my lap, refusing to look at him, the worst part was that he'd been wrong.

I had agreed to help him. I had come to know him.

And now I'd never get him out of my mind. Ever.

"I wanted to give you something else too." Sin reached under his shirt and fished a gold necklace out.

"One might think it's my birthday," I said. "Enough, Sin. I need nothing else."

He cut me off, his tone rigid. "Please," he said, placing the little gold horn on a chain in my palm and his hand over it. "This summons my personal Sluagh whenever you use it."

My brow furrowed.

What?

"You've seen me use it before. At my apartment. If ever you are in danger, you summon a Sluagh. They have been commanded not to harm you but to protect you, Sersa. They will listen to any command you give."

I didn't know what to say.

This was not a gift he—anyone—would give lightly.

"Please just agree to this one thing. Please say you'll keep the horn with you always."

"Just until I leave the Soullands, right?"

He said nothing for a long moment.

"I mean forever, Sersa."

"But you need it."

His eyes narrowed. "No. Keep it. I insist."

My shoulders raised with a deep inhale. Unable to form words, I nodded.

Why was he giving me all these protections? Was this Sin's way of confirming I was in danger—that the Daemon King *was* plotting my death? And did this mean that, even when I returned to Os Íseal, I wouldn't be safe?

At that, Sin stood and headed for the door. Dúma leaped off the bed, wagging her tail at him.

"Where are you going?" I asked.

Sin looked over his shoulder. "I have to be somewhere tonight."

"Tonight?" I looked toward the terrace. The drapes were closed, concealing the sky.

"You slept through an entire day." His lips twisted up. "There are Soul Guards outside your door. You'll be safe here. I'll call for some food, and I believe Helde and Stellera are going to come and keep you company."

I frowned. More than anything I wanted to know where Sin was going. I wondered why he'd cut our moment short. Either he still felt the same way he'd said mere days ago, or he'd heard my thoughts and wanted to avoid them.

Maybe he didn't feel that way anymore.

Maybe I had lost my chance.

Maybe Sin had never felt that way and his head had just been clouded in the moments we'd shared. Mine certainly had.

Sin left me, and I heard the door sweep open a few minutes later.

"I'm in here," I called to Stellera and Helde.

It wasn't either of them.

My gut dipped into my toes as the Daemon King stalked toward the bed. He didn't sit but instead halted at the foot and stared down at me. His hands were clasped in front of him, and his squinted eyes revealed crows' feet.

"You had quite the night, my dear," he said. "It is good to see you unscathed."

I gritted my teeth. My nostrils flared. I said nothing.

"You continue to surprise me more and more, Sersa Scáth. I mean…" The king chuckled. "You killed a daemon with your bare hands last night."

I licked my lips and swallowed. My shoulders raised in a deep breath, but I tried to play it off as straightening my spine to show him I wasn't afraid. A rattle of pain pulsed in my back.

"I did," I replied with words like ice.

"I heard you shout before I saw you throw yourself from the carriage. You terrified my daughter, you know. Likely Nessin too."

"I apologize for that."

"Yes, what was it you yelled? Who was it you *believed* you saw?"

I chewed on the inside of my cheek. "My mother. She never visits Nos Ovscura. She hates your city. I've missed her very much since coming here."

"Ah." The Daemon King raised his eyebrows and adjusted his clasped hands in front of his majestic green robes. The garments reminded me of the deities I'd seen in Nos Nua's woods. "Yes, Ciel tells me how close your family once was. But you understand, dear Sersa, that to be Daemon Queen, you must be of sound mind. You must make the right decisions and dissuade yourself from your impulses. Flinging yourself into a crowd—in a dangerous neighborhood no less—caught more than a few eyes. And after last night, well... My concerns are that the pressure of being Daemon Queen might get to you. Your brother tells me you had some troubles in Os Íseal."

"Oh?" I challenged. "Did you use your special tea on him to learn all about my troubles?"

The Daemon King moved around the side of the bed. He was so swift for his size that my body and mind didn't even have a chance to stiffen or fear him.

He reached forward and squeezed my hand in his before I could pull away. His claws were especially tight. Dúma raised onto her legs and growled, hackles raised.

He afforded her a fleeting, unamused look. He wasn't afraid in the least.

"I make the happenings that take place—and the people who live in my citadel—my business. To rule is to probe and to understand the state of your kingdom with a mania for intel and control that few others can appreciate. I like to know who is living under my roof and what they are doing at all times, Sersa Scáth. And I especially like to know what my subjects are capable of. From here on out, you will uphold the right image. That of a princess. After all, you could be Daemon Queen one day. You need to practice while you can."

The Daemon King discarded my hand and walked away.

Unexpectedly, he turned over his shoulder to look at me under the archway. "You ought to train that dog better too. I would hate for her to be put down for her aggressive tendencies."

At that, he sauntered out of the room.

It wasn't just a threat to Dúma. He was saying he'd put me down if I wasn't careful. The thing was, the Daemon King had already tried.

He'd ignited the war between us, and I was ready for it.

The next few days, Sin left, night after night.

Once I was feeling better and we'd resumed our nightly revelries with the High Houses, he disappeared as soon as we got home each night. While I suspected he was at the White Plume, I didn't know for certain, and the last thing I wanted to do was slip away and go looking for him, only to find he wasn't there.

Or for him to discover I was following him.

When the Daemon King invited his entire court and all the High Houses to a party one night, I'd assumed Sin would stay. But even then, he left a few minutes after the guests did. Worse, none of the Gilders had brought more than two or three servants, and I spent the night trying to check the faces of each one. Their plain clothes and tired or envious expressions made them easy to spot. Some clearly longed for the night to end, while others wanted to be a part of it.

I wanted to tell the servants filled with envy that being a Gilder wasn't all it seemed on the surface.

Each passing day twisted my thoughts into a tighter coil, and the harder I tried to think of what Sin was doing, the harder it was to sleep, to think, to do anything but focus on the fact that he was being more suspicious than ever before.

I wondered constantly if he knew his father had threatened and sent that daemon after me. Sin wanted to be the next Daemon King, and that change would likely occur by force, based on mine and Thane's conversation, but I wondered what he was doing to reach his deceitful objective.

His plots obviously extended far beyond me. As he'd said, I was only a box to be checked. The next Daemon King needed a wife. Even a fake one. But our argument where he'd revealed the fact that he needed to be married to become king had occurred before Sin divulged his feelings for me on Nos Nua.

Had his feelings faded? Was I nothing to him?

Were we nothing?

He'd told me the day we'd met that he dealt in secrets. He stole secrets like he could steal souls. I suspected Sin was more secrets than man at this point. So, which was he gathering? How was he molding the Gilders, if he was, to aid him in expediting his coronation?

Before my thoughts could come full circle or connect themselves, I threw off my covers and dressed. I didn't look for a dress but dug through the rest of the wardrobe Claud and Draea had stocked for me in search of breeches, tunics, and boots in the drawers. Curled into a ball at the foot of the bed, Dúma watched my every move.

I sighed with relief to be out of a dress and changed quickly.

Once finished, I swiped at the gold horn I had gone to bed wearing and pulled it out from under my tunic.

I opened the terrace doors. The three Cradled Moons were high in the sky.

Bracing myself, I blew into the horn.

Its call was silent. Dúma followed onto the terrace dusted in moonlight, and I wondered if she heard the sound it made. "You have to stay here, girl. I'll be back."

The Sluagh flew so fast, almost as if it'd emerged out of thin air. A gust whooshed, throwing me off balance, and the pointed tips of its wings and talons clacked the terrace as it landed.

Though I tried to convince myself Sin wouldn't have given me the horn if he hadn't meant what he'd said, I flinched and staggered backward reflexively. Dúma didn't growl. She and these creatures, these spirits, were both of the Soullands. Kin in a way. All my life, I'd been raised to fear these spirits. But tonight, I needed its help.

I needed the Sluagh to take me to the place I'd first seen Sin summon it.

I slipped the cloak around my shoulders and tried to avoid the wings as I climbed onto its slick silver back. Its veiny skin was almost sheer, allowing the moonlight to pass through the wings.

I scratched Dúma behind the ear and kissed her head in case I fell to my death and never returned.

"Take me to Sin's apartment in the slums," I commanded the Sluagh.

As it lifted us high above the citadel, I held on for dear life.

35

When the Sluagh landed on the rickety terrace, I thought for sure we were going to break it and go plummeting toward the ground. It would have been just my luck after surviving the terrifying flight here. We'd soared over the city, and I'd prayed the entire time no one saw me hanging onto its thick yet bony neck, squeezing my eyes shut in panic.

The window was unlocked. I slid it open and put one leg through then the other. The second I stepped inside, Sin was behind me, a dagger pressed to my neck. His arm wrapped across my chest.

He realized instantly it was me.

"Sersa? What are you doing here?"

"You're hiding things from me. You never stopped. I want to know what, and I want to know why."

Sin sighed and let me go, but I immediately missed the closeness of his body, the press of it, and the warmth against mine. We looked into each other's eyes. My breaths came in quick beats as he raked an ungloved hand through his hair.

"How did you know I'd be here? Also, get over here. You need to send the Sluagh away. You can't let it stay here." He hooked a thin finger around the golden horn's chain, my tunic peeling forward slightly. He quickly looked away and touched the horn to his full lips.

I swallowed.

Sin released the horn's chain, and we moved toward the window as the Sluagh shot into the sky. He slammed the window shut and locked it.

"Well?" he asked.

I allowed my eyes to meet his. They weren't angry but perplexed.

"You seemed like you were thinking. You told me you come here to think," I said.

"You really do hang onto my every word, don't you?"

"Maybe I do. Maybe I have to because you keep pushing me away," I said, pinning the blame back on him. I moved toward the armchairs and took a seat in the one nearest the window. "Thane told me you are trying to dethrone your father—and worse."

"Thane can't keep his mouth shut to save his life." He leaned against the edge of his desk and looked into the fire for a long moment before returning his attention to me. "I wanted you to understand that I am a monster since day one. I've always tried to warn you. So, what is it I plan to do?"

I licked my lips and swallowed.

"You plan to kill your father," I said with a straight face.

Sin slid off the desk and crossed the room. He took the seat opposite me and folded his hands in front of him, his elbows propped up on the armrests. "How do you feel about it? Do you have questions?"

"A hundred," I spluttered, suddenly out of breath. I wanted to laugh. That was all he had to say?

"Then ask."

I leaned forward across the little table between us. "Why?"

"He murdered my mother. Why else? I, too, know what it's like to lose a parent. Only I watched him as he did it. I can still hear her screams when I close my eyes. Niuna is her spitting image. I'm surprised he can even look at her. It proves he feels nothing. No remorse."

I shuddered. "I don't blame you. I haven't taken a particular liking to your father either. He's threatened me. He sent that daemon after me. He must have."

Sin looked lost in thought for a moment. "I thought so too. It's why I've been here and out in the city so much."

"Then let me come with you," I snapped, standing. I moved toward him, but before I could sit in his lap, he stood too, towering over me like a stretched shadow.

I tilted my face up to his, skimming his forearms. "You're trying to keep me out of things, but it will only make me more reckless, Sin. I *want* to be here for you."

When his eyes dropped to my lips, my tongue skimming the surface, I wondered if they screamed the way my thoughts did.

Kiss me.

He didn't.

Instead, Sin took a deep breath and licked his lips as I had a moment ago.

He sighed. "I have a line-up of Gilders scheduled for tonight. You can come with me to hear what secrets they've gathered the last few days."

"When? Now?"

"Yes, now." Sin smiled softly, sliding his hands under my jaw. Though he pressed a kiss to my forehead, I found the sweet gesture, so unlike the daemon I saw in him periodically and the one he claimed to be, satiating enough.

For now.

I walked in front of Sin, guiding me from behind through the dark passageway inside the White Plume. It was even draftier than the last time. He didn't touch me, but somewhere deep in my mind, I convinced myself that it was all he wanted to do.

I wanted to.

As we halted in front of a peephole, he positioned himself behind me as he had last time. Except now, my senses were so heightened, my awareness of him and his body even sharper than ever before. It was the desire coursing through me, unable to be ignored any longer.

When he reached around me to lift the little gold flap, I couldn't help myself. I touched my fingers to his wrist and drew circles on the exposed skin between his glove and sleeve there. Sin inhaled through his nose but somehow managed to make it sound natural.

Maybe my touch did nothing to him anymore.

Maybe it never had.

If not, then why had he kissed my forehead in his apartment? Why offer me any gesture at all?

"Sin?" I swallowed as I turned to look over my shoulder. "Can we talk later?"

"Of course," he whispered.

I was shocked when he stole a kiss. His tongue prodded my lips open and curled around mine as his hand slid over my stomach, flattening my back against his chest. His thumb tested its boundaries, tracing the bottom of my breast until I led his hand upward. He pressed a tender kiss to my jaw and another to my neck, simultaneously teasing my nipple through my clothes. My knees trembled, and I squeezed my thighs together as I felt the need and warmth between them.

The moment ended much too soon.

"I want you," I admitted.

"You have me, love. *Focus*," he whispered in my ear. "You'll want to hear what they have to say."

As I faced forward once more, Sin's breath dusted the nape of my neck, sending my pulse racing faster. I leaned back. More than ever before, being entirely alone with Sin, not an eye in sight to glimpse us, ignited my body and mind. The temptation to spin back around or guide his hands where I wanted them...

He was right. I needed to focus.

I looked through the peephole as a line of people, none I recognized, walked into the room and toward the wall we hid behind. Each held a mask at their side.

A second disguise, I realized.

I straightened my spine. These peepholes were right at my eye level, and I needed to stand tall to be able to see.

"Masks off." Sin's voice projected through the peephole as the line of people spread out, all facing the wall we hid behind.

At once, the line before us fumbled for the edges of their masks.

Their façades fell away into heaps of fallen feathers. Though I recognized each of the Gilders, I couldn't put a name to all their faces. I should have been able to, but I wondered how old that book of Gilders I'd read on Nos Nua had been. I wondered if it'd been an excuse for us to do something, anything, together at the height of the tension on our honeymoon.

"Let's begin on the left," Sin said, a few seconds delayed.

I wondered if my admission had distracted him.

My fingers continued to trace his skin. He spun his hand around mine, pinning my palm against the wall. My fingers curled against the smooth stone, and he laced his fingers on top of mine.

Dúm's teeth.

Sure, I wanted to hear what these Gilders had to say. But I was the distracted one. I couldn't control my impulses. Repressing them as long as I had was backfiring.

With Sin so close, how could I maintain control?

"What information do you have for me tonight?"

Sin's voice startled me, and I returned my gaze to the peephole. He sounded entirely composed while his fiery scent clouded my head further.

The man on the very left cleared his throat. "Stellera Drumghoul is with child. The Daemon King has commented in private circles that this strengthens his views of Prince Lochlainn as his heir."

I stiffened, no longer distracted. My attention snapped fully to the room ahead, though Sin didn't unpin my hand or unlace our fingers.

"Are you certain she is with child? Who is the source?" Sin asked.

"Prince Lochlainn personally went to the Daemon King to share the good news. Though the prince wanted to keep it hushed for at least a few weeks to be sure the princess is in good health, the king shared this information with Arlo Elittes. I was there, my lord."

My lord? Who did they think was behind the wall?

Sin moved a strand of my hair away to whisper in my ear, "Arlo is Thane's father." He moved away slightly and projected his voice again for the Gilders behind the peephole. "Very good. Next."

Another man, lumpier and shorter than the last, smoothed his mustache down on both sides before speaking. He folded his hands in front of him respectfully as if readying himself to address Sin. "The trials for the throne near closer. I bring word that the Daemon King could not leave his bed for an entire day before a Bonemender was summoned. The curse is deeper, further along, than was previously thought, my lord. He tried to placate this spell by consuming over a hundred souls."

I narrowed my eyes through the hole. "What—"

Sin touched a finger to my lips. The leather of his gloves was ice-cold.

"And who was the source?" he pressed.

"Draea Abalon," said the man. "She heard directly from the Daemon King's personal servants."

Draea was in on this too?

Sin swallowed behind me. "Next."

"Another source," said a woman, "claimed the trials will be announced in one week."

"And the source?"

"The Daemon King's concubines. They, too, confirmed the curse's effects. He was too ill to...*ahem*."

Sin shook his head. "Anything else? No? Next."

"Yet another source claims we cannot trust Prince Lochlainn Drumghoul."

My stomach dipped into my toes for Stellera. She was with child. I tried to ball my hands into fists, but Sin wound his fingers tighter around mine, easing the fear. He had none still, no worries that I might reap his magic like I had my clan's.

"They saw Prince Lochlainn," continued the Gilder woman, "speaking with Daigh Hellick and..."

"And?"

"And Lady Alders. She cannot be trusted either, my lord."

Lady Alders scoffed. Standing at the end of the line, she pressed a hand to her chest in offense. Though I'd known she allegedly supported Sin, I only realized now that she was here.

"Me?" she said. "Good gods, never in a million years! My lord—"

"The House of Alders is compromised," urged the other woman.

Sin didn't hesitate. "You know what to do. See who she's spoken to and intercept them."

At once, the Mindbloods from before peeled off the walls they stood against and approached Lady Alders. So focused on the Gilders, I hadn't noticed them either. Lady Alders shrieked, trying to get away from them, but one of the Mindbloods gripped her mind before she could, freezing the Gilder in her steps.

"Take enough that she knows not to do it again," Sin commanded. "And enough that she can't tell anyone anything else."

He slammed the peephole shut and stormed down the passageway. He didn't wait for me. Incensed, Sin lifted the next peephole door right as I filed in front of him. He didn't touch me now, but my heart was racing in my chest as if he had.

This room was filled with daemons.

I widened my eyes and wet my lips, tasting something potent in the air. The hazy room smelled of sweet smoke, like sugar and something florally. Pink clouds coiled around the occupants.

"News?" Sin said.

A daemon flinched alert and nodded. He bowed low, dropping his eyes and his pipe.

"Oh, yes." The daemon nodded feverishly. "Prince Lochlainn Drumghoul visited us the day after last. He set a bounty, my Prin—"

"Ah." Sin flicked the peephole, and the daemon dropped his head.

"Excuse me!" He fumbled the hat in his hands. "I mean, *my lord.*"

"Whose head is the bounty for?"

"Forgive me. You—your..."

"*Me?*" Sin asked, impatient.

"N-n-no, my lord. The bounty was for Princess Sersa Drumghoul," stammered the daemon. "We also discovered who sent the pet after her."

"*Who?*" Sin growled. His body tensed around me.

"Niuna Drumghoul. If I may, my lord, if the true sender is veiled by the young princess's name, we do not know. But I believe someone has accepted Prince Lochlainn's bounty. The deal was made in the Midnight Market. I overheard it myself. Princess Sersa is not safe in the City of Soulless with an order to kill on her head."

"No, she's not," Sin said to himself. Then louder, "Thank you. I will summon you when I require you next. You know how to reach me if you hear anything else."

At that, Sin dropped the little door.

"Niuna warned me I wouldn't be– I wouldn't be Daemon Queen for long," I said.

He stared at me straight-faced in the darkness, but I swore I saw a hundred thoughts swimming in his eyes simultaneously.

"What? Why didn't you tell me?" he asked.

I shook my head. "I figured you would know."

"Niuna has different gifts than any of us. She sees things that have yet to be."

"The future."

"Not necessarily the future. Things that may be."

"Isn't that the same thing?"

"Choices are the difference between possibilities and the things that are." Sin led the way out of the passage, hand tight around mine.

"What'll you do?" I asked when we reached the penthouse. He didn't answer me. He was tugged into his thoughts, eyes tracing the floors and the walls in search of something. A plan, maybe. "Sin?"

"You know exactly what I'll do." He fished the golden horn from beneath my clothes again, this time slipping it off my head, and blew into it not once but three times. "I need to borrow this."

"H-How many can you summon?"

"As many as I like."

All the blood drained from my face. I'd witnessed Reaping Hour more times than I could count, but even still, I had no idea how many Sluagh the Daemon King controlled.

"That excuse for a king does not control the Sluagh," Sin said, quiet yet sharp, every word enunciated.

"Sin, I don't like the look in your eyes. What are you planning to do?"

Deep down, I knew.

"I'm planning to make it look like an accident, that's what." He squared his shoulders at the three Sluagh who'd appeared on the terrace and handed them a dagger I hadn't seen him unsheathe. "Stab Lochlainn Drumghoul with this. Then kill him. And do not return without that dagger."

I staggered back. "Are you sure you know what you're doing?"

By the time I'd found my voice, the Sluagh had already shot into the sky, their enormous wings extending from their bodies like the sails of a ship.

Sin turned and cupped my face in his hands.

"I will not let him take you from me. You're not safe until Loch is dead and the bounty is dropped. So, yes, I know what I'm doing. I will do whatever is necessary to make sure you're safe. I would kill my brother with my bare hands if I must."

"I'm not asking you to do that," I said. "And Stellera—"

"You don't need to ask me to do anything. You'll never need to ask me to instinctively protect you, Sersa. Even if you don't want my protection. Even when I *know* you can protect yourself." He took a deep breath. "As for Stellera, she'll be better off. Trust me." His wild eyes glanced to the side. "I need you to stay here."

"Why? Where are you going?"

"To follow the Sluagh. If they can't finish the job, I'm going to."

"But—"

Sin kissed me long and hard. Frantic. As his hands skimmed the outside of my body, I imagined, under different circumstances, that he might smile as we kissed. Maybe both of us would.

But not now. Not in this dark, dire place trapping us.

Sin sucked on my lower lip before he pulled away.

"Wait for me," he said. "You'll be safest here, I promise. Please do as I ask, Sersa. I love you, and I don't want to lose you. Not tonight. Not ever."

I pressed my lips together and fought back tears as he placed more distance between us. He grabbed a feathered mask before he slipped out into the night on the Sluagh's heels. All I could think was that he might not return. He'd beaten his brother once, but I didn't know whether we had enough luck on our side for him to do it again.

Then I realized what Sin had said.

He loved me.

And I hated myself for my weakness. For what I felt. For not saying it back.

I loved Nessin Drumghoul too.

36

Following Sin was easy. Instinctive.

I slipped down from the terrace and landed in a shadowy, cobbled alleyway outside the White Plume. The drop wasn't far, and though I heard the congested street around the corner bustling with patrons tonight, no one paid me any mind as I slinked forward and joined the crowd.

Including Sin.

So focused, he didn't notice me wading after him through groups of people. I kept a safe distance, but when I made eye contact with a daemon, they tilted their head at me.

I cursed Dúm under my breath, realizing I'd forgotten to grab a mask. As a Daemon Princess, I was now recognizable.

I pulled my hood lower over my eyes and kept them on the ground, only looking up to be sure I hadn't lost Sin. When he arrived at the gate, I froze and hid behind a pastry shop on the corner of the city square. The scent of cinnamon dough and sickly-sweet icing trickled into the air, distracting me for a second.

Through gaps in the foot traffic, I saw Sin crossing the street, waiting for the gate to open for him. He was *leaving* Gilders Eye? I still had the eye bracelet he'd given me weeks ago, but I couldn't understand why Lochlainn would be outside the affluent side of Nos

Ovscura. Could Sin be headed to the Crescendo? Surely, he wouldn't send the Sluagh to such a public place. He was cleverer than that. His brother had to be somewhere Sin had not only known he'd be ahead of time but also somewhere the Sluagh and he wouldn't be seen. To be tied to Lochlainn's death...

I shuddered.

If Sin was discovered, the Daemon King would have his head. But maybe it didn't matter when Sin was already planning to have his father's before then.

As the gates closed, I slipped after him with seconds to spare. He led me deeper and deeper into the derelict parts of the city, where the buildings teetered together and vendors on both sides of the street shouted at passersby, trying to tempt them to buy whatever wares they hoped to swindle people with tonight.

We reached a quiet street, so far within the maze. I was sure I wouldn't be able to get out on my own. I'd have to follow him to get back to Gilders Eye.

Or worse. I might have to reveal myself to him.

That was out of the question.

As Sin approached a row of brownstones that had surprisingly good bones for this side of the city but still the dingy exteriors crowding all other streets, I glimpsed Prince Lochlainn surrounded by the three Sluagh.

Sin had definitely known where Lochlainn would be.

I hung back, hiding behind the corner of a brownstone across the narrow street.

Lochlainn was clutching his shoulder, where a red wound blossomed wider and wider, staining his fingers, dripping down his front, and pooling on the cobblestones. He ripped the dagger free and let it dangle at his side. Blood dripped off the blade. Sin stayed in a pocket of shadows, watching, and my mind raced with thoughts of my own brother.

The sheer thought of harming Ciel made me sick.

"*Do not fight,*" Sin commanded hypnotically under his breath. So quiet I almost couldn't hear. "*Do not fight them, brother.*"

The Sluagh took turns slashing their talons across Lochlainn's front. The other prince was powerless against them—against his own brother's commands.

My gut swirled with unease.

"I know it's you, Sin!" Lochlainn shouted. His labored voice made every bone in my body stiffen, every nerve flicker.

My blood froze in my veins.

"You think I'm foolish enough not to recognize my own brother's magic? You would leave my children fatherless? You would make me leave my son as Mother left us?"

This urged Sin to step out of the shadows. I couldn't see his face from here, but I saw the tension between his shoulder blades. The wild black hair of Sin's façade, courtesy of the White Plume's mask, blew in the wind around him. Likewise, Lochlainn's hair came loose from its ribbon. Sin's ungloved palms flexed at his sides, arms slightly raised like he was controlling each of the Sluagh right now.

I knew he was.

He'd ordered every slash they drew across his brother's body.

"You forget who took Mother from us," Sin said, softer than expected. "I won't let you take Sersa too. I won't let *him* either. Your final mistake was putting a price on her head."

Chills rippled down my spine, along my forearms, into my toes.

Sin couldn't be doing this for me. Not all for me. I hated myself for praying to the High Triad, but it was all I could do as I dug my nails into the stone and gritted my teeth so hard I swore I tasted blood mixing with the bile spinning in my gut.

"You have always refused to believe our father was wrong. You idolize him. You have always believed that blind worship will put you on his throne," Sin said. "But you're wrong. I will put *myself* on that throne."

"Then you would choose her over me. *Her* over your own flesh and blood."

Sin's fingers twitched.

One of the spirits slashed a fatal wound across Lochlainn's gut.

I bit down on my fist, wanting to look away but unable to.

Sin reached the circle of Sluagh as Lochlainn dropped to his knees. The dagger—the one Sin had lent them—clattered to the ground as Lochlainn's fist uncurled. He dropped his other hand that'd been trying to stop the blood flowing from his shoulder.

The Sluagh halted and cleared a path for Sin. He knelt before his brother.

Sin's voice was barely a whisper, but I heard it over the wind that coiled down the street. "I have already chosen her."

"Then do it yourself. Give me mercy in death if not—" Lochlainn's words escaped him as he fell forward, barely catching himself on his palms. Blood dribbled from his mouth. He spit it onto the cobbles.

Sin turned his brother over and set his head against his arm. He picked up the dagger, hands shaking, and whispered words I couldn't hear. A prayer maybe. A last farewell.

Lochlainn reached a bloody hand toward Sin's face, still not his own but the carefully crafted façade.

But the other hand—

Lochlainn's other hand slipped a dagger soundlessly from his coat.

"It was always going to be you, little brother. *Daemon King*. But she will not be your Daemon Queen," Lochlainn said, "and you have always known that. Niuna saw it too. Not all things can be saved."

"The future is not set in stone."

Lochlainn gritted his teeth and lifted his arm, ready to plunge the dagger into Sin's heart.

Instinctively, I fumbled for the dainty daggers at my waist and whipped one across the street, sending it soaring toward Lochlainn's chest.

It buried itself deep.

Sin looked up, horror in his eyes as they landed on me.

Lochlainn dropped his blade. A second clatter echoed where it'd fallen. Sin's brother grew slack in his arms, his eyes fluttering closed. Like nothing had happened, Sin hid the golden horn under his shirt. Then he stood, carefully resting Lochlainn's head on the ground.

He yanked free the dagger I'd thrown and cleaned it on the inside of his coat.

"Take him to Nos Nua," Sin commanded the Sluagh. "Do not

maim his body any more than it already is. Make sure he is somewhere safe. *Hidden.*"

As the Sluagh lifted Lochlainn off the ground, its wings created a short-lived whirlwind.

The door to one of the brownstones swept open. A young, breathtakingly beautiful woman and her boy, no more than three or four, stood in the doorway. Her eyes darted to the sky and the Sluagh carrying Lochlainn away. The boy's gaze found Sin.

As the woman looked upon his face, there was no recognition in her gaze.

She had braided, black hair and dark eyes, while her son—white-haired, pale-skinned, sucking on his thumb—looked lost in a daze. His features were unmistakably Lochlainn, his chin-length hair even braided into a thin, short tail. He pointed to the sky then.

Had the Daemon King known about this boy? If he had, Lochlainn wouldn't have claim to the throne anyway. Would he? The Daemon King had gone so far as to warn me that he and Sin, all the brothers, needed to be certain any and all heirs were legitimate. For this boy to be alive, there was no way the king knew. But how couldn't he in his own city?

Maybe that proved how much he favored his second eldest son.

When the woman looked down the street, her gaze landing on *me*, I flinched hard. She gasped. I hardly managed to step back into the shadows. But the look on her face said it all.

She recognized me, and that was all that mattered.

I had been present for the death—the murder—of her son's father, a Daemon Prince.

No, I had done it.

Sin followed her gaze and glowered at me with all the rage in the world. Wherever I was, Sin was sure to be close.

Would Lochlainn's lover know that?

"You will not speak of this," Sin commanded the woman. Then he stormed forward, grabbed me by the arm, and we dashed into the City of Soulless, never looking back.

Sin said nothing as we moved through the city, back into Gilders Eye, and to the White Plume. I felt like I was going to shatter into a million pieces as he kept silent, never uttering a single word on the walk to the pleasure den. We entered through the White Plume's front entrance, and only then did he release me. He knew I'd follow up to the penthouse. I had nowhere else to go.

He unlocked the door, let me in, and locked it behind us.

I cleared my throat, unable to stand the silence anymore. I licked my lips. "Can't we send a Mindblood to alter the woman's memories?" My voice cracked. "I-In case your command did not work."

Sin shook his head. "It worked, but she could be halfway to the citadel by now. She could try to go there anyway."

"How will she get into Gilders Eye?" I asked. "She can't."

This gave him pause. A glimmer of hope surfaced in his eyes. He tore off his mask, poofing into a heap at my feet before he disappeared into the hall. He'd acted so quickly, almost without thought. So had I, but that was somewhat to be expected.

He'd said he would do anything to protect me, and I'd acted in kind without thinking either.

I stood in the penthouse foyer, unable to move. I watched the door, eyes occasionally looking to the pile of feathers, waiting for Sin to return.

Finally, he did minutes later.

The wait felt like days had passed.

A crazed look consumed his colorless eyes as he dropped onto his hands and knees. He hung his head, and as a furious shriek tore through his body, I knew he was anything but fine.

It was done. His brother was dead at his command.

But I—*I* had ended Lochlainn's life.

Kneeling on the floor beside him, I pulled Sin against me and held him. I stroked his white hair, the strands like spun silk between my fingers as he buried his face in my chest. I breathed a dozen times that I was sorry. That I was so sorry.

After a few minutes, his fury diminished, and his breathing slowed. His shoulders eased. His muscles unwound.

But then, Sin slowly pulled back from my chest and looked into my eyes. His were rimmed in red and his skin more flushed than I'd ever seen, but his cheeks weren't glistening with tears.

He looked murderous yet calm, beautiful and tortured.

A raging sea in some parts while utterly still in others.

The worst part was that I didn't know what he was feeling or what he wanted to do in that moment. I knew better than to touch him right now, but I wished there was something, anything, I could do or say.

Nothing would ease his pain right now. I'd felt it before when I thought I'd lost my father. But it hadn't been a true loss. I'd clung to my sliver of hope because we'd never seen Pa's corpse, and there were no witnesses.

My hands were responsible tonight though.

"Stop that," Sin whispered, gathering my thoughts. "You saved me." He shook his head. "I would be dead without you, and Lochlainn would kill you next. I sent a Mindblood there. I don't know if they'll get there in time. I don't know anything for sure, but if they don't..." His white gaze flicked up. "You may have to leave tonight, Sersa. If the Daemon King learns you were there, he'll go after you. The slashes on Loch's body are all me, but the king knows how to get even with me."

"If it even comes to that," I said. "You sent all evidence away. I don't want to leave." The desperation in my voice made my throat catch. What I wanted was to be with Sin. "As you said, you commanded her. You just need to figure out what you will do with... with Lochlainn gone." *Dead.* "People will think he's missing."

Sin sat up and bent his knees to his chest, hanging his head between them. He took a deep breath and looked back up after a moment. "I don't know. I don't have enough time to find and hire a Changeling at the Midnight Market." Sin shook his head. "Even if I did, they wouldn't know Loch. Not really. They'd need to study him for days, memorize his manner of speaking and phrases, his movements. Everything."

It was true. Though Ailerby wasn't from the Soullands and certainly not a Changeling, he'd spent days studying every clan member in silence when he'd come to live with us. He'd been caught countless times following them around, mimicking others in dark corners, and eerily mirroring everything they did. While Ailerby had refined his ability to imitate others impeccably, even he needed to study the person to do so.

With Lochlainn dead, there was no way we could pull it off.

"I–" Sin swallowed. "I can't stop thinking that I either just secured my throne or ensured I will never sit upon it."

I didn't understand, not really, but I knew if either of us or both of us were caught, my father would be lost forever. How would I return to Os Íseal? I wouldn't, not until Sin finished fulfilling his vendetta. The Soullands wouldn't be safe for me until he had.

Sin stood and offered a hand to help me up. "This will take a few days to come to a head. Perhaps I can forge a note saying he ran off with his lover and son. I could order them to leave the city." He pinched the bridge of his nose. "I don't know yet. But we've been gone too long already. The staff of the White Plume will confirm we were here, but we need to get back. I don't want to give the Daemon King or anyone else any reason to question our whereabouts."

"Of course," I said with a nod.

Sin pulled me close, and I rested my forehead against his chest.

"You bear no guilt in this. Please don't think you do." When I scoffed to hold back tears, Sin stroked my hair. "I'm serious, Sersa. I would kill for you over and over to keep you safe."

He had to know I felt the same—that I would have released that blade a million times for him. But still, I choked on my words.

37

It was madness in Gilders Eye when we reached the gates under a pale red sky. Bloodcurdling screams echoed in the air. People crowded around the square, surrounded by shops selling any little thing the Gilders' hearts desired.

Sin grabbed my hand and pulled me toward the front of the crowd, desperate to see what all the commotion was about. He led with his shoulders, forcing people to part for him until they realized who he was.

We reached the front.

Two mangled bodies lay in the middle of the square. I gasped. Sin held me tight against his side, but I focused ahead, absorbing the sight in horror.

Lochlainn and the Sluagh who'd carried him had fallen from a great height. An arrow pierced the Sluagh's insipid flesh.

They had been shot down.

Jolting me alert, the voices of Soul Guards surrounded the square, ordering people to move on, to disperse and let them through. But Gilders everywhere were crying, cupping hands over their mouths to muffle their sobs.

"Our prince is dead," said someone. "The Daemon Prince is dead! True death!"

It was then that I saw it. One of the Soul Guards carried a powerful crossbow. The *guards* had shot them down. Either they'd been ordered, or they'd seen the Sluagh carrying someone in the light of dawn.

My heart pattered frantically in my chest, but Sin, I sensed, wasn't going to leave. It would look more suspicious than the fact that we were here at the scene of the crime. Rather, the fall of it. Upon seeing Lochlainn again, Sin's eyes widened, and his mouth hung open. He looked shocked, and I had the horrendous thought that it was good. He'd look guilty otherwise.

But me... I didn't know what I looked like. I felt numb. Nothing.

It didn't matter what Sin had said. I was guilty.

The Soul Guard with the crossbow approached us, and I realized it was the same one who'd stopped us on Dúm's Cross the first day Sin and I met. I still didn't know his name, and I still didn't care to know, but he seemed to be everywhere. He'd obviously seen the figure the Sluagh had carried. Perhaps he'd questioned it because it'd been a moment too early for Reaping Hour.

I didn't know why. I'd probably never know why, but I wished we could go back and undo so many things, redo so many.

The guard knelt before Sin. "Prince Nessin, I'm so sorry, but..." He glanced over his shoulder then to the ground at Sin's feet. "It's Prince Lochlainn. He's fallen to his true death. We will find out how this happened. I pledge this promise to you, my prince, and to the Daemon King. I swear this to you on my life."

Sin had almost managed to cover up his brother's death.

Murder.

But if the Soul Guards discovered the truth now, I would be as good as dead.

Two days passed, and Lochlainn's lover still hadn't come forward. No, she hadn't been just a lover. She had mothered his child. An heir. Now, Lochlainn had a second heir on the way if what the Gilders at the White Plume had said about Stellera was true. But she would never be Daemon Queen now that Lochlainn was dead, and I didn't know what that meant for the child she carried.

The funeral took place on the shore behind the citadel at midnight. The sky turned blacker with each passing minute as we made our way toward the Wraithsea. A foamy tide thrashed against the sand, and I couldn't help but think about the time Sin and I had spent on Nos Nua, so far in the distance, I couldn't see it through the fog.

The Gilders wore their finest black clothes for the occasion while the Daemon King wore red from head to toe, including a long cloak that dragged behind him as he walked at the head of the procession. Under the Cradled Moons and set against the backdrop of the dark landscape, his attire seemed to glow like a beacon.

On Os Íseal, the color meant a loved one had been killed in cold blood.

The color meant the wearer *sought* blood.

Revenge.

A death for a death.

Whoever had killed Lochlainn, the Daemon King had a message for them. He would find them and destroy them.

Sin and I walked behind him, standing in a straight line with the rest of his siblings, including Niuna, and their spouses. The only people ahead of the Daemon King were the Soul Guards who carried the pyre Lochlainn laid atop. As soon as we reached the water, the king would ignite the twigs and send his son out to sea in hopes of entering the Otherworld.

Sin squeezed my hand when we reached the shoreline. His eyes were hardened, narrowed on the sea. My mind emptied as the pyre ignited in a blaze, carried forward on the tide.

While he had ordered his brother's death for me, I had thrown the blade. I couldn't stop myself from thinking that, deep down, maybe Sin blamed me.

Maybe he would come to hate me soon enough.

A few days later, I navigated to Stellera and Lochlainn's rooms as soon as I was allowed.

All the revelries had halted in the wake of Prince Lochlainn's death. As had my search for Pa, despite that it felt more important than ever. I needed to get Ciel and Pa out of this city and never look back.

With the complications of my feelings for Sin, that would be easier said than done. But Sin, surprisingly, hadn't retreated from me. Every night since I'd killed Lochlainn, he'd held me close, his deep breaths and lips dusting my neck as if he knew we would be separated soon enough. The night of the funeral, we'd kissed for what felt like minutes, but in reality, we'd savored one another well beyond midnight. His hands had roved my body ravenously, and I knew it meant he felt our time with one another draining.

In our shadowy room, Sin's fingers had again found their way under my tunic that night, and every night thereafter, but they weren't what I craved. I wondered why he held back after everything, how he resisted at all, and why he wouldn't let me touch him. But I chalked it up to the fact that what I'd done affected him more than he would admit.

Stellera was sitting on a deep blue settee in the corner of the room when I entered. She waved me over eagerly. She wore all black, and though she was barely showing, she touched a hand to her lower belly.

It was true, then. Pregnant. With Lochlainn Drumghoul's son.

"Thank the gods someone is here," she said, eyes darting toward the Soul Guards in the entryway. "I have been confined to this room for an entire week, and I will go mad if I'm here alone any longer."

These were not the words of a grieving widow, yet I understood them in my own way.

I approached the settee cautiously.

"Come, sit," she begged.

Instead, I threw her into a hug and tried not to sob in her ear. My secret weighed heavily on me. "I'm so sorry, Stellera. I'm so—"

"Oh, for Aon's sake, it isn't your fault."

If only she knew.

When I pulled back to look at her, there was no sadness on her face.

"Though I am sorry for what happened, I am dedicated to a cause" —Stellera leaned forward and pitched her voice low—"that is bigger than me."

I gritted my teeth to keep my mouth from falling open.

Before I could ask what she meant, she grabbed a black shawl and tugged me toward the door. Down the corridor outside her room, she led me to an elevated terrace garden I hadn't known existed. It looked almost like the one where I'd first met her and Helde, but it was significantly larger.

And Ciel and Devlin lingered there.

Stellera looped her arm through mine after nodding hello to the couple standing near some rose bushes, and then we started to stroll leisurely after both Ciel and his husband passed sorrowful smiles our way.

"So," she said with a long sigh. "The light has been the only thing keeping me from feeling sick lately. I've been out here all week when I can. I walk for what feels like five bells, and then I'm so exhausted I simply fall asleep."

"Then you're not okay," I said.

She passed me a shrewd look. "Oh, I'm okay. If you must know, I have a daemon lover."

"That girl we saw," I said, dropping my voice, "at the White Plume?"

She laughed. "All right, I have many daemon lovers. But no. His name is Feren. I haven't seen him in weeks. My point is, mine and Prince Lochlainn's union wasn't a love match exactly. He wasn't horrible to me by any means. He just made it very clear an heir was all he cared about."

The bassinette he'd given her as a wedding gift still burned in my mind. He'd seen her as useful for one thing and one thing only, like his father had divulged.

"It's sad, of course. Very sad. But..." Stellera never finished her sentence. Instead, she changed the subject. "I hope to bow to *you* one day soon. Since Prince Devlin has been vocal about his aversion to ruling, Prince Nessin will make a fine Daemon King. No one will admit it, but Prince Jestin is hardly an option."

We rounded a bush with vibrant red flowers then approached a tall row of privacy hedges.

"Not that I love to gossip or anything," she went on. "But I heard that all the brothers have informed the Daemon King the consummations are all complete. That means the trials will begin soon. But if Devlin won't compete, I suppose it will be more of a formality after how easily Prince Nessin beat Jestin."

I halted and turned to look at her, but she urged me to keep walking until we were momentarily hidden behind the tall hedges.

"Why in all the bloody gods' names would they tell the king they've lain with their spouses? Is that really anyone else's business other than our own?" I didn't want to tell her Sin had lied—again—either.

Now, Stellera stopped.

Under the shade of a massive oak tree, she turned to look at me. Her blue eyes narrowed. Her skin was darker than the last time I'd seen her. With the Rime season almost here, it was unseasonably warm and bright. It would retreat soon enough, the frigid temperatures replacing it before we knew it. I wondered what it was like back home or if this weather was exclusive to the Soullands.

"The consummation does not mean a tumble in the sheets, Sersa. I am talking about the *actual* consummation. Do you know what I'm alluding to?"

I hadn't the faintest clue. I leaned back against the tree. The bark scratched my back and arms through my long-sleeved dress.

"I ask this as a friend and from a place of realization that I will never be Daemon Queen and would very much like you to be," Stellera said. She chewed the side of her lip, eyes roving across my face. She was thinking of something, and I wondered if she might be trying to find a way to lie to me.

"Just say it. I can handle whatever it is," I snapped.

Her eyes darted to Ciel and Devlin then back to me. Stellera stood tall and strong, her words sharp. "You must give Prince Nessin a sliver of your soul for the union to be official. You cannot become

Daemon Queen if you do not complete the process, nor can he become Daemon King."

For a second, I didn't think it sounded so bad. Sure, it was another thing Sin had withheld from me, but becoming Daemon Queen had never been a part of the plan to begin with.

But then my eyes reflexively found Ciel and Devlin, like Stellera's had moments ago. Surprisingly, they were grinning at one another despite the circumstances. All I could think was how lucky Devlin was to have Ciel, the kindest soul in the world; Ciel, the most caring brother I could have asked for and the only one who understood my moods; Ciel, who accepted me instead of trying to change me; and Ciel, who had more love in his heart than most people I knew, than anyone deserved.

He'd come here for me, given up his chance to become a Druid, and the gods only knew what else. In return, he'd gotten something most people spent years trying to find, something Devlin had spent centuries trying to.

"Then, both you and Helde..." I turned back to her. A wave of dizziness overwhelmed me. Black spots speckled the edges of my vision. "I mean, you both had less than a whole soul already."

"Living under the High Houses, Helde and I grew up understanding the ways. It is a great honor to give a piece of our soul, albeit already incomplete, to support the Daemon Princes' claim to the throne. We also have no need to leave the Soullands. Our lives are here." Stellera's knowing eyes held mine. "Not that you have any reason now that you and the prince are wed, of course. But once someone fully mortal gives a piece of their soul to a soulless, they can never leave the Soullands again, Sersa."

My gaze darted back to Ciel and Devlin, their lips now on one another's. Had my own brother given a piece of his soul to his husband?

Had Ciel risked it all—like he'd said before we came here—to save Pa?

I remembered what he'd said weeks ago.

I also want Pa back, and I'm willing to do whatever is necessary.

I was willing to bet anything Ciel had done just that.

38

"Ciel."

Devlin and my brother turned as they entered the hall the terrace garden connected to.

"May I have a moment alone with my brother, Prince Devlin?" I asked.

"Of course," he said with a slight dip of his head, letting go of Ciel's hand. There were bags under his eyes, and without Ciel's lips on his, the heavy weight of sadness had returned to his expression.

When he was out of earshot, I pulled Ciel toward the end of the hall. There were no doors down this way, only a large window. We stood beside it. The feel of the strange moons on my skin as the light twisted through the glass made me sweat.

I decided bluntness was best—the only way I'd get the words out. "Did you give Prince Devlin a piece of your soul?"

Ciel's gaze pierced through me. He was silent for a long time, clearly thinking. Every moment he stayed quiet shattered my heart even more. My too-smart brother couldn't have.

And yet I swore his silence meant exactly the opposite.

He brushed the long hair out of his eyes. "That's none of your business, Sersa."

"I will ask one more time, and you will answer me. Did you give him *any* of your soul?"

Ciel licked his lips and looked down the hallway where Devlin had disappeared. When he looked back at me, his eyes burned into mine. Black into black.

"I did."

My world spun, and though the sensation was inside my head, my reaction couldn't be contained. My voice trembled through gritted teeth. "Do you know what that means for you?"

"I do."

"Then you know you can never leave the Soullands!"

Ciel took a hasty step forward. *"Be quiet."*

When he finally released me, taking a step back, the red behind my eyes had retreated. Marginally.

"You can never return," I said again, breathless rather than enraged.

"I have made my peace with it, and I would give up the life I had on Os Íseal a million times. Our feelings for one another are real. Realer than imaginable. I take it you haven't given a piece to Prince Nessin then. That's good. You must promise me you won't, Sers."

"What's the point? I might as well now that you're—"

"One of us needs to be able to take Pa back home. You can't do that if you truly want to save him."

Of course I wanted to. My heart thrummed in my chest, and furious tears threatened to fall from my eyes. Ciel. Ciel...

No.

"Save him? We're no closer to finding Pa than we were the first day. I only saw him once and haven't since. We wasted so much time on our honeymoons. Ridiculous."

"I saw him," Ciel said.

Again, my world spun.

"Where? What? Are you sure?"

He nodded. "Devlin was invited to the House of Elittes yesterday for a garden party."

"We weren't invited."

"No," he said tightly. He spoke even quieter, his hands on my upper arms and eyes locked on my face. Strands of black hair fell out of his ponytail into those intense eyes again. "I believe the Elittes want to see Devlin on the Daemon Throne now that Lochlainn is dead. Jestin wasn't invited either, but many Gilders from different High Houses were there."

"Which houses?" I asked as if I could remember which those Gilders in the White Plume had been from. Besides Lady Alders, I couldn't. They'd worn no markers identifying their houses either. "I thought Devlin doesn't want the throne."

"He doesn't want it, but I think he knows about Sin's plans. I think– I think Devlin supports his plan, Sersa. He met with Sin directly after, so he must be funneling him information."

Sin dealt in secrets. I had no doubt.

Ciel shook his head. "I don't know for sure. I accompanied Devlin to the party. Pa didn't see me, and I almost didn't see him through the crowd, but I know it was him. The shaved head again, like you said."

I stared, unblinking, at him. My eyes hadn't deceived me the other night then. It *had* been Pa. He was alive. He was safe or at least mostly. "What was he doing? Did he look all right? Do you think Devlin told Sin about Pa being there?"

"No. He didn't see him, or I don't think. I was alone when I did. But fittingly enough, they had Pa in gold shackles."

Ciel took a deep breath.

"That's not all. The Daemon King was there. I went inside to change into fresh clothes. Lord Elittes's son offered me some of his after one of their sloshed guests spilled on me. I think it was the bloke who sat next to you at the fights. He left me upstairs to change by myself, and the Daemon King and Lord Elittes were in a room down the hall together. I could barely make out the king's face through the crack of the door, but I'd know his voice anywhere."

Lord Elittes's son.

Lord Elittes probably had a few sons, but...

Thane. Had he known? Had he purposely directed Ciel upstairs, where he knew the Daemon King and his father would be? And what about Pa? How could Thane not know who he was?

My heart raced, and my eyes flickered across my brother's face as I listened and picked apart his words.

Ciel took a shuddering breath. "The king suspects one of his sons murdered Prince Lochlainn. He's already ruled out Jestin, claiming he's too soft for that sort of thing, but as a Bonespeaker, he can effortlessly command the Sluagh. As for Devlin, he's no Bonespeaker. He can't control the Sluagh. So, there's only one son he *knows* would be both up to the task and capable. One Lochlainn severely wounded as a child. One with ice in his heart."

I pressed my trembling lips together.

"The king knows Sin can command the Sluagh to do his bidding, and that Jestin's ability is nowhere near his. Supposedly, Sin's always had an unnatural connection to the creatures. Ever since they wounded him, Sers. Devlin has said before that they look at Sin like their king already, and their father has always taken note of it."

I licked my lips, tasting salt. But the horn summoned the Sluagh. Did his father not know? Did the connection go beyond that?

"The king made it known he isn't against killing one of his own sons. He's out for blood. He won't stop. He isn't afraid of losing—in his words—his best heir. But he's trying to find some evidence against Sin first. More than Lochlainn's wounds. Devlin thinks his father doesn't want to incite the Gilders who have lobbied for Sin."

"For centuries," I finished.

"Yes."

"We must get Pa out tonight," I hissed through my gasping breaths.

"Agreed. The only way we can do that is with Sin's help. We need his commands. We can't be caught, or it'll be all of our heads."

So far, Sin's command to Lochlainn's lover had worked. She hadn't come forward. If she had, we'd be dead already. Proof would surface before long though. It had to. And if not, the king could easily fabricate some.

I nodded slowly.

This would work. Sin could command others to stay silent, to keep our secrets, if we ran into anyone.

"Okay," I said. "Tonight it is."

"Tonight," Ciel echoed.

39

I told Sin the loose plan, and he agreed. With the news of what his father had discussed with Lord Elittes, Sin knew it was time, whether or not we wanted it to be.

Standing in his room after we'd changed—he in his finest attire, me in the darkest, most comfortable clothes I had—Sin put his bare hands on my shoulders and looked me in the eye.

"You must promise me something," he said.

"Anything," I said immediately as if he'd commanded me.

"You're going to regret that." A sad smile curled his scarred lips. "I will never command you again, Sersa. Not since that day you washed up on the beach, sopping wet. So please agree even when I tell you."

"There was another time after that," I said, thinking of the night he'd drowned his guard at the Druids' parish.

"Yes. I regret that time." He hesitated for a long moment, studying my face. "When we get your father, you must leave the city. Tonight. You must not look back."

His eyes held mine, incredibly still.

I couldn't bring myself to tell him that it had always been the plan, but learning that Ciel couldn't leave changed everything.

"Ciel. He completed the consummation with Devlin," I said,

hardly louder than a breath. Saying the words aloud shattered me into a million pieces. "When it's time, he can't come with."

Sin pulled me against his chest. With his arms wrapped around me, everything stilled for a second. It felt right. I knew nothing was and it wouldn't be for a long time, but being here with Sin now sustained me.

"I'm sorry. I promise I will take care of Ciel. So will Devlin. I'll send them away before it gets…" He swallowed.

I pulled back to look up at him. "Before what?"

"If what Ciel heard is true—and I wholeheartedly believe my father said and meant it—things are going to unravel. Soon. I don't want you here when they do. If you stay in the Soullands, you will be the sole thing I focus on. Protecting you. Ensuring you're unharmed. I need to act without thought, Sersa."

My stomach dipped into my toes, and my hands trembled at my sides. I pulled away again, fully this time, and turned my back to him. I couldn't look in his eyes.

I couldn't face the reality that I'd never see him again.

I squeezed my eyes shut, biting my lip so hard I swore I'd draw blood.

"What is this really worth to you?" I asked. "Your father killed your mother. I get it. But what *else* do you want from this, Sin? What will you do once you sit on the Daemon Throne?"

He blew out a deep breath and closed the distance between us again. His palms slid to my upper arms, softly squeezing them, letting me know he was here. But that touch—his hands and body, his beautiful face, his smirk, his presence—all of it would vanish before I knew it. Never to be in my reach again.

"I haven't worked that all out. But I love you, Sersa. I said it before, and I will keep saying it. I love you, and I can't lose you. Even if I must…" I felt him shake his head behind me. "My motivation now is so much deeper than it was before. I endangered you by bringing you here, and the only way I can prevent anything from happening is by going straight to the source of that danger. By removing it at once."

My body trembled fiercely, and Sin squeezed my arms as if to hold me up or hold me together. I imagined myself as a glass heart, cupped in his gloved hands, ready to shatter.

No matter how gentle he was in this moment, our fate only had a few possible ends.

I couldn't bring myself to voice the feelings I harbored for Sin when I knew our ending even before it unfolded.

My nostrils burned with the threat of hopeless tears because Sin *was* going to lose me. I was going to return to Os Íseal. Maybe my clan would lock me up. Maybe...

Thinking of all the possibilities would ruin me. Those possibilities wounded me so deeply, in the very center of my stupid heart.

"Under my reign," Sin whispered, "I could stop the Sluagh, their hunting, the Reaping Hours night after night. And you—"

He sounded like he'd been punched in the gut. He hovered behind me, sliding his hands around my shoulders. I closed my eyes, aware only of his touch intoxicating my mind. He'd forgotten for a second what he'd just asked me to do.

To leave and never look back.

"Sin." My words came out shaky with emotion but steadfast. "There is something I want. Something I *need*. A proper farewell."

Behind me, his body tensed against mine.

He swallowed audibly.

"*Anything*," he said as I had before. But his words, his lips, were close to my ears. "Name it, and it's yours. I'm yours."

I spiraled, raised onto my tiptoes, and crushed my lips against his as I had done to the stranger, the façade he'd worn at the White Plume. His lips were as desirous as mine. I ran my hand along his abdomen through his shirt, and he parted my lips with his tongue. I fumbled for his pants, feeling him through the fabric.

But before I could beg him to touch me in our last moments alone together, there came a knock at the door.

I closed my eyes, tipped my head back, and sighed through my nose.

Ciel.

It was time to leave.

My heart shattered. My desire shattered.

And it was replaced by black tendrils of fear and blue waves of sorrow creeping at the edges of my vision.

"Our best bet is the side entrance," Sin said, eyes locked on the dark windows of Elittes Manor. "It's the servant entrance."

We hid in the shadows along the street perpendicular to the manor. The property and the manor itself were wider than a lot of the others we'd visited, sprawling behind enormous metal gates with privacy hedges almost twice Sin's height and a vast, verdant lawn. The manor was a single floor, whereas the other High Houses had been at least three with endless balconies and stone courtyard entrances.

"Did you ask *Thane* which entrance is best?" I asked.

Sin's so-called friend had to have known all along that Pa was here. Under his very own nose.

"No, I know the estate," Sin said.

I didn't press Sin, but if Pa was inside—if he'd been here the entire time—Thane was the first person I was going to murder.

The sky overhead was black and starless, but we had only a few bells till dawn. We needed to make quick work of this. We couldn't risk Pa being stuck in the city another day until it reopened to tourists, especially if other servants noticed his absence.

Luckily, this side of the city was quiet right now. But if we were caught, we wouldn't be able to get ourselves out of it.

Sin took a step toward me and looped his finger around the horn I wore.

My eyes flicked up to his. "How many will you summon?"

"More than two will look suspicious," Sin said. "Especially after Loch." His colorless eyes flickered to Ciel.

Thanks to the Daemon King and what Ciel had overheard, he already knew about Lochlainn. Though I supposed he believed Sin had done it, both of us evidently refused to breathe life into the truth.

Holding my gaze, Sin pressed the horn to his lips. It took a moment for the Sluagh to reach us.

"Onto the lawn," he commanded, pointing.

The spirits obeyed. Their wings flapped against the crisp night air as they flew over the gates surrounding Elittes Manor.

"Oh, before I forget." Sin pulled three masks from the inside of his coat. A fourth poked out of the inner pocket for Pa. "Masks on."

After we slipped on the masks and each of our appearances shifted, we scurried toward the gates, using the hedges to our advantage. Sin signaled for us to hang back when we reached the side. A guard stood a few hundred feet away.

Sin slipped a dagger from a sheath along his waist.

There was a struggle up ahead in the lantern light, and then it was done. He dragged the guard across the street into what was the cleanest alleyway I'd ever seen in this city. Damn Gilders.

Sin walked back toward a break in the hedges. The side entrance into the estate. Looped around his fingers was a set of keys. We hurried toward him.

"Did you..." Ciel swallowed. He looked toward the alleyway where darkness cloaked the guard's body then back to Sin.

I didn't bother reminding Ciel he'd stabbed a man on Dúm's Cross for sending me into the Wraithsea.

Sin slipped the dagger back into its sheath. It was clean, so he must've swiped it on his clothes.

He turned to Ciel and raised an eyebrow. "Yes, I did. He was already 'dead' to begin with. Now, he's doubly dead. Oh, not *that* look." Sin flashed his palms near his chest. "I am a Bonespeaker, Ciel. I can raise him from the dead when we're done if it'll make you feel better."

Ciel tried and failed to hide his emotions. His brows knotted and his mouth puckered into a scowl.

"Can you do that?" Ciel asked.

"No. I was lying. It's a souldagger," Sin said, tipping his head side to side. "Eh, actually that's a complicated answer we don't have time for."

I squeezed Ciel's arm. "You can stay out here if you like. Really. If Sin is right about the servants' quarters, we should be back in no time."

"I'm coming," Ciel said.

Sin tried to unlock the gate with a few keys before he found the correct one. He slid it into the lock and turned until there was a soft click. It was like a symphony to my ears as the knob twisted.

We slid inside and clung to the shadows along the dark lawn.

To our left, the Sluagh's distraction was working. Guards had left their posts to shoo them off like bothersome crows trying to pick at entrails someone had forgotten to clean up.

The entrance to the servants' quarters was a straight shot ahead.

Sin fumbled with the keys yet again, but they all looked the same. I held my breath rather than allowing myself to relax.

The lock clicked, and the door opened.

"Let me go first," Sin said. "If anyone comes, I'll command them." He looked to Ciel. "But understand that if that happens…"

"Do whatever you must," Ciel said.

Sin nodded curtly and faced forward. He prowled ahead, testing the tips of his toes before taking each step with an adeptness that Ciel and I tried to mimic.

Snores trickled into the narrow hall through cracked doors on either side of us. There were too many doors. We couldn't search all of them.

Fear tapped at my mind before those soft sounds turned to heavy beats and echoing shouts from the lawn.

Gods. The guards. Something had to be happening with the Sluagh.

I refocused.

At the very end of the hall was a barred door—but it was ajar. The servants' quarters were like a prison confining them. Someone had opened the door though.

The fear was replaced by a mix of fury and curiosity.

Red tinted my vision.

"Search the rooms that are open first," Ciel whispered.

Sin nodded and doubled back the way we'd come, but I saw a shadow lurking beyond the barred door. Without thought, I pursued it. None of my senses warned me. No, I wanted to harm whichever Elittes it was.

Sin hissed at me, but I ignored him.

"The third door on the right. He closes his door to sleep." A voice came from a few steps away, but I couldn't see the face it belonged to.

Still, I knew who it was.

Thane took a step back. I took a step forward. The new room

beyond the barred servants' cells was filled with barrels of wine, mead, or whiskey.

A stout window near the ceiling spilled light onto the floors.

As I caught a glimpse of Thane's shadow, I lunged around a stack of three barrels in metal shelving and thrust the dagger at him. Moonlight struck his eyes.

"*You*," I snarled.

Thane's hands were hidden in his pockets. He didn't flash his palms or move. He didn't even flinch beneath the bite of my blade. The tip grazed the front of his high-collared coat.

"Tell me why he's here. Tell me why you lied to me, to Sin."

"Because I, Sersa Scáth, am part of something that's bigger than me, than us all," he whispered.

Stellera had said the same thing.

When Thane slid back into the shadows a second later, I couldn't bring myself to follow. My body trembled. My throat went dry and my limbs, sluggish with fear and anger and all things rolled into one.

When I finally gathered the strength to search for him, weaving between the rows of barrels, Thane was gone.

"Sersa?" Sin gripped the barred door. A hint of irritation laced his voice. "We found him. We need to go."

Furious, I rushed past him and back into the servants' quarters. Ciel and Pa were hugging one another, tears in both their eyes, despite that Ciel did not look anything like himself, thanks to the mask—his hair was a shade of ruddy blonde, his chin square, and he looked several inches shorter than usual.

I rammed them, wrapping my arms around both of their backs before either had turned.

Pa looked over Ciel's shoulder. There was no recognition on his face.

"I can't take off my mask," I said. "But hello, Pa."

A soft cry escaped from him. Ciel unwound his arms from ours, allowing me to embrace him alone.

Pa held my face, looking into my eyes. "And yet I imagine your face as clear as the skies over the Western Pointe, my girl. Though neither of you should be here."

Sin took a step into the moonlight spilling through the frosted glass door behind us. "I don't mean to—"

"We need to leave, I know," I said.

Though I wanted to sit and talk to Pa the entire night, there was no time for that.

I grabbed Pa's hand and pulled him down the hall, following Ciel. We stumbled out of the servants' quarters and looked to our right as we crossed the cobbled path between the manor and the hedge perimeter.

The Soul Guards had finally managed to get the pair of Sluagh to flee. They were lifting themselves off the ground, wings sending whooshing air in every direction.

As Sin fumbled for the keys on his belt to unlock the door hidden between two towering hedges, I jangled the knob.

It was unlocked.

"Did you lock it?" I whispered.

We didn't have time to dither. The guards would be making their way back to their posts.

"No," Sin said. "I thought it locked on its own."

"Maybe it doesn't," Ciel said. "Does it, Pa?"

"I haven't the foggiest," he said.

"No time," Sin snapped.

With a glance over my shoulder at the approaching guards, I led the way, creeping the door open—

And halted.

A half-circle of Soul Guards stood before us. Each wielded a short sword, extended with a silent threat.

Sin unsheathed the scythe at his hip, and I handed a dagger each to Ciel and Pa.

"*Halt*," Sin said the instant they took a step forward.

The guards stopped.

"*Set your weapons down.*" Each of them did. "*Move out of our way.*"

They cleared a path.

"A Bonespeaker," said Pa, breathless. A bewildered expression tinged with horror.

We moved toward the opening, but at the last second, the guards turned on us. They lunged and struck from all directions. One slammed a little knife into Pa's thigh. He cried out, dropping the dagger I'd given him a second before. It clattered against the street.

I looked to Sin, knowing what had to be done.

All of them needed to die—to experience true death.

But how had they wriggled free from his command?

I shoved Pa and Ciel away from the guards and shouted, "Stay with him, Ciel! We got this!"

My brother had little choice in the matter. Pa toppled, and Ciel was forced to catch him. He pulled his arm over his shoulder and helped Pa limp off into the shadows along the next street.

I turned my sights back to the guard who'd stabbed Pa and slashed my little blade at the air. I kicked up a short sword off the ground and used it to extend my reach. Finally, the guard stumbled, and I lunged for my prey. I struck and parried with the next guard, but my rage was building. The red behind my eyes deepened. Darkened.

The guard I was fighting halted and touched a finger to the clammy skin under his eyes then.

I couldn't see completely through the red. Not at first.

He bled from the eyes, the mouth, the ears, and after a second, he dropped to his knees.

Then he fell forward in a pool of his own blood.

All the guards had stopped moving. I whirled around. They touched their faces, mouths agape and eyes wide.

"Dúm," one of them whispered as they raised their hand to point at me. "*Dúm.*"

In my rage, I was draining all of them. I allowed the fury to burrow deeper inside me, to build in my blood. I knew all too well that death had claimed them the moment they challenged us.

The moment they stood against their Daemon Prince, against me and my family, it was war.

We stepped over their bodies, leaving them to bleed out.

Sin picked up my fallen dagger, grabbed my hand, and tugged me away. "They probably won't die, but there's no time. *Speak of this to no one. Forget,*" he commanded them all as we fled into the darkness.

"Will that work? They broke free from your command, Sin."

He shook his head. "I don't know."

At the end of the street, Ciel had propped Pa against the side of a white brick wall, supporting him still so he didn't put any weight on his leg.

"Dúm's Cross is too far in his state, Sers." Ciel's brows pinched together, and his forehead wrinkled.

Pa wore a similar expression of pain.

Sin cut in, "He'll lead the Soul Guard right to us with how much blood he's losing. We need to bring him to the White Plume and have a Bonemender heal him. It's only a block away. It'll be more crowded over there, but we can't risk a mask being traced back to the Plume. The illusion will fall when you reach the midpoint of Dúm's Cross."

I swallowed. "Okay. No masks."

"Ailerby," Ciel started. "If we can get a message to Ailerby, Sin can help him get into Gilders Eye—"

"Then Ailerby can get Pa out undetected," I finished. "That's brilliant."

He smiled sadly. He wouldn't be accompanying us out of the Soullands anytime soon. Not unless he told Devlin the truth and the prince returned the shard of his soul.

We looked at Sin, who nodded.

"It will work," Sin said. "We need to hurry back to the Plume."

Though I wanted to get Pa out of the city right now, deep down, I knew they were right. We couldn't drag him all the way to the city's edge and get past the Soul Guards, not without being caught.

40

The second we reached the White Plume, I summoned the Sluagh using Sin's horn and penned a note to Ailerby signed by both Ciel and me.

I knew Ailerby would receive it quickly, but we needed him to be waiting for us at the Devil's Tail in a few bells at most if we hoped to get Pa back home before Reaping Hour at dawn. The risk of keeping Pa in Gilders Eye for an entire day was too great. It was completely out of the question.

Ciel helped Pa limp through the penthouse as Sin directed them to the bathing room to clean his bleeding leg. Once finished, Ciel brought him to the velvet settee at the end of the enormous bed. As soon as Pa sat, his pants soaked through the velvet with blood. He wore a simple pair of trousers and a taupe-colored tunic. We'd caught him sleeping, so he was barefoot. The healer would have to check the soles of his feet for cuts too.

"The Bonemender should be here any minute," Sin said.

"Can we get him fresh clothes?" I asked Sin.

He nodded.

"Ha," Pa spat. "I need no healer. Give me a needle, and I'll sew it myself."

Ciel's eyes softened.

"For a daemon's venom-laced blade, you do," Sin said. "All the Soul Guards carry weapons that are fatal to mortals. Assuming you are, in fact, still a mortal."

"Listen to him," Ciel said. "Please."

"Does anyone else have any wounds?" Sin asked. "Even a tiny cut can be lethal."

I looked at Sin. He had a slash mark right across his scarred cheek.

"I'm immune," he said. "A drop of daemon blood and all."

I found a few thin cuts on my wrists and arms. Sin assessed them as soon as I showed him.

"These too," he said urgently. Then through gritted teeth, "Where is that gods-damned healer?"

I settled next to Pa on the settee and finally removed my mask, letting it trundle into a pile of feathers at my feet.

"While we wait, Pa, we need to know if anyone at Elittes Manor took a piece of your soul. If they did, we need to get it back before we can bring you home. You"—my eyes flickered reflexively to Ciel's—"won't be able to get past Dúm's Cross. You'll have to stay in Nos Ovscura if your soul isn't complete."

Pa shook his head. "No one touched me. I was treated well after I was sold to the new High House."

"And before? Which were you at before the House of Elittes?" I asked.

"The House of Turrian. Nasty place. I wouldn't touch their doorknob again with a ten-foot spear. But they let me keep my soul, Sersy. I'm unharmed."

While I wanted to murder every last Turrian at the moment, my mind circled back to the Elittes. Why would either house leave him untouched?

"May I check you to be sure no one took a sliver of your soul, sir?" Sin asked in his most level voice.

"*Sir?* Like hell, daemon!" Pa staggered backward on the velvet cushion. He didn't get very far with his wounded leg. Pain marked his scrunched face as he grunted.

"Pa, do as he says," Ciel said.

They stared at one another for a long moment.

Finally, Pa relented. "All right. But be quick about it."

Sin nodded curtly. He stood in front of Pa and pressed a hand to his chest. He flinched under Sin's touch, and I couldn't say I blamed him. Sin wasn't the friendliest looking bloke to begin with.

Especially when his eyes turned pure white. No pupil. No colorless iris. Nothing. My eyes flickered between them.

"Does it hurt?" Ciel asked.

Pa shook his head.

After a minute, Sin snapped alert and dropped his hand.

"Your father's soul is intact. He'll be able to get past the veil on Dúm's Cross."

"I can't believe it," I said and kissed Pa on the cheek.

Ciel's brows pinched together. "That doesn't make any sense. Why would the Elittes not take even a shard of his soul? Or the Turrians?" I could see the wheels spinning behind his eyes. "Unless this was all a distraction and they don't care whether Pa escapes."

I turned back to Pa and touched a hand to his shoulder. "Which Turrian bought you originally and which Elittes? Do you know either of their names?"

"I don't remember the first. It was all a blur after the Sluagh snatched me. But the second was certainly a Gilder. Definitely a Gilder. I'd recognize him anywhere, but he never told me who he was. At first, he kept me locked up but fed and clothed and clean until he brought me to Elittes Manor. All he said was that I needed to follow his instructions or my children would get hurt."

"Was his name Thane?" I asked. Did you ever hear the name Thane?"

I felt Sin's eyes on me, but I focused on my father.

He shrugged. "I don't know, Sersy. I heard that name," he said, nodding, "once I was moved to Elittes Manor. But I never saw the same man again."

I thought of the masks we'd worn moments ago.

It was possible Thane had disguised himself, wasn't it? Not to mention, I didn't know what type of magic Thane possessed, let alone whether he did or not.

"Sersa. Ciel. I heard about the two of you while I was there. I couldn't say a word to anyone. I couldn't get a letter to anyone either. But I heard." Pa's voice hardened, and his eyes turned mournful. "Tell me it's not true. You both wed a Daemon Prince."

Sin kept quiet, but Pa's eyes trailed to him anyway.

At once, he tried to stand. "This is one of them, isn't it?"

He thrust his finger at Sin's chest, who didn't so much as take a step back or even flinch. What reason did Sin have to be afraid of Pa, the unblood he was?

"I am," Sin said. "But I assure you I did not and will *never* harm your daughter."

"This is my husband," I said. For the first time, the word didn't make me flinch.

"Sersa, you must be kidding," Pa stammered. "You can't possibly mean to say—"

"That I love him?" I swallowed, feeling my eyes shimmer with emotion. If Pa only knew. But I waved my hand, not wanting to get into it. "This is not important right now. What's important is healing you and getting you out of here."

At once, there was a knock at the door. Sin strode toward the foyer and let the Bonemender in. She swiftly took care of my minor cuts in the entryway.

"Rilla will take good care of you," Sin said as he directed the healer toward the settee where Pa was scowling. "We should get back," he whispered to me, turning his back on Ciel and my father.

"You're not taking my children with you anywhere, daemon," Pa said, "royal or not!"

"With all due respect, Sersa is not a child at all. She can make her own decisions," Sin said. He turned to me. "It's up to you."

I nodded.

Ciel cut in to ease the tension. "Sin's right. It could be a while before Ailerby gets our note. We can't afford to raise any suspicions until then."

"The Sluagh will fly straight to him," Sin said, our fingers now tightly laced. "It shouldn't be long before we can return, maybe even before sunrise. But if there are eyes on us, we may have to delay until the night."

"I won't leave without the two of you. Both of you." Pa dropped his eyes as the Bonemender knelt and started assessing his wound. He grunted as the fabric grazed the hole in his leg.

"We have to get back to the citadel. But we will be back, I promise. *We* promise," I said.

Ciel smiled sadly, but it was nothing compared to the sadness I'd see in him soon enough.

"Yes, *we*," Ciel whispered.

The lies we'd told would come back to haunt us before we knew it.

41

I leaned my head against Sin's chest when we reached our moonlit rooms less than a half bell later.

His rooms. These would no longer be my rooms after tonight. I would return to Os Íseal with Pa.

Without Ciel.

My entire body trembled at the thought. I wrapped my arms tighter around Sin's waist, clasping my hands behind his back to steady myself.

"Thank you. For risking so much. For everything."

My voice betrayed no emotion, but I felt everything and nothing simultaneously.

Sin pulled back to run a hand through my hair, skimming my jaw. "When the sun rises, I'm going to visit Devlin. I'll tell him he must leave, that he must take Ciel somewhere far away and protect him at all costs."

My breath caught in my chest.

"I'll tell him the plan and ensure they have enough time to get away before I challenge the king. He will learn what's happened before we know it."

"What will you tell Devlin? And what about Stellera?"

"My brother has supported this endeavor for a long time coming.

He doesn't know the truth about Lochlainn's death yet, and I won't tell him until it's necessary. As for Stellera, she's safe here. The Daemon King knew Lochlainn was loyal to him, but I will ask her to go with Devlin and Ciel."

"And Jestin?" I asked.

"He–" Sin took a deep breath. "Jestin loves our father. He looks up to him. I may not be able to convince him to flee before our world unravels."

"Will he stand against you?"

"I don't know, but he can't command me. Bonespeakers have no effect on one another. I beat him in the fights, Sersa. I'm not worried about him."

I nodded, pressing my lips together. "I still can't believe Thane knew my father was there the entire time." Fury hummed in my veins, rushing alongside my blood. "You said he's trustworthy, Sin. You trusted him."

"I know," he whispered.

I leaned my forehead into his chest again, inhaling his smell and trying to memorize it. My nostrils stung at the thought of never smelling him again, and I had an image of myself—old, sad, and withered—staring at the City of Soulless across the bridge, trying to summon his scent after years and years.

One nightmare would replace this one before we knew it.

Being away from Sin. The thought destroyed me.

But we could live in a dream together for at least a moment longer. I tilted my head back to look into his eyes. Then I raised onto tiptoes to brush my lips against his. His thumb moved along my jaw, summoning chills up and down my spine, into my toes, and the lowest part of my belly.

He pulled back and brushed my lips with a bare finger. His touch alone summoned pure, blazing fire everywhere it traced.

We shared a knowing look.

My lips parted in a breath before his trailed back to mine, swirling his tongue around mine, biting my lip.

He moved on to my neck, shooting ripples of pleasure down my body. The spectral colors and emotions swarmed me. There was no sadness or anger. No fear. Well, maybe a little fear because I loved

Sin too. I loved him more than I had ever imagined loving anyone was possible, and I wanted every part of him too.

Until I had to leave.

I shoved those thoughts aside and focused on his lips, his hands.

He kissed lower and lower until he reached my collarbone. He planted a chaste kiss there too, and my body arched against his, pleading to maintain our closeness. Pleading to be even closer.

A soft moan escaped me.

The sound set Sin into feverish motions.

Before I could register his adept hands, they were clawing at my tunic. He pulled the loose fabric down my shoulders as I fumbled with the bralette I wore, freeing my breasts and letting it fall to the floor.

Then I stepped back and out of my breeches. The little lace shorts I wore underneath were all that remained.

Sin halted and took in every inch of me as he drew his thumb around my nipple. He pinched it between his thumb and forefinger, and I rolled my head as I released another moan.

His lips curled into a devilish smile.

"You are so perfect. Do you know that? Do you know how I feel about you—how much I love you, Sersa?"

There were those words again. My heart would've started pattering faster if not for the wave of bright colors surging inside me even louder, like a tide crashing against me. I could only focus on so much, and the colors won. As they always did.

It was the third time he'd told me he loved me.

Sin prowled forward, and it was then I saw the hunter in his eyes. The man he'd always claimed to be.

He walked me backward, piercing white eyes locked on mine and his chest rising slowly, mine swift and shallow, until we reached the bed. I slid onto it and instinctively reached for his waistband to pull him closer. But he pulled back to slide his own shirt over his head, revealing the lean muscles of his abdomen, his chest, his arms. Then he reached for the clasps of his breeches. He moved unhurriedly, a smirk curling his lips.

Sin dropped them, proudly revealing he wore nothing underneath.

With a swallow, I flushed as I took in every inch of him in return but not from embarrassment. I imagined him being inside me, and yet my imagination did me no justice.

I needed to feel him.

"I'll be gentle, love."

I nodded in understanding, but heat built inside my body. Not just love for Sin but immense desire too, like the most potent of poisons reaching my head in an instant.

He moved forward on hands and knees until we were a few inches from the pillows. My hair fanned around me as I laid back, lips searching for his. Sin positioned himself over me, his hard hips and arousal grinding against me.

I wanted to tear my lace shorts away, but he pinned me with his body, and I kneaded my fingers against his back, pulling him ever closer, savoring him through the thin fabric. The muscles in his back twitched and tightened with every movement, as did his corded arms while my fingers explored his bare skin with delirious urgency.

What I felt was not a want. No, it'd been a need I had repressed for some time now, and I would no longer.

I gasped as his motions grew swifter—

Then he halted abruptly, a smirk tainting his face with mischief.

Sin loved what he was doing to me.

I had the urge to shout at him, to tell him to keep going, but he was busy skimming my inner thigh then my hip under the shorts. His adept fingers changed their mind, finding the ties of my shorts. He only traced them, knowing *exactly* what he was doing.

On his knees, he straightened to stare into my eyes. His were wild as his head tilted. "What do you want, Sersa?"

My eyes lowered then raised again.

"This time I won't tease you," he said. "No, this time I'm going to do everything to you that I've been imagining since I first saw you."

I lifted my hips slightly, a silent signal, and Nessin undid the first crisscrossing tie of my shorts. I fisted the sheets on either side of me. His fingers moved so slowly, torturously slow. I lifted my hips again when his fingers retreated to my navel. I reached toward him. I wanted to touch him now, but his hand shot out and gently lowered mine to the pillows behind me.

"I want to savor every second I touch you, not think of how badly I want you to touch me." Sin's words were hardly a whisper now, but he slowly trailed his fingers back toward the laces of my shorts.

He released another tie. Another. The final one. He pulled them down my hips and pressed a kiss just below my navel. Heat continued to build inside me as he squeezed my hip, working his way closer to my center until his contact set me ablaze.

My hips moved against his fingers of their own volition as he traced unhurried, practiced circles. He moved downward a little and slid a finger inside me. I threw my head back.

I had never wanted anything more. Never *needed* another more.

His every movement was slow and gentle until he slid another finger inside me, his knuckle pressed against my center as he worked me deeper. I said his name, and he stopped. I gasped. With a devilish chuckle, he moved down my body, tracing a line of kisses back toward my navel, then lower and lower until he was between my legs.

Sin took my fingers and threaded them in his hair.

The way his tongue and fingers moved together...

He left me lightheaded. If I weren't flat on my back, I'd faint.

It felt even better because of how much I felt for Sin, not just for his body. I cried out his name again, fisting the sheets as my entire body started to tremble.

And then he stopped again.

"Would you stop that?" I snapped.

"Stop what, love?"

With a wicked gleam in his eyes, Sin repositioned himself, kneeling over me. He spread my knees and adjusted his hips against mine, rubbing himself against my center. As a shiver rolled down my body, I closed my eyes for a second, unable to stand the feeling of Sin there. He pressed forward the tiniest amount, and as our gazes locked, all I saw inside him was an irrepressible craving there.

All the sweet whispers were gone, and in their place was a daemon with the most lascivious desires.

But if he was a daemon, then he was my daemon.

"*Is* this *what you want?*" he asked.

It was. It was everything I wanted, but that didn't stop my thoughts from going to another truth. When I hesitated to answer,

Sin's dark brows pulled together, aware of exactly what was on my mind.

"You've never—" His words cut off in his throat, almost breathless. "Our honeymoon. We almost—you almost let me have you, Sersa Drumghoul, without warning, I might add."

I bit my lip. "So? I've done everything else." *With lots of young men.*

Sin turned his head to the side for a second, evidently wanting to dodge the thought.

"Just not..." My eyes flicked down his body again.

"Sersa, I don't want to hurt you. There are a hundred other ways I can *pleasure* you instead, as you just learned, which is my aim for tonight if that's not perfectly clear—"

"Are you implying you want another to be the one?"

His eyes turned murderous. Before his mind spiraled, I sat up slightly to pull him closer.

"I knew what I wanted that night, and I know now. I want all of you."

Sin seemed to forget my teasing. We kissed deeply, roughly, for minutes straight while his hands kneaded my body and dipped between my legs repeatedly, preparing me for precisely *what* I wanted.

When I tried to stroke him, he pinned my wrists in a single hand against the pillows behind me. I couldn't stand it any longer. The feeling between my legs was killing me.

Finally, Sin slid his fingers between them again, and this time, I knew it was different. He was assessing my readiness.

I gripped his arms tightly. Pleading.

Sin pulled his lips away from mine. His stare was serious. "Are you sure this is what you want? Right now?"

I nodded as I reached forward to grab him, summoning a growl from deep within his chest. I positioned him against my center. Sin licked his lips, and as he eased into me inch by inch, the fullness made me gasp sharply. I squeezed my eyes shut, and Sin tensed, holding still while I adjusted.

The pain was more intense than I'd been expecting.

"Breathe for me, please, Sersa," he whispered, voice softer than before. "I don't want to hurt you," he repeated.

I did as he told me, taking one deep breath after another, waiting for it to pass. He lowered his mouth to my breast and sucked, maybe in hopes of distracting me.

It worked.

The feel of his tongue there was perfect. I focused on the sensation and my breath, and my body slowly started to unfurl for him, the tension lessening when I'd thought there was no way it could. Sin brought his lips back to mine, and I moved my hips once, testing how he felt.

He repressed another growl, nostrils flaring.

Biting my lip and closing my eyes, I nodded against Sin, and he started to move. Slowly. After a few minutes, I began to move my hips against his, the pain dispelling one breath at a time, and he took my rhythm as a signal. He pulled out and re-entered me.

The feel.

I gasped sharply again, but it wasn't from pain. The pressure between my legs shifted. When he pressed further into me still, I realized he'd been holding back. A lot.

Dúm's teeth.

Sin paused, noting my openmouthed expression before his lips curled into a grin. Strips of white hair hung in his face. Closing my eyes, I palmed his lower back, urging him to continue.

Begging.

He continued his movements, so deep inside me now, and I moaned his name repeatedly as the sensations shifted to pleasure with only a hint of the pain from before until it was gone entirely.

"Please, Sin. Please," I pleaded, feeling his hot breath dust the top of my breasts.

We moved this way until our rising chests fought against one another, gasping for air. Sin tilted my face to his, locking our lips, our tongues finding one another wistfully. His arms framed my face as our foreheads pressed together, and he worked against me harder, one hand sliding down to grip my hip as he kissed my neck until I cried out. As pleasure rippled through me, I almost couldn't stand his continued motions, but a moment later, he stiffened and pressed a final kiss to my shoulder.

I traced the scars on Sin's chest with my fingers.

"Why did you deny me the first time if you knew you wanted and loved me?"

Sin studied me raptly, a hand on my shoulder and the other toying with loose strands of black hair. "*I* was sure. But I wanted you to be sure. The last thing I wanted was for you to regret being with me. Especially after you ran away from me in the gallery. It's what stopped me so many other times before."

"For a man who can delve into others' minds, I'm unimpressed, Nessin. You could have easily seduced me in that apartment of yours. If only you had stayed the day," I said.

"And risk the woman I am obsessed with, in love with, thinking I only wanted one thing from her?" He raised his eyebrows. "Then again, you haven't said it back."

I clung to those words like air, knowing I'd be out of it soon enough.

I dusted a kiss against Sin's ribs. "Well, I would have read my mind more if I were you," I said. "Also, I doubt anyone would regret you."

His eyes softened. A smirk tugged at his scarred upper lip.

I traced it too.

"I only read your thoughts when I couldn't help myself. Or when your mind was so loud that I couldn't avoid it. Believe it or not, I never wanted to know your thoughts. I was afraid I'd find the distaste you claimed to have for me."

I propped myself up slightly and brushed the white hair from his eyes.

"I hate to break it to you, but I could never so much as dislike you, let alone hate you, Nessin Drumghoul. I am in love with you. I love you. And I will never not love you."

"You have no idea how happy that makes me."

"The devil himself—happy? Are you sure that's possible?"

"You know how I crave your flattery."

We both grinned, and he peeled off the pillows to brush his lips against mine. But the moment ended as the Sluagh landed on the terrace. Its wings draped the stone like a cape. I closed my eyes and dropped my forehead to Sin's chest before I gathered all my strength.

Then I pressed my lips to his one final time before we had to say goodbye.

42

Ciel, Pa, and I waited in the Devil's Tail at a table tucked behind a metal beam in the corner. It was the only somewhat private area, but even nearing dawn and Reaping Hour, the tavern was still drowning in patrons.

Sin was retrieving Ailerby from Dúm's Cross, but I'd warned him in the note that Sin would stand back to avoid being seen by the Soul Guards. Lucky for Ailerby, he would veil himself and go undetected as he crossed the bridge to join Sin. I'd had to warn him of other things too, but I didn't want to think about Ciel right now.

The little bell on the door kept jangling every time a new patron entered or left. The crowd was a mix of daemons, unidentifiable wraiths, and mortals with their flushed cheeks and rowdy demeanor.

I tapped my foot under the table and tried to make the rest of myself—especially my face—look natural, but it proved impossible. My body was thrumming, my nerves screeching, and my mouth dry. I couldn't bring myself to drink the mead we'd ordered, again in hopes of looking natural, and the cloying scent of honey twisted my gut into knots.

The thought of what Pa would do when he learned Ciel had to stay behind sickened me with shame and fear.

When the little bell on the door rang again, my eyes widened and landed on Sin. He and Ailerby, who hadn't dropped the veil to reveal himself, had made it. Sin stiffly headed for our table in the back.

Once he reached us, an unseen body slid onto the bench beside me, trying to be quiet as a feather. I fought the urge to throw my arms around Ailerby. Two moons had passed since I'd seen him—never mind that I couldn't see him right now. His presence flushed away some of my sadness and fear. I'd missed him so much, and I'd buried those feelings ever since I left him on Dúm's Cross.

"I don't know what we'd do without you tonight, Ail," I said.

"I know," he replied flippantly. "I hope the Council doesn't try to lock you in the tower again. But if they do, I'll sit in there with you and gorge myself on pastries too."

"Is that my boy Ailerby?" Pa whispered.

"Hi, Chief. Lovely to see your face. Though I'm not sure about the hair."

Pa snorted, but the humor faded as he turned to me. He squeezed my hand. "Why would the Council try to lock you in the tower?"

I turned to look at him, sitting beside me.

Words failed to pass my lips.

"Sersa," he said sternly this time. "What happened since I've been gone?"

"It'll take too long to explain," I said. "Later."

Still standing next to the table because there was no room on the benches and no other chairs, Sin turned his gaze to me. "Are you ready to leave? It's nearing Reaping Hour."

"I'm ready if you two are," Pa said.

Pursing my lips into a thin line, I nodded. I knew it was time. I didn't need reminders of what was about to come. Across from me, Ciel's hands moved in his lap under the table while he kept his eyes down. I fought tears. My nostrils burned.

I was about to leave the City of Soulless without my brother.

Swallowing hard, I followed Ailerby. Sin led the way toward the entrance but halted and grabbed my hand.

The others lingered outside.

I turned to face Sin reluctantly. His colorless eyes were soft yet sharp. Afraid yet sad.

"I'll walk you to the bridge's edge, but I think it's best I stay back again. I don't want to risk being seen and endangering you or your father."

I nodded, biting my lip. I couldn't look Sin in the eye.

Sensing this, he touched a gloved hand to my chin, turning my face toward his. "I'll broach the topic of getting your brother's soul back from Devlin as soon as I'm able. Once my task is complete, I'll send word. I promise."

I nodded again. I couldn't say anything. If I did, I'd break. My tears would fall. I might even drop to my knees right here and find myself too weak to leave. An ever-present question swirled in my mind.

What if you can't kill your father?

Gods. Suddenly the weight of the fact that I'd murdered his brother, that he was about to commit both regicide and patricide now, terrified me. I realized I should have been afraid of Sin and maybe he should have been afraid of me after what I'd done.

But we were a pair, and if Sin didn't act, his father was going to kill him. I convinced myself if Sin hadn't acted against Lochlainn, I would be dead. If I hadn't acted against Lochlainn, *Sin* would be dead.

I might still die.

I had to leave. For Pa. He needed me. While waiting had never been my thing, I would have to for a moment. I couldn't get Ciel's soul back on my own. Only a Soulreaper could.

When it was safe, Sin would do it.

"I love you, Sersa Scáth," Sin said with a swallow.

He'd called me Sersa *Drumghoul* before.

This was the truth I'd been too afraid to face.

The second I stepped through the veil between our worlds, I was no longer his, and he was no longer mine.

Sin kissed me long and slow. The time to separate came sooner than I was ready. The realization that it might be our last kiss settled like a weight on my shoulders, but it was already over. I hadn't even savored the taste of him or the feel of his lips, and I knew I'd come to regret it.

As we headed outside, I walked with that weight. Sin released his hand from mine, likely knowing I would not let go until he did. My knees felt wobbly. Every part of me protested. My mind screamed. My body trembled. My heart.

My *stupid* heart.

We had always said our betrothal would be fake, and, thus, our union annulled when the deal was done. But now... The only difference now was that I didn't want it to end. I'd never wanted to be married, especially not so young, but I didn't want to lose Sin.

When we reached a less crowded street, I took Pa and Ciel's hands. Ailerby at the front veiled the three of us. He kept himself veiled too.

Then we started our trek toward Dúm's Cross, Sin trailing a few feet behind us. His feet slowed until he wasn't moving at all, and his eyes grew farther and farther away with each step I took.

Before I knew it, our boots clomped on the smooth black stone.

The first step.

The second.

The tenth.

I looked over my shoulder, eyes searching the crowd beyond the bridge for Sin. The distance between us continued to swell until it was a chasm. And so was my bleeding heart. Tears didn't fall from my eyes. I tried to convince myself I could return to the city at any time, but I didn't know if that was true.

Before I knew it, we were approaching the middle of the bridge. My legs and feet had only cooperated this far because Ciel was behind me, his palm sweating around mine, and Pa tugging me onward.

But when Ciel finally unwound his hand, letting me slip away, my body stiffened.

We were past the middle.

I whipped my head around to look at him, realizing instantly that his hand hadn't slipped away. He could no longer hold on. His form had faded to a gossamer, beautiful state.

Ciel was a wraith in the world we belonged to.

No. Ciel belonged to the Soullands now.

I couldn't give anything away. I needed Pa to keep walking, so I forced my feet to obey. He never looked behind. Never noticed.

We reached the end of the bridge and then the beach until finally we were headed toward the cliff stairs. Either there weren't many people leaving the city right now, or I somehow blocked them all out.

"Should you drop the veil now?" Pa asked.

"N-No," Ailerby said. "Not yet."

Ailerby, who could hide his emotions or mimic others' emotions even better than me, had stammered on the lie.

Rocks scattered at our feet as we ascended the cliff stairs. The crowd thinned further. In the sparse throng of people, we were able to walk without fear of falling to our deaths.

But inside—inside I felt like part of me had fallen. Cracked. I'd left the shards in Nos Ovscura, and I would never recover. Not without Ciel. And not without...

I squeezed my eyes shut for a second. I refused to think it. If I let myself think of Sin as a need, I wouldn't be able to keep walking, to keep my back turned on them.

We reached the top of the cliff stairs.

Tears trickled down my cheeks.

"Drop the veil, Ail," I finally said.

Ailerby hesitated when Pa tugged on his arm. I felt the ripple of his movement through our clasped hands.

"Chief."

"Do it," I urged. "It's okay."

As soon as Ailerby did, Pa looked around us. He craned his neck around groups of people, urging them to walk past us.

"Where's my boy?" Pa said, stumbling on his words. Again, he looked along the cliff overlooking the beach then toward the bridge.

While I could see Ciel's silhouette now moving through the people leaving the city, Pa and Ailerby wouldn't be able to. Not in this wraithlike form. Not until Ciel was behind the midpoint of the bridge's other side again.

I'd always seen shadows others couldn't.

"I-I don't see him," Pa shouted. He licked his lips, eyes scanning at a furious pace.

Finally, Ciel's body solidified. He looked as alive as ever.

I choked back a sob. I had entered the Soullands to get back one family member only to leave another behind.

I'd failed.

Ciel walked until he halted next to Sin and turned to watch us. Sin squeezed his shoulder and said something I so badly wanted to hear. Their cloaks blew in the wind, tangling with one another.

Pa finally glimpsed Ciel. When he skittered toward the cliff's edge, Ailerby and I gripped his arms, tugging him backward. He was ready to descend the stairs again and cross the bridge.

The bells tolled, signaling the first warning for Reaping Hour.

"We need to get to House Scáth, Pa," I said. "Please. The bridge will be lowering."

"What's he doing? Let me go!" Pa whirled around, his green eyes wide. Terrified. Incredulous. Furious.

"Ciel." I blinked, but it forced another tear to roll down my cheek. "You couldn't see Ciel before because..." My voice turned hoarse. "He turns into a wraith when he enters our world."

Pa scoffed. "Our world? Sersa, now you are talking madness!"

Though I tried not to let it show, his words wounded me.

"Ciel gave a piece of his soul to his husband. He can't get past the veil between our worlds anymore. Sin will keep him safe. He'll be safe from the Sluagh like this."

Pa tore free of Ailerby. "How could you let this happen? I can't believe how foolish you both are! Marrying Soullander princes. Thinking you're invincible!"

"I don't know," I stammered. "But I'm going to make it right, I promise. Sin is going to help get the sliver back from his brother. Then Ciel *will* come home."

"Stop saying that prince's name like–like you..." Pa shook his head and let whatever he'd wanted to say fade on the wind that rippled across the top of the cliff. "All I know is that you had better be right, or the Daemon King himself will have me to answer to!"

Pa had hardly yelled at me when I was a child. It was usually Ma, so his tone made me flinch. I swallowed as I searched his face, but he couldn't even look at me. He turned back to the shore, his jaw working with anger as he studied Ciel from afar.

Then the crowd closed in around Ciel and Sin, and we lost sight of them both.

43

The Council was called into session the second Pa and I walked into House Scáth. Servants flew out of the way as if they were seeing a ghost. Or maybe it was me.

I couldn't go to the oubliettes in the woods to eavesdrop on the Council even if I wanted to because as soon as Ma saw us, her eyes twisted with rage and her mouth into a scowl, and she ordered Dawnwatchers and Duskwatchers at every door.

There was nowhere for me to go but to escape to my rooms and lock myself in.

Chest rising and falling feverishly, I leaned against the door and tried to calm down. Nothing worked. Not counting to the top of a breath and holding it like the Druids had told me. Not thinking of the faces of those I loved—Sin's face made it decidedly worse, and Ciel's sent me sobbing again.

But these tears weren't sad. These were all fury.

I released a roar mixed with a grunt and shoved the contents off the nearest table. Knickknacks. Books from Ciel I'd never read tumbled to the floor. Glass shattered. Pages tore. Ancient book spines twisted like broken necks. Jewelry scattered the floor.

But the rage didn't dissipate.

I slammed my fist into the wall and dropped to my knees from the pain. Blood bloomed on my knuckles. I hung my head as I cried, no longer caring if anyone heard me. Clan members outside surely did.

I slid to the ground and lay on my side, clutching my hand to my chest as reality settled over me like a dark cloud.

I had saved Pa, but I'd lost Ciel.

I had helped Sin somewhat, and in the process, I'd fallen in love with him. I'd *fallen in love* with him. I hated myself for my weakness, for my impulses, for every desire I'd felt for him. Every part of my body throbbed in agony and loss, and I was only grateful because it distracted me from my physical pain.

Minutes or bells passed—I didn't care, I didn't know—and I eventually stilled. Even when I heard someone picking the lock, I didn't bother getting up.

The door swept open a minute later, and Ailerby entered before closing and locking it behind him. He crossed the room and lowered onto the ground beside me. The stone was rough and cold, but I hardly felt it until he wrapped his warm arms around me. I wasn't deserving of his kindness, but he held me even as I started to cry again. Now, I not only hated myself for leaving Ciel and Sin, but I felt guilty for needing Ailerby. For needing anyone.

Why couldn't I sort through my feelings on my own?

A few minutes passed, the crying dissipated, and then Ailerby propped himself up on one elbow. He reached for my fist and held it to the light. "We'll need to get a healer for this, Sers. The bones need to be set."

I nodded. I'd heard a crunch, and the pain, like the rest of my mental anguish currently, wasn't merely a bruise or a cut. It went so much deeper, down to the bone. The pain in my mind manifested so deep that it became tangible, alive, and eager to control me.

It could too.

An urgent knock on the door echoed through the room.

I closed my eyes for a second and sighed. "Here we go."

A servant's voice on the other side trembled.

"Lady Sersa, the Council summons you at once."

After Ailerby cleaned my knuckles in a basin of water and wrapped up my hand, we headed to the Council Room together. He held my hand, the one I hadn't broken, and we walked side by side. A united front.

Incense coiled through the wide corridors of House Scáth, and bright morning light streamed through the lofty stone cloisters on either side. A courtyard to our left contained at least twenty clan members—way too many for so early—whose eyes all watched me approach the Council Room at the end of the hall.

I rolled my eyes and faced forward. Let them watch. I was sure they already knew where I'd been and what I'd done. I wondered if Pa had told my uncles I'd married a Daemon Prince. I didn't care what they thought about it, but they would have likely spewed the gossip by now.

Two guards opened the double doors, and the Council Room unfolded beyond the threshold. Eyes darted my way. The members who sat in the seats with their backs to me craned over the edges of their chairs. I wanted to say something snarky, to snap at them to turn around. I'd be in the middle of the triangle where they interrogated their subjects soon enough. But I bit my tongue.

Before we reached the triangle inside the chairs, Ma's voice echoed through the lofty room. "Ailerby. You were not summoned. I must ask you to leave."

He waited until we stopped in the middle of the room, inside the grips of every member but especially Ma. My father stood behind her throne, slightly to the side. After he'd disappeared, his seat had been filled by another. His return would likely see someone kicked off the Council.

Ailerby squeezed my uninjured hand tighter and stood tall beside me. His tone was polite. "I must apologize then, Chieftess, because I will not."

Some of the Council members, namely Uncle Bardic, groaned with disgust.

"Sersa deserves someone to stand with her," Ailerby said firmly.

"Do you want him to stay?" Ma asked. I nodded. "Very well."

There were no protests this time because Ma silenced Uncle Bardic with a glare.

I faced Ma, sitting at one of the triangle's points, but my eyes darted to the sides in my line of sight. Luckily, Uncle Bardic was behind me, closest to the doors a few hundred feet away. The vast room felt even larger standing in the center.

Ma wasted no time launching into the questioning. "You enter the Council's triangle with the knowledge that only truth is accepted here. And should you lie, may the..." She faltered. "May the gods strike you down, Sersa Scá—*Drumghoul*. Do you not?"

I cleared my dry throat. "I do."

Her eyes narrowed. She knew me better.

"Bain Scáth comes to the Council with claims that you and your brother, Ciel Scáth, entered the Soullands precisely two moons ago and each married a Daemon Prince, heirs to the Daemon Throne."

I looked at the Druidess in the corner of the room. Her hands were clasped in front of her, and she was nodding as Ma spoke. Though I didn't know her name, I did know that she was here as a judge, a hand of the clans' widespread laws throughout Clais.

Yet I couldn't wrap my mind around why she'd been summoned. What were they going to do, try to lock me up again?

"Is this correct?" Ma pressed.

Snapping my gaze back to her, I licked my lips.

"Yes." My voice still sounded raspy from crying.

"And what was the reason for this unplanned, unsanctioned union?"

"I went there to find Pa. Then I got married."

"Were there no other reasons?" Ma pressed.

"No. I mean, yes." I shook my head. What was I to say? The Daemon Prince needed to present an intended? I married him so that I could find Pa in Gilders Eye?

Then I fell for the gods-damned prince.

Pa opened his mouth to speak. His hands were balled into fists, and he leaned forward slightly, one foot in front of the other. Ma waved her hand. His eyes dropped, and he filed back into line behind her throne, gripping the edge tightly.

I glared at him. My parents had always said when Ciel or I were sick or had gotten hurt that they would gladly take our pain if they could. Pa deemed Ciel's life more valuable than his own.

Maybe Ciel's life was more valuable to me too.

"And..." Ma got stuck on the next question.

Uncle Bardic stepped in gladly, giving her no chance to recover. "And was the union consummated with this Daemon Prince?"

"That's hardly your business," I snapped, squeezing Ailerby's hand tighter. My other hand reflexively balled into a fist, and I had to bite the inside of my cheek when the pain reminded me the wall had broken it.

Bardic sighed long and loud, eyes circling to another Council member to his right. "That's a yes then."

"I don't see the problem regardless of the answer," I said. "Women can serve as chieftess, can they not? Women can divorce as easily as men, can they not? Why should I not be afforded the same exact treatment?"

"Divorce from the Daemon King's heir?" Uncle Bardic challenged. Gripping the armrests, he leaned forward slightly.

"Again, I don't see why it matters who he is."

The Druidess cleared her throat from the outskirts of the room.

Ma held up her hand. "Silence. Bardic, I will ask the questions here. Speak out of turn again, and you will be forced to leave the room."

He should have been forced *off* the Council years ago based on the way he spoke to his chieftess.

Ma proceeded. "Why has your brother not returned with you?"

I returned my eyes to hers and swallowed. "While there, I learned that a mortal cannot leave the Soullands once they are missing even a shard of their soul, whether willingly granted or taken by force. Ciel gave a piece of his soul to his husband willingly."

Ma hid whatever she was feeling.

I did not. My teeth fumbled over my lips, tasting rusty blood. My eyes burned with the threat of new tears, but I was thankful none fell as I stood before them. Still, the anger, fear, and sadness overwhelmed me. They festered in my gut and turned my mind cloudy, the colors all swirling in uncontrollable patterns through the air around me.

I looked down at my hands and realized my magic was out in the open for all the Council members to see. It wasn't in my mind.

They pressed themselves back into their seats, trying to get away.

Though I tried to let go, Ailerby held onto me tighter.

A silent gesture of solidarity. But what if I stole his magic too? I couldn't bear it.

"Everyone, out. I want to talk to my daughter alone." Ma stood and pointed at the doors. "Shall I repeat myself?"

They scurried out of their seats. I looked toward the corner, and the Druidess also moved for the door.

"I'm going to give you some privacy," Ailerby said.

I nodded, trying to catch my breath.

He winked at me as he released my hand and headed for the door.

"Bain," Ma said. "You too, please."

I'd never seen any strain in my parents' union, but now I did. Pa's jaw firmed as he gritted his teeth, and his hands balled into fists. He may have been named Chief of Clan Scáth by association, but Ma was the true head. The formidable Shadowess of Os Íseal. She'd always had the last say.

Pa exited a little noisily in my opinion, leaving Ma and me alone. We stared into one another's eyes for a few minutes, neither of us saying anything.

"Tell me for my own curiosity," she said. "Do you love the Daemon Prince you wed?"

"Sometimes I don't want to."

Ma smiled like she had when I was a child. Like she had before Pa disappeared.

"After you love and get hurt, hesitation always stays with you. But the thrill of it—it never convinces us to stay away, does it?" Her eyes crinkled in a reminiscent way. She studied my face. "You must know the Druidess will advise me to strip you of your inheritance. The Council will vote against you too. Your father is so angry, even he might vote against you."

I swallowed again, but there was no moisture in my mouth. "I told him I will make things right. And I meant it."

"If there's one thing I know about my daughter, it's that she always keeps her word."

"You taught me that."

She smiled again. "I did." She gripped the armrests of her throne and used them to push herself up. "There are so many things I do not understand, Sersa. But most of all, I cannot understand why you did it, why you went there and imperiled yourself."

"I wanted to find Pa, and you agreed to lock me in the tower!" I hollered at her so loud that the red flooded my vision. Black and blue still streaked it. I wanted to break everything in the Council Room suddenly. When I managed to slow my breathing, I added, "I did it for us. To reunite us all."

Ma strode forward and touched a hand to my cheek. "I know I have put so much weight on your shoulders as heir to the clan. But reuniting us, making us whole, was never your responsibility to begin with."

"The opportunity presented itself. What was I supposed to do?"

She nodded reassuringly. "I would have done the same if I were in your place. And if I had fallen for a prince."

While this bolstered me, I dropped my eyes in shame for my previous outburst.

Ma tipped my chin back to look at her. "You are entitled to your anger. I should not have agreed to what your uncles suggested. I was not acting as a chieftess should, and you were right to run. Again, I'd have done the same." She sighed sadly, but there was some hope behind it. "You are old enough to make your own choices now, Sersa. Just know what the choices might lead to and make sure those choices are yours and yours alone."

She dropped her hand from my chin and stood taller.

"Once we're announced an unblood clan with no heir, the unbloods and subjects we oversee may try to ransack House Scáth. Maybe worse. The city may become almost as unsafe as Nos Ovscura. No matter what you decide, I must stay with the clan and protect House Scáth. Our kin. You understand."

I nodded before her words set in. Ma was talking like I was going back to the City of Soulless when I hadn't made that decision. Not yet.

Haven't you? said the voice in my head. It sounded an awful lot like Nev. Was she saying that I ought to leave the clan?

"Ma." I swallowed. "I would give your magic back if I could. You know that, right?"

"I know. But you are the daughter of the Shadowess, and in turn, a Shadowess yourself. You deserve all the power you have been given, Sersa. But," she added sharply, "do not let it consume or conquer you. Learn to see the difference or you will lose yourself in it. The day pretends to be the night during the Dark season, does it not?"

Her words were a riddle of sorts. Lessons always were with her.

"Thank you," I said.

When I turned on my heels, Ma halted me.

"One last thing." She brandished a piece of wax-sealed parchment from her robes. But the seal was broken. "The Druids sent a letter for Ciel. Somehow they knew of his marriage when even I did not. Due to his union with the Daemon Prince, he's no longer allowed to study in the Redthorne Wood parish. He should receive the letter from you—and if he is restored—please tell him to come visit at the very least. I will pray to the gods every day he does."

At that, Ma offered me her old spear with a wink. It was shortened to a quarter of its length, hidden inside her robes.

"And remember. You are in charge of yourself. Always. Whatever you decide, I will support you. Your father will too. In time. You were born to be queen. Of one world or another."

44

I didn't know what I was going to do, not really, and I especially couldn't think straight enough to decide after a guard brought a letter to my door that night. It was from the Daemon King himself, inviting me back to his citadel.

My eyes froze on the last line before I'd read any of the others.

They didn't escape in time. I have Ciel.

I collapsed onto the edge of my bed as Ailerby snatched the letter from me. He scanned it quickly, but I kept my eyes on the floor, flickering across every meaningless object in my room.

"Then the decision is made for me," I whispered.

Ailerby whirled around to stare at me. "What?"

"Sin must have failed. He must have failed to kill his father."

Gods. I leaned forward, wrapping my arms around my waist to stop the spinning in my gut. It didn't help. Did that mean... What if Sin...

"He has Ciel? Could he be lying? We have to go if he does," Ailerby said, his voice higher pitched than normal.

I knew what I had to do.

I didn't know how, but I was going to kill the Daemon King myself.

Ailerby was taking deep breaths, trying to stop his lungs from bursting in his chest, but he doubled over and put his hands on his knees. "Sersa, I'm coming with. I *have* to."

"It's too dangerous."

"No, it's not!" He straightened. His eyes burned with frenzy. "You both left me behind like I mean nothing to you. What if your soul had been taken too? What if you had become stuck there? What? Were you going to never come back?" he shouted. "It's Ciel we're talking about."

"Ailerby—"

"No! I love Ciel just as much as you do. I'm coming, and you're not going to stop me."

"O-Okay. Okay. You can come. But once we reach the citadel, I want you to veil yourself."

Ailerby wiped his mouth. Though I hadn't seen any spittle fly from it, I didn't doubt it the way he'd shouted at me.

I tilted my head at him. "Ail, what's wrong? I've known you long enough to tell that something is."

He licked his lips. A blush bloomed in his cheeks. "I need to tell you something."

"You can tell me anything. Always. You know that."

"Not this. This..."

Ailerby shook his head and crossed the room then. He sat on the bed beside me, fumbling in his pocket, and fished out a tiny piece of parchment with deep creases as if it'd been opened and re-folded a hundred times. He unfolded it now, and my curiosity piqued when he offered it to me.

Another note.

But this one—it was not a threat. It was a love letter. Simple and to the point.

Ailerby,
   I'll always love you — to the Otherworld and back.
   Yours in heart and spirit,
   Ciel

. . .

So many secrets between us all, never written down, save for this small memento, never uttered. I folded the note back up and handed it to Ailerby, sensing it was the last thing he had of Ciel. The last reminder.

These secrets weighed so much.

Had Ciel loved Ailerby but loved Prince Devlin more? My heart ached for Ailerby's. For both of them. But mostly because I knew who Ciel would choose over and over.

"I told him we couldn't be together," Ailerby whispered.

"Why?"

"So many reasons."

I threw my arms around Ailerby. His chest stiffened against mine like he was holding something back, but then he wrapped his arms around me too.

"I'm here if you ever want to tell me those reasons, Ail. For now, all I can say is I'm so sorry. I'm so sorry he followed me. If I had known, I'd have done anything to stop him."

"So am I. So would I. But it's not your fault. Ciel's as stubborn as you. He just hides it better."

"I think I'm done trying to hide myself," I replied.

I didn't ask Ailerby to veil us as we made our way back into Nos Ovscura. With Ma's old spear hidden under my cloak, Sin's three daggers dangling at my waist, and my own magic thrumming in my blood, I had what I needed.

I was ready. Killing the Daemon King would be no easy feat, but if he thought he was going to keep Ciel and steal the rest of his soul or whatever he had planned, he was dead wrong.

Soul Guards seized us as soon as we crossed the midpoint on Dúm's Cross. Neither Ailerby nor I fought them as they wrapped thick hands around our arms and tugged us into the city.

But as we stepped off the bridge on the other side, the ground quaked under us. The Soul Guards turned back, and my gaze followed. The bridge wasn't lowering. People were scurrying back and forth along it, running into one another as the tremors continued to echo through the city. Some tried to run back toward Os Íseal, but others seemed to know they wouldn't make it.

But from what?

It all happened so fast.

The Daemon King in Colossi form strode toward the bridge and stepped right through it. Stone crumbled beneath his weight, and people screamed—bloodcurdling, gut-wrenching screams that were so terrible my gut dropped into my toes. Hundreds fell to their death, tumbling into the waters or crushed under the Daemon King's weight. A massive cloud of dust formed in the air, so thick I couldn't see through it.

Finally, it started to settle.

The Daemon King stood between Os Íseal and Nos Ovscura in the permanent chasm he'd left behind. Through the crowd he found me, surrounded by guards, with ease.

For a second, I thought he might turn back the way he'd come, but then he leaned forward and extended a massive arm toward the bridge's edge.

"Veil yourself," I snapped at Ailerby. "Do it—now!"

His hesitation made the difference of a second, and before I knew it, the Daemon King had picked both of us up, pinching us between his fingers. Both of us shrieked as he dangled us upside down, squeezing my leg in a way that was sure to snap the bone.

The Daemon King's voice boomed when he spoke.

"Is this another person you care for? Good." He eyed Ailerby with a mix of disinterest and a thirst for blood. "As they say, dear Sersa, the more the merrier."

The Daemon King turned on his heels and stalked toward the enormous pipes to the left of the city. In seconds, he walked for what would have been a full bell to a normal-sized man. The Colossi were anything but normal.

Finally, we reached the city limits. He strode past the slums then Gilders Eye. People along the Eye froze and watched the king, their mouths open in utter shock.

We reached the shore behind the citadel in no more than a few minutes.

Someone was tied to an upright pyre in the middle of the beach where the water lapped at the sand. Even swaying upside down, I didn't need to strain to know who it was.

Ciel.

The Daemon King had enough sense not to drop me or Ailerby. Instead, he let us fall when we were a reasonable distance from the sand. I dropped onto my shoulder and grunted. Ailerby, beside me, made a similar noise. He'd landed on his face, but at least it wasn't his neck.

I rolled onto my side, trying to gather the strength to rise to my feet. I searched the beach for others, but it was only us.

Me. Ailerby. Ciel. The Daemon King.

As my eyes found the tied-up figure though, a sharp ripple of chills whipped up my spine, raising the hairs on my arms.

It was not Ciel.

Nessin.

All the blood drained from my face as realization set in. The king had lied to get me here.

Of course he did, snapped the chiding voice in my head. Nev, again.

A blade stood upright, pressed deep into the center of Sin's chest. His hands, bound behind his back, twisted his shoulders in a way that was painful just to look at.

"Where's Ciel?" My voice was as coarse as the sand I fisted. "Tell me where he is."

"Nessin told your brother," the king said like a cuss, "to flee with my son. They're long gone by now. But I will find them. I will find Ciel. I knew Nessin wouldn't be enough. I knew if I told you I was going to kill him, you wouldn't come. Look, Nessin. She doesn't even care. She came for her brother, not *you.*"

Sin tried to raise his head but failed. White hair wet from the saltwater hung in his face. The wind stirred the strands around his temples.

I looked down at my hands. "Then Ciel is s-safe."

Ailerby pressed his forehead into the sand. From my peripheral, I couldn't tell if he was crying or relieved.

"For now," the Daemon King purred.

He decreased his size right before our eyes, but he was still ten times my size, able to pick me up and crush me in his fist if he wanted. The king reached toward the unlit pyre and pinched the straight log Sin's head rested against as if he might lift and toss him into the Wraithsea to drown.

"No, stop," I said. "You can have me instead."

"Sersa, no!" Ailerby rolled over and sat up.

I took a step forward.

"You know my soul is whole," I said. "You can have it—if you leave Sin alone and allow him to be healed."

"No—" Sin started.

The Daemon King released the log and turned the dagger in Sin's chest the tiniest bit. In his fingers, the hilt looked like the tip of a feather. Smaller even. The twisting of the blade summoned a bloodcurdling scream from Sin. I cupped a hand over my mouth to stop from screaming myself.

All the blue I'd ever felt returned to me in a gust of color, tinting and tilting my world. It drowned me like never before. "Please!"

He can be healed. I forced myself to focus on this fact.

"Let him go," I pleaded. "Let a healer tend to him. Let him and Ailerby leave. Then you can have my soul."

The Daemon King took a step away from Sin.

"You are so naïve. What is to stop me from taking your soul?" He snickered. "Do you know, dear Sersa, how to kill a soulless?"

I knew instantly what he'd done. The Daemon King hadn't plunged any old dagger into his son's chest.

"You used a souldagger."

"Very good," he said, like I was a child to be praised. The Daemon King nodded at the dagger. "And do you know what can save him? Your *soul*. Your soul can save him, my dear. The remedy to his true death is so close yet so unattainable."

I rushed forward, but the king closed the distance between us.

"Would you really try it?" He raised an eyebrow, testing me. "I will let you watch Nessin's true death before I deliver yours. But first..."

When the Daemon King minimized his form yet again, I wondered what he was doing. Why wouldn't he stay in Colossi form?

Surely, he was the strongest then. He was certainly the most intimidating that way. He twirled a dagger in his hand as he stalked toward the pyre.

I took several more steps forward. I needed to get closer.

"First, I want to tell you about another of Nessin's betrayals, Sersa. It may help you deal with his death more easily." The Daemon King grinned as he called over his shoulder, "Nessin, do you want to tell her or shall I?"

Sin grunted, trying to raise his head again. He managed halfway. Blood spluttering in his throat, he shouted, "Go to hell!"

The Daemon King tsked. "We're already there, my boy. I could show you true hell if you like. I could take your bride as my own once you're dead, subject her to an eternity with *me*. Perhaps I will let Sersa live tonight to think on it. Niuna could use a mother."

While the Daemon King spoke, I closed the rest of the distance between us. He caught on, eyes sliding to me languidly but with crinkled edges that were once again amused.

"Since Nessin is in no state to speak, I will. You know Thane Elittes as I am aware. Well, Thane—oddly enough—made a purchase in my citadel's weekly auction through an unknown servant...say, oh, two moons ago, Nessin?"

Sin raised his eyes, studying me through strips of sweat-matted hair. So close to true death, his gaze didn't focus. Likewise, I felt the shore blurring before me.

"Thane Elittes bid on your father. More than he should have too," the Daemon King said. "All because someone told him to do it."

45

As I unraveled the Daemon King's suffocating words, I shook with rage. Thane Elittes had bought Pa.

"Oh, come, dear Sersa. I am only the messenger." He gestured with open arms. "As you might have already guessed, Nessin and Thane have been friends since they were children, and my son ordered Thane to buy your father before he asked you to be his bride. He'd been keeping tabs on you for weeks. Unsettling, if you ask me. But it is the way it's done if you want a mortal. And Nessin, evidently, has a *taste* for them."

There had to be an explanation. Sin couldn't be involved.

My heart pounded. Red and black blossomed at the edges of my vision, but I wasn't afraid of what I felt. I couldn't let my fear consume and control me. Not now.

I wanted to hurt the Daemon King. I wanted to kill him with my bare hands.

Before I could act, he grabbed me by the wrist and yanked me forward. My bandaged, broken hand throbbed louder as he cut off my circulation. Pressing the dagger against my throat, he forced me to move.

"Now..." The Daemon King threw me to the ground, summoning the Colossi's strength, despite his normal size.

I landed on the same shoulder I had when he'd dropped me before. I cried out and bit down hard, refusing to recognize the pain. I needed to keep my strength.

The king reached over the pyre and gave the dagger in Sin's chest one final twist before yanking it free. He threw it onto the sand. Though Sin's clothes were black, I saw the wound in the center of his chest and the gleam of wetness on the fabric. Blood flowed freely down his stomach, dripping onto the wood that formed the pyre.

Drip. Drip. Drip.

I watched it.

Three drops of blood was the High Triad's symbol. If ever I needed those pesky gods to intervene, it was now.

Yet I knew they wouldn't get involved.

This was between me and the king.

"Now, we watch Nessin experience true death, dear Sersa. Now, we watch how the souldagger drains a soulless of every last drop of blood. Forged by the Druids, it prevents us from healing. While our soul is gone," the Daemon King whispered, yanking my hair so I moved toward him, "the souldagger releases our body of this world. Do we go to the Otherworld? Do we go anywhere? No one knows, dear Sersa. That is the fate you delivered Lochlainn, after all, is it not?"

His voice and breath prickled the hairs on the back of my neck.

I cringed.

"Souldagger," I whispered under my breath.

My uninjured hand fumbled my hip, reaching for the three little objects dangling there. My fingertips barely caught hold of one, but once it did, my mind ignited.

I freed it silently, slowly.

"What are you whispering about?" the king hissed.

"I already knew what a souldagger does, Gearóid. Your son gifted me three."

I shoved his hand away, dropped to a crouch, and popped back up, driving my dagger into his shoulder.

Even in the shock that flashed across his face, the Daemon King managed to shove me to the ground, but the timing was perfect. Ailerby rushed up behind him and drove another blade into his back.

His grunt echoed in the salty air, but it turned to a dark chuckle that developed into a full-blown laugh.

The king didn't pull the daggers from his body. Instead, he yanked a sword from the sheath at his hip—a weapon I hadn't noticed before. Soul Guards surrounded him at all times.

So, the question was, could the king defend himself?

"I am much harder to kill than that," he said. "I am trained in nearly every form of combat. You will never beat me, Sersa."

"Yet, you're not shifting," I said with a nod.

Something else occurred to me.

I narrowed my eyes at him. "Sin wounded you. Didn't he? It's why you can't maintain your form."

The glare that sharpened the Daemon King's eyes told me everything I needed to know. Sin had already wounded his father using a souldagger. He must have.

I glimpsed the sweat beading on his forehead then and the strain in his otherwise unwrinkled forehead.

I pulled the spear from my belt, and its pointed tip extended. My broken hand couldn't grip it though. I quickly swapped the dagger and spear, holding one in each hand. It'd been a long time—an entire moon—since I'd wielded it, but the art of the spear was like second nature to me. It was Ma's weapon of choice, and, thus, our clan's weapon of choice.

"If, as you say, I'll never beat you," I said, "I bet your wounds will level those odds."

"A fraction, perhaps. But I see you're wounded too." The Daemon King nodded at my fist.

"A fraction is all I need. And I'm not wounded as badly as you, I suspect."

I let him strike first.

He charged me, and I moved to the side, letting the spear slide against his blade.

Ma always said to tire them out first.

Let them waste all their energy trying to strike.

I kept an eye on the king's gait and the tilt of his body. He was compensating for his left side, holding his nondominant arm close to his body. The wound wasn't bleeding through his clothes, but these cues were all I needed to fortify me.

The Daemon King charged me again, and I scoffed. He was trying to power through this fight while I was partaking in an elegant dance with him. He wanted this over with as soon as possible because he knew he didn't have long.

He needed to win this because he needed my soul.

"Veil yourself, Ailerby," I said between parries.

His eyes were a question. *You too?*

I shook my head.

Tonight, I would fight and end the Daemon King fairly.

To my surprise, Ailerby obeyed and veiled himself with magic. Not a minute later, sounds at my back assured me that he was making quick work of the pyre and taking Sin down.

I seized my first opening to attack when the king's breaths grew labored. The souldagger had done more damage than he'd feigned—quicker too.

I twirled my spear in the air, blinding him to which side I was going to strike before it whacked him behind the knees. He didn't fall but grunted, and his legs buckled.

His guard down, I used the opportunity to get closer. Tearing the dagger free from his shoulder summoned another grunt from him. Blood bubbled from the wound, and I cherished *every* drop, knowing his lifeblood was now flowing freely.

One drop of blood hit the sand.

Two drops.

Three.

As soon as the third drop of blood landed, the crimson stain bloomed like a diseased flower. It turned *silver*. And from it, Nev appeared. My eyes flickered to the deity as they sauntered out of the Daemon King's path; he couldn't see Nev, and he couldn't harm them, but that didn't mean they weren't there. Nev's robes were no longer green but the richest shade of red, like the blood they'd emerged from.

"We don't come here, Sersa Scáth, to ask whether you wish to never feel again. Not this time."

We can take away your ability to feel at all. No pain. No anger. No sadness. No fear.

If they weren't here to taunt me like the last time, then why?

Nev's appearance shifted like it had on Nos Nua. Aon appeared in their place. Hair like a flame coiled around her shoulders, and her feet were bare as she circled us in the sand. Her voice sounded like the wind.

"We are only here to warn you. Leave the Daemon King and his son. Let them both perish..."

Finally, Dúm appeared. Dark hair hung in the god of death's eyes, and his lips twisted into a smirk that reminded me far too much of Sin.

Sin, dying a few feet away.

I needed to end the Daemon King. Now. Before it was too late.

"You may never leave the City of Soulless again if you do not leave now," Dúm said in his velvety voice.

Sensing my distraction, the Daemon King lunged.

His sword swiped my waist, and my grip on the souldagger faltered. I almost dropped it.

Fear surged inside me like a wave. But the black was mixed with red—a cloud of it. From my peripheral, I saw the gods had vanished. I didn't have time to puzzle out why.

I cupped the slash the Daemon King had drawn in my side, but it was hardly a flesh wound. I told myself the pain didn't matter. The souldagger had him fading far worse than me.

But then he lunged again, and I moved aside yet again.

This time, the cloud of my magic swarmed him like a thousand crows. It poured from me like a tidal wave, and I let it crash around me without trying to be in control.

The king shrieked as it circled him.

"What are you doing? Stop it—stop!"

Blood dripped from the Daemon King's nose. I urged my anger to sharpen, and the teeming crimson tendrils closed in on him, snaking up and down his body, encircling him.

Red.

Why weren't the tendrils black?

Focus.

I felt everything all at once.

The fear of Sin's death.

The fear that I'd never see Ciel again. That he'd be trapped forever.

The anger that Sin had lied to me so many times. That he'd ordered Thane to buy my father. Maybe even used a Bonespeaker's command on him.

I closed my eyes, not wanting to feel these things but knowing that these emotions bolstered me. I was me *because* of my ability to feel so deeply, to pick myself up when the blue drowned me. To quell my fear even when it consumed me each day.

To love.

I didn't need the gods' help. I didn't need control at all but to untether myself, to let myself *be*. This was something I'd live with forever—and it was going to be okay. I hoped with everything I had that I'd be strong enough to handle the tides as Pa had told me once.

I took a deep breath, standing tall despite the blood seeping through my fingers.

"And you said I could never beat you," I whispered.

The Daemon King dropped to his knees. His fingers uncurled and released the sword.

I pressed my hand tighter to my side. While the bleeding wasn't life-threatening, the wound throbbed fiercely.

"But," I wheezed. "It seems I've already won."

He reached over his shoulder to pull the dagger from his upper back. I walked toward him, then halted far enough away that he couldn't reach me with his hands or his sword.

"You can save my son if you like," he said unevenly. "You can help him sit on my throne. But know, dear Sersa, that he *is* the monster I made him. All my sons are, even Devlin. But especially Nessin. He always has been. He has always eyed my throne, even before I killed my wife. He has always had ice in his heart, and it will not thaw. Even for you."

As a silvery substance began to ooze from the Daemon King's shoulder wound, my stomach knotted tighter. Sin had been stabbed minutes ago. Before I'd gotten here.

Was he bleeding silver too?

I glanced over my shoulder. Ailerby had reappeared and was pressing his coat to the center of Sin's chest, trying to stop whatever flowed from him.

"That won't work," the king taunted, eyes darting to Ailerby and Sin in a final attempt to jolt me.

"No. But I know what will."

I took another step forward, dropping my spear and passing the dagger to my good hand. Then I plunged the tip into the Daemon King's heart, painfully aware that I had killed two Soullander royals now.

As he stared up at the darkening sky, I whispered, "Say hello to the High Triad for me."

His eyes turned glassy as he opened his mouth to speak. But he never got the chance to say whatever it was.

I released him and rushed over to Sin, pulling him onto my lap. Ailerby continued to press on the coat he held against Sin's chest. It wasn't doing anything.

Silver blood pooled on Sin's lips. He tried to reach a hand toward my cheek.

"Sin? Sin, stay with us! Please..." I wiped the tears from my cheeks suddenly and sat up straighter. "You can take a piece of my soul. Your father *said*." Between sobs, I grabbed his hand and pressed it to my chest. "Take it!"

"Sersa..." He grinned through bloody teeth. "I want to kiss you one last time."

"No! Stop it. I don't want to kiss you once! I want to kiss you forever," I said, voice cracking. "Take it. Live!"

When Sin leaned forward to press his lips to mine a final time as promised, all I tasted was his blood. Even still, I didn't want to pull away from him.

But then, something unfurled inside me.

It was an unbearable coldness, an iciness I'd never felt before.

Sin taking an infinitesimal shard of my soul.

I gasped as it left me, leaving a perceptible cavity. The emptiness felt like more than a shard. It felt like he'd taken so much more.

Gasping still, I pressed a hand to my chest, iced with an infusible coldness. I tried to focus on Sin's face. The little color he'd had before returned almost instantly, and the hole in his own chest began to close as the one in my soul widened.

A minute passed, and he managed to speak through still-bloodied lips and teeth.

"Sersa, are you okay? I promise I bought your father so that I could get him out. But we couldn't," Sin explained. "Not until everything was set in stone. We couldn't draw attention to Bain or to Thane. I bought him because I knew even then—"

I hushed him. "Focus on healing. We will—we'll talk later."

But Sin never did as anyone said. He pulled himself to sitting and then stood. How he healed so quickly, right before my eyes, I couldn't fathom. But he was soulless.

And now so was I in a way.

Sin strode toward his father's corpse, focused on one thing.

I assumed the Daemon King was dead by now, but maybe he was still fading into the Otherworld—or the Underworld if this wasn't it. As Sin knelt before his father, I wondered what he was doing. Whispering a prayer? Saying farewell?

I realized instantly that he was doing neither of those things, and it was then I saw in his gaze the daemon I'd seen a few times before.

Sin reached behind his father's neck and tugged, like he were uprooting a weed.

I only saw what he held when he turned around.

A thick gold neck ring dangled from his steady hand. He studied the horizon then the Daemon King's torc, and without any further hesitation, he widened the two metal ends so it could fit around his neck. When he slipped it on, lightning rippled across the sky. The wind gusted furiously, and the tide crashed against the shore, taking the abandoned pyre out to sea.

Horns sprouted at Sin's temples where a crown might have been. The new Daemon King stood tall, staring out at his realm as he released a shriek that summoned all the Sluagh in the Soullands.

EPILOGUE

Still sitting on the ground, my legs tucked under me, I gaped at Sin in awe as all around us the Soullands seemed to awaken for the new Daemon King.

Sin. I couldn't believe it. He was the Daemon King. The Soullands were his.

I cast a look at his father. There was no doubt he was dead. His mouth hung agape, frozen in a last breath, while he gazed at the heavens. Sin hadn't so much as closed his father's eyes before he'd ripped the torc free and staked his claim over the realm.

The Sluagh swarmed overhead, their leather wings adding to the gusts blowing across the beach, and *thousands* of wraiths and Iarsmaí walked to the edge of the Wraithsea confining them like the walls of a prison.

As another bolt of lightning struck the sky, all the wraiths knelt for Sin. I didn't know what I'd have done if I weren't already sitting.

Would I bow to him?

Worse, would he *expect* me to bow to him? I had played a hand in him taking the throne.

The ice in my heart hadn't gone away. Instead, my body was growing used to it with each passing second. It was an unshakable coldness, one I hoped would disappear the instant Sin replaced the shard of my soul I'd lent him.

Out of nowhere, there were two shrieks—one of the Sluagh followed by Ailerby.

I realized a half second too late that Ailerby had screamed my name.

As a spear came spiraling toward me from the sky, the moment seemed to slow, every minuscule detail of Sin's expression warning me I was as good as dead. He ceased staring out at the sea, the sky, and whipped his head in my direction. His mouth opened, brow furrowed.

The wind swept his hair across his eyes.

Sin sprinted for me.

I shoved myself to the side, but the spear managed to swipe my shoulder. With a cry, I gritted my teeth. The spear pierced the sand behind me.

But if I'd thrown that spear, I wouldn't have missed.

As I looked up, dying to know who had thrown it, I glimpsed a head of white hair, not quite cropped like Devlin's, nor long like Lochlainn's, lingering in the sea of Sluagh.

Jestin glared at me from the back of one. He hung onto its thick neck one handed, his boots digging into its spine.

By the time Sin reached me, falling to his knees to check me over, Jestin grew farther and farther until he was so far away that I was sure there was no reaching or following him.

But even from afar, his gesture was clear. Arm outstretched, he pointed right at me.

A threat.

Sin stopped tearing at the fabric the spear had pierced to assess my wound and traced my gaze to the sky. A slow smile spread Jestin's lips, mimicking the demonic look Sin always wore.

Jestin dropped his arm and faced the sea, commanding the Sluagh onward.

Neither Sin nor I said a thing. We knew what that look meant. His smile. He'd come for Sin—maybe even the throne he'd stolen.

And Jestin would come for me too.

My broken hand still throbbed as I walked to Nessin's private quarters two days later. The recurrent reminder that these were no longer my rooms ached in my chest. Soon enough, I would know what Sin and I were going to do.

In no more than a few minutes, I'd know where we stood.

He would return the sliver of my soul, but the rest of it…

The rest of it was far more complicated.

There were dozens of Soul Guards and Sluagh outside his rooms. One pushed open the door for me, and I glimpsed through the entryway.

Sin was out on the terrace.

Hands clasped behind his back, he stood beneath the light of the Cradled Moons. His shoulders were tense, and he wore a thin black shirt tucked in. Dúma slept beside him, but when she heard my entrance, she bolted toward me.

Sin turned a moment later when Dúma and I approached together. He didn't look pleased to see me in the least. In the two days since I'd seen him, I'd almost forgotten he now had horns. They looked so strange. I didn't think I'd ever get used to them.

You may not have to, whispered the voice of the gods in my head.

"Hello," I said, guarded.

"Sersa. Hello. Please, sit." Sin's voice was as cold as his eyes, and if I recognized the undertones correctly, this conversation wasn't going to be easy.

I sat, and Dúma put her paws on my lap. Her weight made it hard to breathe. I scratched her ears and told her to get down. She sat right beside me, squinting up at the moons dusting bizarre light, tinted blue, onto us.

"How are you feeling?" Sin asked.

"Fine. Better. And you?" My voice was thin.

"Like new. Thanks to you."

These words were genuine, and they carved out a hole inside my heart.

Sin cleared his throat and straightened. He still hadn't sat. I gestured, a question in my eyes. He reluctantly took the seat across the table from me. It was far—the seat he'd chosen sent a deliberate message.

"You don't need to dance around whatever it is you have to say," I said. "I think I've earned the right to the truth by now."

He licked his lips. "You have. You have more than earned the truth, and I have failed to earn your trust. And I'm afraid..." He swallowed. "It will only get worse from here."

I held his gaze, but he looked away. Sin squinted at the sea in the distance, and I wondered whether he couldn't look at me.

My eyes darted to the horns jabbing the air. Right from his head. They were strange to look at, marbled black and white. As the Cradled Moons shifted though, I thought I saw a red streak here or there.

"I am not going to return the shard of your soul I possess, Sersa."

That snapped me alert.

I stiffened. My brow furrowed.

"I don't understand. Why wouldn't you?"

A muscle worked in Nessin's jaw. "Because with a broken soul, you are safe in the Soullands from daemons and Sluagh alike. My own brother, Jestin, sends threats that he *will* be Daemon King next. His message from the sky was also clear enough. You are not safe out in the world—rather, your world. But when a soulless holds a piece of someone's soul, it not only strengthens the holder. It strengthens the one it was taken from. In this case, *you*. Only a souldagger can kill you now, and those are incredibly rare."

I had three.

I gritted my teeth.

With Jestin's threat out in the open, how was I safe in the Soullands?

"You will heal from wounds that would have been otherwise fatal. You will not get sick, with few exceptions. You are untraceable to other soulless, blending in with all of us so the rest of your soul cannot be detected by even the best hunters. In other words, you will be safer here than in Os Íseal, or anywhere else, for that matter."

"I don't understand what you're saying. I– You lied to me, Nessin. You told Thane to buy my father. To use me. You owe me the courtesy of at least giving my soul back, though I'd argue that you owe me a lot more than that."

"It was more than that, and you know it. I knew who I wanted as my—" He stopped abruptly. "I told Thane to buy Bain with the intention of sending him home right away, but I knew I would be thrust out of the running for heir. I knew you'd... The thought of marrying another." He shook his head.

"Whatever your excuses, you still lied. You deceived me repeatedly, Nessin."

"That, I know."

"Then I don't get why you're doing this on top of it all!"

"Then let me be forthright." Nessin stood and walked toward the terrace. He spread his arms and dug his palms into the stone before he turned around. "I have ordered the dissolution of our union. Once the Gilders realize you were the one who murdered the Daemon King, they will tear us apart anyway."

Tear us apart? I wanted to laugh and scream at the same time.

He'd already seen that much through.

"He was your father, and yes, I murdered him to protect you," I said. "I will never be able to take that back. You have no idea how truly sorry I am that it came to it—and with Lochlainn—but I couldn't let him kill you. Too much damage has already been done everywhere. To everyone."

"My father." Nessin sneered with disgust. "He meant nothing to me, Sersa. Lochlainn's death was every bit necessary too. You know that. But the Gilders will do everything to try you for your crimes. I cannot protect you if you remain in Nos Ovscura. I failed before."

"Then let me go home!" I pointed toward the Wraithsea, to the bridge that his father had demolished. "Let me go where they can't reach me."

But was that really an option? Devlin and Ciel had fled. I still didn't know where they'd gone for sure—maybe Fient again—but I needed to see Ciel.

"My sources tell me your clan is being stripped of its title,"

Nessin said. "You will not be safe there anymore either. You know that."

"You would rather me abandon my clan? Me, the only one left with magic?"

He swept forward and slammed his fists into the table. "I would rather you live, and I'd do *anything* to ensure that—even if it means you hating me!"

"And maybe you will get that wish," I said, hard as stone.

"Then the gods are merciful," he said calmly, having regained his composure. "All I want is your safety, Sersa, and here beside me, you are not safe. You will never be safe as Daemon Queen. Perhaps your hatred for me will make this easier." He took a deep breath. "Devlin knows everything. He supports my reign. He has vowed to keep Ciel from harm. I did not even have to ask Devlin. You have my word on that."

Another deep breath. His horned shadow expanded behind him.

"I have arranged sanctuary for you on a nearby isle. It's not luxurious by any means because I didn't want to draw attention, but you will be safe. And that is all that matters."

"How will they know you didn't kill your father? The Gilders," I interrupted.

"Because they have requested the services of a Mindblood to verify my claims. As Daemon King, they cannot punish me. But they would try to punish you at all costs or simply have you killed."

"A Mindblood can alter memories or remove them entirely."

"They would see the gap. Even the best Mindbloods often leave behind hints of their magic, like a torn seam that's only been partially repaired."

I froze, realizing what all of this meant. What he meant.

"Then you want me to stay, but you want me to leave. Make up your mind."

"I have arranged safe passage for you tonight."

I choked on my breath. After everything, he wanted me to go into hiding. Tonight. So soon.

"And what about my brother? Will I at least get to see him? Stay with him?"

"I will reunite the two of you when I can," Nessin said, raking his ungloved hand through his hair.

I stood, took a step forward, and reached for him. He pulled his hands away and took a step back. At the edge of the terrace, there was nowhere else to go. It was clear. He would not be convinced otherwise.

I blinked, disbelieving that he had refused to let me touch him. But I stood my ground.

"That is not all," Nessin said.

Furious tears welled in my eyes. "What else? What else, Nessin?"

Nessin spoke with such a straight face, now masterfully hiding the shred of emotion he'd displayed a moment ago.

Either that, or he really felt nothing.

"I have said under oath that we never consummated our union. I have selected a new Daemon Queen, a Gilder's daughter from one of the High Houses. She does not yet know, of course, but I will marry her in a few weeks once everything settles. It's for pretenses, Sersa. Unlike what we shared. Every bit we experienced was real, I swear. But my hope is that a new queen will ease the talk of the Daemon King's murder—give them something else to focus on. Distraction is essential right now."

"For them or for you?" I asked quietly.

My tears did not match my voice. They rolled down my face, one after another.

"Nos Ovscura needs it. The Soullands beyond—*my realm*—needs it." Nessin hesitated only long enough for me to realize how serious he was. "I don't want to do this."

"Then don't!"

"I must." Though his voice turned quiet, it remained as cold as ice. "We always knew this deceit of ours was going to end, Sersa. In another life, maybe it wouldn't have to, but in this one, it must."

As I backed away, over the threshold of our room—*his* room—I bowed, spreading my arms wide. Dúma followed.

I hated myself, hated him, hated everything, every lie, that I'd believed.

A final furious tear dropped at my feet.

"Then I had better let you get back to your redecorating," I said, eyeing the parlor that was once more being turned into a bedroom for his new betrothed. "Have a lovely life with your new Daemon Queen. May she shatter your heart like you have mine, Nessin."

End of Book 1

PRONUNCIATION GUIDE

Clais | *CLAASH*
    Daemon | *DEE-MON*
    Hwain | *HWEEN*
    Iarsmaí | *EAR-SMY-EE*
    Nos Nua | *NAAS NOO-AH*
    Nos Ovscura | *NAAS AHV-SKUR-AH*
    Os Íseal | *OSS EE-SHAWL*
    Sluagh | *SLOO-AH*

Characters

Sersa Scáth | S*IR-SA* S*KA*
    Nessin Drumghoul | N*ESS-IN* D*RUM-GHOUL*
    Ciel Scáth | K*EEL* S*KA*
    Devlin Drumghoul | D*EV-LIN* D*RUM-GHOUL*
    Gearóid Drumghoul (Daemon King) | G*AIR-O-ID* D*RUM-GHOUL*
    Lochlainn Drumghoul | L*OCK-LIN* D*RUM-GHOUL*
    Jestin Drumghoul | J*ESS-TIN* D*RUM-GHOUL*
    Niuna Drumghoul | N*OO-NA* D*RUM-GHOUL*
    Ailerby Ipswich | A*L-IR-BEE* I*PS-WITCH*
    Thane Elittes | T*HANE* A*H-LEE-TISS*

PRONUNCIATION GUIDE

Stellera Caise | STEL-LAIR-UH CASE
Helde Hellick | HELL-DEE HELL-ICK
Sorcha Scáth | SOR-KA SKA
Bain Scáth | BAIN SKA
Aislinn Hellick | ASH-LINN HELL-ICK
Nev | NEV
Aon | AY-AWN
Dúm | DOOM

ACKNOWLEDGMENTS

Writing a book requires a great deal of time in one's own head. There are so many people who supported this story's existence by allowing me just that. Thank you to the few who know where I disappear to, who let me be for long stretches of time, and who've been here the entire way.

Mom, your squealing excitement at the mere idea of publishing this book fueled me every step of the way. Thanks for listening to me talk about plot endlessly, partaking in a month-long debate about book covers, and everything in between. I'm so thankful to have inherited your compulsion to create and wouldn't be here if it weren't for your encouragement. Thanks for being both, with double the strength of one. Also, my bad for breaking your laptop when I discovered writing as a tween.

Alex, you once said I could probably achieve anything I put my mind to, and though you might not remember it, those words have stayed with me for years. Thank you for being you and for being my balance when I am up or down. Love you!

Jaime, if you had told me twenty years ago that a big sister can become your best friend, I'd have died laughing. Especially us. I am so grateful for you. Thank you for listening to my writing and publishing breakdowns and always reminding me that these things take time.

Amelia! You read this book before it even had a title and raved in all caps not a hundred pages in. I will never forget your enthusiasm for these characters and their story. As tradition, I'm granting you the right to read every book in this series first. But I will be withholding the last chapters moving forward. Who reads the end first?? In all seriousness, thank you for telling me to rest, write, or take deep breaths. You're awesome.

This manuscript became a book because of the finishing touches. Thank you to my outstanding sensitivity and beta readers, Bérénice, Dimitra, Jasmin, and Neff. Both your excitement for this story and your critique meant so much to me. A huge thank you to K.D. Ritchie/Story Wrappers for the most stunning cover artwork I ever could have imagined. Thank you to my editor Jeni Chappelle for polishing this book...and removing a lot of *useless* italics and random ellipsis...

Finally, a huge thank you to each and every reader. I hope you enjoy the first part of Sersa's story as much as I enjoyed writing it!

ABOUT THE AUTHOR

Shannon R. Lir is an adult fantasy romance author. Her favorite stories are about young women with sharp daggers, perpetually smirking love interests, and all shades of morally gray characters. She loves anything to do with magical worlds and has been trying to immerse herself in the ones between the pages of books she loves or the ones she writes all her life. She briefly studied creative writing at the University of Southern California before leaving to pursue a major deemed to be more practical. She's written every day since.

This Deceit of Ours is Shannon's debut novel and the first book in the Reign of Soulless series. Connect with her at shannonrlir.com or follow her on Instagram.

shannonrlir.com

 instagram.com/shannonrlir

Printed by BoD™in Norderstedt, Germany